The
COLD MOON

Jeffery
DEAVER

HODDER

Copyright © 2006 by Jeffery Deaver
First published in the United States of America in 2006 by Simon & Schuster
First published in Great Britain in 2006 by Hodder & Stoughton
A division of Hodder Headline

This Hodder paperback edition 2006

The right of Jeffery Deaver to be identified as the Author
of the Work has been asserted by him in accordance with the
Copyright, Designs and Patents Act 1988.

A Hodder Book

4

A CIP catalogue record for this title is available from the British Library

ISBN 978 0 340 83383 4

Typeset in Fairfield Light by Palimpsest Book Production Limited,
Grangemouth, Stirlingshire

Printed and bound by Clays Ltd, St Ives plc

Hodder Headline's policy is to use papers that are natural, renewable and recyclable
products and made from wood grown in sustainable forests. The logging and
manufacturing processes are expected to conform to the environmental
regulations of the country of origin.

Hodder & Stoughton Ltd
A division of Hodder Headline
338 Euston Road
London NW1 3BH

Also by Jeffery Deaver

Mistress of Justice
The Lesson of Her Death
Praying for Sleep
Speaking in Tongues
A Maiden's Grave
The Devil's Teardrop
The Blue Nowhere
Garden of Beasts

The Rune series

Manhattan is my Beat
Death of a Blue Movie Star
Hard News

The Location Scout series

Shallow Graves
Bloody River Blues
Hell's Kitchen

The Lincoln Rhyme thrillers

The Bone Collector
The Coffin Dancer
The Empty Chair
The Stone Monkey
The Vanished Man
The Twelfth Card

Short stories

Twisted
More Twisted

You can't see me, but I'm always around you.
Run as fast as you can, but you'll never escape me.
Fight me with all your strength, but you'll never defeat
    me.
I kill when I wish, but can never be brought to justice.
    Who am I?

                                                    Old Man Time

I

12:02 A.M. TUESDAY

Time is dead as long as it is being clicked off
by little wheels; only when the clock stops does
time come to life.

— WILLIAM FAULKNER

Chapter
ONE

'How long did it take them to die?'

The man this question was posed to didn't seem to hear it. He looked in the rearview mirror again and concentrated on his driving. The hour was just past midnight and the streets in lower Manhattan were icy. A cold front had swept the sky clear and turned an earlier snow to slick glaze on the asphalt and concrete. The two men were in the rattling Band-Aid-mobile, as Clever Vincent had dubbed the tan SUV. It was a few years old; the brakes needed servicing and the tires replacing. But taking a stolen vehicle in for work would not be a wise idea, especially since two of its recent passengers were now murder victims.

The driver – a lean man in his fifties, with trim black hair – made a careful turn down a side street and continued his journey, never speeding, making precise turns, perfectly centered in his lane. He'd drive the same whether the streets were slippery or dry, whether the vehicle had just been involved in murder or not.

Careful, meticulous.

How long did it take?

Big Vincent – Vincent with long, sausage fingers, always

damp, and a taut brown belt stretching the first hole – shivered hard. He'd been waiting on the street corner after his night shift as a word-processing temp. It was bitterly cold but Vincent didn't like the lobby of his building. The light was greenish and the walls were covered with big mirrors in which he could see his oval body from all angles. So he'd stepped into the clear, cold December air and paced and ate a candy bar. Okay, two.

As Vincent was glancing up at the full moon, a shockingly white disk visible for a moment through a canyon of buildings, the Watchmaker reflected aloud, 'How long did it take them to die? Interesting.'

Vincent had known the Watchmaker – whose real name was Gerald Duncan – for only a short time but he'd learned that you asked the man questions at your own risk. Even a simple query could open the door to a monologue. Man, could he talk. And his answers were always organized, like a college professor's. Vincent knew that the silence for the last few minutes was because Duncan was considering his answer.

Vincent opened a can of Pepsi. He was cold but he needed something sweet. He chugged it and put the empty can in his pocket. He ate a packet of peanut butter crackers. Duncan looked over to make sure Vincent was wearing gloves. They always wore gloves in the Band-Aid-mobile.

Meticulous . . .

'I'd say there are several answers to that,' Duncan said in his soft, detached voice. 'For instance, the first one I killed was twenty-four, so you could say it took him twenty-four years to die.'

Like, *yeah* . . . thought Clever Vincent with the sarcasm of a teenager, though he had to admit that this obvious answer hadn't occurred to him.

'The other was thirty-two, I think.'

A police car drove by, the opposite way. The blood in

Vincent's temples began pounding but Duncan didn't react. The cops showed no interest in the stolen Explorer.

'Another way to answer the question,' Duncan said, 'is to consider the elapsed time from the moment I started until their hearts stopped beating. That's probably what you meant. See, people want to put time into easy-to-digest frames of reference. That's valid, as long as it's helpful. Knowing the contractions come every twenty seconds is helpful. So is knowing that the athlete ran a mile in three minutes, fifty-eight seconds, so he wins the race. Specifically how long it took them tonight to die . . . well, that isn't important, as long as it wasn't fast.' A glance at Vincent. 'I'm not being critical of your question.'

'No,' Vincent said, not caring if he was critical. Vincent Reynolds didn't have many friends and could put up with a lot from Gerald Duncan. 'I was just curious.'

'I understand. I just didn't pay any attention. But the next one, I'll time it.'

'The girl? Tomorrow?' Vincent's heart beat just a bit faster.

He nodded. 'Later today, you mean.'

It was after midnight. With Gerald Duncan you had to be precise, especially when it came to time.

'Right.'

Hungry Vincent had nosed out Clever Vincent now that he was thinking of Joanne, the girl who'd die next.

Later today . . .

The killer drove in a complicated pattern back to their temporary home in the Chelsea district of Manhattan, south of Midtown, near the river. The streets were deserted; the temperature was in the teens and the wind flowed steadily through the narrow streets.

Duncan parked at a curb and shut the engine off, set the parking brake. The men stepped out. They walked for a half block through the icy wind. Duncan glanced down at his shadow on the sidewalk, cast by the moon. 'I've thought of another answer. About how long it took them to die.'

Vincent shivered again – mostly, but not only, from the cold.

'When you look at it from their point of view,' the killer said, 'you could say that it took forever.'

Chapter
TWO

What *is* that?

From his squeaky chair in the warm office, the big man sipped coffee and squinted through the bright morning light toward the far end of the pier. He was the morning supervisor of the tugboat repair operation, located on the Hudson River north of Greenwich Village. There was a Moran with a bum diesel due to dock in forty minutes but at the moment the pier was empty and the supervisor was enjoying the warmth of the shed, where he sat with his feet up on the desk, coffee cradled against his chest. He wiped some condensation off the window and looked again.

What is it?

A small black box sat by the edge of the pier, the side that faced Jersey. It hadn't been there when the facility had closed at six yesterday, and nobody would have docked after that. Had to come from the land side. There was a chain-link fence to prevent pedestrians and passers-by from getting into the facility, but, as the man knew from the missing tools and trash drums (go figure), if somebody wanted to break in, they would.

But why *leave* something?

He stared for a while, thinking, It's cold out, it's windy,

the coffee's just right. Then he decided, Oh, hell, better check. He pulled on his thick gray jacket, gloves and hat and, taking a last slug of coffee, stepped outside into the breathtaking air.

The supervisor made his way through the wind along the pier, his watering eyes focused on the black box.

The hell is it? The thing was rectangular, less than a foot high, and the low sunlight sharply reflected off something on the front. He squinted against the glare. The whitecapped water of the Hudson slushed against the pilings below.

Ten feet away from the box he paused, realizing what it was.

A clock. An old-fashioned one, with those funny numbers – Roman numerals – and a moon face on the front. Looked expensive. He glanced at his watch and saw the clock was working; the time was accurate. Who'd leave a nice thing like that here? Well, all right, I got myself a present.

As he stepped forward to pick it up, though, his legs went out from under him and he had a moment of pure panic thinking he'd tumble into the river. But he went straight down, landing on the patch of ice he hadn't seen, and slid no further.

Wincing in pain, gasping, he pulled himself to his feet. The man glanced down and saw that this wasn't normal ice. It was reddish brown.

'Oh, Christ,' he whispered as he stared at the large patch of blood, which had pooled near the clock and frozen slick. He leaned forward and his shock deepened when he realized how the blood had gotten there. He saw what looked like bloody fingernail marks on the wooden decking of the pier, as if someone with slashed fingers or wrists had been holding on to keep from falling into the churning waters of the river.

He crept to the edge and looked down. No one was floating in the choppy water. He wasn't surprised; if what he imagined was true, the frozen blood meant the poor bastard had been here a while ago and, if he hadn't been saved, his body'd be halfway to Liberty Island by now.

Fumbling for his cell phone, he backed away and pulled his glove off with his teeth. A final glance at the clock, then he hurried back to the shed, calling the police with a stubby, quaking finger.

Before and After.

The city was different now, after that morning in September, after the explosions, the huge tails of smoke, the buildings that disappeared.

You couldn't deny it. You could talk about the resilience, the mettle, the get-back-to-work attitude of New Yorkers, and that was true. But people still paused when planes made that final approach to LaGuardia and seemed a bit lower than normal. You crossed the street, wide, around an abandoned shopping bag. You weren't surprised to see soldiers or police dressed in dark uniforms carrying black, military-style machine guns.

The Thanksgiving Day parade had come and gone without incident and now Christmas was in full swing, crowds everywhere. But floating atop the festivities, like a reflection in a department store's holiday window, was the persistent image of the towers that no longer were, the people no longer with us. And, of course, the big question: What would happen next?

Lincoln Rhyme had his own Before and After and he understood this concept very well. There was a time he could walk and function and then came the time when he could not. One moment he was as healthy as everyone else, searching a crime scene, and a minute later a beam had snapped his neck and left him a C-4 quadriplegic, almost completely paralyzed from the shoulders down.

Before and After . . .

There are moments that change you forever.

And yet, Lincoln Rhyme believed, if you make too grave an icon of them, then the events become more potent. And the bad guys win.

Now, early on a cold Tuesday morning, these were Rhyme's thoughts as he listened to a National Public Radio announcer, in her unshakable FM voice, report about a parade planned for the day after tomorrow, followed by some ceremonies and meetings of government officials, all of which logically should have been held in the nation's capital. But the up-with-New-York attitude had prevailed and spectators, as well as protesters, would be present in force and clogging the streets, making the life of security-sensitive police around Wall Street far more difficult. As with politics, so with sports: Play-offs that should occur in New Jersey were now scheduled for Madison Square Garden — as a display, for some reason, of patriotism. Rhyme wondered cynically if next year's Boston Marathon would be held in New York City.

Before and After . . .

Rhyme had come to believe that he himself really wasn't much different in the After. His physical condition, his skyline, you could say, had changed. But he was essentially the same person as in the Before: a cop and a scientist who was impatient, temperamental (okay, sometimes obnoxious), relentless and intolerant of incompetence and laziness. He didn't play the gimp card, didn't whine, didn't make an issue of his condition (though good luck to any building owners who didn't meet the Americans with Disabilities Act requirements for door width and ramps when he was at a crime scene in their buildings).

As he listened to the report now, the fact that certain people in the city seemed to be giving in to self-pity irritated him. 'I'm going to write a letter,' he announced to Thom.

The slim young aide, in dark slacks, white shirt and thick sweater (Rhyme's Central Park West town house suffered from a bad heating system and ancient insulation), glanced up from where he was overdecorating for Christmas. Rhyme enjoyed the irony of his placing a miniature evergreen tree on a table below which a present, though an unwrapped one, already waited: a box of adult disposable diapers.

'Letter?'

He explained his theory that it was more patriotic to go about business as usual. 'I'm going to give 'em hell. The *Times*, I think.'

'Why don't you?' asked the aide, whose profession was known as 'care-giver' (though Thom said that, being in the employ of Lincoln Rhyme, his job description was really 'saint').

'I'm going to,' Rhyme said adamantly.

'Good for you . . . though, one thing?'

Rhyme lifted an eyebrow. The criminalist could – and did – get great expression out of his extant body parts: shoulders, face and head.

'Most of the people who *say* they're going to write a letter don't. People who *do* write letters just go ahead and write them. They don't announce it. Ever notice that?'

'Thank you for the brilliant insight into psychology, Thom. You know that nothing's going to stop me now.'

'Good,' repeated the aide.

Using the touchpad controller, the criminalist drove his red Storm Arrow wheelchair closer to one of the half dozen large, flat-screen monitors in the room.

'Command,' he said into the voice-recognition system, via a microphone attached to the chair. 'Word processor.'

WordPerfect dutifully opened on the screen.

'Command, type. "Dear sirs." Command, colon. Command, paragraph. Command, type, "It has come to my attention—"'

The doorbell rang and Thom went to see who the visitor was.

Rhyme closed his eyes and was composing his rant to the world when a voice intruded. 'Hey, Linc. Merry Christmas.'

'Uhm, ditto,' Rhyme grumbled to paunchy, disheveled Lon Sellitto, walking through the doorway. The big detective had to maneuver carefully; the room had been a quaint parlor in the Victorian era but now was chockablock with forensic science gear: optical microscopes, an electron microscope, a gas chromatograph, laboratory beakers and racks, pipettes, petri dishes, centrifuges, chemicals, books and magazines, computers – and thick wires, which ran everywhere. (When Rhyme began doing forensic consulting out of his town house, the power-hungry equipment frequently would blow circuit breakers. The juice running into the place probably equaled the combined usage by everyone else on the block.)

'Command, volume, level three.' The environmental control unit obediently turned down NPR.

'Not in the spirit of the season, are we?' the detective asked.

Rhyme didn't answer. He looked back at the monitor.

'Hey, Jackson.' Sellitto bent down and petted a small, long-haired dog curled up in an NYPD evidence box. He was temporarily living here, his former owner, Thom's elderly aunt, had passed away recently in Westport, Connecticut, after a long illness. Among the young man's inheritances was Jackson, a Havanese. The breed, related to the bichon frise, originated in Cuba. Jackson was staying here until Thom could find a good home for him.

'We got a bad one, Linc,' Sellitto said, standing up. He started to take off his overcoat but changed his mind. 'Jesus, it's cold. Is this a record?'

'Don't know. Don't spend much time on the Weather Channel.' He thought of a good opening paragraph of his letter to the editor.

'Bad,' Sellitto repeated.

Rhyme glanced at Sellitto with a cocked eyebrow.

'Two homicides, same M.O. More or less.'

'Lots of "bad ones" out there, Lon. Why're these any badder?'

As often happened in the tedious days between cases Rhyme was in a bad mood; of all the perps he'd come across, the worst was boredom.

But Sellitto had worked with Rhyme for years and was immune to the criminalist's attitudes. 'Got a call from the Big Building. Brass want you and Amelia on this one. They said they're insisting.'

'Oh, insisting?'

'I promised I wouldn't tell you they said that. You don't like to be insisted.'

'Can we get to the "bad" part, Lon? Or is that too much to ask?'

'Where's Amelia?'

'Westchester, on a case. Should be back soon.'

The detective held up a wait-a-minute finger as his cell phone rang. He had a conversation, nodding and jotting notes. He disconnected and glanced at Rhyme. 'Okay, here we have it. Sometime last night our perp, he grabs—'

'He?' Rhyme asked pointedly.

'Okay. We don't know the gender for sure.'

'Sex.'

'What?'

Rhyme said, 'Gender's a linguistic concept. It refers to designating words male or female in certain languages. Sex is a biological concept differentiating male and female organisms.'

'Thanks for the grammar lesson,' the detective muttered. 'Maybe it'll help if I'm ever on *Jeopardy!* Anyway, *he* grabs some poor schmuck and takes 'em to that boat repair pier on the Hudson. We're not exactly sure how he does it, but he forces the guy, or woman, to hang on over the river and then cuts their wrists. The vic holds on for a while, looks like – long enough to lose a shitload of blood – but then just lets go.'

'Body?'

'Not yet. Coast Guard and ESU're searching.'

'I heard plural.'

'Okay. Then we get another call a few minutes later. To check out an alley downtown, off Cedar, near Broadway. The perp's got *another* vic. A uniform finds this guy duct-taped and on his back. The perp rigged this iron bar – weighs maybe seventy-five pounds – above his neck. The vic has to hold it up to keep from getting his throat crushed.'

'Seventy-five pounds? Okay, given the strength issues, I'll grant you the perp's sex probably is male.'

Thom came into the room with coffee and pastries. Sellitto, his weight a constant issue, went for the Danish first, his diet hibernated during the holidays. He finished half and, wiping his mouth, continued. 'So the vic's holding up the bar. Which maybe he does for a while – but he doesn't make it.'

'Who's the vic?'

'Name's Theodore Adams. Lived near Battery Park. A nine-one-one came in last night from a woman said her brother was supposed to meet her for dinner and never showed. That's the name she gave. Sergeant from the precinct was going to call her this morning.'

Lincoln Rhyme generally didn't find soft descriptions helpful. But he conceded that 'bad' fit the situation.

So did the word 'intriguing.' He asked, 'Why do you say it's the same M.O.?'

'Perp left a calling card at both scenes. Clocks.'

'As in tick-tock?'

'Yup. The first one was by the pool of blood on the pier. The other was next to the vic's head. It was like the doer wanted them to see it. And, I guess, hear it.'

'Describe them. The clocks.'

'Looked old-fashioned. That's all I know.'

'Not a bomb?' Nowadays – in the time of the After – every item of evidence that ticked was routinely checked for explosives.

'Nope. Won't go bang. But the squad sent 'em up to Rodman's Neck to check for bio or chemical agents. Same brand of clock, looks like. Spooky, one of the respondings said. Has this face of a moon on it. Oh, and just in case we were slow, he left a note under the clocks. Computer printout. No handwriting.'

'And they said . . . ?'

Sellitto glanced down at his notebook, not relying on memory. Rhyme appreciated this in the detective. He wasn't brilliant but he *was* a bulldog and did everything slowly and with perfection. He read, '"The full Cold Moon is in the sky, shining on the corpse of earth, signifying the hour to die and end the journey begun at birth."' He looked up at Rhyme. 'It was signed "the Watchmaker".'

'We've got two vics and a lunar motif.' Often, an astronomical reference meant that the killer was planning to strike multiple times. 'He's got more on the agenda.'

'Hey, why d'you think I'm here, Linc?'

Rhyme glanced at the beginning of his missive to the *Times*. He closed his word-processing program. The essay about Before and After would have to wait.

Chapter
THREE

A small sound from outside the window. A crunch of snow.

Amelia Sachs stopped moving. She glanced out at the quiet, white backyard. She saw no one.

She was a half hour north of the city, alone in a pristine Tudor suburban house that was still as death.

An appropriate thought, she reflected, since the owner of the place was no longer among the living.

The sound again. Sachs was a city girl, used to the cacophony of urban noises – threatening and benign. The intrusion into the excessive suburban quiet set her on edge.

Was its source a footstep?

The tall, red-haired detective, wearing a black leather jacket, navy blue sweater and black jeans, listened carefully for a moment, absently scratching her scalp. She heard another crunch. Unzipped her jacket so her Glock was easily accessible. Crouching, she looked outside fast. Saw nothing.

And returned to her task. She sat down on the luxurious leather office chair and began to examine the contents of a huge desk. This was a frustrating mission, the problem being that she didn't know exactly what she was looking for. Which often happened when you searched a crime scene that was secondary or tertiary or whatever four-times-removed might be called. In fact, you'd be hard-pressed to call this a crime scene at all. It was unlikely that any perpetrators had ever been present, nor had any bodies been discovered here, any loot hidden. This was simply a little-used residence of a man named Benjamin Creeley, who'd died miles away and had not been to this house for a week before his death.

Still she had to search, and search carefully – because Amelia Sachs was not here in the role she usually worked: crime scene cop. She was the lead detective in the first homicide case of her own.

Another snap outside. Ice, snow, branch, deer, squirrel . . . She ignored it and continued the search that had started a few weeks earlier, all thanks to a knot in a piece of cotton rope.

It was this length of clothesline that had ended the life of fifty-six-year-old Ben Creeley, found dangling from the banister of his Upper East Side town house. A suicide note was on the table, no signs of foul play evident.

Just after the man's death, though, Suzanne Creeley, his widow, went to the NYPD. She simply didn't believe that he'd killed himself. The wealthy businessman and accountant had been moody lately, yes. But only, she believed, because he'd been working very long hours on some particularly difficult projects. His occasionally dour moods were a far cry from suicidal depression. He had no history of mental or emotional problems and wasn't taking antidepressants. Creeley's finances were solid. There'd been no recent changes to his will or insurance policy. His partner, Jordan Kessler, was on a business trip to a client's office in Pennsylvania. But he and Sachs had spoken briefly and he confirmed that while Creeley *had* seemed depressed lately he hadn't, Kessler believed, ever mentioned suicide.

Sachs was permanently assigned to Lincoln Rhyme for crime

scene work but she wanted to do more than forensics exclusively. She'd been lobbying Major Cases for the chance to be lead detective on a homicide or terrorist investigation. Somebody in the Big Building had decided that Creeley's death warranted more looking into and gave her the case. Aside from the general consensus that Creeley wasn't suicidal, though, Sachs at first could find no evidence of foul play. But then she made a discovery. The medical examiner reported that at the time of his death Creeley had a broken thumb; his entire right hand was in a cast.

Which simply wouldn't've let him tie the knot in his hangman's noose or secure the rope to the balcony railing.

Sachs knew because she'd tried a dozen times. Impossible without using the thumb. Maybe he'd tied it before the biking accident, a week prior to his death, but it just didn't seem likely that you'd tie a noose and keep it handy, waiting for a future date to kill yourself.

She decided to declare the death suspicious and opened a homicide file.

But it was shaping up to be a tough case. The rule in homicides is either they're solved in the first twenty-four hours or it takes months to close them. What little evidence existed (the liquor bottle he'd been drinking from before he died, the note and the rope) had yielded nothing. There were no witnesses. The NYPD report was a mere half-page long. The detective who'd run the case had spent hardly any time on it, typical for suicides, and he provided Sachs with no other information.

The trail to any suspects had pretty much dried up in the city, where Creeley had worked and where the family spent most of their time; all that remained in Manhattan was to interview the dead man's partner, Kessler, in more depth. Now, she was searching one of the few remaining sources for leads: the Creeleys' suburban home, at which the family spent very little time.

But she was finding nothing. Sachs now sat back, staring at a recent picture of Creeley shaking the hand of someone who appeared to be a businessman. They were on the tarmac of an airport, in front of some company's private jet. Oil rigs and pipelines loomed in the background. He was smiling. He didn't look depressed – but who does in snapshots?

It was then that another crunch sounded, very close, outside the window behind her. Then one more, even closer.

That's no squirrel.

Out came the Glock, one shiny 9-millimeter round in the chamber and thirteen underneath it. Sachs made her way quietly out the front door and circled around to the side of the house, pistol in both hands, but close to her side (*never* in front of you when rounding a corner, where it can be knocked aside; the movies always get it wrong). A fast look. The side of the house was clear. Then she moved toward the back, placing her black boots carefully on the walkway, which was thick with ice.

A pause, listening.

Yes, definitely footsteps. The person was moving hesitantly, maybe toward the back door.

A pause. A step. Another pause.

Ready, Sachs told herself.

She eased closer to the back corner of the house.

Which is when her foot slid off a patch of ice. She gave a faint, involuntary gasp. Hardly audible, she thought.

But it was loud enough for the trespasser.

She heard the pounding of feet fleeing through the back-yard, crunching through the snow.

Damn . . .

In a crouch – in case it was a feint to draw her to target – she looked around the corner and lifted the Glock fast. She saw a lanky man in jeans and a thick jacket sprinting away through the snow.

Hell . . . Just *hate* it when they run. Sachs had been dealt a tall body and bum joints – arthritis – and the combination made running pure misery.

'I'm a police officer. Stop!' She started sprinting after him.

Sachs was on her own for the pursuit. She'd never told Westchester County Police that she was here. Any assistance would have to come through a 911 call and she didn't have time for that.

'I'm not going to tell you again. Stop!'

No response.

They raced in tandem through the large yard then into the woods behind the house. Breathing hard, a pain below her ribs joining the agony in her knees, she moved as fast as she could but he was pulling ahead of her.

Shit, I'm gonna lose him.

But nature intervened. A branch protruding from the snow caught his shoe and he went down hard, with a huge grunt that Sachs heard from forty feet away. She ran up and, gasping for breath, rested the side of the Glock against his neck. He stopped squirming.

'Don't hurt me! Please!'

'Shhhh.'

Out came the cuffs.

'Hands behind your back.'

He squinted. 'I didn't do anything!'

'Hands.'

He did as he was told but in an awkward way that told her he'd probably never been collared. He was younger than she'd thought – a teenager, his face dotted with acne.

'Don't hurt me, please!'

Sachs caught her breath and searched him. No ID, no weapons, no drugs. Money and a set of keys. 'What's your name?'

'Greg.'

'Last name?'

A hesitation. 'Witherspoon.'

'You live around here?'

He sucked in air, nodding to his right. 'The house there, next door to the Creeleys'.'

'How old are you?'

'Sixteen.'

'Why'd you run?'

'I don't know. I was scared.'

'Didn't you hear me say I was police?'

'Yeah, but you don't look like a cop . . . a policewoman. You really are one?'

She showed him her ID. 'What were you doing at the house?'

'I live next door.'

'You said that. What were you *doing*?' She pulled him up into a sitting position. He looked terrified.

'I saw somebody inside. I thought it was Mrs Creeley or maybe somebody in the family or something. I just wanted to tell her something. Then I looked inside and saw you had a gun. I got scared. I thought you were with them.'

'Who's them?'

'Those guys who broke in. That's what I was going to tell Mrs Creeley about.'

'Broke in?'

'I saw a couple of guys break into their house. A few weeks ago. It was around Thanksgiving.'

'Did you call the police?'

'No. I guess I should have. But I didn't want to get involved. They looked, like, tough.'

'Tell me what happened.'

'I was outside, in our backyard, and I saw 'em go to the back door, look around and then kind of, you know, break the lock and go inside.'

'White, black?'

'White, I think. I wasn't that close. I couldn't see their faces. They were just, you know, guys. Jeans and jackets. One was bigger than the other.'

'Color of their hair?'

'I don't know.'

'How long were they inside?'

'An hour, I guess.'

'You see their car?'

'No.'

'Did they take anything?'

'Yeah. A stereo, CDs, a TV. Some games, I think. Can I stand up?'

Sachs pulled him to his feet and marched him to the house. She noted that the back door *had* been jimmied. Pretty slick job too.

She looked around. A big-screen TV was still in the living room. There was lots of nice china in the cabinet. The silver was there too. And it was sterling. The theft wasn't making sense. Had they stolen a few things as cover for something else?

She examined the ground floor. The house was immaculate – except for the fireplace. It was a gas model, she noted, but inside there was a lot of ash. With gas logs, there was no need for paper or kindling. Had the burglars set a fire?

Without touching anything inside, she shone her flashlight over the contents.

'Did you notice if those men had a fire going when they were here?'

'I don't know. Maybe.'

There were also streaks of mud in front of the fireplace. She had basic crime scene equipment in the trunk of her car. She'd dust for prints around the fireplace and desk and collect the ash and mud and any other physical evidence that might be helpful.

It was then that her cell phone vibrated. She glanced at the screen. An urgent text message from Lincoln Rhyme. She was needed back in the city ASAP. She sent an acknowledging message.

What had been burned? she wondered, staring at the fireplace.

'So,' Greg said. 'Like, can I go now?'

Sachs looked him over. 'I don't know if you're aware of it, but after any death the police conduct a complete inventory of everything in the house the day the owner dies.'

'Yeah?' He looked down.

'In an hour I'm calling Westchester County Police and having them check the list against what's here now. If anything's missing they'll call me and I'll give them your name and call your parents.'

'But—'

'The men didn't steal anything at all, did they? After they left, you went in through the back door and helped yourself to . . . what?'

'I just borrowed a few things is all. From Todd's room.'

'Mr Creeley's son?'

'Yeah. And one of the Nintendos was mine. He never returned it.'

'The men? Did they take anything?'

A hesitation. 'Didn't look like it.'

She undid the handcuffs. Sachs said, 'You'll have everything back by then. Put it in the garage. I'll leave the door open.'

'Oh, like, yeah. I promise,' he said breathlessly. 'Definitely . . . Only . . .' He started to cry. 'The thing is I ate some cake. It was in the refrigerator. I don't . . . I'll buy them another one.'

Sachs said, 'They don't inventory food.'

'They don't?'

'Just get everything else back here.'

'I promise. Really.' He wiped his face on his sleeve.

The boy started to leave. She asked, 'One thing? When you heard that Mr Creeley killed himself were you surprised?'

'Well, yeah.'

'Why?'

The boy gave a laugh. 'He had a seven-forty. I mean, the long one. Who's going to kill themselves, they drive a BMW, right?'

Chapter
FOUR

They were terrible ways to die.

Amelia Sachs had pretty much seen it all, or so she thought. But these were as cruel means of death as she could recall.

She'd spoken to Rhyme from Westchester and he'd told her to hurry to lower Manhattan, where she was to run two scenes of homicides committed apparently hours apart by somebody calling himself the Watchmaker.

Sachs had already run the simpler of the two – a pier in the Hudson River. It was a fast scene to process; there was no body and most of the trace had been swept away or contaminated by the abrasive wind flowing along the river. She'd photographed and videoed the scene from all angles. She noted where the clock had been – troubled that the scene had been disturbed by the bomb squad when they'd collected it for testing. But there was no alternative, with a possible explosive device.

She collected the killer's note, too, partly crusted with blood. Then she'd taken samples of the frozen blood. She noted finger-nail marks on the pier where the victim had held on, dangling above the water, then slid off. She collected a torn nail – it was wide, short and unpolished, suggesting that the victim was a man.

The killer had cut his way through the chain-link fence protecting the pier. Sachs took a sample of the wire to check for tool marks. She found no fingerprints, footprints or tire tread marks near the point of entry or the pool of frozen blood.

No witnesses had been located.

The medical examiner reported that if the victim had indeed fallen into the Hudson, as seemed likely, he would have died of hypothermia within ten minutes or so. NYPD divers and the Coast Guard were continuing their search for the body and any evidence in the water.

Sachs was now at the second scene, the alleyway off Cedar Street, near Broadway. Theodore Adams, mid-thirties, was lying on his back, duct tape gagging him and binding his ankles and wrists. The killer had looped a rope over a fire escape, ten feet above him, and tied one end to a heavy, six-foot-long metal bar with holes in the ends like the eye of a needle. This the killer had suspended above the victim's throat. The other end of the rope he'd placed in the man's hands. Being bound, Adams couldn't slide out from under the bar. His only hope was to use all his strength to keep the massive weight suspended until someone happened along to save him.

But no one had.

He'd been dead for some time and the bar had continued to compress his throat until the body froze solid in the December cold. His neck was only about an inch thick under the crushing metal. His expression was the chalky, neutral gaze of death but she could imagine how his face must have looked for the – what? – ten or fifteen minutes he'd struggled to stay alive, growing red from the effort, then purple, eyes bulging.

Who on earth would murder in these ways, which were obviously picked for prolonged deaths?

Wearing a white Tyvek bodysuit to prevent trace from her clothes and hair from contaminating the scene, Sachs readied the evidence collection equipment, as she discussed the scene with two of her colleagues in the NYPD, Nancy Simpson and Frank Rettig, officers based at the department's main crime scene facility in Queens. Nearby was their Crime Scene Unit's rapid response vehicle – a large van filled with the essential crime scene investigation equipment.

She slipped rubber bands around her feet to distinguish her prints from the perp's. (Another of Rhyme's ideas. 'But why bother? I'm in the Tyvek, Rhyme, not street shoes,' Sachs had once pointed out. He'd looked at her wearily. 'Oh, excuse me. I guess a perp would *never* think to buy a Tyvek suit. How much do they cost, Sachs? Forty-nine ninety-five?')

Her first thoughts were that the killings were either organized-crime hits or the work of a psychopath; OC clips were often staged like these to send messages to rival gangs. A sociopath, on the other hand, might set up such an elaborate killing out of delusion or for gratification, which might be sadistic – if it had a sexual motivation – or simply cruel for its own sake, apart from lust. In her years on the street she'd learned that inflicting pain was a source of power in itself and could even be addictive.

Ron Pulaski, in uniform and leather jacket, approached. The blond NYPD patrolman, slim and young, had been helping out Sachs on the Creeley case and was on call to assist on cases that Rhyme was handling. After a bad run-in with a perp had put him in the hospital for a long stay, he'd been offered medical disability retirement.

The rookie had told Sachs that he'd sat down with Jenny, his young wife, and discussed the issue. Should he go back on duty or not? Pulaski's twin brother, also a cop, provided input too. And in the end he chose to undergo therapy and return to the force. Sachs and Rhyme had been impressed with his youthful zeal and pulled some strings to get him assigned to them whenever possible. He later confessed to Sachs (never to Rhyme, of course) that the criminalist's refusal to be sidelined by his quadriplegia and his aggressive regimen of daily therapy were Pulaski's main inspiration to get back on active duty.

Pulaski wasn't in Tyvek, so he stopped at the yellow tape marking the scene. 'Jesus,' he muttered as he stared at the grotesque sight.

Pulaski told her that Sellitto and other officers were checking with security guards and office managers in the buildings around the alley to learn if anyone had seen or heard the attack or knew Theodore Adams. He added, 'The bomb squad's still checking on the clocks and'll deliver 'em to Rhyme's later. I'm going to get all the license plates of the cars parked around here. Detective Sellitto told me to.'

Her back to Pulaski, Sachs nodded. But she really wasn't paying much attention to this information; it wasn't useful to her at the moment. She was about to search the scene and was trying to clear her thoughts of distractions. Despite the fact that by definition crime scene work involves inanimate objects, there's a curious intimacy to the job; to be effective, CS cops have to mentally and emotionally *become* the perps. The whole horrific scenario plays itself out in their imaginations: what the killer was thinking, where he stood when he lifted the gun or club or knife, how he adjusted his stance, whether he lingered to watch the victim's death throes or fled immediately, what caught his attention at the scene, what tempted and repulsed him, what was his escape route. This wasn't psychological profiling – that occasionally helpful, media-chic portrait-painting of suspects; this was the art of mining the huge clutter at crime scenes for those few important nuggets that could lead to a suspect's door.

Sachs was now doing this, becoming someone else – the killer who'd engineered this terrible end to another human being.

Eyes scanning the scene, up and down, sideways: the cobblestones, the walls, the body, the iron weight . . .

I'm him . . . I'm him . . . What do I have in mind? Why did I want to kill these vics? Why in these ways? Why on the pier, why here?

But the cause of death was so unusual, the killer's mind so removed from hers, that she had no answers to these questions, not yet. She pulled on her headset. 'Rhyme, you there?'

'And where else would I be?' he asked, sounding amused. 'I've been waiting. Where are you? The second scene?'

'Yes.'

'What are you seeing, Sachs?'

I'm him . . .

'Alleyway, Rhyme,' she said into the stalk mike. 'It's a cul-de-sac for deliveries. It doesn't go through. The vic's close to the street.'

'How close?'

'Fifteen feet out of a hundred-foot alley.'

'How'd he get there?'

'No sign of tread marks but he was definitely dragged to the place he was killed; there's salt and crud on the bottom of his jacket and pants.'

'Are there doors near the body?'

'Yes. He's pretty much in front of one.'

'Did he work in the building?'

'No. I've got his business cards. He's a freelance writer. His work address is the same as his apartment.'

'He might've had a client there or in one of the other buildings.'

'Lon's checking now.'

'Good. The door that's closest? Would that've been someplace the perp could have waited for him?'

'Yeah,' she replied.

'Have a guard open it up and I want you to search what's on the other side.'

Lon Sellitto called from the perimeter of the scene, 'No

witnesses. Everybody's fucking blind. Oh, and deaf too . . . And there must be forty or fifty different offices in the buildings around the alley. If anybody knew him, it may take a while to find out.'

Sachs relayed the criminalist's request to open the back door near the body.

'You got it.' Sellitto headed off on this mission, blowing warming breath into his cupped hands.

Sachs videotaped and photographed the scene. She looked for and found no evidence of sexual activity involving the body or nearby. She then began walking the grid – walking over every square inch of the scene twice, looking for physical evidence. Unlike many crime scene professionals, Rhyme insisted on a single searcher – except in the case of mass disasters, of course – and Sachs always walked the grid alone.

But whoever'd committed the crime had been very careful not to leave anything obvious behind, except the note and the clock, the metal bar, the duct tape and rope.

She told him this.

'Not really in their nature to make it easy for us, is it, Sachs?'

His cheerful mood grated; *he* wasn't right next to a victim who'd died this fucking lousy death. She ignored the comment and continued working the scene: performing a basic processing of the corpse so it could be released to the medical examiner, collecting his effects, dusting for fingerprints and doing electrostatic prints of shoe treads, collecting trace with an adhesive roller, like the sort used for removing pet hairs.

It was likely that the perp had driven here, given the weight of the bar, but there were no tread marks. The center of the alley was covered with rock salt to melt the ice, and the grains prevented good contact with the cobblestones.

Then she squinted. 'Rhyme, something odd here. Around

the body, for probably three feet around it, there's something on the ground.'

'What do you think it is?'

Sachs bent down and with a magnifier examined what seemed to be fine sand. She mentioned this to Rhyme.

'Was it for the ice?'

'No. It's only around him. And there's none anywhere else in the alley. They're using salt for the snow and ice.' Then she stepped back. 'But there's only a fine residue left. It's like . . . yes, Rhyme. He swept up. With a broom.'

'Swept?'

'I can see the straw marks. It's like he scattered handfuls of sand on the scene and then swept it up . . . But maybe he didn't do it. There wasn't anything like this at the first scene, on the pier.'

'Is there any sand on the victim or the bar?'

'I don't know . . . Wait, there is.'

'So he did it *after* the killing,' Rhyme said. 'It's probably an obscuring agent.'

Diligent perps would sometimes use a powdery or granular material of some kind – sand, kitty litter or even flour – to spread on the ground after committing a crime. They'd then sweep or vacuum up the material, taking most of the trace particles with it.

'But why?' Rhyme mused.

Sachs stared at the body, stared at the cobblestone alley.

I'm him . . .

Why would I sweep?

Perps often wipe fingerprints and take the obvious evidence with them but it's very rare when someone goes to the trouble of using an obscuring agent. She closed her eyes and, as hard as it was, pictured herself standing over the young man, who was struggling to keep the bar off his throat.

'Maybe he spilled something.'

But Rhyme said, 'Doesn't seem likely. He wouldn't be that careless.'

She continued to think: I'm careful, sure. But why would I sweep?

I'm him . . .

'Why?' Rhyme whispered.

'He—'

'Not *he*,' the criminalist corrected. 'You're him, Sachs. Remember. *You*.'

'*I'm* a perfectionist. I want to get rid of as much evidence as possible.'

'True, but what you gain by sweeping up,' Rhyme said, 'you lose by staying on the scene longer. I think there has to be another reason.'

Going deeper, feeling herself lifting the bar, putting the rope in the man's hands, staring down at his struggling face, his bulging eyes. I put the clock next to his head. It's ticking, ticking . . . I watch him die.

I leave no evidence, I sweep up . . .

'Think, Sachs. What's he up to?'

I'm him . . .

Then she blurted, 'I'm coming back, Rhyme.'

'What?'

'I'm coming back to the scene. I mean, *he's* coming back. That's why he swept up. Because he absolutely didn't want to leave anything that'd give us a description of him: no fibers, hairs, shoe prints, dirt in his soles. He's not afraid we'll use it to track him to his hidey-hole – he's too good to be leaving trace like that. No, he's afraid we'll find something that'll help us recognize him when he comes back.'

'Okay, that could be it. Maybe he's a voyeur, likes to watch people die, likes to watch cops at work. Or maybe he wants to see who's hunting for him . . . so he can start a hunt of his own.'

Sachs felt a trickle of fear down her back. She looked around her. There was, as usual, a small crowd of gawkers standing across the street. Was the killer among them, watching her right now?

Then Rhyme added, 'Or maybe he's already been back. He came by earlier this morning to see that the vic was really dead. Which means—'

'That he might've left some evidence somewhere else, outside the scene. On the sidewalk, the street.'

'Exactly.'

Sachs slipped under the tape out of the designated crime scene and looked over the street. Then the sidewalk in front of the building. There she found a half dozen shoe prints in the snow. She had no way of knowing if any of them were the Watchmaker's but several – made by wide, waffle-stomper boots – suggested that somebody, a man probably, had stood in the mouth of the alley for a few minutes, shifting weight from foot to foot. She looked around and decided there was no reason for anybody to be standing there – no pay phones, mailboxes or windows were nearby.

'Got some unusual boot prints here in the mouth of the alley, by the curb on Cedar Street,' she told Rhyme. 'Large.' She searched this area too, digging into a snowbank. 'Got something else.'

'What?'

'A gold metal money clip.' Her fingers stinging from the cold through the latex gloves, she counted the cash inside. 'It's got three hundred forty in new twenties. Right next to the boot prints.'

'Did the vic have any money on him?'

'Sixty bucks, also pretty fresh.'

'Maybe the perp boosted the clip and then dropped it getting away.'

She placed it in an evidence bag, then finished searching other portions of the scene, finding nothing else.

The back door of the office building opened. Sellitto and a uniformed guard from the security staff of the building were there. They stood back as Sachs processed the door itself – finding and photographing what she described to Rhyme as a million fingerprints (he only chuckled) and the dim lobby on the other side. She didn't find anything obviously relevant to the murder.

Suddenly a woman's panicky voice cut through the cold air. 'Oh, my God, no!'

A stocky brunette in her thirties ran up to the yellow tape, where she was stopped by a patrol officer. Her hands were at her face and she was sobbing. Sellitto stepped forward. Sachs joined them. 'Do you know him, ma'am?' the big detective asked.

'What happened, what happened? No . . . oh, God . . .'

'Do you know him?' the detective repeated.

Wracked with crying, the woman turned away from the terrible sight. 'My brother . . . No, is he – oh, God, no, he can't be . . .' She sank to her knees on the ice.

This would be the woman who'd reported her brother missing last night, Sachs understood.

Lon Sellitto had the personality of a pitbull when it came to suspects. But with victims and their relatives he showed a surprising tenderness. In a soft voice, thickened by a Brooklyn drawl, he said, 'I'm so sorry. He's gone, yes.' He helped her up and she leaned against the wall of the alley.

'Who did it? Why?' Her voice rose to a screech as she stared at the terrible tableau of her brother's death. 'Who'd do something like this? Who?'

'We don't know, ma'am,' Sachs said. 'I'm sorry. But we'll find him. I promise you.'

Gasping for breath, she turned. 'Don't let my daughter see, please.'

Sachs looked past her to a car, parked half on the curb,

where she'd left it in her panic. In the passenger seat was a teenage girl, who was staring at Sachs with a frown, her head cocked. The detective stepped in front of the body, blocking off the girl's view of her uncle.

The sister, whose name was Barbara Eckhart, had jumped from her car without her coat and was huddling against the cold. Sachs led her through the open door into the service lobby that she'd just run. The hysterical woman asked to use the restroom and when she emerged she was still shaken and pale, though the crying was under control.

Barbara had no idea what the killer's motive might be. Her brother, a bachelor, worked for himself, a freelance advertising copywriter. He was well liked and had no enemies that she knew of. He wasn't involved in any romantic triangles – no jealous husbands – and had never done drugs or anything else illegal. He'd moved to the city two years earlier.

That he had no apparent OC connection troubled Sachs; it moved the psycho factor into first place, far more dangerous to the public than a mob pro.

Sachs explained how the body would be processed. It would be released by the medical examiner to the next of kin within twenty-four to forty-eight hours. Barbara's face grew stony. 'Why did he kill Teddy like that? What was he thinking?'

But that was a question for which Amelia Sachs had no answer.

Watching the woman return to her car, Sellitto helping her, Sachs couldn't take her eyes off the daughter, who was staring back at the policewoman. The look was hard to bear. The girl must know by now that this man was in fact her uncle and he was dead, but Sachs could see what seemed to be a small bit of hope in the girl's face.

Hope, about to be destroyed.

*

Hungry.

Vincent Reynolds lay on his musty bed in their temporary home, which was, of all things, a former church, and felt his soul's hunger, silently mimicking the grumbling of his bulging belly.

This old Catholic structure, in a deserted area of Manhattan near the Hudson River, was their base of operation for the killings. Gerald Duncan was from out of town and Vincent's apartment was in New Jersey. Vincent had said they could stay at his place but Duncan had said, no, they could hardly do that. They should have no contact whatsoever with their real residences. He'd sounded sort of like he was lecturing. But not in a bad way. It was like a father instructing his son.

'A church?' Vincent had asked. 'Why?'

'Because it's been on the market for fourteen and a half months. Not a hot property. And nobody's going to be showing it this time of year.' A fast look at Vincent. 'Don't worry. It's desanctified.'

'It is?' asked Vincent, who figured that he'd committed enough sins to be guaranteed a direct route to hell, if there was one; trespassing in a church, sanctified or de-, was the very least of his offenses.

The real estate agent kept the doors locked, of course, but a watchmaker's skills are essentially those of a locksmith (the first clock makers, Duncan had explained, were lock-smiths) and the man easily picked one of the back door locks then fitted it with a padlock of his own, so they could come and go, unseen by anyone on the street or sidewalk. He changed the lock on the front door too and left a bit of wax on it so they'd know if anybody tried to get in when they were away.

The place was gloomy and drafty and smelled of cheap cleansers.

Duncan's room was the former priest's bedroom on the

second floor in the rectory portion of the structure. Across the hall was Vincent's room, where he was now lying, the old office. It contained a cot, table, hotplate, microwave and refrigerator (Hungry Vincent, of course, got the kitchen, such as it was). The church still had electricity in case brokers needed the lights, and the heat was on so the pipes wouldn't burst, though the thermostat was set very low.

When he'd first seen it, knowing Duncan's obsession with time, Vincent had said, 'Too bad there's no clock tower. Like Big Ben.'

'That's the name of the bell, not the clock.'

'On the Tower of London?'

'In the clock tower,' the older man had corrected again. 'At the Palace of Westminster, where Parliament sits. Named after Sir Benjamin Hall. In the late eighteen fifties it was England's largest bell. In early clocks, the bells were the only thing that told you the time. There were no faces or hands.'

'Oh.'

'The word "clock" comes from the Latin *clocca*, which means bell.'

This man knew *everything*.

Vincent liked that. He liked a lot of things about Gerald Duncan. He'd been wondering if these two misfits could become real friends. Vincent didn't have many. He'd sometimes go out for drinks with the paralegals and other word-processing operators. But even Clever Vincent tended not to say too much because he was afraid he'd let slip the wrong thing about a waitress or the woman sitting at a table nearby. Hunger made you careless (just look at what had happened with Sally Anne).

Vincent and Duncan were opposites in many ways but they had one thing in common: dark secrets in their hearts. And anyone who's ever shared that knows it makes up for vast differences in lifestyle and politics.

Oh, yes, Vincent was definitely going to give their friendship a shot.

He now washed up, again thinking of Joanne, the brunette they'd be visiting today: the flower girl, their next victim.

Vincent opened the small refrigerator. He took out a bagel and cut it in half with his hunting knife. It had an eight-inch blade and was very sharp. He smeared cream cheese on the bagel and ate it while he drank two Cokes. His nose stung from the chill. Meticulous Gerald Duncan insisted that they wear gloves here too, which was kind of a pain, but today, because it was so cold, Vincent didn't mind.

He lay back on the bed, imagining what Joanne's body looked like.

Later today . . .

Feeling hungry, starving to death. His gut was drying up from the craving. If he didn't have his little heart-to-heart with Joanne pretty soon, he'd waste away to steam.

Now he drank a can of Dr Pepper, ate a bag of potato chips. Then some pretzels.

Starving . . .

Hungry . . .

Vincent Reynolds would not on his own have come up with the idea that the urge to sexually assault women was a hunger. That idea was courtesy of his therapist, Dr Jenkins.

When he was in detention because of Sally Anne – the only time he'd been arrested – the doctor had explained that he had to accept that the urges he felt would never go away. 'You can't get rid of them. They're a hunger in a way . . . Now, what do we know about hunger? It's natural. We can't help feeling hungry. Don't you agree?'

'Yessir.'

The therapist had added that even though you couldn't stop hunger completely you could 'satisfy it appropriately. You understand what I mean? With food, you'd have a healthy meal when it's the appropriate time, you don't just snack. With people, you have a healthy, committed relationship, leading up to marriage and a family.'

'I get it.'

'Good. I think we're making progress. Don't you agree?'

And the boy had taken great heart in the man's message, though it translated into something a little different from what the good doctor intended. Vincent reasoned that he'd use the hunger analogy as a helpful guide. He'd only eat, that is, have a little heart-to-heart with a girl, when he really needed to. That way he wouldn't become desperate – and careless, the way he had with Sally Anne.

Brilliant.

Don't you agree, Dr Jenkins?

Vincent finished the pretzels and soda and wrote another letter to his sister. Clever Vincent drew a few cartoons in the margins. Pictures he thought she might like. Vincent wasn't a terrible artist.

There was a knock on his door.

'Come in.'

Gerald Duncan pushed the door open. The men said good morning to each other. Vincent glanced into Duncan's room, which was perfectly ordered. Everything on the desk was arranged in a symmetrical pattern. The clothes were pressed and hanging in the closet exactly two inches apart. This could be one hurdle to their friendship. Vincent was a slob.

'You want something to eat?' Vincent asked.

'No, thanks.'

That's why the Watchmaker was so skinny. He rarely ate, he was never hungry. That could be another hurdle. But Vincent decided he'd ignore that fault. After all, Vincent's sister never ate much either and he still loved her.

The killer made coffee for himself. While the water was heating he took the jar of beans out of the refrigerator and measured out exactly two spoons' worth. These clattered as he poured them into the hand grinder and turned the handle a dozen times until the noise stopped. He carefully poured the grounds into a paper cone filter inside a drip funnel. He tapped it to make sure the grounds were level. Vincent loved watching Gerald Duncan make coffee.

Meticulous . . .

Duncan looked at his gold pocket watch. He wound the stem very carefully. He finished the coffee – he drank it fast like medicine – and then looked at Vincent. 'Our flower girl,' he said, 'Joanne. Will you go check on her?'

A thud in his gut. So long, Clever Vincent.

'Sure.'

'I'm going to the alley on Cedar Street. The police will be there by now. I want to see whom we're up against.'

Whom . . .

Duncan pulled his jacket on and slung his bag over his shoulder. 'You ready?'

Vincent nodded and donned his cream-colored parka, hat and sunglasses.

Duncan was saying, 'Let me know if people are coming by the workshop to pick up orders or if she's working alone.'

The Watchmaker had learned that Joanne spent a lot of time in her workshop, a few blocks away from her retail flower store. The workshop was quiet and dark. Picturing the woman, her curly brown hair, her long but pretty face, Hungry Vincent couldn't get her out of his mind.

They walked downstairs and into the alley behind the church.

Duncan hooked the padlock. He said. 'Oh, I wanted to say something. The one for tomorrow? She's a woman too. That'd be two in a row. I don't know how often you like to have your . . . what do you call it? A heart-to-heart?'

'That's right.'

'Why do you say that?' Duncan asked. The killer, Vincent had learned, had a tireless curiosity.

That phrase too came from Dr Jenkins, his buddy the detention center doc, who'd tell him to come to his office anytime he wanted and talk about how he was feeling; they'd have themselves a good old heart-to-heart.

For some reason, Vincent liked the words. The phrase also sounded a lot better than 'rape'.

'I don't know. I just do.' He added that he'd have no problem with two women in a row.

Sometimes eating makes you even hungrier, Dr Jenkins.

Don't you agree?

As they stepped carefully over the icy patches on the sidewalk, Vincent asked, 'Um, what are you going to do with Joanne?'

In killing his victims Duncan had one rule: Their deaths could not be quick. This wasn't as easy at it sounded, he'd explained in that precise, detached voice of his. Duncan had a book titled *Extreme Interrogation Techniques*. It was about terrifying prisoners into talking by subjecting them to tortures that would eventually kill them if they didn't confess: putting weights over their throats, cutting their wrists and letting them bleed, a dozen other.

Duncan explained, 'I don't want to take too long, in her case. I'll gag her and tie her hands behind her. Then get her on her stomach and wrap a wire around her neck and her ankles.'

'Her knees'll be bent?' Vincent could picture it.

'That's right. It was in the book. Did you see the illustrations?'

Vincent shook his head.

'She won't be able to keep her legs at that angle for very long. When they start to straighten, it pulls the wire around her neck taut and she'll strangle herself. It'll take about eight, ten minutes, I'd guess.' He smiled. 'I'm going to time it. As you suggested. When it's over I'll call you and she's all yours.'

A good old heart-to-heart . . .

They stepped out of the alley as a blast of freezing wind struck them. Vincent's parka, which was unzipped, blew open.

He stopped, alarmed. On the sidewalk a few feet away was a young man. He had a scrawny beard and wore a threadbare jacket. A backpack was slung over a shoulder. A student, Vincent guessed. Head down, he kept walking briskly.

Duncan glanced at his partner. 'What's the matter?'

Vincent nodded at his side, where the hunting knife, in a scabbard, was stuck into his waistband. 'I think he saw it. I'm . . . I'm sorry. I should've zipped my jacket, but . . .'

Duncan's lips pressed together.

No, no . . . Vincent hoped he hadn't made Duncan unhappy. 'I'll go take care of him, if you want. I'll—'

The killer looked toward the student, who was walking quickly away from them.

Duncan turned to Vincent. 'Have you ever killed anyone?'

He couldn't hold the man's piercing blue eyes. 'No.'

'Wait here.' Gerald Duncan studied the street, which was deserted, except for the student. He reached into his pocket and took out the box cutter he'd used to slash the wrists of the man on the pier last night. Duncan walked quickly after the student. Vincent watched him catching up until the killer was only a few feet behind him. They turned the corner, heading east.

This was terrible . . . Vincent hadn't been meticulous. He'd put everything at risk: his chance for friendship with Duncan, his chance for the heart-to-hearts. All because he'd been careless. He wanted to scream, he wanted to cry.

He reached into his pocket, found a KitKat and wolfed it down, eating some of the wrapper with the candy.

Five agonizing minutes later Duncan returned, holding a wrinkled newspaper.

'I'm sorry,' Vincent said.

'It's all right. It's okay.' Duncan's voice was soft. Inside the paper was the bloody box cutter. He wiped the blade with the paper and retracted the razor blade. He threw away the bloody paper and gloves. He put a new pair on. He insisted they carry two or three pairs with them at all times.

Duncan said, 'The body's in a Dumpster. I covered it up with trash. If we're lucky it'll be in a landfill or out to sea before somebody notices the blood.'

'Are you all right?' Vincent thought there was a red mark on Duncan's cheek.

The man shrugged. 'I got careless. He fought back. I had to slash his eyes. Remember that. If somebody resists, slash their eyes. That stops them resisting right away and you can control them however you want.'

Slash their eyes . . .

Vincent nodded slowly.

Duncan asked, 'You'll be more careful?'

'Oh, yes. Promise. Really.'

'Now go check on the flower girl and meet me at the museum at quarter past four.'

'Okay, sure.'

Duncan turned his light blue eyes on Vincent. He gave a rare smile. 'Don't be upset. There was a problem. It's been taken care of. In the great scheme of things, it was nothing.'

Chapter
FIVE

The body of Teddy Adams was gone, the grieving relatives too.

Lon Sellitto had just left for Rhyme's and the scene was officially released. Ron Pulaski, Nancy Simpson and Frank Rettig were removing the crime scene tape.

Still stung by the look of desperate hope in the face of Adams's young niece, Amelia Sachs had gone over the scene yet again with even more diligence than usual. She checked other doorways and possible entrance and escape routes the perp might've used. But she found nothing else. She didn't remember the last time a complicated crime like this had yielded so little evidence.

After packing up her equipment she mentally shifted back to the Benjamin Creeley case and called the man's wife, Suzanne, to tell her that several men had broken into their Westchester house.

'I didn't know that. Do you have any idea what they stole?'

Sachs had met the woman several times. She was very thin – she jogged daily – and had short frosted hair, a pretty face. 'It didn't look like much was missing.' She decided to say nothing about the neighbor boy; she figured she'd scared him into going straight.

Sachs asked if anyone would have been burning something in the fireplace, and Suzanne replied that no one had even been to the house recently.

'What do you think was going on?'

'I don't know. But it's making the suicide look more doubtful. Oh, by the way, you need a new lock on your back door.'

'I'll call somebody today . . . Thank you, Detective. It means a lot that you believe me. About Ben not killing himself.'

After they hung up, Sachs filled out a request for analysis of the ash, mud and other evidence at the Creeleys' house and packed these materials separately from the Watchmaker evidence. She then completed the chain-of-custody cards and helped Simpson and Rettig pack up the van. It took two of them to wrap the heavy metal bar in plastic and stow it.

She was just swinging shut the van's door when she glanced up, across the street. The cold had driven off most of the spectators but she noted a man standing with a *Post* in front of an old building being renovated on Cedar Street, near Chase Plaza.

That's not right, Sachs thought. Nobody stands on the street corner and reads a newspaper in this weather. If you're worried about the stock market or curious about a recent disaster, you flip through quickly, find out how much money you lost or how far the church bus plummeted and then keep on walking.

But you don't just stand in the windy street for Page Six gossip.

She couldn't see the man clearly – he was partially hidden behind the newspaper and a pile of debris from the construction site. But one thing was obvious: his boots. They'd have a traction tread, which could have left the distinctive impressions she found in the snow at the mouth of the alley.

Sachs debated. Most of the other officers had left. Simpson and Rettig were armed but not tactically trained and the suspect was on the other side of a three-foot-high metal barricade set up for an upcoming parade. He could escape easily if she approached him from where she was now, across the street. She'd have to handle the take-down more subtly.

She walked up to Pulaski, whispered, 'There's somebody at your six o'clock. I want to talk to him. Guy with the paper.'

'The perp?' he asked.

'Don't know. Maybe. Here's what we're going to do. I'm getting into the RRV with the CS team. They're going to drop me at the corner to the east. Can you drive a manual?'

'Sure.'

She gave him the keys to her bright red Camaro. 'You drive *west* on Cedar toward Broadway, maybe forty feet. Stop fast, get out and vault the barricade, come back this way.'

'Flush him.'

'Right. If he's just out reading the paper, we'll have a talk, check his ID and get back to work. If not, I'm guessing he'll turn and run right into my arms. You come up behind and cover me.'

'Got it.'

Sachs made a show of taking a last look around the scene and then climbed into the big brown RRV van. She leaned forward. 'We've got a problem.'

Nancy Simpson and Frank Rettig glanced toward her. Simpson unzipped her jacket and put her hand on the grip of her pistol.

'No, don't need that. I'll tell you what's going down.' She explained the situation then said to Simpson, who was behind the wheel, 'Head east. At the light make a left. Just slow up. I'll jump out.'

Pulaski climbed into the Camaro, fired it up and couldn't resist pumping the gas to get a sexy whine out of the Tubi exhausts.

Rettig asked, 'You don't want us to stop?'

'No, just slow up. I want the suspect to be sure I'm leaving.'

'Okay,' Simpson said. 'You got it.'

The RRV headed east. In the sideview mirror Sachs saw Pulaski start forward – easy, she told him silently; it was a monster engine and the clutch gripped like Velcro. But he controlled the horses and rolled forward smoothly, the opposite direction from the van.

At the intersection of Cedar and Nassau the RRV turned and Sachs opened the door. 'Keep going. Don't slow up.'

Simpson did a great job keeping the van steady. 'Good luck,' the crime scene officer called.

Sachs leapt out.

Whoa, a little faster than she'd planned. She nearly stumbled, caught herself and thanked the Department of Sanitation for the generous sprinkling of salt on the icy street. She started along the sidewalk, coming up behind the man with the newspaper. He didn't see her.

A block away, then a half block. She opened her jacket and gripped the Glock that rode high on her belt. About fifty feet past the suspect, Pulaski suddenly pulled to the curb, climbed out and – without the guy's noticing – easily jumped over the barricade. They had him sandwiched in, separated by a barrier on one side and the building being renovated on the other.

A good plan.

Except for one glitch.

Across the street from Sachs were two armed guards, stationed in front of the Housing and Urban Development building. They'd been helping with the crime scene and one of them glanced at Sachs. He waved to her, calling, 'Forget something, Detective?'

Shit. The man with the newspaper whirled around and saw her.

He dropped the paper, jumped the barrier and sprinted as fast as he could down the middle of the street toward Broadway, catching Pulaski on the other side of the metal fence. The rookie tried to leap it, caught his foot and went down hard in the street. Sachs paused but saw he wasn't badly hurt and she continued after the suspect. Pulaski rolled to his feet and together they sprinted after the man, who had a thirty-foot head start and was increasing his lead.

She grabbed her walkie-talkie and pressed TRANSMIT. 'Detective Five Eight Eight Five,' she gasped. 'In foot pursuit of a suspect in that homicide near Cedar Street. Suspect is heading west on Cedar, wait, now south on Broadway. Need backup.'

'Roger, Five Eight Eight Five. Directing units to your location.'

Several other RMPs – radio mobile patrols, squad cars – responded that they were nearby and en route to cut off the suspect's escape.

As Sachs and Pulaski approached Battery Park, the man suddenly stopped, nearly stumbling. He glanced to his right – at the subway.

No, not the train, she thought. Too many bystanders in close proximity.

Don't do it . . .

Another glance over his shoulder and he plunged down the stairs.

She stopped, calling to Pulaski, 'Go after him.' A deep breath. 'If he shoots, check your backdrop real carefully. Let him go rather than fire if there's any doubt at all.'

His face uneasy, the rookie nodded. Sachs knew he'd never been in a firefight. He called, 'Where're you—'

'Just go!' she shouted.

The rookie took a breath and started sprinting again. Sachs ran to the subway entrance and watched Pulaski descend three steps at a time. Then she crossed the street and trotted a half block south. She drew her gun and stepped behind a newsstand.

Counting down . . . four . . . three . . . two . . .

One.

She stepped out, turning to the subway exit, just as the suspect sprinted up the stairs. She trained the gun on him. 'Don't move.'

Passers-by were screaming and dropping to the ground. The suspect's reaction, though, was simply disgust, presumably that his trick hadn't worked. Sachs had thought he might be coming this way. The surprise in his eyes when he saw the subway could've been phony she'd decided. It told her that maybe he'd been making for the station all along – as a possible feint. He raised his hands lethargically.

'On the ground, face down.'

'Come on. I—'

'Now!' she snapped.

He glanced at her gun and then complied. Winded from the run, her joints in pain, she dropped a knee into the middle of his back to cuff him. He winced. Sachs didn't care. She was just in one of those moods.

'They got a suspect. At the scene.'

Lincoln Rhyme and the man who delivered this interesting news were sitting in his lab. Dennis Baker, fortyish, compact and handsome, was a supervisory lieutenant in Major Cases – Sellitto's division – and had been ordered by City Hall to make sure the Watchmaker was stopped as fast as possible. He'd been one of those who'd 'insisted' that Sellitto get Rhyme and Sachs on the case.

Rhyme lifted an eyebrow. Suspect? Criminals often did return to the scene of the crime, for various reasons, and Rhyme wondered if Sachs had actually collared the killer.

Baker turned back to his cell phone, listening and nodding. The lieutenant – who bore an uncanny resemblance to the actor George Clooney – had that focused, humorless quality that makes for an excellent police administrator but a tedious drinking buddy.

'He's a good guy to have on your side,' Sellitto had said of Baker just before the man arrived from One Police Plaza.

'Fine, but is he going to meddle?' Rhyme had asked the rumpled detective.

'Not so's you'd notice.'

'Meaning?'

'He wants a big win under his belt and he thinks you can deliver it. He'll give you all the slack – and support – you need.'

Which was good, because they were down some manpower. There was another NYPD detective who often worked with them, Roland Bell, a transplant from the South. The detective had an easy-going manner, very different from Rhyme's, though an equally methodical nature. Bell was on vacation with his two sons down in North Carolina, visiting his girl-friend, a local sheriff in the Tarheel State.

They also often worked with an FBI agent, renowned for his antiterrorism and undercover work, Fred Dellray. Murders of this sort aren't usually federal crimes but Dellray often helped Sellitto and Rhyme on homicides and would make the resources of the Bureau available without the typical red tape. But the Feds had their hands full with several massive Enron-style corporate fraud investigations that were just getting under way. Dellray was stuck on one of these.

Hence, Baker's presence – not to mention his influence at the Big Building – was a godsend. Sellitto now disconnected his cell phone call and explained that Sachs was interviewing the suspect at the moment, though he wasn't being very co-operative.

Sellitto was sitting next to Mel Cooper, the slightly built, ballroom-dancing forensic technician that Rhyme insisted on using. Cooper suffered for his brilliance as a crime scene lab man; Rhyme called him at all hours to run the technical side of his cases. He'd hesitated a bit when Rhyme called him at the lab in Queens that morning, explaining that he'd planned to take his girlfriend and his mother to Florida for the weekend.

Rhyme's response was, 'All the more incentive to get here as soon as possible, wouldn't you say?'

'I'll be there in a half hour.' He was now at an examination table in the lab, awaiting the evidence. With a latex-gloved hand, he fed some biscuits to Jackson; the dog was curled up at his feet.

'If there's any canine hair contamination,' Rhyme grumbled, 'I won't be happy.'

'He's pretty cute,' Cooper said, swapping gloves.

The criminalist grunted. 'Cute' was not a word that figured in the Lincoln Rhyme dictionary.

Sellitto's phone rang again and he took the call, then disconnected. 'The vic at the pier – Coast Guard and our divers haven't found any bodies yet. Still checking missing persons' reports.'

Just then Crime Scene arrived and Thom helped an officer cart in the evidence from the scenes Sachs had just run.

About time . . .

Baker and Cooper lugged in a heavy, plastic-wrapped metal bar.

The murder weapon in the alleyway killing.

The CS officer handed over chain-of-custody cards, which Cooper signed. The man said goodbye but Rhyme didn't acknowledge him. The criminalist was looking at the evidence. This was the moment that he lived for. After the spinal cord accident, his passion – really an addiction – for the sport of going one-on-one with perps continued undiminished, and the evidence from crimes was the field on which this game was played.

He felt eager anticipation.

And guilt too.

Because he wouldn't be filled with this exhilaration if not for someone else's loss: the victim on the pier and Theodore Adams, their families and friends. Oh, he felt sympathy for their sorrow, sure. But he was able to wrap up the sense of tragedy and put it somewhere. Some people called him cold, insensitive, and he supposed he was. But those who excel in a field do so because a number of disparate traits happen to come together within them. And Rhyme's sharp mind and relentless drive and impatience happened to coincide with the emotional distance that is a necessary attribute of the best criminalists.

He was squinting, gazing at the boxes, when Ron Pulaski arrived. Rhyme had first met him when the young man had been on the force only a short time. Although that was a year earlier – and Pulaski was a family man with two children – Rhyme couldn't stop thinking of him as the 'rookie'. Some nicknames you just can't shake.

Rhyme announced, 'I know Amelia has somebody in custody but in case it isn't the perp, I don't want to lose time.' He turned to Pulaski. 'Give me the lay of the land. First scene, the pier.'

'All right,' he began uneasily. 'The pier is located approximately at Twenty-second Street in the Hudson River. It extends into the river fifty-two feet at a height of eighteen feet above the surface of the water. The murder—'

'So they've recovered the body?'

'I don't think so.'

'Then you meant *apparent* murder?'

'Right. Yessir. The apparent murder occurred at the far end of the pier, that is, the west end, sometime between six last night and six this morning. The dock was closed then.'

There was very little evidence: just the fingernail, probably a man's, the blood, which Mel Cooper tested and found to be human and type AB positive, which meant that both A and B antigens – proteins – were present in the victim's plasma, and neither anti-A nor anti-B antigens were. In addition a separate protein, Rh, was present. The combination of AB antigens and Rh positive made the victim's the third-rarest blood type, accounting for about 3.5 percent of the population. Further tests confirmed that the victim was a male.

In addition, they concluded that he was probably older and had coronary problems since he was taking an anticoagulant – a blood thinner. There were no traces of other drugs or indications of infection or disease in the blood.

There were no fingerprints, trace or footprints at the scene and no tire tread marks nearby, other than those left by employees' vehicles.

Sachs had collected a piece of the chain link and Cooper examined the cut edges, learning that the perp had used what seemed to be standard wire cutters to get through the fence. The team could match these marks with those made by a tool if they found one but there was no way to trace the cutter back to its source by the impressions alone.

Rhyme looked over the pictures of the scene, particularly the pattern the blood had made as it flowed onto the pier. He guessed that the victim had been hanging over the edge of the deck, at chest level, his fingers desperately wedged into the space between the planks. The fingernail marks showed that eventually he'd lost his grip. Rhyme wondered how long the vic had been able to hang on.

He nodded slowly. 'Tell me about the next scene.'

Pulaski replied, 'All right, that homicide occurred in an alley off Cedar Street, near Broadway. This alley featured a dead end. It was fifteen feet wide and one hundred and four feet long and was surfaced with cobblestones.'

The body, Rhyme recalled, was fifteen feet from the mouth of the alley.

'What's the time of death?'

'At least eight hours before he was found, the ME tour doc said. The body was frozen solid so it'll take a while to determine with any certainty.' The young officer suffered from the habit of copspeak.

'Amelia told me about the service and fire doors in the alley. Did anybody ask what time they were locked for the night?'

'Three of the buildings're commercial. Two of them lock their service doors at eight thirty and one at ten. The other's a government administration building. That door's locked at six. There's a late-night garbage pickup at ten.'

'Body discovered when?'

'Around seven A.M.'

'Okay, the vic in the alley was dead at least eight hours, last door was locked at ten and garbage picked up then. So the killing took place between, say, ten fifteen and eleven P.M. Parking situation?'

'I got the license plates of every car in a two-block radius.' Pulaski was holding up a *Moby-Dick* of a notebook.

'What the hell's that?'

'Oh, I wrote down notes about all the cars. Thought it might be helpful. You know, where they were parked, anything suspicious about them.'

'Waste of time. We just needed the tag numbers for names and addresses,' Rhyme explained. 'To cross-check DMV with NCIC and the other databases. We don't care who needed bodywork or had bald tires or a crack pipe in the backseat . . . Well, did you?'

'What?'

'Run the tags?'

'Not yet.'

Cooper went online but found no warrants on any of the registered owners of the cars. At Rhyme's instruction he also checked to see if any parking tickets were issued in that area around the time of the killing. There were none.

'Mel, run the vic's name. Warrants? Anything else about him?'

There were no state warrants on Theodore Adams, and Pulaski recounted what his sister had said about him – that he apparently had no enemies or personal life issues that might result in his murder.

'Why these vics, though?' Rhyme asked. 'Are they random? . . . I know Dellray's busy but this's important. Give him a call and have him run Adams's name. See if the Feds have anything on him.'

Sellitto made a call to the federal building and got through to Dellray – who was in a bad mood because of the 'fucking quagmire' of a financial fraud case he'd been assigned. Still, he managed to look through the federal databases and active case files. But the results were negative on Theodore Adams.

'Okay,' Rhyme announced, 'until we find something else let's assume they're random victims of a crazy man.' He squinted at the pictures. 'Where the hell're the clocks?'

A call to the bomb squad revealed that they'd been cleared of any bio or toxic threat and were on their way to Rhyme's right now.

The cash in the faux gold money clip appeared fresh out of an ATM machine. The bills were clean but Cooper found some good prints on the clip. Unfortunately, when he ran them through IAFIS, the FBI's Integrated Automated Fingerprint Identification System, there were no hits. The few prints on the cash in Adams's pocket came back negative as well, and the serial numbers revealed the bills hadn't been flagged by the Treasury Department for possible involvement in money laundering or other crimes.

'The sand?' Rhyme asked, referring to the obscuring agent.

'Generic,' Cooper called, not looking up from the microscope.

'Sort used in playgrounds rather than construction. I'll check it for other trace.'

And no sand at the pier, Rhyme recalled Sachs telling him. Was that because, as she'd speculated, the perp was planning to return to the alley? Or simply because the substance wasn't needed on the pier, where the brutal wind from the Hudson would sweep the scene clean?

'What about the span?' Rhyme asked.

'The what?'

'The bar the vic's neck was crushed with. It's a needle-eye span.' Rhyme had made a study of construction materials in the city, since a popular way to dispose of bodies was to dump them at job sites. Cooper and Sellitto weighed the length of metal – it was eighty-one pounds – and got it onto the examining table. The span was about six feet long, an inch wide and three inches high. A hole was drilled in each end. 'They're used mostly in shipbuilding, heavy equipment, cranes, antennas and bridges.'

'That's gotta be the heaviest murder weapon I've ever seen,' Cooper said.

'Heavier than a Suburban?' asked Lincoln Rhyme, the man for whom precision was everything. He was referring to the case of the wife who'd run over her philandering husband with a very large SUV in the middle of Third Avenue several months earlier.

'Oh, that . . . his cheatin' heart,' Cooper sang in a squeaky tenor. Then he tested for fingerprints and found none. He filed off some shavings from the rod. 'Probably iron. I see evidence of oxidation.' A chemical test revealed that this was the case.

'No identifying markings?'

'Nope.'

Rhyme grimaced. 'That's a problem. There've got to be fifty sources in the metro area . . . Wait. Amelia said there was some construction nearby—'

'Oh,' Pulaski said, 'she had me check there and they weren't using any metal bars like that. I forgot to mention it.'

'You forgot,' Rhyme muttered. 'Well, I know the city's doing some major work on the Queensboro Bridge. Let's give 'em a try.' Rhyme said to Pulaski, 'Call the work crew at the Queensboro and find out if spans're being used there and, if so, are any missing.'

The rookie nodded and pulled out his mobile phone.

Cooper looked over the analysis of the sand. 'Okay, got something here. Thallium sulfate.'

'What's that?' Sellitto asked.

'Rodent poison,' said Rhyme. 'It's banned in this country but you sometimes find it in immigrant communities or in buildings where immigrants work. How concentrated?'

'Very . . . and there's none in the control soil and residue that Amelia collected. Which means it's probably from some-place the perp's been.'

'Maybe he's planning to kill somebody with it,' Pulaski suggested, as he waited on hold.

Rhyme shook his head. 'Not likely. It's not easy to administer and you need a high dosage for humans. But it could lead us to him. Find out if there've been any recent confiscations or environmental agency complaints in the city.'

Cooper made the calls.

'Let's look at the duct tape,' Rhyme instructed.

The tech examined the rectangles of shiny gray tape, which had been used to bind the victim's hands and feet and gag him. He announced that the tape was generic, sold in thousands of home improvement, drug and grocery stores around the country. Testing the adhesive on the tape revealed very little trace, just a few grains of snow-removal salt, which matched samples Sachs had taken from the general area, and the sand that the Watchmaker had spread to help him clean up trace.

Disappointed that the duct tape wasn't more helpful, Rhyme turned to the photos Sachs had shot of Adams's body. Then he wheeled closer to the examination table and peered at the screen. 'Look at the edges of the tape.'

'Interesting,' Cooper said, glancing from the digital photos to the tape itself.

What had struck the men as odd was that the pieces of tape had been cut with extreme precision and applied very carefully. Usually it was just torn off the roll, sometimes ripped by the attacker's teeth (which often left DNA-laden saliva), and wrapped sloppily around the victim's hands, ankles and mouth. But the strips used by the Watchmaker were perfectly cut with a sharp object. The lengths were identical.

Ron Pulaski hung up, then announced, 'They don't use needle-eye spans on the work they're doing now on the bridge.'

Well, Rhyme hadn't expected easy answers.

'And the rope he was holding on to?'

Cooper looked it over, examined some databases. He shook his head. 'Generic.'

Rhyme nodded at several whiteboards that stood empty in the corner of the lab. 'Start our charts. You, Ron, you have good handwriting?'

'It's good enough.'

'That's all we need. Write.'

When running cases Rhyme kept charts of all the evidence they found. They were like crystal balls to him; he'd stare at the words and photos and diagrams to try to understand who the perp might be, where he was hiding, where he was going to strike next. Gazing at his evidence boards was the closest Lincoln Rhyme ever came to meditating.

'We'll use his name as the heading, since he was *so* courteous to let us know what he wants to be called.'

As Pulaski wrote what Rhyme dictated, Cooper picked up a tube containing a tiny sample of what seemed to be soil.

He looked it over through the microscope, starting on 4x power (the number-one rule with optical scopes is to start low, if you go right to higher magnifications you'll end up looking at artistically interesting but forensically useless abstract images).

'Looks like your basic soil. I'll see what else's in it.' He prepared a sample for the chromatograph/mass spectrometer, a large instrument that separates and identifies substances in trace evidence.

When the results were ready Cooper looked over the computer screen and announced, 'Okay, we've got some oils, nitrogen, urea, chloride . . . and protein. Let me run the profile.' A moment later his computer filled with additional information. 'Fish protein.'

'So maybe the perp works in a fish restaurant,' Pulaski said enthusiastically. 'Or a fish stand in Chinatown. Or, wait, maybe the fish counter at a grocery store.'

Rhyme asked, 'Ron, you ever hear a public speaker say, "Before I begin, I'd like to say something"?'

'Uhm. I think.'

'Which is a little odd, because if he's talking he's already begun, right?'

Pulaski lifted an eyebrow.

'My point is that in analyzing the evidence you do something before you start.'

'Which is what?'

'Find out where the evidence *came* from. Now, where did Sachs collect the fish protein dirt?'

He looked at the tag. 'Oh.'

'Where is "oh"?'

'Inside the victim's jacket.'

'So whom does the evidence tell us something about?'

'The victim, not the perp.'

'Exactly! Is it helpful to know that he has it on his jacket?

Who knows? Maybe it will be. But the important point is to not blindly send the troops to every fishmonger in the city too fast. You comfortable with that theory, Ron?'

'Real comfortable.'

'I'm so pleased. Write down the fishy soil under the victim's profile and let's get on with it, shall we? When's the medical examiner sending us a report?'

Cooper said, 'Could be a while. Coming up on Christmastime.'

Sellitto sang, ''Tis the season to be killing . . .'

Pulaski gave a frown. Rhyme explained to him, 'The deadliest times of the year are hot spells and holidays. Remember, Ron: Stress doesn't kill people; people kill people – but stress makes 'em do it.'

'Got fibers here, brown,' Cooper announced. He glanced at the notes attached to the bag. 'Back heel of the victim's shoe and his wristwatch band.'

'What kind of fibers?'

Cooper examined them closely and ran the profile through the FBI's fiber database. 'Automotive, it looks like.'

'Makes sense he'd have a car – you can't really carry an eighty-one-pound iron bar around on the subway. So our Watchmaker parked in the front part of the alley and dragged the vic to his resting place. What can we tell about the vehicle?'

Not much, as it turned out. The fiber was from carpet used in more than forty models of cars, trucks and SUVs. As for tread marks, the part of the alley where he'd parked was covered with salt, which had interfered with the tires' contact with the cobblestones and prevented the transfer of tread marks.

'A big zero in the vehicle department. Well, let's look at his love note.'

Cooper slipped the white sheet of paper out of a plastic envelope.

The full Cold Moon is in the sky,
shining on the corpse of earth,
signifying the hour to die
and end the journey begun at birth.

— THE WATCHMAKER

'Is it?' Rhyme asked.

'Is it what?' Pulaski asked, as if he'd missed something.

'The full moon. Obviously. Today.'

Pulaski flipped through Rhyme's *New York Times*. 'Yep. Full.'

'What's he mean by the Cold Moon in caps?' Dennis Baker asked.

Cooper did some searching on the Internet. 'Okay, it's a month in the lunar calendar . . . We use the solar calendar, three hundred and sixty-five days a year, based on the sun. The lunar calendar marks time from new moon to new moon. The names of the months describe the cycle of our lives from birth to death. They're named according to milestones in the year: the Strawberry Moon in the spring, the Harvest Moon and Hunter Moon in the fall. The Cold Moon is in December, the month of hibernation and death.'

As Rhyme had noted earlier, killers referencing the moon or astrological themes tended to be serial perps. There was some literature suggesting that people were actually motivated by the moon to commit crimes but Rhyme believed that was simply the influence of suggestion – like the increase in alien abduction reports just after Steven Spielberg's film *Close Encounters of the Third Kind* was released.

'Run the name Watchmaker through the databases, along with "Cold Moon". Oh, and the other lunar months too.'

After ten minutes of searching through the FBI's Violent Criminal Apprehension Program and the National Crime Information Center, as well as state databases, they had no hits.

Rhyme asked Cooper to find out where the poem itself had come from but he found nothing even close in dozens of poetry websites. The tech also called a professor of literature at New York University, a man who helped them on occasion. He'd never heard of it. And the poem was either too obscure to turn up in a search engine or more likely it was the Watchmaker's own creation.

Cooper said, 'As for the note itself, it's generic paper from a computer printer. Hewlett-Packard LaserJet ink, nothing distinctive.'

Rhyme shook his head, frustrated at the absence of leads. If the Watchmaker was in fact a cyclical killer he could be somewhere right now, checking out – or even murdering – his next victim.

A moment later Amelia Sachs arrived, pulled off her jacket. She was introduced to Dennis Baker, who told her he was glad she was on the case; her reputation preceded her, the wedding-ring-free cop added, smiling a bit of flirt her way. Sachs responded with a brisk, professional hand-shake. All in a day's work for a woman on the force.

Rhyme briefed her on what they'd learned from the evidence so far.

'Not much,' she muttered. 'He's good.'

'What's the story on the suspect?' Baker asked.

Sachs nodded toward the door. 'He'll be here in a minute. He took off when we tried to get him but I don't think he's our boy. I checked him out. Married, been a broker with the same firm for five years, no warrants. I don't even think he could carry it.' She nodded at the iron span.

There was a knock on the door.

Behind her, two uniformed officers brought in an unhappy-looking man in handcuffs. Ari Cobb was in his mid-thirties, good-looking in a dime-a-dozen businessman way. The slightly built man was wearing a nice coat, probably cashmere, though it was stained with what looked like street sludge, presumably from his arrest.

'What's the story?' Sellitto asked him gruffly.

'As I told *her*' – a cool nod toward Sachs – 'I was just walking to the subway on Cedar Street last night and I dropped some money. That's it right there.' He nodded toward the bills and money clip. 'This morning I realized what happened and came back to look for it. I saw the police there. I don't know, I just didn't want to get involved. I'm a broker. I have clients who're real sensitive about publicity. It could hurt my business.' It was only then that the man seemed to realize that Rhyme was in a wheelchair. He blinked once, got over it, and resumed his indignant visage once more.

A search of his clothing found none of the fine-grained sand, blood or other trace to link him to the killings. Like Sachs, Rhyme doubted this was the Watchmaker, but given the gravity of the crimes he wasn't going to be careless. 'Print him,' Rhyme ordered.

Cooper did so and found that the friction ridges on the money clip were his. A check of DMV revealed that Cobb didn't own a car, and a call to his credit card companies showed that he hadn't rented one recently using his plastic.

'When did you drop the money?' Sellitto asked.

He explained that he'd left work about seven thirty the previous night. He'd had some drinks with friends, then left about nine and walked to the subway. He remembered pulling a subway pass out of his pocket when he was walking along Cedar, which was probably when he lost the clip. He continued on to the station and returned home, the Upper East Side, about 9:45. His wife was on a business trip so he went to a bar near his apartment for dinner by himself. He got home about one.

Sellitto made some calls to check out his story. The night guard at his office confirmed he'd left at seven thirty, a credit card receipt showed he was at a bar down on Water Street around nine, and the doorman in his building and a neighbor confirmed that he had returned to his apartment at the time that he said. It seemed impossible for him to have abducted two victims, killed one at the pier and then arranged the death of Theodore Adams in the alley, all between nine fifteen and one.

Sellitto said, 'We're investigating a very serious crime here. It happened near where you were last night. Did you notice *anything* that could help us?'

'No, nothing at all. I swear I'd help if I could.'

'The killer could be going to strike again, you know.'

'I'm sorry about that,' he said, not sounding very sorry at all. 'But I panicked. That's not a crime.'

Sellitto glanced at his guards. 'Take him outside for a minute.'

After he was gone, Baker muttered, 'Waste of time.'

Sachs shook her head. 'He knows something. I've got a hunch.'

Rhyme deferred to Sachs when it came to what he called – with some condescension – the 'people' side of being a cop: witnesses, psychology and, God forbid, hunches.

'Okay,' he said. 'But what do we *do* with your hunch?'

It wasn't Sachs who responded, though, but Lon Sellitto. He said, 'Got an idea.' He opened his jacket, revealing an impossibly wrinkled shirt, and fished out his cell phone.

Chapter
SIX

Vincent Reynolds was walking down the chilly streets of SoHo, in the blue light of this deserted part of the neighborhood, east of Broadway, some blocks from the area's chic restaurants and boutiques. He was fifty feet behind his flower girl – Joanne, the woman who would soon be his.

His eyes were on her, and he felt a hunger, keen and electric, as intense as the one he'd felt the night he met Gerald Duncan for the first time, which had proved to be a very important moment for Vincent Reynolds.

After the Sally Anne incident – when Vincent got arrested because he lost control – he told himself that he'd have to be smarter. He'd wear a ski mask, he'd take the women from behind so they couldn't see him, he'd use a condom (which helped him slow down, anyway), he'd never hunt close to home, he'd vary the techniques and the neighborhoods of the attacks. He'd plan the rapes carefully and be prepared to walk away if there was a risk he'd get caught.

Well, that was his theory. But in the past year it'd been getting harder and harder to control the hunger. Impulse would take over and he'd see a woman by herself on the street and think, I *have* to have her. Now! I don't care if anybody sees me.

The hunger does that to you.

Two weeks earlier he'd been having a piece of chocolate cake and a Coke at a diner up the street from the office where he regularly temped. He glanced at the waitress, a new one. She had a round face and a slim figure, curls of golden hair. He noticed her tight blue blouse had two buttons open and, in his soul, the hunger erupted.

She smiled at him as she brought his check and he decided he had to have her. Right away.

He heard her say to her boss she was going into the alley for a cigarette. Vincent paid and stepped outside. He walked to the alley and then glanced into it. There she was, in her coat, leaning against the wall, looking away from him. It was late – he preferred the three to eleven P.M. shift – and though there were some passers-by on the sidewalk, the alley was completely empty. The air was cold, the cobblestones would be colder, but he didn't care; her body would keep him warm.

It was then that he heard a voice whisper in his ear, 'Wait five minutes.'

Vincent jumped and swiveled around to look at a man with a round face and lean body, in his fifties, with a calm way about him. He was gazing past Vincent into the alley.

'What?'

'Wait.'

'Who're you?' Vincent wasn't afraid, exactly – he was two inches taller, fifty pounds heavier – but the odd look in the man's shockingly blue eyes spooked him.

'That doesn't matter. Pretend we're just friends, talking.'

'Fuck that.' Heart pounding, hands shaking, Vincent started to walk away.

'Wait,' the man said softly once more. His voice was almost hypnotic.

The rapist waited.

A minute later he saw a door open in a building across the

alley from the back of the restaurant. The waitress walked to the doorway and spoke to two men. One was in a suit, the other was in a police uniform.

'Jesus,' Vincent whispered.

'It's a sting,' the man said. 'She's a cop. The owner's running numbers out of the restaurant, I think. They're setting him up.'

Vincent recovered fast. 'So? That doesn't matter to me.'

'If you'd done what you had in mind you'd be in cuffs now. Or shot dead.'

'Had in mind?' Vincent asked, trying to sound innocent. 'I don't know what you're talking about.'

The stranger only smiled, motioning Vincent up the street. 'Do you live here?'

A pause then Vincent answered, 'New Jersey.'

'You work in the city?'

'Yeah.'

'You know Manhattan well?'

'Pretty good.'

The man nodded, looking Vincent up and down. He identified himself as Gerald Duncan and suggested they go someplace warm to talk. They walked three blocks to a diner and Duncan had coffee and Vincent had another piece of cake and a soda.

They talked about the weather, the city budget, downtown Manhattan at midnight.

Then Duncan said, 'Just a thought, Vincent. If you're interested in a little work I could use somebody who isn't overly concerned with the law. And it might let you practice your . . . hobby.' He nodded back in the direction of the alley.

'Collecting sitcoms from the seventies?' asked Clever Vincent.

Duncan smiled again and Vincent decided he liked the man.

'What do you want me to do?'

'I've only been to New York a few times. I need a man who knows the streets, the subways, traffic patterns, neighborhoods . . . who knows something about the way police work. The details, I'll save for later.'

Hmm.

'What line are you in?' Vincent had asked.

'Businessman. We'll let it go at that.'

Hmm.

Vincent told himself to leave. But he felt the lure of the man's comment – about practicing his hobby. Anything that might help him feed the hunger was worth considering, even if it was risky. They continued to talk for a half hour, sharing some information, withholding some. Duncan explained that *his* hobby was collecting antique watches, which he repaired himself. He'd even built a few from scratch.

As he'd finished his fourth dessert of the day Vincent asked, 'How did you know she was a cop?'

Duncan seemed to debate for a moment. Then he said. 'I've been checking out somebody at the diner. The man at the end of the counter. Remember him? He was in the dark suit.'

Vincent nodded.

'I've been following him for the past month. I'm going to kill him.'

Vincent smiled. 'You're kidding.'

'I don't really kid.'

And Vincent had learned that was true. There was no Clever Gerald. Or Hungry Gerald. There was just one – Calm and Meticulous Gerald, who expressed his intention that night to kill the man in the diner – Walter somebody – in the same matter-of-fact way that he'd made good on that promise by cutting the son of a bitch's wrists and watching him struggle until he fell from a pier into the freezing brown water of the Hudson River.

The Watchmaker had gone on to tell Vincent that he was in town to kill other people too. Among them were some women. As long as Vincent was careful and didn't spend more than twenty or thirty minutes, he could have their bodies after they were dead – to do what he wished. In exchange, Vincent would help him – as a guide to the city and its roads and transportation system, and to stand guard and sometimes drive the getaway car.

'So. You interested?'

'I guess,' Vincent said, though his private response was a lot more enthusiastic than that.

And Vincent was now hard at work on this job, following the third victim: Joanne Harper, their flower girl, Clever Vincent had dubbed her. He watched her take out a key and disappear through the service door to her workshop. He eased to a stop, ate a candy bar and leaned against a lamp pole, looking through the shop's grimy window.

His hand touched the bulge at his waistband, where the Buck knife rested. Staring at the vague form of Joanne, turning on lights, taking her coat off, moving around the workshop. She was alone.

Gripping the knife.

He wondered if she had freckles, he wondered what her perfume smelled like. He wondered if she whimpered when she was in pain. Did she—

But, no, he shouldn't think like this! He was here only to get information. He couldn't break the rules, couldn't disappoint Gerald Duncan. Vincent inhaled the painfully cold air. He should wait.

But then Joanne walked near the window. He got a good look at her. Oh, she's pretty . . .

Vincent's palms began to sweat. Of course, he could simply take her now and leave her tied up for Duncan to kill later. That would be something that a friend would understand. They'd both get what they wanted.

After all, sometimes you just *can't* wait.

The hunger does that to you . . .

Next time, pack warm. What *were* you thinking?

Riding in a pungent cab, thirty-something Kathryn Dance held her hands out in front of a backseat heater exhaling air that wasn't hot, wasn't even warm; at best, she decided, it was uncold. She rubbed together her fingers, tipped in dark red nails, and then gave her black-stockinged knees a chance at the air.

Dance came from a locale where the temperature was seventy-five, give or take, all year round and you had to drive up Carmel Valley Road a long, long way to find enough sledding snow to keep your son and daughter happy. In her last-minute packing for the seminar here in New York, somehow she'd forgotten that the North East plus December equals the Himalayas.

She was reflecting: Here I can't drop the last five pounds of what I gained in Mexico last month (where she'd done nothing but sit in a smoky room, interrogating a suspected kidnapper). If I can't lose it, at least the extra weight ought to do its duty as insulation. Ain't fair . . . She pulled her thin coat more tightly around her.

Kathryn Dance was a special agent with the California Bureau of Investigation, based in Monterey. She was one of the nation's preeminent experts in interrogation and kinesics – the science of observing and analyzing the body language and verbal behavior of witnesses and suspects. She'd been in New York for the past three days presenting her kinesics seminar to local law enforcement agencies.

Kinesics is a rare specialty in policework, but to Kathryn Dance there was nothing like it. She was a people addict. They fascinated her, they electrified her. Confounded and challenged her too. These billions of odd creatures moving through the world, saying the strangest and most wonderful and terrible things . . . She felt what they felt, she feared what scared them, she got pleasure from their joy.

Dance had been a reporter after college: journalism, that profession tailor-made for the aimless with insatiable curiosities. She ended up on the crime beat and spent hours in courtrooms, observing lawyers and suspects and jurors. She realized something about herself: She could look at a witness, listen to his words and get an immediate sense of when he was telling the truth and when he wasn't. She could look at jurors and see when they were bored or lost or angry or shocked, when they believed the suspect, when they didn't. She could tell which lawyers were ill-suited to the bar and which were going to shine.

She could spot the cops whose whole heart was in their jobs and the ones that were only biding their time. (One of the former in particular caught her eye: a prematurely silver-haired FBI agent out of the San Jose field office, testifying with humor and panache in a gang trial she was covering. She finagled an exclusive interview with him after the guilty verdicts, and he finagled a date. Eight months later she and William Swenson were married.)

Eventually bored with the reporter's life, Kathryn Dance decided on a career change. Life turned crazy for a time as she juggled her roles as mother of two small children and wife and grad student, but she managed to graduate from UC-Santa Cruz with a joint master's in psych and communications. She opened a jury consulting business, advising attorneys which jurors to choose and which to avoid during voir dire jury selection. She was talented and made very good money. But six years ago, she decided to change course once again. With the help of a supportive, tireless husband and her mother and father, who lived in nearby Carmel, she headed back to school once more: the California State Bureau of Investigation training academy in Sacramento.

Kathryn Dance became a cop.

The CBI doesn't break out kinesics as a specialty so Dance was technically just another investigative agent, working homicides, kidnappings, narcotics, terrorism and the like. Still, in law enforcement, talents are spotted early and news of her talent quickly spread. She found herself the resident expert in interview and interrogation (fine with her, since it gave her some bargaining power to trade off undercover and forensic work, which she had little interest in).

She now glanced at her watch, wondering how long this volunteer mission would take. Her flight wasn't until the afternoon but she'd have to give herself plenty of time to get to JFK; traffic in the city was horrendous, even worse than the 101 Freeway around San Jose. She couldn't miss the plane. She was eager to get back to her children, and – funny about caseloads – the files on your desk never seem to disappear when you're out of the office; they only multiply.

The cab squealed to a stop.

Dance squinted out the window. 'Is this the right address?'

'It's the one you gave me.'

'It doesn't look like a police station.'

He glanced up at the ornate building. 'Sure don't. That'll be six seventy-five.'

Yes and no, Dance thought to herself.

It was a police station and yet it wasn't.

Lon Sellitto greeted her in the front hallway. The detective had taken her course in kinesics the day before at One Police Plaza and had just called, asking if she could come by now to give them a hand on a multiple homicide. When he'd telephoned he'd given her the address and she'd assumed it was a precinct house. It happened to be filled with nearly as much forensic equipment as the lab at the Monterey CBI headquarters but was, nonetheless, a private home.

And it was owned by Lincoln Rhyme, no less.

Another fact Sellitto had neglected to mention.

Dance had heard of Rhyme, of course – many law enforcers knew of the brilliant quadriplegic forensic detective – but wasn't aware of the details of his life or his role in the NYPD. The fact he was disabled soon failed to register; unless she was studying body language intentionally, Kathryn Dance tended to pay most attention to people's eyes. Besides, one of her colleagues in the CBI was a paraplegic and she was accustomed to people in a wheelchair.

Sellitto now introduced her to Rhyme and a tall, intense police detective named Amelia Sachs. Dance noted at once that they were more than professional partners. No great kinesic deductions were necessary to make this connection; when she walked in, Sachs had her fingers entwined with Rhyme's and was whispering something to him with a smile.

Sachs greeted her warmly and Sellitto introduced her to several other officers.

Dance was aware of a tinny sound coming from over her shoulder – earbuds dangling behind her. She laughed and shut off her iPod, which she carried with her like a life-support system.

Sellitto and Sachs told her about the homicide case they needed some help on – a case that Rhyme seemed to be in charge of, though he was a civilian.

Rhyme didn't participate much in the discussion. His eyes continually returned to a large whiteboard, on which were notations of the evidence. The other officers were giving her details of the case, though she couldn't help but observe Rhyme – the way he squinted at the board, would mutter something under his breath and shake his head, as if chastising himself for missing something. Occasionally his eyes would close. Once or twice he offered a comment about the case but he largely ignored Dance.

She was amused. The agent was used to skepticism. Most often it arose because she simply didn't look like a typical cop, this five-foot-five woman with dark blond hair worn usually, as now, in a tight French braid, light purple lipstick, iPod earbuds dangling, the gold and abalone jewelry her mother had made, not to mention her passion – quirky shoes (chasing perps didn't usually figure in Dance's daily life as a cop).

Now, though, she suspected she understood Lincoln Rhyme's lack of interest. Like many forensic scientists, he wouldn't put much stock in kinesics and interviewing. He'd probably voted against calling her.

As for Dance herself, well, she recognized the value of physical evidence, but it had no appeal to her. It was the human side of crime and crime solving that made her own heart race.

Kinesics versus forensics . . .

Fair enough, Detective Rhyme.

While the handsome, sardonic and impatient criminalist continued to gaze at the evidence charts, Dance absorbed the details of the case, which was a strange one. The murders by the self-anointed Watchmaker were horrific, sure, but Dance wasn't shocked. She'd worked cases that were just as gruesome. And, after all, she lived in California, where Charles Manson had set the standard for evil.

Another detective from the NYPD, Dennis Baker, now told her specifically what they needed. They'd found a witness who might have some helpful information but he wasn't forthcoming with details.

'He claims he didn't see anything,' Sachs added. 'But I have a feeling he did.'

Dance was disappointed that it wasn't a suspect but a witness she'd be interviewing. She preferred the challenge of confronting criminals, and the more deceitful the better. Still, interviewing witnesses took much less time than breaking suspects and she couldn't miss her flight.

'I'll see what I can do,' she told them. She fished in her Coach purse and put on round glasses with pale pink frames.

Sachs gave her the details about Ari Cobb, the reluctant witness, laying out the chronology of the man's evening, as they'd been able to piece it together, and his behavior that morning.

Dance listened carefully as she sipped coffee that Rhyme's caregiver had poured for her and indulged in half a Danish.

When she'd gotten all the background Dance organized her thoughts. Then she said to them, 'Okay, let me tell you what I've got in mind. First, a crash course. Lon heard this yesterday at the seminar but I'll let the rest of you know how I handle interviewing. Kinesics traditionally was studying somebody's physical behavior – body language – to understand their emotional state and whether they were being deceptive or not. Most people, including me, use the term now to mean all forms of communication – not just body language but spoken comments and written statements too.

'First, I'll take a baseline reading of the witness – see how he acts when he's answering things that we know are truthful – name, address, job, things like that. I'll note his gesturing, posture, word choice and the substance of what he says.

'Once I have the baseline I'll start asking questions and find out where he exhibits stress reactions. Which means he's either lying or has some important issues with the topic I'm asking him about. Up until then, what I've been doing is "interviewing" him. Once I suspect he's lying, then the session shall become an "interrogation". I start to whittle away at him, using a lot of different techniques, until we get to the truth.'

'Perfect,' said Baker. Although Rhyme was apparently in charge, Dennis Baker, Dance deduced, was from headquarters; he had the belabored look of a man on whose shoulders an investigation like this ultimately – and politically – rested.

'You have a map of the area we're talking about,' Dance said. 'I'd like to know the geography of the area involved. You can't be an effective interrogator without it. I like to say I need to know the subject's terrarium.'

Lon Sellitto gave a fast laugh. Dance smiled in curiosity. He explained, 'Lincoln says exactly the same about forensics. If you don't know the geography, you're working in a vacuum. Right, Linc?'

'Sorry?' the criminalist asked.

'Terrarium, you like that?'

'Ah.' His polite smile was the equivalent of Dance's son saying, 'Whatever.'

Dance examined the map of lower Manhattan, memorizing the details of the crime scene and of Ari Cobb's after-work schedule the previous day, as Sachs and a young patrol officer, named Pulaski, pointed them out.

Finally she felt comfortable with the facts. 'Okay, let's get to work. Where is he?'

'A room across the hall.'

'Bring him in.'

Chapter
SEVEN

A moment later an NYPD patrol officer brought in a short, trim businessman wearing an expensive suit. Dance didn't know if they'd actually arrested him but the way he touched his wrists told her that he'd been in cuffs recently.

Dance greeted the man, who was uneasy and angry, and nodded him to a chair. She sat across from him – nothing between them – and scooted forward until she was in a neutral proxemic zone, the term referring to the physical space between a subject and an interviewer. This zone can be adjusted to make the subject more or less comfortable. She was not too close to be invasive but not so far away as to give him a sense of security. ('You push the edge of edgy,' she'd say in her lectures.)

'Mr Cobb, my name's Kathryn Dance. I'm a law enforcement agent and I'd like to talk to you about what you saw last night.'

'This is ridiculous. I already told them' – a nod at Rhyme – 'everything I saw.'

'Well, I just arrived. I don't have the benefit of your previous answers.'

Jotting responses, she asked a number of simple questions

– where he lived and worked, marital status, and the like – which gave her Cobb's baseline reaction to stress. She listened carefully to his answers. ('Watching and listening are the two most important parts of the interview. Speaking comes last.')

One of the first jobs of an interviewer is to determine the personality type of the subject – whether he's an introvert or extrovert. These types aren't what most people think; they're not about being boisterous or retiring. The distinction is about how people make decisions. An introvert is governed by intuition and emotion more than logic and reason; an extrovert, the opposite. Assigning personalities helps the interviewer in framing the questions and picking the right tone and physical demeanor to adopt when asking them. For instance, taking a gruff, clipped approach with an introvert will make him withdraw into his shell.

Ari Cobb, though, was a classic extrovert and an arrogant one at that – no kid gloves were needed. This was Kathryn Dance's favorite kind of subject. She got to kick serious butt when interviewing them.

Cobb cut off a question. 'You've held me way too long. I have to get to work. What happened to that man isn't my fault.'

Respectful but firm, Dance said, 'Oh, it's not a question of fault . . . Now, Ari, let's talk about last night.'

'You don't believe me. You're calling me a liar. I wasn't *there* when the crime happened.'

'I'm not suggesting you're lying. But there still might've been something you saw that could help us. Something you think isn't important. See, part of my job is helping people remember things. I'll walk you through the events of last night and maybe something'll occur to you.'

'Well, there's nothing I saw. I just dropped some money. That's all. I handled the whole thing badly. And now it's a federal case. This is such bullshit.'

'Let's just go back to yesterday. One step at a time. You were working in your office. Stenfeld Brothers Investments. In the Hartsfield Building.'

'Yeah.'

'All day?'

'Right.'

'You got off work at what time?'

'Seven thirty, a little before.'

'And what did you do after that?'

'I went to Hanover's for drinks.'

'That's on Water Street,' she said. Always keep your subjects guessing exactly how much you know.

'Yeah. It was a martini and Karaoke thing. They call it Martuney Night. Like "tunes".'

'Clever.'

'I've got a group I meet there. We go a lot. Some friends. Close friends.'

She noticed that his body language meant he was about to add something – probably he was anticipating her asking for their names. Being too ready with an alibi is an indicator of deception – the subject tends to think that offering it is good enough and the police won't bother to check it out, or won't be smart enough to figure out that having a drink at eight P.M. doesn't exculpate you from a robbery that happened at seven thirty.

'You left when?'

'At nine or so.'

'And went home?'

'Yes.'

'To the Upper East Side.'

A nod.

'Did you take a limo?'

'Limo, right,' he said sarcastically. 'No, the subway.'

'From which station?'

'Wall Street.'

'Did you walk?'

'Yes.'

'How?'

'Carefully,' he said, grinning. 'It was icy.'

Dance smiled. 'The route?'

'I walked down Water Street, cut over on Cedar to Broadway then south.'

'And that's where you lost your money clip. On Cedar. How did that happen?' Her tone and the questions were completely nonthreatening. He was relaxing now. His attitude was less aggressive. Her smiles and low, calm voice were putting him at ease.

'As near as I can figure, it fell out when I was getting my subway pass.'

'How much money was it again?'

'Over three hundred.'

'Ouch . . .'

'Yeah, ouch.'

She nodded at the plastic bag containing the money and clip. 'Looks like you just hit the ATM too. Worst time to lose money, right? After a withdrawal.'

'Yep.' He offered a grimacing smile.

'When did you get to the subway?'

'Nine thirty.'

'It wasn't later, you sure?'

'I'm positive. I checked my watch when I was on the platform. It was nine thirty-five, to be exact.' He glanced down at his big gold Rolex. Meaning, she supposed, that a watch this expensive was sure to tell accurate time.

'And then?'

'I went back home and had dinner in a bar near my building. My wife was out of town. She's a lawyer. Does corporate financing work. She's a partner.'

'Let's go back to Cedar Street. Were there any lights on? People home in their apartments?'

'No, it's all offices and stores there. Not residential.'

'No restaurants?'

'A few but they're only open for lunch.'

'Any construction?'

'They're renovating a building on the south side of the street.'

'Was anybody on the sidewalks?'

'No.'

'Cars driving slowly, suspiciously?'

'No,' Cobb said.

Dance was vaguely aware of the other officers watching her and Cobb. They were undoubtedly impatient, waiting, like most people, for the big Confession Moment. She ignored them. Nobody really existed except the agent and her subject. Kathryn Dance was in her own world – a 'zone', her son, Wes, would say (he was the athlete of the family).

She looked over the notes she'd taken. Then she closed the notebook and replaced one pair of glasses with another, as if she were exchanging reading for distance glasses. The prescriptions were the same, but instead of the larger round lenses and pastel frames these were small and rectangular, with black metal frames, making her look predatory. She called them her 'Terminator specs'. Dance eased closer to Cobb. He crossed his legs.

In a voice much edgier, she asked, 'Ari, where did that money really come from?'

'The—'

'Money? You didn't get it at an ATM.' It was during his comments about the cash that she noticed an increased stress level – his eyes stayed locked on to hers, but the lids lowered slightly and his breathing altered, both major deviations from his nondeceptive baseline.

'Yes, I did,' he countered.

'What bank?'

A pause. 'You can't make me tell you that.'

'But we can subpoena your bank records. And we'll detain you until we get them. Which could take a day or two.'

'I went to the fucking ATM!'

'That's not what I asked. I asked where the cash in your money clip came from.'

He looked down.

'You haven't been honest with me, Ari. Which means you're in serious trouble. Now, the money?'

'I don't know. Probably some of it was from petty cash at my firm.'

'Which you got yesterday?'

'I guess.'

'How much?'

'I—'

'We'll subpoena your employer's books too.'

He looked shocked at this. He said quickly, 'A thousand dollars.'

'Where's the rest of it? Three hundred forty in the money clip. Where's the rest?'

'I spent some at Hanover's. It's a business expense. It's legitimate. As part of my job—'

'I was asking where the rest of it is.'

A pause. 'I left some at home.'

'At home? Is your wife back now? Could she confirm that?'

'She's still away.'

'Then we'll send an officer to look for the money. Where is it, exactly?'

'I don't remember.'

'Over six hundred dollars? How could you forget where six hundred dollars is?'

'I don't know. You're confusing me.'

She leaned closer still, into a more threatening proxemic zone. 'What were you really doing on Cedar Street?'

'Walking to the fucking subway.'

Dance grabbed the map of Manhattan. 'Hanover's is *here*. The subway's *here*.' Her finger made a loud sound with every tap on the heavy paper. 'It makes no sense to walk down Cedar to get from Hanover's to the Wall Street subway station. Why would you walk that way?'

'I wanted some exercise. Walk off the Cosmopolitans and chicken wings.'

'With ice on the sidewalks and the temperature in the teens? You do that often?'

'No. I just happened to last night.'

'If you don't walk it often then how do you know so much about Cedar Street? The fact there're no residences, the closing time of the restaurants and the construction work?'

'I just do. What the hell's this all about?' Sweat was dotting his forehead.

'When you dropped the money, did you take your gloves off to get your subway pass out of your pocket?'

'I don't know.'

'I assume you did. You can't reach into a pocket with winter gloves on.'

'Okay,' he snapped. 'You know so much, then I did.'

'With the temperature as cold as it was, why would you do that ten minutes before you got to the subway station?'

'You can't talk to me this way.'

She said in a firm, low voice, 'And you didn't check the time on the subway platform, did you?'

'Yes, I did. It was nine thirty-five.'

'No, you didn't. You're not going to be flashing a five-thousand-dollar watch on the subway platform at night.'

'Okay, that's it. I'm not saying anything else.'

When an interrogator confronts a deceptive subject, that person experiences intense stress and responds in various ways to try to escape from that stress – barriers to the truth,

Dance called them. The most destructive and difficult response state to break through is anger, followed by depression, then denial, and finally bargaining. The interrogator's role is to decide what stress state the suspect is in and neutralize it – and any subsequent ones – until finally the subject reaches the accept-ance state, that is, confession, in which he finally will be honest.

Dance had assessed that though Cobb displayed some anger he was primarily in the denial state – such subjects are very quick to plead memory problems and to blame the interrogator for misunderstandings. The best way to break down a subject in denial is to do what Dance had just done – it's known as 'attacking on the facts'. With an extrovert you slam home weaknesses and contradictions in their stories one after another until their defenses are shattered.

'Ari, you got off work at seven thirty and went to Hanover's. We know that. You were there for about an hour and a half. After that you walked two blocks out of your way to Cedar Street. You know Cedar real well because you go there to pick up hookers. Last night between nine and nine thirty, one of them stopped her car near the alley. You negotiated a price and paid her. You got into the car with her. You got out of the car around ten fifteen or so. That's when you dropped the money by the curb, probably checking your cell phone to see if your wife had called or getting a little extra cash for a tip. Meanwhile, the killer had pulled into the alley and you noticed it and saw something. What? What did you see?'

'No . . .'

'Yes,' Dance said evenly. She stared at him and said nothing more.

Finally his head lowered and his legs uncrossed. His lip was trembling. He wasn't confessing but she'd moved him up a step in the chain of stress response states – from denial to bargaining. Now Dance had to change tack. She had both to offer sympathy and to give him a way to save face. Even the most cooperative subjects in the bargaining state will continue to lie or stonewall if you don't leave them some dignity and a way to escape the worst consequences of what they've done.

She pulled her glasses off and sat back. 'Look, Ari, we don't want to ruin your life. You got scared. It's understandable. But this is a very dangerous man we're trying to stop. He's killed two people and he may be going to kill some more. If you can help us find him, what we've learned about you here today doesn't have to come out in public. No subpoenas, no calls to your wife or boss.'

Dance glanced at Detective Baker, who said, 'That's absolutely right.'

Cobb sighed. Eyes on the floor, he muttered, 'Fuck. It was three hundred goddamn dollars. Why the hell did I go back there this morning?'

Greed and stupidity, thought Kathryn Dance. But she said kindly, 'We all make mistakes.'

A hesitation. Then he sighed again. 'See, this's the crazy thing. It wasn't much – what I saw, I mean. You're probably not going to believe me. I hardly saw anything. I didn't even see a person.'

'If you're honest with us we'll believe you. Go on.'

'It was about ten thirty, a little after. After I got out of the . . . girl's car I started to walk to the subway. You're right. I stopped and pulled my cell phone out of my pocket. I turned it on to check messages. That's when the money fell out, I guess. It *was* at the alley. I glanced down it and saw some tail-lights at the end.'

'What kind of car?' Sachs asked.

'I didn't see the car, just taillights. I swear.'

Dance believed this. She nodded to Sachs.

'Wait,' Rhyme said abruptly. 'The *end* of the alley?'

So the criminalist had been listening after all.

'Right. All the way at the end. Then the reverse lights came on and it started backing toward me. The driver was moving pretty fast so I kept walking. Then I heard the squeal of brakes and he stopped and shut the engine off. He was still in the alley. I kept on walking. I heard the door slam and this noise. Like a big piece of metal falling to the ground. That was it. I didn't see anybody. I was past the alley at that point. Really.'

Rhyme glanced at Dance, who nodded that he was telling the truth.

'Describe the girl you were with,' Dennis Baker said. 'I want to talk to her too.'

Cobb said quickly, 'Thirties, African-American, short curly hair. Her car was a Honda, I think. I didn't see the license plate. She was pretty.' He added this as some pathetic justification.

'Name?'

Cobb sighed. 'Tiffanee. With two *e*s. Not a *y*.'

Rhyme gave a faint laugh. 'Call Vice, ask about girls working regularly on Cedar,' he ordered his slim, balding assistant.

Dance asked a few more questions, then nodded, glanced at Lon Sellitto and said, 'I think Mr Cobb here has told us as much as he knows.' She looked at the businessman and said sincerely, 'Thanks for your cooperation.'

He blinked, unsure what to make of her comment. But Kathryn Dance wasn't being sarcastic. She never took personally the words or glares (occasionally even spittle or flung objects) from the subjects. A kinesic interviewer has to remember that the enemy is never the subject himself but simply the barriers to truth that he raises, sometimes not even intentionally.

Sellitto, Baker and Sachs debated for a few minutes and decided to release the businessman without charging him. The skittish man left, with a look at Dance that she was very familiar with: part awe, part disgust, part pure hatred.

After he'd left, Rhyme, who was looking at a diagram of the scene of the killing in the alley, said, 'This's curious. For some reason the perp decided he didn't want the vic at the end of the alley, so he backed up and picked the spot about fifteen feet from the sidewalk . . . Interesting fact. But is it *useful*?'

Sachs nodded. 'You know, it might be. The far end of the alley didn't get any snow, it looked like. They might not've used salt there. We could lift some footprints or tire treads.'

Rhyme made a call – with an impressive voice recognition program – and sent some officers back to the scene. They called back a short time later and reported that they had found fresh tire treads at the end of the alley, along with a brown fiber, which seemed to match the ones on the victim's shoe and wristwatch. They uploaded the digital pictures of the fiber and treads and gave the wheelbase dimensions.

Despite her lack of interest in forensics, Dance found herself intrigued by this choreography. Rhyme and Sachs were a particularly insightful team. She couldn't help but be impressed when ten minutes later, the technical man, Mel Cooper, looked up from a computer screen and said, 'With the wheelbase and those particular brown fibers, it's probably a Ford Explorer, either two or three years old.'

'Odds are it's the older one,' Rhyme said.

Why did he say that? Dance wondered.

Sachs saw the frown on her face and answered, 'The brakes squealed.'

Ah.

Sellitto turned to Dance. 'That was good, Kathryn. You nailed him.'

Sachs asked, 'How'd you do it?'

She explained the process she'd used. 'I went fishing. I reviewed everything he'd told us – the after-work bar, the subway, the cash and money clip, the alleyway, the chronology of events and the geography. I checked out his kinesic reaction to each response. The cash was a particularly sensitive subject. What was he doing with the money that he shouldn't've been? An extroverted, narcissistic businessman like him? I figured it was either drugs or sex. But a Wall Street broker's not buying street drugs; he'd have a connection. That left hookers. Simple.'

'That's slick, don't you think, Lincoln?' Cooper asked.

Dance was surprised to see that the criminalist could shrug. He then said noncommitally, 'Worked out well. We got some evidence it might've taken us a while to find.' His eyes went back to the board.

'Linc, come on. We got his vehicle make. We wouldn't have if it hadn't been for her.' Sellitto said to Dance, 'Don't take it personal. He doesn't trust witnesses.'

Rhyme frowned at the detective. 'It's not a contest, Lon. Our goal is the truth, and my experience has been that the reliability of witnesses is somewhat less than that of physical evidence. That's all. Nothing personal about it.'

Dance nodded. 'Funny you say that. I tell people in my lectures the same thing: that our main job as cops isn't throwing bad guys in jail, it's getting to the truth.' She too shrugged. 'We just had a case in California – death row prisoner exonerated the day before his scheduled execution. A private eye friend of mine spent three years working for his lawyer to get to the bottom of what happened. He just wouldn't accept that everything was what it seamed to be. The prisoner was thirteen hours away from dying and it turned out he was innocent . . . If that PI hadn't kept looking for the truth all those years, he'd be dead now.'

Rhyme said, 'And I know what happened. The defendant was convicted because of a witness's perjured testimony, and DNA analysis freed him, right?'

Dance turned. 'No, actually there were no witnesses to the

killing. The real killer planted fake physical evidence implicating him.'

'How 'bout that,' said Sellitto and he and Amelia Sachs shared a smile. Rhyme glanced at them both coolly. 'Well,' he said to Dance, 'it's fortunate that things worked out for the best . . . Now I better get back to work.' His eyes returned to the whiteboard.

Dance said goodbye to them all and pulled on her coat as Lon Sellitto showed her out. On the street Dance walked to the curb, where she plugged the iPod earbuds back in and clicked the unit on. This particular playlist contained folk rock, Irish and some kick-ass Rolling Stones (once at a concert she'd done a kinesic analysis of Mick Jagger and Keith Richards for her friends' benefit).

She was waving down a cab when she realized there was an odd, unsettled feeling within her. A moment passed before she recognized it. She was feeling a nagging sense of regret that her brief involvement in the Watchmaker case was now over.

Joanne Harper was feeling good.

The trim thirty-two-year-old was in the workshop a few blocks east of her retail flower store in SoHo. She was among her friends.

That is to say, roses, cymbidium orchids, birds-of-paradise, lilies, heliconia, anthurium and red ginger.

The workshop was a large ground-floor area in what had been a warehouse. It was drafty and cold and she kept most of the rooms dark to protect the flowers. Still, she loved it here, the coolness, the dim light, the smells of lilac and fertilizer. She was in the middle of Manhattan, yes, but it seemed more like a quiet forest.

The woman added some more florist's foam to the huge ceramic vase in front of her.

Feeling good.

For a couple of reasons: because she was working on a lucrative project that she had complete discretion to design.

And because of the buzz from her date the previous night.

With Kevin, who knew that angel trumpets needed exceptionally good drainage to thrive, and that creeping red sedum flowered in brilliant crimson all the way through September, and that Donn Clendenon whacked three over the wall to help the Mets beat Baltimore in 1969 (her father had captured two of the homers with his Kodak).

Kevin the cute guy, Kevin with the dimple and grin. *Sans* present or past wives.

Did it get any better than that?

A shadow crossed the front window. She glanced up, but saw no one. This was a deserted stretch of east Spring Street and pedestrians were rare. She scanned the windows. Really ought to have Ramon clean them. Well, she'd wait till warmer weather.

She continued assembling the vase, thinking again about Kevin. Would something work out between them?

Maybe.

Maybe not.

Didn't really matter (okay, sure it did, but a thirty-two-year-old SUW – single urban woman – had to take the didn't-really-matter approach). But the *important* thing was she had fun with him. Having played the post-divorce dating game in Manhattan for a few years, she felt entitled to have some fun with another man.

Joanne Harper, who bore a resemblance to the redhead on *Sex and the City*, had come here ten years earlier to become a famous artist, live in a storefront studio in the East Village and sell her paintings out of a Tribeca gallery. But the art world had other ideas. It was too harsh, too petty, too, well, *un*artistic. It was about being shocking or troubled or fuckable or rich. Joanne gave up on fine arts and tried graphic design for a while but was dissatisfied with that too. On a whim she took a job in an interior landscaping company in Tribeca and fell in love with the business. She decided that if she was going to starve at least she'd be hungry doing what she was passionate about.

The joke, though, was that she became a success. She managed to open her own company a few years ago. It now included both the Broadway retail store and this – the Spring Street commercial operation, which serviced companies and organizations, providing daily flowers for offices and large arrangements for meetings, ceremonies and special events.

She continued to add foam, greens, eucalyptus and marbles to the vases – the flowers would be added at the last minute. Joanne shivered slightly from the chill air. She glanced at the clock on the dim wall of the workshop. Not too long to wait, she reflected. Kevin had to make a couple of deliveries in the city today. He'd called this morning and told her he'd be at the retail shop in the afternoon. And, hey, if you're not doing anything, maybe we could go for some cappuccino or something.

Coffee the *day* after a date? Now that—

Another shadow fell on the window.

She looked up again quickly. No one. But she felt uneasy. Her eyes strayed to the front door, which she never used. Boxes were stacked up in front of it. It was locked . . . or was it?

Joanne squinted but with the glare from the bright sun she couldn't tell. She walked around the worktable to check.

She tested the latch. Yes, it was locked. Joanne looked up, and gasped.

A few feet from her, on the sidewalk outside, was a huge man, staring at her. Tall and fat, he was leaning forward and staring through the window of the workshop, shielding his eyes. He was wearing old-fashioned aviator sunglasses with mirrored lenses, a baseball cap and cream-colored parka. Because of the glare, and the grime on the windows, he couldn't see that she was right in front of him.

Joanne froze. People sometimes peeked in, curious about the place, but there was an intensity about his posture, the way he hovered, that bothered her a lot. The front door wasn't special glass; anyone with a hammer or brick could break in. And with the sparse foot traffic in this part of SoHo an assault here might go completely unnoticed.

She backed up.

Perhaps his eyes grew accustomed to the light or he found a bit of clean window and noticed her. He jerked back, surprised. He seemed to debate something. Then he turned and disappeared.

Stepping forward, Joanne pressed her face against the window, but she couldn't see where he'd gone. There was something way creepy about him – the way he'd just stood there, hunched over, head cocked, hands stuffed into his pockets, staring through those weird sunglasses.

Joanne wheeled the vases to the side and glanced outside again. No sign of the man. Still, she gave in to the temptation to leave and go to the retail store, check the morning's receipts and chat with her clerks until Kevin arrived. She put on her coat, hesitated and left via the service door. She looked up the street. No sign of him. She started toward Broadway, west, the direction the big man had gone. She stepped into a thick beam of perfectly clear sunlight, which seemed nearly hot. The brilliance blinded her and she squinted, alarmed that she couldn't see clearly. Joanne paused, not wanting to walk past the alley up the street. Had the man gone in there? Was he hiding, waiting for her?

She decided to walk east, the opposite direction, and loop around to Broadway on Prince Street. It was more deserted that way, but at least she wouldn't have to walk past any alleys. She pulled her coat tighter around her and hurried up the street, head down. Soon the image of the fat man had slipped from her mind and she was thinking once again about Kevin.

Dennis Baker went downtown to report on their progress, and the rest of the team continued to examine the evidence.

The fax phone rang and Rhyme looked at the unit eagerly in hopes it was something helpful. But the pages were for Amelia Sachs. Rhyme was watching her face closely as she read them. He knew the look. Like a dog after a fox.

'What, Sachs?'

She shook her head. 'The analysis of the evidence from Ben Creeley's place in Westchester. No IAFIS hits on the prints but there were leather texture marks on some of the fireplace tools and on Creeley's desk. Who opens desk drawers wearing gloves?'

There was, of course, no database of glove marks but if Sachs could find a pair in a suspect's possession that matched this pattern, that would be solid circumstantial evidence placing him at the scene, nearly as good as a clear friction-ridge print.

She continued to read. 'And the mud I found in front of the fireplace? It doesn't match the soil in Creeley's yard. Higher acid content and some pollutants. Like from an industrial site.' Sachs continued. 'There were also some traces of burned cocaine in the fireplace.' She looked at Rhyme and gave a wry smile. 'A bummer if my first murder vic turns out to be not so innocent.'

Rhyme shrugged. 'Nun or dope dealer, Sachs, murder's still murder. What else do you have?'

'The ash I found in the fireplace – the lab couldn't recover much but they found these.' She held up a photo of financial records, like a spreadsheet or ledger, which seemed to show entries totaling millions of dollars. 'They found part of a logo or something on it. The techs're still checking it out. And they'll send the entries to a forensic accountant, see if he can make any sense of it. And they also found part of his calendar. Stuff about getting his car oil changed, a haircut appointment – hardly the agenda for the week you're going to kill yourself, by the way . . . Then the day before he died he went to the St James Tavern.' She tapped a sheet – the recovered page from his calendar.

A note from Nancy Simpson explained about the place. 'Bar on East Ninth Street. Sleazy neighborhood. Why'd a rich accountant go there? Seems funny.'

'Not necessarily.'

She glanced Rhyme's way then walked to the corner of the room. He got the message and followed in the red Storm Arrow wheelchair.

Sachs crouched down beside him. He wondered if she'd take his hand (since some sensation had returned to his right fingers and wrist, holding hands had taken on great importance to them both). But there was a very thin line between their personal and their business lives and she now remained purely professional.

'Rhyme,' she whispered.

'I know what—'

'Let me finish.'

He grunted.

'I have to follow up on this.'

'Priorities. Your case is colder than the Watchmaker, Sachs. Whatever happened to Creeley, even if he was murdered, the perp's probably not a multiple doer. The Watchmaker is. He has to be our priority. Whatever evidence there is about Creeley'll still be there after we nail our boy.'

She was shaking her head. 'I don't think so, Rhyme. I've pushed the button. I've started asking questions. You know how that works. Word's starting to spread about the case. Evidence and suspects could be disappearing right now.'

'And the *Watchmaker*'s probably targeting somebody else right now too. He could be *killing* somebody else right now . . . And, believe me, if there's another murder and we drop the ball there'll be hell to pay. Baker told me the request for us came from the top floor.'

Insisted . . .

'I won't drop the ball. You get another scene, I'll run it. If Bo Haumann stages a tactical op, I'll be there.'

Rhyme gave an exaggerated frown. 'Tactical? You don't get dessert until you finish your vegetables.'

She laughed, and now he felt the pressure of her hand. 'Come on, Rhyme, we're in copland. Nobody runs just one case at a time. Most Major Cases desks're littered with a dozen files. I can handle *two*.'

Troubled by a foreboding he couldn't articulate, Rhyme hesitated then said, 'Let's hope, Sachs. Let's hope.'

It was the best blessing he could give.

Chapter
EIGHT

He came *here*?

Amelia Sachs, standing beside a planter that smelled of urine and sported a dead yellow stalk, glanced through the grimy window.

She suspected the place would be bad, knowing the address, but not *this* bad. Sachs was standing outside the St James Tavern, on a wedge of broken concrete rising from the sidewalk. The bar was on East Ninth Street, in Alphabet City, the nickname referring to the north-south avenues that ran through it: A, B, C and D. The place had been a terror some years ago, a remnant of the gang wastelands on the Lower East Side. It had improved somewhat (crack houses were morphing into expensive fix-'em-uppers w/vu) but it was still a rough-and-tumble 'hood; sitting in the snow at Sachs's feet was a discarded hypodermic needle, and a spent 9-millimeter shell casing rested on the window ledge six inches from her face.

What the hell had accountant/venture capitalist, two-home-owning, Beemer-driving Benjamin Creeley been doing in a place like this the day before he died?

At the moment, the large, shabby tavern wasn't too crowded. Through the greasy window she spotted aging locals at the bar or tables: spongy women and scrawny men who'd get a lot, or most, of their daily calories from the bottle. In a small room in the back were some white men in jeans, dungarees, work shirts. Four of them, all loud – even through the window she could hear their crude voices and laughter. She thought immediately of the punks who'd spend hour after hour in the Mafia social clubs, some slow, some lazy – but all of them dangerous. One glance told her these were men who'd hurt people.

Entering the place, Sachs found a stool at the small end of the bar's L, where she was less visible. The bartender was a woman of around fifty, with a narrow face, red fingers, hair teased up like a country-western singer's. There was a weariness about her. Sachs thought, It's not that she's seen it all; it's that everything she *has* seen has been in places just like this.

The detective ordered a Diet Coke.

'Hey, Sonja,' called a voice from the back room. In the filthy mirror behind the bar Sachs could see it belonged to a blond man in extremely tight blue jeans and a leather jacket. He had a weasely face and appeared to have been drinking for some time. 'Dickey here wants you. He's a shy boy. Come on over here. Come on and visit the shy boy.'

'Fuck you,' somebody else shouted. Presumably Dickey.

'Come 'ere, Sonja, sweetheart! Sit on shy boy's lap. It'll be comfy. Real smooth. No bumps.'

Some guffaws.

Sonja knew that she too was the butt of their mean humor but she called back gamely, 'Dickey? He's younger'n my son.'

'That's okay – everybody knows he's a motherfucker!'

Huge laughter.

Sonja's eyes met Sachs's and then looked away quickly, as if she'd been caught aiding and abetting the enemy. But one advantage of drunks is that they can't sustain anything – cruelty or euphoria – for very long and soon they were on to sports and rude jokes. Sachs sipped her soda, asked Sonja, 'So. How's it going?'

The woman offered an unbreakable smile. 'Just fine.' She had no interest in sympathy, especially from a woman who was younger and prettier and didn't tend bar in a place like this.

Fair enough. Sachs got down to business. She flashed her badge, subtly, and then showed her a picture of Benjamin Creeley. 'Do you remember seeing him in here?'

'Him? Yeah, a few times. What's this about?'

'Did you know him?'

'Not really. Just sold him some drinks. Wine, I remember. He wanted red wine. We got shitty wine but he drank it. He was pretty decent. Not like some people.' No need to glance into the back room to indicate whom she meant. 'But I haven't seen him for a while. Last time he came in he got into a big argument. So I figured he wouldn't be coming back.'

'What happened?'

'I don't know. Just heard some shouting and then he was storming out the door.'

'Who was he arguing with?'

'I didn't see it. I just heard.'

'He ever do drugs that you saw?'

'No.'

'Were you aware that he killed himself?'

Sonja blinked. 'No shit.'

'We're following up on his death . . . I'd appreciate keeping it to yourself, my asking you about it.'

'Yeah, sure.'

'Can you tell me anything about him?'

'God, I don't even know his name. I guess he was in here maybe three times. He have a family?'

'Yes, he did.'

'Oh, that's tough. That's harsh.'

'Wife and a teenage boy.'

Sonja shook her head. Then she said, 'Gerte might've known him better. She's the other bartender. She works more'n me.'

'Is she here now?'

'Naw, should be here in a while. You want I should have her call you?'

'Give me her number.'

The woman jotted it down. Sachs leaned forward and nodded toward the picture of Creeley and said, 'Did he meet anybody in particular here that you can remember?'

'All I know is it was in there. Where *they* usually hang.' She nodded at the back room.

A millionaire businessman and that crowd? Had two of them been the ones who'd broken into the Creeley's Westchester house and had the marshmallow roast in his fireplace?

Sachs looked into the mirror, studying the men's table, littered with beer bottles, ashtrays and gnawed chicken wing bones. These guys had to be in a crew. Maybe young capos in an organized crime outfit. There were a lot of *Sopranos* franchises around the city. They were usually petty criminals but often it was the smaller crews who were more dangerous than the traditional Mafia, which avoided hurting civilians and steered clear of crack and meth and the seamier side of the underworld. She tried to get her head around a Benjamin Creeley gang connection. It was tough.

'You see them with pot, coke – *any* drugs?'

Sonja shook her head. 'Nope.'

Sachs leaned forward and whispered to Sonja, 'You know what crew're they connected with?'

'Crew?'

'A gang. Who's their boss, who they report to? Anything?'

Sonja didn't speak for a moment. She glanced at Sachs to see if she was serious and then gave a laugh. 'They're not in a gang. I thought you knew. They're cops.'

At last the clocks – the Watchmaker's calling cards – arrived from the bomb squad with a clean bill of health.

'Oh, you mean they didn't find any really tiny weapons of mass destruction inside?' Rhyme asked caustically. He was irritated that they'd been out of his possession – more risk of contamination – and at the delay in their arrival.

Pulaski signed the chain-of-custody cards and the patrolman who'd delivered the clocks left.

'Let's see what we've got.' Rhyme moved his wheelchair to the examination table as Cooper unpacked the clocks from plastic bags.

They were identical, the only difference being the blood crusted on the base of the clock that had been left on the pier. They seemed old – they weren't electric; you wound them by hand. But the components were modern. The works inside were in a sealed box, which had been opened by the bomb squad, but both clocks were still running and showed the correct time. The housing was wood, painted black, and the face was antiqued white metal. The numbers were Roman numerals, and the hour and minute hands, also black, ended in sharp arrows. There was no second hand but the clocks clicked loudly every second.

The most unusual feature was a large window in the top half of the face that displayed a disk on which were painted the phases of the moon. Centered in the window now was the full moon, depicted with an eerie human face, staring outward with ominous eyes and thin lips.

The full Cold Moon is in the sky . . .

Cooper went over the clocks with his usual precision and reported that there were no friction-ridge prints and only minimal trace evidence, all of which matched samples that Sachs had collected around both scenes, meaning that none of it had been picked up in the Watchmaker's car or residence.

'Who makes them?'

'Arnold Products. Framingham, Massachusetts.' Cooper did a Google search and read from the website. 'They sell clocks, leather goods, office decorations, gifts. Upscale. The stuff's not cheap. A dozen different models of clocks. This is the Victorian. Genuine brass mechanism, oak, modeled after a British clock sold in the eighteen hundreds. Costs fifty-four dollars whole-sale. They don't sell to the public. Have to go through the dealer.'

'Serial numbers?'

'Only on the mechanisms. Not the clocks themselves.'

'Okay,' Rhyme ordered, 'make the call.'

'Me?' Pulaski asked, blinking.

'Yup. You.'

'I'm supposed to—'

'Call the manufacturer and give them the serial numbers of the mechanism.'

Pulaski nodded. 'Then see if they can tell us which store it was shipped to.'

'One hundred percent,' Rhyme said.

The rookie took out his phone, got the number from Cooper and dialed.

Of course, the killer might not have been the purchaser. He could've stolen them from a store. He could've stolen them from a residence. He could've bought them used at a garage sale.

But 'could've' is a word that goes with the territory of crime scene work, Rhyme reflected.

You have to start somewhere.

THE WATCHMAKER

CRIME SCENE ONE

Location:
- Repair pier in Hudson River, 22nd Street.

Victim:
- Identity unknown.
- Male.
- Possibly middle-aged or older, and may have coronary condition (presence of anticoagulants in blood).
- No other drugs, infection or disease in blood.
- Coast Guard and ESU divers checking for body and evidence in New York Harbor.
- Checking missing persons' reports.

Perp:
- See below.

M.O.:
- Perp forced victim to hold on to deck, over water, cut fingers or wrists until he fell.
- Time of attack: between 6 P.M. Monday and 6 A.M. Tuesday.

Evidence:
- Blood type AB positive.
- Fingernail torn, unpolished, wide.
- Portion of chain-link fence cut with common wire cutters, untraceable.
- Clock. See below.
- Poem. See below.
- Fingernail markings on deck.
- No discernible trace, no fingerprints, no footprints, no tire tread marks.

CRIME SCENE TWO

Location:
- Alley off Cedar Street, near Broadway, behind three commercial buildings (back doors closed at 8:30 to 10 P.M.) and one government administration building (back door closed at 6 P.M.).
- Alley is a cul-de-sac. Fifteen feet wide by one hundred and four feet long, surfaced in cobblestones, body was fifteen feet from Cedar Street.

Victim:
- Theodore Adams.
- Lived in Battery Park.
- Freelance copywriter.
- No known enemies.
- No warrants, state or federal.
- Checking for a connection with buildings around alley. None found.

Perp:
- The Watchmaker.
- Male.
- No database entries for the Watchmaker.

M.O.:
- Dragged from vehicle to alley, where iron bar was suspended over him. Eventually crushed throat.
- Awaiting medical examiner's report to confirm.
- No evidence of sexual activity.
- Time of death: approximately 10:15 P.M. to 11 P.M. Monday night. Medical examiner to confirm.

Evidence:
- Clock.
  - No explosives, chemical or bioagents.
  - Identical to clock at pier.
  - No fingerprints, minimal trace.
  - Arnold Products, Framingham, MA. Calling to find distributors and retailers.
- Poem left by perp at both scenes.
  - Computer printer, generic paper, HP LaserJet ink.
  - Text:
    The full Cold Moon is in the sky,
    shining on the corpse of earth,
    signifying the hour to die
    and end the journey
    begun at birth.
    – The Watchmaker
  - Not in any poetry databases; probably his own.
  - Cold Moon is lunar month, the month of death.
- $60 in pocket, no serial number leads; prints negative.
- Fine sand used as 'obscuring agent'. Sand was generic. Because he's returning to the scene?
- Metal bar, 81 pounds, is needle-eye span. Not being used in construction across from the alleyway. No other source found.
- Duct tape, generic, but cut precisely, unusual. Exactly the same lengths.
- Thallium sulfate (rodent poison) found in sand.
- Soil containing fish protein found inside victim's jacket.
- Very little trace found.
- Brown fibers, probably auto-motive carpeting.

Other:
- Vehicle.
  - Probably Ford Explorer, about three years old. Brown carpet.
  - Review of license tags of cars in area Tuesday morning reveals no warrants. No tickets issued Monday night.
- Checking with Vice about pros-titutes, re: witness.

There's a good-old-boy network in urban government, a matrix of money, patronage and power extending like a steel cobweb everywhere, high and low, connecting politicos to civil servants to business associates to labor bosses to workers . . . It's endless.

New York City is no exception, of course, but the good-old-boy network Amelia Sachs found herself enmeshed in at the moment had one difference: a prime player was a good old girl.

The woman was in her mid-fifties, wearing a blue uniform with plenty of gingerbread on the front – commendations, ribbons, buttons, bars. An American flag pin, of course. (Like politicians, NYPD brass who appear in public *have* to wear the red, white and blue.) She had a pageboy cut of dull salt-and-pepper hair, framing a long, somber face.

Marilyn Flaherty was an inspector, one of the few women at this level in the department (the rank of inspector trumps captain). She was a senior officer in the Operations Division. This was a command that reported directly to the chief of department – the NYPD designation for police chief. Op Div had many functions, among them liaising with other organizations and agencies about major events in the city – planned ones, like dignitaries' visits, and unexpected, like terrorist attacks. Flaherty's most important role was being the police department's contact with City Hall.

Flaherty had come up through the ranks, like Sachs (coincidentally, both women had also grown up in adjacent Brooklyn neighborhoods). The inspector had worked in Patrol Services – walking a beat – then the Detective Bureau, then she'd run a precinct. Stern and brittle, thick and broad, she was a formidable woman in all ways, with the where-withal – okay, the *balls* – to maneuver through the minefield a woman in the upper ranks of law enforcement faces.

To observe that she'd succeeded, you had only to glance at the wall and take note of the framed pictures of friends:

city officials, union bosses and wealthy real estate developers and businessmen. One depicted her and a stately bald man sitting on the porch of a big beach house. Another showed her at the Metropolitan Opera, on the arm of a man Sachs recognized – a businessman as rich as Donald Trump. Another indicator of her success was the size of the One Police Plaza office in which they now sat; Flaherty somehow had landed a massive corner model with a view of the harbor, while all the command inspectors Sachs knew didn't have such nice digs.

Sachs was sitting opposite Flaherty, the inspector's expansive and polished desk between them. The other person present in the room was Robert Wallace, a deputy mayor. He sported a jowly, self-confident face and a head of silver hair sprayed into a politician's perfect coif.

'You're Herman Sachs's daughter,' Flaherty said. Without waiting for a response she looked at Wallace. 'Patrolman. Good man. I was at the ceremony where they gave him that commendation.'

Sachs's father had been given a number of commendations over the years. She wondered which one this had been for. The time he talked a drunken husband into giving up the knife he was holding to his wife's throat? The time he went through a plate-glass window, disarming a robber in a convenience store while he was off duty? The time he delivered a baby in the Rialto theater, with Steve McQueen fighting bad guys up on the silver screen while the Latina mother lay on the popcorn-littered floor, grunting in her rigorous labor?

Wallace asked, 'What's this all about? We understand there might be some crimes police officers're involved in?'

Flaherty turned her steel gray eyes to Sachs and nodded. Go.

'It's possible . . . We have a drug situation. And a suspicious death.'

'Okay,' Wallace said, stretching the syllables out with a sigh and wincing. The former Long Island businessman, now on the mayor's senior staff, served as special commissioner to root out corruption in city government. He'd been ruthlessly efficient at the job; in the past year alone he'd closed up major fraud schemes among building inspectors and teachers' union officials. He was clearly troubled at the thought of crooked cops.

Flaherty's creased face, though, unlike Wallace's, gave nothing away.

Under the inspector's gaze, Sachs explained about the suicide of Benjamin Creeley, suspicious because of the broken thumb, as well as the burned evidence at his house, traces of cocaine and the possible connection to some cops who frequented the St James.

'The officers're from the One One Eight.'

Meaning the 118th Precinct, located in the East Village. The St James, she'd learned, was the watering hole for the station house.

'There were four of them in the bar when I was there, but others hang out there too from time to time. I have no idea who Creeley met with. Whether it was one or two or a half dozen.'

Wallace asked, 'You get their names?'

'No. I didn't want to ask too many questions at this point. And I didn't even get a confirmation that Creeley actually met with anyone from the house. It's likely, though.'

Flaherty touched a diamond ring on her right middle finger. It was huge. Other than this, and a thick gold bracelet, she wore no jewelry. The inspector remained emotionless but Sachs knew this particular news would trouble her a great deal. Even the hint of dirty cops sent a chill throughout city government, but a problem at the 118 would be especially awkward. It was a showcase house, with a higher share of collars, as well as a higher rate of casualties among its officers, than other precincts. More senior cops moved from the 118 to positions in the Big Building than from anywhere else.

'After I found out there might be a connection between them and Creeley,' Sachs said, 'I hit an ATM and took out a couple of hundred bucks. I exchanged that for all the cash in the till at the St James. Some of the bills had to come from the officers there.'

'Good. And you ran the serial numbers.' Flaherty rolled a Mont Blanc pen absently along the desk blotter.

'That's right. Negative on the numbers from Treasury and Justice. But nearly all the bills tested positive for cocaine. One for heroin.'

'Oh, Jesus,' Wallace said.

'Don't jump to conclusions,' Flaherty said. Sachs nodded and explained to the dep mayor what the inspector was referring to: Many twenty-dollar bills in general circulation contained some drugs. But the fact that nearly every bill the cops in the St James had paid with showed trace was a cause for concern.

'Same composition as the coke that was found in Creeley's fireplace?' Flaherty asked.

'No. And the bartender said she'd never seen them with drugs.'

Wallace asked, 'Do you have *any* evidence that police officers were directly involved in the death?'

'Oh, no. I'm not even suggesting that. The scenario I'm thinking of is that, if any cops're involved at all, it was just hooking Creeley up with some crew, looking the other way and taking some points if he was laundering money or a percentage of the profit from the drugs. Then burying any complaints or stepping on investigations from other houses.'

'Any arrests in the past?'

'Creeley? No. And I called his wife. She said she never saw

him doing any drugs. But a lot of users can keep a secret pretty well. Dealers definitely can if they're not using the product themselves.'

The inspector shrugged. 'Of course, it could be completely innocent. Maybe Creeley just met a business acquaintance at the St James. You mentioned he was arguing with somebody there just before he died?'

'Seems that way.'

'And so one of his business deals went bad. Real estate or something. Might have nothing to do with the One One Eight.'

Sachs nodded emphatically. 'Absolutely. It could be a pure coincidence that the St James is a hangout for cops. Creeley could've been killed because he borrowed money from the wrong people or was a witness to something.'

Wallace looked out the window at the bright, cold sky. 'With the death, I think we've got to jump on this. Fast. Let's get IAD involved.'

Internal Affairs would be the logical outfit to investigate any crimes involving police. But Sachs didn't want that, at least not at this point. She'd turn the case over to them later, but not until she'd nailed the perps herself.

Flaherty touched the marbled pen once more then seemed to think better. Men can get away with all kinds of careless mannerisms; women can't afford to, not at this level. With fingers tipped in perfectly manicured nails, the polish clear, Flaherty placed the pen in her top drawer. 'No, not IAD.'

'Why not?' Wallace asked.

The inspector shook her head. 'It's too close to the One One Eight. Word could get back.'

Wallace nodded slowly. 'If you think it's best.'

'I do.'

But Sachs's elation that Internal Affairs wasn't going to take over her case didn't last long. Flaherty added, 'I'll find some-body here to give it to. Somebody senior.'

Sachs hesitated only a moment. '*I'd* like to follow up on it, Inspector.'

Flaherty said, 'You're new. You've never handled anything internal.' So the inspector'd been doing her homework too. 'These're different sorts of cases.'

'I understand that. But I can handle it.' Sachs was thinking: I'm the one who broke the case. I've taken it this far. And it's my first homicide. Goddamn it, don't take it away from me.

'This isn't just crime scene work.'

Calmly she said, 'I'm lead investigator on the Creeley homi-cide. I'm not doing tech work.'

'Still, I think it's best . . . So. If you could get me all the case files, everything you have.'

Sachs was sitting forward, her index fingernail digging into her thumb. What could she do to keep the case?

It was then that the deputy mayor frowned. 'Wait. Aren't you the one who works with that ex-cop in the wheelchair?'

'Lincoln Rhyme. That's right.'

He considered this for a moment then looked at Flaherty. 'I say let her run with it, Marilyn.'

'Why?'

'She's got a solid-gold reputation.'

'We don't need a reputation. We need somebody with ex-perience. No offense.'

'None taken,' Sachs replied evenly.

'These are very sensitive issues. Inflammatory.'

But Wallace liked his idea. 'The mayor'd love it. She's asso-ciated with Rhyme and he's good press. *And* he's civilian. People'll look at it like she's an independent investigator.'

People . . . meaning reporters, Sachs understood.

'I don't want a big, messy investigation,' Flaherty said.

Sachs said quickly, 'It won't be. I've got only one officer working with me.'

'Who?'

'Out of Patrol. Ronald Pulaski. He's a good man. Young but good.'

After a pause Flaherty asked, 'How would you proceed?'

'Find out more about Creeley's connection with the One One Eight and the St James. And about his life – see if there might've been another reason to murder him. I want to talk to his business partner. Maybe there was a problem with clients or some work he was doing. And we need to find out more about the connection between Creeley and the drugs.'

Flaherty wasn't completely convinced but she said, 'Okay, we'll try it your way. But you keep me informed. Me and nobody else.'

A huge sense of relief flooded through Sachs. 'Of course.'

'Informed by phone or in person. No e-mails or memos . . .' Flaherty frowned. 'One thing, you have any other cases on your plate?'

Inspectors don't rise to this level without a sixth sense. The woman had asked the one question Sachs was hoping she wouldn't.

'I'm assisting on the homicide – the Watchmaker.'

Flaherty frowned. 'Oh, you're on *that* one? I didn't know that . . . Compared with a serial doer, this St James situation isn't as important.'

Rhyme's words, echoing: *Your case is colder than the Watchmaker* . . .

Wallace was lost in thought for a moment. Then he glanced at Flaherty. 'I think we have to be adults here. What's going to look worse for the city? A man who kills a few people or a scandal in the police department that the press breaks before we control it? Reporters go for crooked cops like sharks after blood. No, I want to move on this. Big.'

Sachs bridled at Wallace's comment – *kills a few people* – but she couldn't deny that their goals were the same. She wanted to see the Creeley case through to the end.

For the second time in one day she found herself saying, 'I can handle both cases. I promise you it won't be a problem.'

In her mind she heard a skeptical voice saying, *Let's hope, Sachs.*

Chapter
NINE

Amelia Sachs collected Ron Pulaski from Rhyme's, a kidnapping she gathered the criminalist wasn't too pleased about, though the rookie didn't seem very busy at the moment.

'How fast've you had her up to?' Pulaski touched the dashboard of her 1969 Camaro SS. Then he said quickly, 'I mean "it", not "her".'

'You don't need to be so politically correct, Ron. I've been clocked at one eighty-seven.'

'Whoa.'

'You like cars?'

'More, I like cycles, you know. My brother and I had two of 'em when we were in high school.'

'Matching?'

'What?'

'The cycles.'

'Oh, because we're twins, you mean. Naw, we never did that. Dress alike and stuff. Mom wanted us to but we were dorky enough as it was. She laughs now, of course – 'cause of our uniforms. Anyway, when we were riding, it wasn't like we could just go out and buy whatever we wanted, two matching Honda 850s or whatever. We got whatever we could, second- or third-hand.' He gave a sly grin. 'One night, Tony was asleep, I snuck into the garage and swapped out the engines. He never caught on.'

'You still ride?'

'God gives you a choice: children or motorcycles. The week after Jenny got pregnant, some lucky dude in Queens got himself a real fine Moto Guzzi at a good price.' He grinned. 'With a particularly sweet engine.'

Sachs laughed. Then she explained their mission. There were several leads she wanted to follow up on: The other bartender at the St James – Gerte was her name – would be arriving at work soon and Sachs needed to talk to her. She also wanted to talk to Creeley's partner, Jordan Kessler, who was returning from his Pittsburgh business trip.

But first there was one other task.

'How'd you like to go undercover?' she asked.

'Well, okay, I guess.'

'Some of the crew from the One One Eight might've gotten a look at me at the St James. So this one's up to you. But you won't be wearing any wires, anything like that. We're not getting evidence, just information.'

'What do I do?'

'In my briefcase. On the backseat.' She downshifted hard, skidded through a turn, straightened the powerful car. Pulaski picked up the briefcase from the floor. 'Got it.'

'The papers on top.'

He nodded, looking them over. The heading on an official-looking form was *Hazardous Evidence Inventory Control*. Accompanying it was a memo that explained about a new procedure for doing periodic spot checks of dangerous evidence, like firearms and chemicals, to make sure they were properly accounted for.

'Never heard about that.'

'No, because I made it up.' She explained that the point

was to give them a credible excuse to go into the bowels of the 118th Precinct and compare the evidence logs with the evidence actually present.

'You tell them you're checking all the evidence but what I want you to look at is the logs of the narcotics that've been seized in the past year. Write down the perp, date, quantity and the arrests. We'll compare it with the district attorney's disposition report on the same cases.'

Pulaski was nodding. 'So we'll know if any drugs disappeared between the time they were logged in and when the perp went to trial or got pled out . . . Okay, that's good.'

'I hope so. We won't necessarily know who took them but it's a start. Now, go play spy.' She stopped a block away from the 118th, on a shabby street of tenements in the East Village. 'You comfortable with this?'

'Never done anything quite like it, gotta say. But, sure, I'll give it a shot.' He hesitated, looking over the form, then took a deep breath and climbed out of the car.

When he was gone, Sachs made some calls to trusted, and discreet, colleagues in the NYPD, the FBI and the DEA to see if any organized crime, homicide or narcotics cases at the 118th had been dropped or were stalled under circumstances that might be suspicious. No one had heard of anything like that but the statistics revealed that despite its shining conviction record, there'd been very few organized crime investigations out of the house. Which suggested that detectives might be protecting local gangs. One FBI agent told her that some of the traditional mob had been making forays into the East Village once again, now that it was becoming gentrified.

Sachs then called a friend of hers running a gang task force in Midtown. He told her that there were two main posses in the East Village – one Jamaican, one Anglo. Both dealt in meth and coke and wouldn't hesitate to kill a witness or take out somebody who'd tried to cheat them or wasn't paying on time.

Still, the detective said, staging a death to look like a suicide by hanging just wasn't the style of either gang. They'd cap him on the spot with a Mac-10 or an Uzi and head off for a Red Stripe or a Jameson.

A short time later, Pulaski returned, with his typical voluminous notes. This boy writes down *everything*, Sachs reflected.

'So how'd it go?'

Pulaski was struggling to keep from grinning. 'Okay, I guess.'

'You nailed it, hm?'

A shrug. 'Well, the desk sergeant wasn't going to let me in but I gave him this look, like what the hell're you doing, stopping me. *You* want to call Police Plaza and tell 'em they're not getting the form thanks to you? He backed right down. Surprised me.'

'Good job.' She tapped her fist to his, and she could see how pleased the young man was at his performance.

Sachs pulled away from the curb and they headed out of the East Village. When she thought they were far enough away from the house, she pulled over and they started comparing the two sets of figures.

After ten minutes they had the results. The quantities noted in the precinct log and the DA's report were very close. Only about six or seven ounces of pot and four of cocaine were unaccounted for, over the entire year.

Pulaski said, 'And none of the evidence logs looked doctored. I figured that might be something to look for too.'

So one motive – that the St James crew and Creeley were selling drugs boosted from the 118th's evidence locker – wasn't in play. This small amount missing could've been lost because of crime scene testing or spillage or inaccurate logging at the scene.

But even if the cops weren't stealing from the locker, they might still have been dealing, of course. Maybe the cops scored the drugs directly from a source. Or they were perped at a bust before they were logged into evidence. Or Creeley himself might've been the supplier.

Pulaski's first undercover operation answered one question but others remained.

'Okay, onward and upward, Ron. Now, tell me, you want a bartender or a businessman?'

'I don't really care. How 'bout we flip a coin?'

'The Watchmaker probably bought the clocks at Hallerstein's Timepieces,' Mel Cooper announced to Rhyme and Sellitto, hanging up the phone. 'The Flatiron District.'

Before he'd been dragged off by Sachs on the Creeley case, Pulaski had tracked down the Northeast wholesaler for Arnold Products. The head of the distribution company had just returned the rookie's call.

Cooper reported that the distributor didn't keep records by serial number, but that if the clocks *had* been sold in the New York area, it would have been at Hallerstein's, the only outlet there. The store was located south of Midtown in the neighborhood named after the historic triangular building on Fifth Avenue and Twenty-third Street, which resembled an old-time flatiron.

'Check out the store,' Rhyme instructed.

Cooper searched online. Hallerstein's didn't have its own website but was listed in several sites that sold antique clocks and watches. It had been in operation for years. The owner was a man named Victor Hallerstein. A check on him revealed no record. Sellitto punched in caller ID block and called, not identifying himself, just to check on the store hours. He pretended he'd been in before and asked if he was speaking to Hallerstein himself. The man said he was. Sellitto thanked him and hung up.

'I'll go talk to him, see what he has to say.' Sellitto pulled on his coat. It was always better to drop in on witnesses unexpectedly. Phoning ahead gave them a chance to think up lies, whether or not they had anything to hide.

'Wait, Lon,' Rhyme said.

The big detective glanced his way.

'What if he didn't *sell* the clock to the Watchmaker?'

Sellitto nodded. 'Yeah, I thought of that – what if he *is* the Watchmaker or a partner or buddy of his?'

'Or maybe he's behind the whole thing and the Watchmaker's working for him.'

'Thought of that too. But, hey, not to worry. I've got it covered.'

With a soundtrack of Irish harp music pulsing in her ears, California Bureau of Investigation agent Kathryn Dance was absently watching the streets of lower Manhattan stream past, en route to Kennedy Airport.

Christmas decorations, tiny lights and tacky cardboard.

Lovers too. Arm in arm, gloved hands in gloved hands. Out shopping. On vacation.

She was thinking of Bill. Wondered if he would've liked it here.

Funny, the small things you remember so perfectly – even after two and a half years, which is such a huge gulf of time under other circumstances.

Mrs Swenson?

This is Kathryn Dance. My husband's name is Swenson.

Oh. Well, this is Sergeant Wilkins. CHP.

Why would the Highway Patrol call her at home and not refer to her as Agent Dance?

Forever challenged in the kitchen, Dance had been making dinner, singing a Roberta Flack song, sotto voce, and trying to figure out a food processor attachment. She was making split pea soup.

I'm afraid I have to tell you something, Mrs Dance. It's about your husband.

Holding the phone in one hand, the cookbook in the other, she'd stopped moving and stared at the recipe as she took in his words. Dance could still picture the page in the cookbook perfectly, though she'd read it only that one time. She even remembered the caption under the picture. *A hearty, tasty soup that you can whip up in no time. And it's nutritious too.*

She could make the soup from memory.

Though she never had.

Kathryn Dance knew it would still be some time before she healed – well, 'heal' was the word her grief counselor used. But that wasn't right, because you never did heal, she'd come to realize. A scar that replaces slashed skin is still a scar. In time a numbness replaces the pain. But the flesh is forever changed.

Dance smiled to herself now, in the cab, as she noted that she'd crossed her arms and curled up her feet. A kinesics expert knows what *those* gestures are all about.

The streets seemed identical to her – dark canyons, gray and dim brown, punctuated with bright neon: *ATM. Salad Bar. Nails $9.95.* Such a contrast to the Monterey Peninsula, with the pine and oak and eucalyptus and sandy patches dotted with succulent groundcover. The passage of the smelly Chevy taxi was slow. The town she lived in, Pacific Grove, was a Victorian village 120 miles south of San Francisco. Populated with eighteen thousand souls and nestled between chic Carmel and hardworking Monterey, of Steinbeck's *Cannery Row* fame, Pacific Grove could be traversed in the time it had taken the cab to drive four blocks.

Gazing at the city streets, she was thinking, dark and congested, chaotic, utterly frantic, yes . . . Still, she loved New York City. (She was, after all, a people addict, and she'd never seen so many of them in one place.) Dance wondered how the children would respond to the city.

Maggie would go for it, Dance knew without doubt. She

could easily picture the ten-year-old, her pigtail sweeping back and forth as she stood in the middle of Times Square and glanced from billboard to passers-by to hawkers to traffic to Broadway theaters, enthralled.

Wes? He'd be different. He was twelve and had had a tough time since his father died. But finally his humor and confidence seemed to be returning. At last Dance had been comfortable enough to leave him with his grandparents while she went to Mexico on the kidnapper extradition, her first international trip since Bill's death. According to Dance's mother, he'd seemed fine when she was away and so she'd scheduled a seminar here; the NYPD and state police had been after her for a year to present one in the area.

Still, though, she knew she'd have to keep an eye on the lean, handsome boy, with curly hair and Dance's green eyes. He continued to grow sullen at times, detached and angry. Some of it typical male adolescence, some of it the residue of losing his father at a young age. Typical behavior, her counselor had explained, nothing to worry about. But Dance felt that it might take a little time before he'd be ready for the chaos of New York, and she'd never push him. When she got home she'd ask him whether he wanted to visit. Dance couldn't understand parents who seemed to believe they needed magic incantations or psychotherapy to find out what their children wanted. All you really needed to do was ask and listen carefully to their answers.

Yep, Dance decided that, if he was comfortable, she'd bring them here next year, before Christmas. A Boston girl, born and bred, Dance's main objection to the central California coast was the lack of seasons. The weather was lovely – but for the holidays you longed for the bite of the cold in your nose and mouth, the snowstorms, the glowing logs in the fireplace, the frost spiderwebbing the windows.

Dance was now pulled from her reverie by her cell phone's

musical chirp, which changed frequently – a joke by the children (though the number-one rule – Never program a cop's phone to SILENT – was adhered to).

She looked at the caller ID.

Hm. Interesting. Yes or no?

Kathryn Dance gave in to impulse and hit the ANSWER button.

Chapter
TEN

As he drove, the big detective fidgeted, he touched his belly, he tugged at his collar.

Kathryn Dance took in the body language of Lon Sellitto as he drove the unmarked Crown Vic – the same official vehicle she had in California – fast through the streets of New York, grille lights flashing, no siren.

The call she'd taken in the cab was from him, once again asking if she'd help them in the case. 'I know you've got a flight, I know you've got to get home, but . . .'

He explained that they'd discovered a possible source for the clocks left at the Watchmaker's crime scenes and wanted her to interview the man who might've sold them. There was a possibility, though slight, that he had some connection with the Watchmaker and they wanted her opinion about him.

Dance had debated only a brief moment before agreeing. She'd regretted her abrupt departure from Lincoln Rhyme's town house earlier; Kathryn Dance hated leaving a case unfinished, even if it wasn't hers. She'd had the cab turn around and return to Rhyme's, where Lon Sellitto was waiting for her.

Now, in the detective's car, Dance asked, 'It was your idea to call me, wasn't it?'

'How's that?' Sellitto asked.

'Not Lincoln's. He's not sure what to make of me.'

His one-second pause was a flashing sign. Sellitto said, 'You did a good job with that witness, Cobb.'

Dance smiled. 'I know I did. But he's not sure what to make of me.'

Another pause. 'He likes his evidence.'

'Everybody has their weaknesses.'

The detective laughed. He hit the siren button and they sped through a red light.

As he drove, Dance glanced at him, watched his hands and eyes, listened to his voice. She assessed: He's truly obsessed with getting the Watchmaker, and the other cases undoubtedly sitting on his desk now are as insubstantial as steam. And, as she'd observed when he was in her class yesterday, he was dogged and savvy, with no problem taking as much time as he needed to understand a problem or to get an interrogation technique right; if anybody grew impatient with him, well, that was their problem.

His energy's nervous but very different from that of Amelia Sachs, who has harm issues. He grumbles out of habit but he's essentially a very content man.

This was something Dance did automically, the analysis. A gesture, a glance, an offhand statement became to her another piece of that miraculous puzzle that was a human being. She was usually able to shut it off when she wished – it's no fun to be out for a Pinot Grigio or Anchor Steam beer and finding yourself analyzing your drinking buddies (and it's a lot less fun for them). But sometimes the thoughts just flowed; this habit went with the territory of being Kathryn Dance.

The people addict . . .

'You have a family?' he asked.

'Two children, yes.'

'And what's your husband do?'

'I'm a widow.' Dance's job was recognizing the effect of different tones of voice, and she now delivered these words in a particular way, both offhand and grave, which he would take to mean 'I don't want to talk about it.' A woman might grip her arm in sympathy; Sellitto did what most of his sex would: muttered a genuine but awkward 'sorry' and moved on. He began talking about the evidence they'd found in the case and the leads – which were primarily nonleads. He was funny and gruff.

Ah, Bill . . . Know what? I think you'd've liked this guy. Dance knew that she did.

He told her about the store where it was likely the clocks came from. 'I was saying, we don't think this Hallerstein's the doer. But that doesn't mean he's not involved. There's a chance this could get a little, you know, hairy.'

'I'm not armed,' Dance pointed out.

The laws about carrying guns from one jurisdiction to another are very strict and most cops are prohibited from bringing weapons from their home state to another. Not that it mattered; Dance had never fired her Glock except on the range and hoped to be able to say the same at her retirement party.

'I'll stay close,' Sellitto reassured.

Hallerstein's Timepieces sat by itself in the middle of a gloomy block next to some wholesaler storefronts and warehouses. She eyed the place. The facade of the building was covered with scabby paint and grime but inside Hallerstein's shop window, protected by thick steel bars, the displayed clocks and watches were immaculate.

As they walked to the door Dance said, 'If you don't mind, Detective, you establish the credentials, then let me handle things. That okay?'

Some cops, on their local turf, would have had a problem with her taking over. She'd sensed, though, that Sellitto would not (he had self-confidence to burn) but she needed to ask the question. He replied, 'It's your, you know, ball game. That's why we called you.'

'I'm going to say some things that sound a little odd. But it's part of the plan. Now, if I sense he's the perp, I'll lean forward and intertwine my fingers.' A gesture that would make her more vulnerable and put the killer subconsciously at ease – less likely to go for a weapon. 'If I think he's innocent, I'll take my purse off my shoulder and put it on the counter.'

'Got it.'

'Ready?'

'After you.'

Dance pushed a button and they were buzzed into the shop. It was a small place, filled with every kind of clock imaginable: tall grandfather clocks, similar but smaller tabletop clocks, ornate sculptures containing timepieces, sleek, modern-style clocks, a hundred others, as well as fifty or sixty pristine watches.

They walked to the back, where a stocky man, balding, around sixty, was watching them cautiously from behind a counter. He was sitting in front of a dismantled clock mechanism that he was working on.

'Afternoon,' Sellitto said.

The man nodded. 'Hello.'

'I'm Detective Sellitto with the police department and this is Agent Dance.' Sellitto showed his ID. 'You're Victor Hallerstein?'

'That's right.' He pulled off a pair of glasses with an extra magnifying lens on a stalk at the side and glanced at Sellitto's badge. He smiled, with his mouth, though not his eyes, and he shook their hands.

'You're the owner?' Dance asked.

'Owner, right. Chief cook and bottle washer. I've had the store for ten years. Same location. Almost eleven.'

Unnecessary information. Often a sign of deception. But it also could simply have been offered because he was uneasy at the unexpected appearance of two cops. One of the most important rules in kinesics is that a single gesture or behavior means very little. You can't accurately judge a response in isolation but only by looking at 'clusters' – for instance, the body language of crossing one's arms has to be considered in light of the subject's eye contact, hand movement, tone of voice and the substance of what he's saying, as well as his choice of words.

And to be meaningful, the behavior has to be consistent when the same stimuli are repeated.

Kinesic analysis, Kathryn Dance would lecture, isn't about home runs; it's about a consistently well-played game.

'How can I help you? Police, huh? Another robbery around the neighborhood?'

Sellitto glanced at Dance, who didn't respond but gave a laugh and looked around. 'I have never seen so many clocks in one place in my life.'

'Been selling them for a long time.'

'Are these all for sale?'

'Make me an offer I can't refuse.' A laugh. Then: 'Seriously, some I wouldn't sell. But most, sure. Hey, it's a store, right?'

'That one is beautiful.'

He glanced at the one she was indicating. An Art Nouveau style in gold metal, with a simple face. 'Seth Thomas, made in nineteen oh five. Stylish, dependable.'

'Expensive?'

'Three hundred. It's only gold plate, mass produced . . . Now, you want expensive?' Hallerstein pointed to a ceramic clock, in pink, blue and purple, painted with flowers. Dance found it irritatingly gaudy. 'Five times as much.'

'Ah.'

'I see that reaction. But in the clock collecting world, one man's tacky is another man's art.' He smiled. The caution and concern weren't gone but Hallerstein was slightly less defensive.

She frowned. 'At noon what do you do? Wear earplugs?'

A laugh. 'Most of them, you can shut the chimes off. The cuckoos're the ones that drive me crazy. So to speak.'

She asked a few more questions about his business, filing away a library of gestures and glances and tones and words – establishing the baseline for his behavior.

Finally, keeping her tone conversational, she asked, 'Sir, we'd like to know: Did someone recently buy two clocks like this one?' She showed him the picture of one of the Arnold Products clocks left at the crime scenes. Her eyes scanned him as he stared at the photo, his face neutral. She decided he was studying it for too long, an indication that his mind was engaged in a debate.

'Can't say I recall. I sell a lot of clocks, believe me.'

Faulty memory – a flag for the stress state of denial in a deceptive person, just like Ari Cobb earlier. His eyes scanned the photo again carefully, as if trying to be helpful, but his shoulder turned toward her slightly, his head dipped and his voice rose in pitch. 'No, I really don't think so. Sorry, I can't help.'

She sensed he was deceptive, not only from the kinesics but his recognition response (in his case, the neutral visage, which deviated from his expressive baseline); most likely he knew the clock. But was he deceptive because he simply didn't want to get involved, or because he sold clocks to someone he thought might be a criminal, or because he was involved in the killings himself?

Hands clasped in front of her, or purse on the counter?

In determining personality type, Dance had categorized the reluctant witness earlier, Cobb, as an extrovert; Hallerstein was the opposite, an introvert, someone who makes decisions based on intuition and emotion. She drew this conclusion about the dealer because of his clear passion for his clocks and the fact he was only a moderately successful businessman (he'd rather sell what he loved than run a mass-market operation and make more profit).

To get an introvert to tell the truth, she'd have to bond with him, make him feel comfortable. An attack like the one on Cobb would make Hallerstein freeze up instantly.

Dance sighed, her shoulders slumping. 'You were our last hope.' She sighed, glancing at Sellitto, who, bless him, gave a good portrayal of a disappointed cop, shaking his head with a grimace.

'Hope?' Hallerstein asked.

'The man who bought these clocks committed a very serious crime. They're the only real leads we have.'

The concern that blossomed in Hallerstein's face seemed genuine but Kathryn Dance had met a lot of good actors. She put the paper back into her purse. 'Those clocks were found next to his murder victims.'

Eyes frozen for a moment. This is one stressed-out shop-keeper we've got ourselves here.

'Murder?'

'That's right. Two people were killed last night. The clocks might've been left as messages of some kind. We're not sure.' Dance frowned. 'The whole thing is pretty confusing. If *I* were going to murder someone and leave a message I wouldn't hide it thirty feet away from the victim. I'd leave it a lot closer and out in the open. So we just don't know.'

Dance watched his reaction carefully. To her calculated misstatement, Hallerstein gave the same response as would anyone unfamiliar with the situation, a shake of the head at the tragedy but no other reaction. Had he been the killer, he would most likely have given a recognition response – usually centering around the eyes and nose – that her words didn't coincide with his knowledge of the facts. He would've thought: But the killer *did* leave it by the body; why would somebody move it? And that thought would have been accompanied by very specific gestures and body language.

A good deceiver can minimize a recognition response so that most people aren't aware of it but Dance's radar was operating at full strength and she believed the dealer passed the test. She was convinced he hadn't been at the crime scenes or knew the Watchmaker.

She put her purse on the counter.

Lon Sellitto moved his hand away from his hip, where it had been resting.

But her job had just begun. They'd established that the dealer wasn't the killer or didn't know him, but he definitely had information.

'Mr Hallerstein, the people who were killed died in very unpleasant ways.'

'Wait, they were on the news, right? A man was crushed? And then somebody was thrown into the river.'

'Right.'

'And . . . that clock was there?'

Almost 'my' clock. But not quite.

Play the fish carefully, she told herself.

She nodded. 'We think he's going to hurt somebody again. And like I said, you were our last hope. If we have to track down other dealers who might've sold the killer the clocks it could take weeks.'

Hallerstein's face clouded.

Dismay is easily recognized in a person's face but it can arise in response to many different emotions – sympathy, pain, disappointment, sorrow, embarrassment – and only kinesics can reveal the source if the subject doesn't volunteer the information. Kathryn Dance now examined the man's eyes, his fingers caressing the clock in front of him, his tongue touching the corner of his lips. Suddenly she understood: Hallerstein was displaying the flight-or-fight response.

He was afraid – for his own safety.

Got it.

'Mr Hallerstein, if you could remember anything to help us, we'd guarantee you were safe.' A glance at Sellitto, who nodded. 'Oh, you bet. We'll put an officer outside your shop if we need to.'

The unhappy man toyed with a tiny screwdriver.

Dance took the picture out of her purse again. 'Could you just take another look? See if you can remember anything.'

But he didn't need to look. His posture caved in slightly, chest receding, head forward. Hallerstein sprinted into the acceptance response state. 'I'm sorry. I lied.'

Which you hardly ever heard. She'd given him the chance to claim that he'd looked at the picture too fast or was confused. But he didn't care about that. Do not pass go – it was confession time, pure and simple.

'I knew the clock right away. The thing is, though, he said if I told anybody, he'd come back, he'd hurt me, he'd destroy all my watches and clocks, my whole collection! But I didn't know anything about any murder. I swear! I thought he was a crank.' His jaw was trembling and he put his hand back on the casing of the clock he'd been working on. A gesture that Dance interpreted to mean he was desperately seeking comfort.

She sensed something else as well. Kinesic experts have to judge if the subject's responses are appropriate to the questions they've been asked or the facts they've been told. Hallerstein was troubled by the murders, yes, and afraid for himself and his treasures, but his reaction was out of proportion to what they'd been discussing.

She was about to explore this when the clock dealer explained exactly why he was so upset.

'He's leaving these clocks at the places where he kills his victims?' Hallerstein asked.

Sellitto nodded.

'Well, I have to tell you.' His voice clutched and he continued in a whisper. 'He didn't just buy two clocks. He bought ten.'

Chapter
ELEVEN

'*How* many?' Rhyme said, shaking his head as he repeated what Sellitto had just told him. 'He's planning *ten* victims?'

'Looks that way.'

Sitting on either side of Rhyme in the lab, Kathryn Dance and Sellitto showed him the composite picture of the Watchmaker that the detective had made at the clock store, using EFIT – Electronic Facial Identification Technology, a computerized version of the old Identi-Kit, which reconstructed a suspect's features from witness prompts. The image was of a white man in his late forties or early fifties, with a round face, double chin, thick nose and unusually light blue eyes. The dealer had added that the killer was a little over six feet tall. His body was lean and his hair black and medium length. He wore no jewelry. Hallerstein recalled dark clothes but couldn't remember exactly what he was wearing.

Dance then recounted Hallerstein's story. A man had called the shop a month earlier, asking for a particular kind of clock – not a specific brand but any one that was compact, had a moon-phase feature and a loud tick. 'Those were the most important,' she said. 'The moon and a loud tick.'

Presumably so that the victims could hear the sound as they died.

The dealer ordered ten clocks. When they'd arrived the man came in and paid cash. He didn't give his name or where he was from or why he wanted the clocks but he knew a great deal about timepieces. They talked about collectibles, who'd recently bought certain well-known timepieces at auctions and what horological exhibits were presently in the city.

The Watchmaker wouldn't let Hallerstein help him out to the car with the clocks. He'd made several trips, carrying them himself.

As for evidence at the shop, there was very little. Hallerstein didn't do much cash business, so most of the nine hundred dollars and change that the Watchmaker had paid him was still in the till. But the dealer had told Sellitto, 'Won't do you much good if you want fingerprints. He wore gloves.'

Cooper scanned the money for prints anyway and found only the dealer's, which Sellitto had taken as controls. The serial numbers on the bills weren't registered anywhere. Brushing the cash for trace revealed nothing but dust with no distinguishing characteristics.

They'd tried to determine exactly when the Watchmaker had contacted the dealer and, reviewing the telephone logs, they found the likely calls. But it turned out that they'd been made from pay phones, located in downtown Manhattan.

Nothing else at Hallerstein's was of any help.

A call came in from Vice, reporting that the officers had no luck finding the prostitute Tiffanee, with *e* or *y*, in the Wall Street area. The detective said he'd keep on it but since there'd been a murder most of the girls had vanished from the neighborhood.

It was then that Rhyme's eyes settled on one entry on the evidence chart.

Soil with fish protein . . .

Dragged from vehicle to alley . . .

He then looked at the crime scene photos again. 'Thom!'

'What?' the aide called from the kitchen.

'I need you.'

The young man appeared instantly. 'What's wrong?'

'Lie down on the floor.'

'You want me to do what?'

'Lie down on the floor. And, Mel, drag him over to that table.'

'I thought something was wrong,' Thom said.

'It is. I need you to lie down on the floor. Now!'

The aide looked at him with an expression of wry disbelief. 'You're kidding.'

'Now! Hurry.'

'Not on this floor.'

'*I* tell you to wear jeans to work. You're the one who insists on overpriced slacks. Put that jacket on – the one on the hook. Then hurry up. On your back.'

A sigh. 'This is going to cost you big-time.' The aide pulled the jacket on and lay down on the floor.

'Wait, get the dog out of there,' Rhyme called. Jackson the Havanese had jumped out of his box, apparently thinking it was playtime. Cooper scooped the dog up and handed him to Dance.

'Can we get on with it? No, zip up the jacket. It's supposed to be winter.'

'It *is* winter,' Cooper replied. 'It's just not winter inside.'

Thom zipped the jacket up to the neck and lay back.

'Mel, put some aluminum dust on your fingers and then drag him across the room.'

The tech didn't even bother to ask the purpose of the exercise. He dipped his fingers in the dark gray fingerprint powder and stood over Thom.

'How do I drag him?'

'That's what I want to figure out,' Rhyme said. He squinted. 'What's the most efficient way?' He told Cooper to grab the bottom of the jacket and pull it up over Thom's face and drag him that way, headfirst.

Cooper pulled off his glasses and gripped the jacket.

'Sorry,' he muttered to the aide.

'I know, you're just following orders.'

Cooper did as Rhyme told him. The tech was breathing heavily from the effort but the aide moved smoothly along the floor. Sellitto watched impassively and Kathryn Dance was trying to keep from smiling.

'That's far enough. Take the jacket off and hold it open for me.'

Sitting, Thom disrobed. 'Can I get up off the floor now?'

'Yes, yes, yes.' Rhyme was staring at the jacket. The aide climbed to his feet and dusted himself off.

'What's this all about?' Sellitto asked.

Rhyme grimaced. 'Damnit, the rookie was right and he didn't even know it.'

'Pulaski?'

'Yep. He assumed the fish trace was from the Watchmaker. *I* assumed it was the victim's. But look at the jacket.'

Cooper's fingers had left traces of the aluminum fingerprint powder *inside* the garment, in exactly the places where the soil had been found on Theodore Adams's jacket. The Watchmaker himself had left the substance on the victim when he was dragging him in the alley.

'Stupid,' Rhyme repeated. Careless thinking infuriated him – especially his own. 'Now, next step. I want to know everything there is to know about fish protein.'

Cooper turned back to the computer. Rhyme then noticed Kathryn Dance glancing at her watch. 'Missed your plane?' he asked.

'I've got an hour. Doesn't look good, though. Not with security and Christmas crowds.'

'Sorry,' the rumpled detective offered.

'If I helped, it was worth it.'

Sellitto pulled his phone off his belt. 'I'll have a squad car sent round. I can get you to the airport in a half hour. Lights and sirens.'

'That'd be great. I might make it.' Dance pulled on her coat and started for the door.

'Wait. I've got an offer for you.'

Both Sellitto and Dance turned their heads to the man who'd spoken.

Rhyme looked at the California agent. 'How'd you like an all-expenses-paid night in beautiful New York City?'

She cocked an eyebrow.

The criminalist continued. 'I'm wondering if you could stay for another day.'

Sellitto was laughing. 'Linc, I don't believe it. You're always complaining that witnesses are useless. Changing your ways?'

Rhyme frowned. 'No, Lon. What I complain about is how most people *handle* witnesses – visceral, gut feel, all that woo-woo crap. Pointless. But Kathryn does it right – she applies a methodology based on repeatable and observable responses to stimuli and draws verifiable conclusions. Obviously it's not as good as friction ridges or reagent A-ten in drug analysis but what she does is . . .' He looked for a word. 'Helpful.'

Thom laughed. 'That's the best compliment you could get. Helpful.'

'No need to fill in, Thom,' Rhyme snapped. He turned to Dance. 'So? How 'bout it?'

The woman's eyes scanned the evidence board and Rhyme noticed she wasn't focused on the cold notations of the clues, but on the pictures. Particularly the photographs of Theodore Adams's corpse, his frosted eyes staring upward.

'I'll stay,' she said.

*

Vincent Reynolds walked slowly up the steps of the Metropolitan Museum on Fifth Avenue, out of breath by the time he got to the top. His hands and arms were very strong – helpful for when he had his heart-to-hearts with the ladies – but he got zero aerobic exercise.

Joanne, his flower girl, floated into his thoughts. Yes, he'd followed and come close to raping her. But at the last minute another of his incarnations had taken charge, Smart Vincent, who was the rarest of the brood. The temptation had been great but he couldn't disappoint his friend. (Vincent also didn't think it was a wise idea to give any grief to a man whose advice for dealing with conflict was to 'slash the eyes'.) So he had merely checked upon her again, eaten a huge lunch and taken the train here.

He now paid and entered the museum, noticing a family – the wife resembled his sister. He'd just written the previous week asking her to come to New York for Christmas but hadn't heard back. He'd like to show her the sights. She could hardly come at the moment, of course, not while he and Duncan were busy. He hoped she'd visit soon, though. Vincent was convinced that having her more in his life would make a difference. It would provide a stability that would make him less hungry, he believed. He wouldn't need heart-to-hearts quite so often.

I really *wouldn't* mind changing a little bit, Dr Jenkins. *Don't you agree?*

Maybe she'd get here for New Year's. They could go to Times Square and watch the ball drop.

Vincent headed into the museum proper. There wasn't any doubt about where to find Gerald Duncan. He'd be in the area that held the important touring exhibits – the treasures of the Nile, for instance, or jewels from the British Empire. Now, the exhibit was 'Horology in Ancient Times'.

Horology, Duncan had explained, was the study of time and timepieces.

The killer had come here several times recently. It drew the older man the way porn shops drew Vincent. Normally distant and unemotional, Duncan always lit up when he was staring at the displays. It made Vincent happy to see his friend actually enjoying something.

Duncan was looking over some old pottery things called incense clocks. Vincent eased up next to him.

'What'd you find?' asked Duncan, who didn't turn his head. He'd seen Vincent's reflection in the glass of the display case. He was like that – always aware, always seeing what he needed to see.

'She was alone in the workshop all the time I was there. Nobody came in. She went to her store on Broadway and met this delivery guy there. They left. I called and asked for her—'

'From?'

'A pay phone. Sure.'

Meticulous.

'And the clerk said she'd gone out for coffee. She'd be back in about an hour but she wouldn't be in the store. Meaning, I guess, she'd go back to the workshop.'

'Good.' Duncan nodded.

'And what'd *you* find?'

'The pier was roped off but nobody was there. I saw police boats in the river, so they haven't found the body yet. At Cedar Street I couldn't get very close. But they're taking the case real seriously. A lot of cops. There were two that seemed in charge. One of them was pretty.'

'A girl, really?' Hungry Vincent perked up. The thought of having a heart-to-heart with a policewoman had never occurred to him. But he suddenly liked the idea.

A lot.

'Young, in her thirties. Red hair. You like red hair?'

He'd never forget Sally Anne's red hair, how it cascaded on

the old, stinky blanket when he was lying on top of her.

The hunger soared. He was actually salivating. Vincent dug into his pocket, pulled out a candy bar and ate it fast. He wondered where Duncan was going with his comments about red hair and the pretty policewoman but the killer said nothing more. He stepped to another display, containing old-time pendulum clocks.

'Do you know what we have to thank for precise time-telling?'

The professor is at the lectern, thought Clever Mr V, having replaced Hungry Mr V for the moment, now that he'd had his chocolate.

'No.'

'Trains.'

'How come?'

'When people's entire lives were limited to a single town they could start the day whenever they decided. Six A.M. in London might be six eighteen in Oxford. Who cared? And if you *did* have to go to Oxford, you rode your horse and it didn't matter if the time was off. But with a railroad, if one train doesn't leave the station on time and the next one comes barreling through, well, the results are going to be unpleasant.'

'That makes sense.'

Duncan turned away from the display. Vincent was hoping they'd leave now, go downtown and get Joanne. But Duncan walked across the room to a large case of thick glass. It was behind a velvet rope. A big guard stood next to it.

Duncan stared at the object inside, a gold-and-silver box about two feet square, eight inches deep. The front was filled with a dozen dials that were stamped with spheres and pictures of what looked like the planets and stars and comets, along with numbers and weird letters and symbols, like in astrology. The box itself was carved with images too and was covered with jewels.

'What is it?' Vincent asked.

'The Delphic Mechanism,' Duncan explained. 'It's from Greece, more than fifteen hundred years old. It's on tour around the world.'

'What does it do?'

'Many things. See those dials there? They calculate the movement of the sun and moon and planets.' He glanced at Vincent. 'It actually shows the earth and planets moving *around* the sun, which was revolutionary, and heretical, for the time – a thousand years before Copernicus's model of the solar system. Amazing.'

Vincent remembered something about Copernicus from high school science – though what he remembered most was a girl in the class, Rita Johansson. The recollection he enjoyed most was of the pudgy brunette, late one autumn afternoon, lying on her tummy in a field near the school, a burlap bag over her head, and saying in a polite voice, 'Please, no, please don't.'

'And look at that dial,' Duncan said, interrupting Vincent's very pleasant memory.

'The silver one?'

'It's platinum. Pure platinum.'

'That's more valuable than gold, right?'

Duncan didn't answer. 'It shows the lunar calendar. But a very special one. The Gregorian calendar – the one we use – has three hundred and sixty-five days and irregular months. The *lunar* calendar's more consistent than the Gregorian – the months are always the same length. But they don't corre-spond to the sun, which means that the lunar month that starts on, say, April fifth of this year will fall on a different day next year. But the Delphic Mechanism shows a *lunisolar* calendar, which combines the two. I hate the Gregorian and the pure lunar.' There was passion in his voice. 'They're sloppy.'

He hates them? Vincent was thinking.

'But the lunisolar – it's elegant, harmonious. Beautiful.'

Duncan nodded at the face of the Delphic Mechanism. 'A lot of people don't believe it's authentic because scientists can't duplicate its calculations without computers. They can't believe that somebody built such a sophisticated calculator that long ago. But I'm convinced it's real.'

'Is it worth a lot?'

'It's priceless.' After a moment he added, 'There've been dozens of rumors about it – that it contained answers to the secrets of life and the universe.'

'You think that?'

Duncan continued to stare at the light glistening off the metal. 'In a way. Does it do anything supernatural? Of course not. But it does something important: It unifies time. It helps us understand that it's an endless river. The Mechanism doesn't treat a second any differently than it does a millennium. And somehow it was able to measure all of those intervals with nearly one hundred percent accuracy.' He pointed at the box. 'The ancients thought of time as a separate force, sort of a god itself, with powers of its own. The Mechanism is an emblem of that view, you could say. I think we'd all be better off looking at time that way: how a single second can be as powerful as a bullet or knife or bomb. It can affect events a thousand years in the future. Can change them completely.'

The great scheme of things . . .

'That's something.'

Though Vincent's tone must have revealed that he didn't share Duncan's enthusiasm.

But this was apparently all right. The killer looked at his pocket watch. He gave a rare laugh. 'You've had enough of my crazy rambling. Let's go visit our flower girl.'

Patrolman Ron Pulaski's life was this: his wife and children, his parents and twin brother, his three-bedroom detached house in Queens and the small pleasures of cookouts with buddies and their wives (he made his own barbecue sauce and salad dressings), jogging, scraping together babysitter money and sneaking off with his wife to the movies, working in a backyard so small that his twin brother called it a grass throw rug.

Simple stuff. So Pulaski was pretty uneasy meeting Jordan Kessler, Benjamin Creeley's partner. When the coin toss in Sachs's Camaro earned him the businessman, rather than the bartender, he'd called and arranged to see Kessler, who'd just returned from a business trip. (His jet, meaning really *his*, not *a*, jet, had just landed, and *his* driver was bringing him into the city.)

He now wished he'd picked the bartender. Big money made him uneasy.

Kessler was at a client's office in lower Manhattan and wanted to postpone seeing Pulaski. But Sachs had told him to be insistent and he had been. Kessler agreed to meet him in the Starbucks on the ground floor of his client's building.

The rookie walked into the lobby of Penn Energy Transfer, quite a place – glass and chrome and filled with marble sculptures. On the wall were huge photographs of the company's pipelines, painted different colors. For factory accessories they were pretty artistic. Pulaski really liked those pictures.

In the Starbucks a man squinted the cop's way and waved him over. Pulaski bought himself a coffee – the businessman already had some – and they shook hands. Kessler was a solid man, whose thin hair was distractingly combed over a shiny crown of scalp. He wore a dark blue shirt, starched smooth as balsa wood. The collar and cuffs were white and the cuff links rich gold knots.

'Thanks for meeting down here,' Kessler said. 'Not sure what a client would think about a policeman visiting me on the executive floor.'

'What do you do for them?'

'Ah, the life of an accountant. Never rests.' Kessler sipped his coffee, crossed his legs and said in a low voice, 'It's terrible, Ben's death. Just terrible. I couldn't believe it when I heard . . . How're his wife and son taking it?' Then he shook his head and answered his own question. 'How *would* they be taking it? They're devastated, I'm sure. Well, what can I do for you, Officer?'

'Like I explained, we're just following up on his death.'

'Sure, whatever I can do to help.'

Kessler didn't seem nervous to be talking to a police officer. And there was nothing condescending in the way he talked to a man who made a thousand times less money than he did.

'Did Mr Creeley have a drug problem?'

'Drugs? Not that I ever saw. I know he took pain pills for his back at one time. But that was a while ago. And I don't think I ever saw him, what would you say? I never saw him impaired. But one thing: We didn't socialize much. Kind of had different personalities. We ran our business together and we've known each other for six years but we kept our private lives, well, private. Unless it was with clients we'd have dinner maybe once, twice a year.'

Pulaski steered the conversation back on track. 'What about illegal drugs?'

'Ben? No.' Kessler laughed.

Pulaski thought back to his questions. Sachs had told him to memorize them. If you kept looking at your notes, she said, it made you seem unprofessional.

'Did he ever meet with anybody who you'd describe as dangerous, maybe someone who gave you the impression they were criminals?'

'Never.'

'You told Detective Sachs that he was depressed.'

'That's right.'

'You know what he was depressed about?'

'Nope. Again, we didn't talk much about personal things.' The man rested his arm on the table and the massive cuff link tapped loudly. Its cost was probably equal to Pulaski's monthly salary.

In Pulaski's mind, he heard his wife telling him, Relax, honey. You're doing fine.

His brother chimed in with: He may have gold links but you've got a big fucking gun.

'Apart from the depression, did you notice anything out of the ordinary about him lately?'

'I did, actually. He was drinking more than usual. And he'd taken up gambling. Went to Vegas or Atlantic City a couple times. Never used to do that.'

'Could you identify this?' Pulaski handed the businessman a copy of the images lifted from the ash that Amelia Sachs had recovered at Creeley's house in Westchester. 'It's a financial spreadsheet or balance sheet,' the patrolman said.

'Understand that.' A little condescending now but it seemed unintentional.

'They were in Mr Creeley's possession. Do they mean anything to you?'

'Nope. They're hard to read. What happened to them?'

'That's how we found them.'

Don't say anything about them being burned up, Sachs had told him. Play it close to the chest, you mean, Pulaski offered, then decided he shouldn't be using those words with a woman. He'd blushed. His twin brother wouldn't have. They shared every gene except the one that made you shy.

'They seem to show a lot of money.'

Kessler looked at them again. 'Not so much, just a few million.'

Not so much.

'Getting back to the depression. How did you know he was depressed, if he didn't talk about it?'

'Just moping around. Irritated a lot. Distracted. Something was definitely eating at him.'

'Did he ever say anything about the St James Tavern?'

'The . . . ?'

'A bar in Manhattan.'

'No. I know he'd leave work early from time to time. Meet friends for drinks, I think. But he never said who.'

'Was he ever investigated?'

'For what?'

'Anything illegal.'

'No. I would've heard.'

'Did Mr Creeley have any problems with his clients?'

'No. We had a great relationship with all of them. Their average return was three, four times the S and P Five Hundred. Who wouldn't be happy?'

S and P . . . Pulaski didn't get this one. He wrote it down anyway. Then the word 'happy.'

'Could you send me a client list?'

Kessler hesitated. 'Frankly, I'd rather you didn't contact them.' He lowered his head slightly and stared into the rookie's eyes.

Pulaski looked right back. He asked, 'Why?'

'Awkward. Bad for business. Like I said before.'

'Well, sir, when you think about it, there's nothing embarrassing about the police asking a few questions after someone's death, is there? It *is* pretty much our job.'

'I suppose so.'

'And all your clients know what happened to Mr Creeley, don't they?'

'Yes.'

'So us following up – your clients'd expect us to.'

'Some might, others wouldn't.'

'In any case, you *have* done something to control the situation, haven't you? Hired a PR firm or maybe met with your clients yourself to reassure them?'

Kessler hesitated. Then he said, 'I'll have a list put together and sent to you.'

Yes! Pulaski thought, three-pointer! And forced himself not to smile.

Amelia Sachs had said to save the big question till the end. 'What'll happen to Mr Creeley's half of the company?'

Which contained the tiny suggestion that Kessler had murdered his partner to take over the business. But Kessler either didn't catch this or didn't take any offense if he did. 'I'll buy it out. Our partnership agreement provides for that. Suzanne – his wife – she'll get fair market value of his share. It'll be a good chunk of change.'

Pulaski wrote that down. He gestured at the photo of the pipelines, visible though the glass door. 'Your clients're big companies like this one?'

'Mostly we work for individuals, executives and board members.' Kessler added a packet of sugar to his coffee and stirred it. 'You ever involved in business, Officer?'

'Me?' Pulaski grinned. 'Nope. I mean, worked summers for an uncle one time. But he went belly up. Well, not him. His printshop.'

'It's exciting to create a business and grow it into something big.' Kessler sipped the coffee, stirred it again and then leaned forward. 'It's pretty clear you think there's something more to his death than just a suicide.'

'We like to cover all bases.' Pulaski had no clue what he meant by that; it just came out. He thought back to the questions. The well was dry. 'I think that'll be it, sir. Appreciate your help.'

Kessler finished his coffee. 'If I can think of anything else I'll give you a call. You have a card?'

Pulaski handed one to the businessman, who asked, 'That woman detective I talked to. What was her name again?'

'Detective Sachs.'

'Right. If I can't get through to you, should I call her? Is she still working on the case?'

'Yessir.'

As Pulaski dictated, Kessler wrote Sachs's name and mobile number on the back of the card. Pulaski also gave him the phone number at Rhyme's.

Kessler nodded. 'Better get back to work.'

Pulaski thanked him again, finished his coffee and left. One last look at the biggest of the pipeline photographs. That was really something. He wouldn't mind getting a little one to hang up in his rec room. But he supposed a company like Penn Energy hardly had a gift shop, like Disney World.

Chapter
TWELVE

A heavyset woman walked into the small coffee shop. Black coat, short hair, jeans. That's how she'd described herself. Amelia Sachs waved from a booth in the back.

This was Gerte, the other bartender at the St James. She was on her way to work and had agreed to meet Sachs before her shift.

There was a no-smoking sign on the wall but the woman continued to strangle a live cigarette between her ruddy index and middle fingers. Nobody on the staff here said anything about it; professional courtesy in the restaurant world, Sachs guessed.

The woman's dark eyes narrowed as she read the detective's ID.

'Sonja said you had some questions. But she didn't say what.' Her voice was low and rough.

Sachs sensed that Sonja had probably told her everything. But the detective played along and gave the woman the relevant details – the ones that she could share, at least – and then showed her the picture of Ben Creeley. 'He committed suicide.' No surprise in Gerte's eyes. 'And we're looking into his death.'

'I seen him, I guess, a couple, three times.' She looked at the menu blackboard. 'I can eat for free at the St James. But I'm going to miss dinner. Since I'm here. With you.'

'How 'bout I buy you some food?'

Gerte waved at the waitress and ordered.

'You want anything?' the waitress asked Sachs.

'You have herbal tea?'

'If Lipton's a herb, we got it.'

'I'll have that.'

'Anything to eat?'

'No, thanks.'

Gerte looked at the detective's slim figure and gave a cynical laugh. She then asked, 'So that guy who killed himself – did he leave a family?'

'That's right.'

'Tough. What's his name?'

A question that didn't instill confidence that Gerte would be a source of good info. And, sure enough, it turned out that she really wasn't any more helpful than Sonja. All she recalled was that she'd seen him in the bar about once a month for the past three months. She too had the impression that he'd been hanging out with the cops in their back room but wasn't positive. 'The place is pretty busy, you know.'

Depends on how you define busy, Sachs reflected. 'You know any of the officers there personally?'

'From the precinct? Yeah, some of them.'

As the beverages arrived, Gerte recited a few first names, some descriptions. She didn't know anybody's last name. 'Most of 'em who come in're okay. Some're shits. But ain't that the whole world? . . . About him.' A nod at Creeley's picture. 'I remember he didn't laugh much. He was always looking around, over his shoulder, out the windows. Nervous like.' The woman poured cream and Equal into her coffee.

'Sonja said he had an argument the last time he came in. Do you remember any other fights?'

'Nope.' Sipping coffee loudly. 'Not while I was there.'

'You ever see him with any drugs?'

'Nope.'

Useless, Sachs was thinking. This seemed like a dead end.

The bartender drew deeply on her cigarette and shot the smoke toward the ceiling. She squinted at Sachs and gave a meaningless smile with her bright red lips. 'So why you so interested in this guy?'

'Just routine.'

Gerte gave a knowing look and finally said, '*Two* guys come into the St James and not long after that they're both dead. And that's routine, huh?'

'Two?'

'You didn't know.'

'No.'

'Figured you didn't. Otherwise you woulda said something up front.'

'Tell me.'

Gerte fell silent and looked off; Sachs wondered if the woman was spooked. But she was merely staring at the hamburger and fries coming in for a landing on the table.

'Thanks, honey,' she growled. Then looked back at Sachs. 'Sarkowski. Frank Sarkowski.'

'What happened?'

'Killed in a robbery, I heard.'

'When?'

'Early November. Something like that.'

'Who'd he see at the St James?'

'He was in the back room some is all I know.'

'Did they know each other?' A nod toward Creeley's picture.

The woman shrugged and eyed her hamburger. She pulled

the bun off, spread a little mayonnaise on it and struggled with the ketchup lid. Sachs opened it for her.

'Who was he?' The policewoman asked.

'Businessman. Looked like a bridge-and-tunnel guy. But I heard he lived in Manhattan and had money. They were Gucci jeans he wore. I never talked to him except to take his order.'

'How'd you find out about his death?'

'Overheard something. Them talking.'

'The officers from the precinct?'

She nodded.

'Any *other* deaths that you heard of?'

'Nope.'

'Any other crimes? Shakedowns, assaults, bribes?'

She shook her head, pouring ketchup on the burger and making a pool for dunking the fries. 'Nothing. That's all I know.'

'Thanks.' Sachs put ten down on the table to cover the woman's meal.

Gerte glanced at the money. 'The desserts're pretty good. The pie. You ever eat here, have the pie.'

The detective added another five.

Gerte looked up and gave an astute smile. 'Why'm I telling you all this stuff? You're wondering, right?'

Sachs nodded with a smile. She'd been wondering exactly that.

'You wouldn't understand. Those guys in the back room, the cops? The way they look at us, Sonja and me, the things they say, the things they *don't* say. The way they joke about us when they think we can't hear 'em . . .' She gave a bitter smile. 'Yeah, I pour drinks for a living, okay? That's all I do. But that don't give 'em the right to make fun of me. Everybody's got the right to some dignity, don't they?'

Joanne Harper, Vincent's dream girl, had not returned to the workshop yet.

The men were in the Band-Aid-mobile, parked on east Spring Street across from the darkened workshop where Duncan was about to kill his third victim and Vincent was about to have his first heart-to-heart in a long, long time.

The SUV wasn't anything great but it was safe. The Watchmaker had stolen it from someplace where he said it wouldn't be missed for a while. It also sported New York plates that'd been stolen from another tan Explorer – to pass an initial call-in by the cops if they happened to get spotted (they rarely checked the VIN number, only plates, the Watchmaker lectured Vincent).

That was smart, Vincent allowed, though he'd asked what they'd do if some cop *did* check the VIN. It wouldn't match the tag and he'd know the Explorer was stolen.

Duncan had replied, 'Oh, I'd kill him.' As if it was obvious.

Moving right along . . .

Duncan looked at his pocket watch and replaced it, zipped up the pocket. He opened his shoulder bag, which contained the clock and other tools of the trade, all carefully organized. He wound the clock, set the time and zipped the cover of the bag closed. Through the nylon, Vincent could hear the ticking.

They hooked up hands-free headsets to their mobile phones and Vincent set a police scanner on the seat next to him (Duncan's idea, of course). He clicked it on and heard a mundane clatter of transmissions about traffic accidents, the progress of street closings for some event on Thursday, an apparent heart attack on Broadway, a chain snatching . . .

Life in da big city . . .

Duncan looked himself over carefully, made sure all his pockets were sealed. He rolled a dog-hair remover over his body, to pick up trace evidence, and reminded Vincent to do the same before he came inside for his heart-to-heart with Joanne.

Meticulous . . .

'Ready?'

Vincent nodded. Duncan climbed out of the Band-Aid-mobile, looked up and down the street, then walked to the service door. He picked the lock in about ten seconds. Amazing. Vincent smiled, admiring his friend's skill. He ate two candy bars, chewed them down with fierce bites.

A moment later the phone vibrated and he answered. Duncan said, 'I'm inside. How's the street look?'

'A few cars from time to time. Nobody on the sidewalks. It's clear.'

Vincent heard a few metallic clicks. Then the man's voice in a whisper: 'I'll call you when she's ready.'

Ten minutes later Vincent saw someone in a dark coat walking toward the workshop. The stance and motion suggested it was a woman. Yep, it was his flower girl, Joanne.

A burst of hunger filled him.

He ducked low, so she wouldn't see him. He pushed the TRANSMIT button on the phone.

He heard the click of Duncan's phone. No 'hello' or 'yes'.

Vincent lifted his head slightly and saw her walk up to the door. He said into the phone, 'It's her. She's alone. She should be inside any minute.'

The killer said nothing. Vincent heard the click of the phone hanging up.

Okay, he was a keeper.

Joanne Harper and Kevin had had three coffees at Kosmo's Diner, otherwise just another functional, boring eatery in SoHo, but as of today a very special place. She was now walking to the back door of the workshop, reflecting that she wished she could have lingered for another half hour or so. Kevin had wanted to – there were more jokes to tell, more stories to share – but her job loomed. It wasn't due till tomorrow night, but this was an important client and she needed to make sure the arrangements were perfect. She'd reluctantly told him she had to get back.

She glanced up and down the street, still a bit uneasy about the pudgy man in the parka and the weird sunglasses. But the area was deserted. Stepping inside the workshop, she slammed the door and double-locked it.

Hanging up her coat, Joanne inhaled deeply, the way she always did when she first walked inside, enjoying the myriad scents inside the shop: jasmine, rose, lilac, lily, gardenia, fertilizer, loam, mulch. It was intoxicating.

She flicked on the lights and started toward the arrangements she'd been working on earlier. Then she froze and gave a scream.

Her foot had struck something. It scurried away from her. She leapt back, thinking: Rat!

But then she looked down and laughed. What she'd kicked was a large spool of florist wire in the center of the aisle. How had it gotten there? All of the spools hung from hooks on the wall nearby. She squinted through the dimness and saw that somehow this one had slipped off and rolled across the floor. Odd.

Must be ghosts of florists past, she said to herself, then regretted the joke. The place was eerie enough and an image of the fat man in the sunglasses came back immediately. Don't go spooking yourself.

She picked up the spool and saw why it had fallen: the hook had slipped out of the wood. That's all. But then she noticed something else curious. This spool was one of the new ones; she hadn't used any wire from it yet, she thought. But she *must* have; some was missing.

She laughed. Nothing like love to make a girl forgetful.

Then she paused, cocking her head. She was listening to a sound she was unaccustomed to.

What was it?

Very odd . . . dripping water?

No, it was mechanical. Metal . . .

Weird. It sounded like a ticking clock. Where was it coming from? The workshop had a large wall clock in the back but it was electric and didn't tick. Joanne looked around. The noise, she decided, was coming from a small, windowless work area just beyond the refrigerated room. She'd check it out in a minute.

Joanne bent down to repair the hook.

Chapter
THIRTEEN

Amelia Sachs skidded to a stop in front of Ron Pulaski. After he jumped in she pointed the car north and gunned the engine.

The rookie gave her the details of the meeting with Jordan Kessler. He added, 'He seemed legit. Nice guy. But I just thought I ought to check with Mrs Creeley myself to confirm everything – about what Kessler gets because of Creeley's death. She said she trusts him and everything's on the up-and-up. But I still wasn't sure so I called Creeley's lawyer. Hope that was okay.'

'Why wouldn't it be okay?'

'Don't know. Just thought I'd ask.'

'It's always okay to do too *much* work in this business,' Sachs told him. 'The problems're when somebody doesn't do enough.'

Pulaski shook his head. 'Hard to imagine somebody working for Lincoln and being lazy.'

She gave a cryptic laugh. 'And what'd the lawyer say?'

'Basically the same thing Kessler and the wife said. He buys out Creeley's share at fair market value. It's all legit. Kessler said his partner had been drinking more and had taken up gambling. His wife told me she was surprised he did that. Never was an Atlantic City kind of guy.'

Sachs nodded. 'Gambling – maybe some mob connections there. Dealing to them, or just taking along recreational drugs. Money laundering maybe. He win or lose, you know?'

'Dropped some big money, seems like. I was wondering if he hit a loan shark to cover the loss. But his wife said the losses were no big deal, what with his income and everything. A couple hundred thousand didn't hurt much. *She* wasn't real happy about it, you can imagine . . . Kessler said he had a good relationship with all his clients. But I asked for a list. I think we ought to talk to them ourselves.'

'Good,' Sachs told him. Then she added, 'Things're getting gluier. There was another death. Murder/robbery, maybe.' She explained about her meeting with Gerte and told him about Frank Sarkowski. 'I need you to track down the file.'

'You bet.'

'I—'

She stopped speaking. She'd glanced into the rearview mirror and felt a tug in her gut. 'Hm.'

'What?' Pulaski asked.

She didn't answer but made a leisurely turn to the right, went several blocks more and then made a sharp left. 'Okay, we may have a tail. Saw it a few minutes ago. Merc made those turns with us just now. No, don't look.'

It was a black Mercedes with darkened windows.

She turned again, abruptly, and braked to a stop. The rookie grunted at the tug from the belt. The Merc kept going. Sachs glanced back, missed the tag but saw that the car was an AMG, the expensive, souped-up version of the German car.

She spun the Camaro in a U-turn but just then a delivery truck double-parked in front of her. By the time she got around it the Merc was gone.

'Who do you think it was?'

Sachs shifted hard. 'Probably a coincidence. Real rare to get tailed. And, believe me, it *never* happens by some dude in a hundred-and-forty-thousand-dollar car.'

Touching the cold body, the florist lying on the concrete, her face as pale as white roses scattered on the floor.

The cold body, cold as the Cold Moon, but still soft; the hardness of death had not yet set in.

Cutting the cloth off, the blouse, the bra . . .

Touching . . .

Tasting . . .

These were the images cascading through Vincent Reynolds's thoughts as he sat in the driver's seat of the Band-Aid-mobile, staring into the dark workshop across the street, breathing fast, anticipating what he was about to do to Joanne. Consumed with hunger.

Noise intruded. *'Traffic Forty-two, can you . . . they want to add some barriers at Nassau and Pine. By the reviewing stand.'*

'Sure, we can do that. Over.'

The words represented no threat to him or Gerald Duncan and so Vincent continued his fantasy.

Tasting, touching . . .

Vincent imagined that the killer would probably be pulling Joanne down on the floor, trussing her up right now. Then he frowned. Would Duncan be touching her in certain places? Her chest, between her legs?

Vincent was jealous.

Joanne was *his* girlfriend, not Duncan's. Goddamn it! If he wanted to fuck something, let him go find a nice girl on his own . . .

But then he told himself to calm down. The hunger did that to you. It made you crazy, possessed you like the people in those gory zombie films Vincent watched. Duncan's your friend. If he wants to play around with her, let him. They could share her.

Vincent looked at his watch impatiently. It was taking soooo long. Duncan had told him that time wasn't absolute. Some scientists once did an experiment where they put one clock way high in the air on a tower and one at sea level. The higher one ran more quickly than the one on the ground. Some law of physics. Psychologically, Duncan had added, time is relative too. If you're doing something you love, it goes by fast. If you're waiting for something, it moves slowly.

Just like now. Come on, come on.

The radio sitting on the dashboard crackled again. More traffic info, he assumed.

But Vincent was wrong.

'Central to any available unit in lower Manhattan. Proceed to Spring Street, east of Broadway. Be advised, looking for florist shops in the vicinity, in connection with the homicides on the pier at Two Two Street and the alley off Cedar Street last night. Proceed with caution.'

'Jesus, Lord,' Vincent muttered aloud, staring at the scanner. Hitting REDIAL on the phone, he glanced up the street – no sign of any police yet.

One ring, two . . .

'Pick up!'

Click. Duncan didn't say anything – this was according to their plans. But Vincent knew he was on the line.

'Get out, now! Move! The cops're coming.'

Vincent heard a faint gasp. The phone disconnected.

'This is RMP Three Three Seven. We're three minutes from scene.'

'Roger that, Three Three Seven . . . Further to that call – we have a report, a ten-three-four, assault in progress, at

four-one-eight Spring. All available units respond.'

'Roger.'

'RMP Four Six One, we're on the way too.'

'Come on, for Christ sake,' Vincent muttered. He put the Explorer in gear.

Then a huge crash as a ceramic urn slammed through the glass front door of the florist's workshop. Duncan came charging outside. He sprinted over the shattered glass shards, nearly fell on the ice and then raced to the Explorer, leaping into the passenger seat. Vincent sped away.

'Slow down,' the killer commanded. 'Turn at the next street.'

Vincent eased off the gas. It was just as well he brought the speed down because, just as he did, a squad car skidded around the corner in front of them.

Two more converged on the street, the officers leaping out.

'Stop at the light,' Duncan said calmly. 'Don't panic.'

Vincent felt a quiver run through his body. He wanted to punch it, just take the chance. Duncan sensed this. 'No. Just behave like everybody else here. You're curious. Look at the police cars. That's okay to do.'

Vincent looked.

The light changed.

'Slow.'

He eased away from the light.

More cop cars streaked past, responding to the call.

The scanner reported several other cars were en route. An officer radioed that there was no ID of the suspected perp. No one said anything about the Band-Aid-mobile. Vincent's hands were shaking but he kept the big SUV steady, square in the middle of his lane, speed never wavering. Finally, after they'd put some distance between them and the florist shop Vincent said softly, 'They knew it was us.'

Duncan turned to him. 'They what?'

'The police. They were sending cars to look for florists around here, like it had something to do with the murders last night.'

Gerald Duncan considered this. He didn't seem shaken or mad. He frowned. 'They knew we were there? That's curious. How could they possibly know?'

'Where should I go?' Vincent asked.

His friend didn't answer. He continued to look out at the streets. Finally he said in a calm voice, 'For now, just drive. I have to think.'

'He got away?' Rhyme's voice snapped through the speaker of the Motorola. 'What happened?'

Standing beside Sachs at the scene in front of the florist shop, Lon Sellitto replied, 'Timing. Luck. Who the fuck knows?'

'Luck?' Rhyme snapped harshly, as if it were a foreign word he didn't understand. Then he paused. 'Wait . . . Are you using a scrambled frequency?'

Sellitto said, 'We are for tactical, but Central isn't, not for nine-one-one calls. He must've heard the initial call. Shit. Okay, we'll make sure they're all scrambled on the Watchmaker case.'

Rhyme then asked, 'What does the scene say, Sachs?'

'I just got here.'

'Well, *search* it.'

Click.

Brother . . . Sellitto and Sachs glanced at each other. As soon as she'd gotten the call about the 10–34 on Spring, she'd dropped Pulaski off to find the Sarkowski homicide file and sped here to search the scene.

I can do both.

Let's hope, Sachs . . .

She tossed her purse onto the backseat of the Camaro, locked the door and headed to the florist shop. She saw Kathryn Dance walking up the street from the main retail shop, where she'd interviewed the owner, Joanne Harper, who'd narrowly escaped being the Watchmaker's third victim.

An unmarked car pulled up to the curb, the emergency lights in the grille flashing. Dennis Baker shut them off and climbed out. He hurried toward Sachs.

'It *was* him?' Baker asked.

'Yep,' Sellitto told him. 'Respondings found another clock inside. Same kind.'

Three down, Sachs thought grimly. Seven to go . . .

'Another love note?'

'Not this time. But we were real close. I'm guessing he didn't have a chance to leave one.'

'I heard the call,' Baker said. 'How'd you figure out it was him?'

'There'd been an environmental agency bust a block from here – a spill at an exterminating company stockpiling illegal thallium sulfate, rat poison. Then Lincoln learned the main use of the fish protein found at the Adams killing was fertilizer for orchids. Lon had dispatch send out cars to florists and landscaping companies near the extermination operation.'

'Rat poison.' Baker gave a laugh. 'That Rhyme, he thinks of everything, doesn't he?'

'And then some,' Sellitto added.

Dance joined them. She explained what she'd learned from the interview: Joanne Harper had returned from coffee and found some wire misplaced in the store. 'That didn't bother her too much. But she heard this ticking and then thought she heard somebody in a back room. She called nine-one-one.'

Sellitto continued, 'And since we had squad cars headed

to the area anyway, we got there before he killed her. But *just* before.'

Dance added that the florist had no clue why anyone would want to hurt her. She'd been through a divorce a long time ago but hadn't heard from her ex in years. She had no enemies that she could think of.

Joanne also told Dance that she'd seen someone watching her through the window earlier that day, a heavyset white man in a cream-colored parka, old-style sunglasses and baseball cap. She hadn't seen much else because of the dirty windows. Dance wondered if there was a connection with Adams, the first victim, but Joanne had never heard of him.

Sachs asked, 'How's she doing?'

'Shook up. But going back to work. Not in the workshop, though. At her store on Broadway.'

Sellitto said, 'Until we get this guy or figure out a motive I'll order a car outside the store.' He pulled out his radio and arranged for it.

Nancy Simpson and Frank Rettig, the CS officers, walked up to Sachs. Between them was a young man in a stocking cap and baggy jacket. He was skinny and looked freezing cold. 'Gentleman here wants to help,' Simpson said. 'Came up to us at the RRV.'

With a glance at Sachs, who nodded, Dance turned to him and asked what he'd seen. There was no need for a kinesics expert, though. The kid was happy to play good citizen. He explained that he'd been walking down the street and saw somebody jump out the florist's workshop. He was a middle-aged man in a dark jacket. Glancing at the EFIT composite Sellitto and Dance had made at the clock store, he said, 'Yeah, could be him.'

He'd run to a tan SUV, driven by a white guy with a round face and wearing sunglasses. But he hadn't seen anything more specific about the driver.

'There're *two* of them?' Baker sighed. 'He's got a partner.'

Probably the one Joanne had seen at her workshop earlier.

'Was it an Explorer?'

'I don't know an Explorer from a . . . any other kind of SUV.'

Sellitto asked about the license number. The witness hadn't seen it.

'Well, we've got the color at least.' Sellitto put out an Emergency Vehicle Locator. An EVL would alert all Radio Mobile Patrol cars as well as most other law enforcers and traffic cops in the area to look for a tan Explorer with two white men inside.

'Okay, let's move on this,' Sellitto called.

Simpson and Rettig helped Sachs assemble equipment to run the scenes. There were several of them: the store itself, the alley, the sidewalk area where he'd escaped, as well as where the Explorer had been parked.

Kathryn Dance and Sellitto returned to Rhyme's, while Baker kept canvassing for witnesses, showing pictures of the Watchmaker's composite to people on the street and workers in the warehouses and businesses along Spring.

Sachs collected what evidence she could locate. Since the first clock hadn't been an explosive device, there was no need to get the bomb squad involved; a simple field test for nitrates was sufficient to make sure. She packed it up, along with the remaining evidence, then stripped off the Tyvek and pulled on her leather jacket. She hurried up the street and dropped into the front seat of the Camaro, fired the car up and turned on the heater full blast.

She reached behind the passenger seat for her purse to get her gloves. But when she picked up the leather bag, the contents spilled out.

Sachs frowned. She was very careful always to keep the purse latched. She couldn't afford to lose the contents, which included two extra ammunition clips for her Glock, as well as a can of tear gas. She clearly remembered twisting the latch when she'd arrived.

She looked at the passenger-side window. Smears on the glass made by gloves were consistent with somebody using a slimjim to pop the door lock. And some of the insulating fuzz around the window was pushed aside.

Burglarized while doing a crime scene. This's a first.

She looked through the bag, item by item. Nothing was gone. The money and charge cards were all there – though she'd have to call the credit card companies in case the thief had jotted down the numbers. The ammunition and CS tear-gas spray were intact. Hand straying to her Glock, she looked around. There was a small crowd gathered nearby, curious about the police activity. She climbed out and approached them, asking if anybody had seen the break-in. Nobody had.

Returning to the Chevy, Sachs got her bare-bones crime scene kit from the trunk and ran the car just like any other crime scene – checking for footprints, fingerprints and trace inside and out. She found nothing. She replaced the equipment and dropped into the front seat once again.

Then she saw, a half block away, a big black car edge out of an alleyway. She thought of the Mercedes she'd seen earlier, when she'd picked up Pulaski. She couldn't see the make, though, and the car disappeared in traffic before she could turn her vehicle around and head after it.

Coincidence or not? she wondered.

The big Chevy engine began to push heat into the car and she strapped in. She pushed the transmission into first. Easing forward, she thought to herself, Well, no harm done.

She was halfway up the block, shoving the shifter into third, when the thought hit her: What *was* he looking for?

The fact that her money and plastic were still there suggested that the perp was after something else.

Amelia Sachs knew that it's the people with motives you can't figure out who are always the most dangerous.

Chapter
FOURTEEN

At Rhyme's, Sachs delivered the evidence to Mel Cooper.

Before she put on her latex gloves, she walked to a canister and pulled out a few dog biscuits, fed them to Jackson. He ate them down fast.

'You ever think about getting a helper dog?' Kathryn Dance asked Rhyme.

'He is a helper dog.'

'Jackson?' Sachs frowned.

'Yep. He helps plenty. He distracts people so I don't have to entertain them.'

The women laughed. 'I mean a real one.'

One of his therapists had suggested a dog. Many para-plegics and quadriplegics had helper animals. Not long after the accident, when the counselor had first brought it up, he'd resisted the idea. He couldn't explain why, exactly, but believed it had to do with his reluctance to depend on something, or someone, else. Now, the idea didn't seem so bad.

He frowned. 'Can you train them to pour whiskey?' The criminalist looked from the dog to Sachs. 'Oh, you got a call when you were at the scene. Someone named Jordan Kessler.'

'Who?'

'He said you'd know.'

'Oh, wait – sure, Creeley's partner.'

'He wanted to talk to you. I told him you weren't here so he left a message. He said that he talked to the rest of the company employees and that Creeley definitely had been depressed lately. And Kessler's still putting together a client list. But it'll take a day or two.'

'A couple of days?'

'What he said.'

Rhyme's eyes were on the evidence she was assembling on an examination table next to Cooper. His mind drifted away from the St James situation – what he was calling the 'Other Case'. As opposed to 'His Case', the Watchmaker. 'Let's get to the evidence,' he announced.

Sachs pulled on latex gloves and began unpacking the boxes and bag.

The clock was the same as the first two, ticking and showing the correct time. The moon face just slightly past full.

Together, Cooper and Sachs dismantled it but found no trace of any significance.

No footprints, friction-ridge prints, weapons or anything else had been left behind in the florists shop. Rhyme wondered if there was some special tool the killer had used to cut the florist's wire or some technique that might reveal a past or present career or training. But, no, he'd used Joanne's own clippers. Like the duct tape, though, the wire had been cut in precise lengths. Each one was exactly six feet long. Rhyme wondered whether he was going to bind her with the wire or whether it was the intended murder weapon.

Joanne Harper had locked the door when she left the shop to meet a friend for coffee. It was clear that the killer had picked the lock to get inside. This didn't surprise Rhyme; a man who knows the mechanics of timepieces could easily learn the skills of lockpicking.

A search of DMV resort revealed 423 owners of tan Explorers in the metropolitan area. They cross-referenced the list against warrants and found only two: a man in his sixties, wanted as a scofflaw for dozens of parking tickets, and a younger man busted for selling coke. He wondered if this was the Watchmaker's assistant but it turned out he was still in jail for the offense. The Watchmaker might well be among the remaining names on the list but there was no way to talk to every one, though Sellitto was going to have someone check those whose addresses were in lower Manhattan. There'd also been a few hits on the Emergency Vehicle Locator but none of the drivers' descriptions fit those of the Watchmaker or his partner.

Sachs had collected samples of trace from the shop itself and found that, yes, the soil and fish protein, in the form of fertilizer, had indeed come from Joanne's. There was some inside the building but Sachs had also found considerable amounts outside, in and around discarded bags of the fertilizer.

Rhyme was shaking his head.

'What's the problem?' Sellitto asked.

'It's not the protein itself. It's the fact it was on the *second* victim. Adams.'

'Because?'

'It means the perp was checking out the workshop earlier – presumably the victim and looking for alarms or security cameras. He's been staking out his locations. Which means there's a reason he's picking these particular victims. But what the hell is it?'

The man crushed to death in the alley wasn't apparently involved in any criminal activities and had no enemies. The same was true with Joanne Harper. And she'd never heard of

Adams – no link between them. Yet they'd both been targeted by the Watchmaker. Why them? Rhyme wondered. An unknown victim at the pier, a young businessman, a florist . . . and seven others to go. What is there about them that's driving him to kill? What's the connection?

'What else did you find?'

'Black flakes,' Cooper said, holding up a plastic envelope. Inside were dots like dried black ink.

Sachs said, 'They were from where he got the wire spool and where he was probably hiding. Also, I found a few of them outside the front door where he'd stepped on the glass running to the Explorer.'

'Well, run them through the GC.'

Cooper fired up the gas chromatograph/mass spectrometer and loaded a sample of the flakes. In a few minutes the results came up on the screen.

'So, what do we have, Mel?'

The tech shoved his glasses higher on his nose. He leaned forward. 'Organic . . . Looks like about seventy-three percent n-alkanes, then polycyclic aromatic hydrocarbons and thiaarenes.'

'Ah, roofing tar.' Rhyme squinted.

Kathryn Dance gave a laugh. 'You know that?'

Sellitto said, 'Oh, Lincoln used to wander around the city collecting everything he could find for his evidence databases . . . Must've been fun going out to dinner with you, Linc. You bring test tubes and bags with you?'

'My ex could tell you all about it,' Rhyme replied with an amused grunt. His attention was on the black spots of tar. 'I'll bet he's been checking out another victim from a place that's getting a new roof.'

'Or maybe they're reroofing his place,' Cooper offered.

'Doubt he's spending time enjoying cocktails and the sunset on his *own* roof in this weather,' Rhyme replied. 'Let's assume it's somebody else's. I want to find out how many buildings are being reroofed right now.'

'There could be hundreds of them, thousands,' Sellitto said.

'Probably not in this weather.'

'And how the hell do we find them anyway?' the rumpled detective asked.

'ASTER.'

'What's that?' Dance asked.

Rhyme recited absently, 'Advanced Spaceborne Thermal Emission and Reflection Radiometer. It's an instrument and data package on the Terra satellite – a joint venture between NASA and the Japanese government. It captures thermal images from space. Orbits every . . . what, Mel?'

'About ninety-eight minutes. But it takes sixteen days to cover the entire Earth.'

'Find out when it was over New York most recently. I want thermal images and see if they can delineate heat over two hundred degrees – I imagine tar's at least that temperature when it's applied. Should narrow down where he's been.'

'The whole city?' Cooper asked.

'He's hunting in Manhattan, looks like. Let's go with that first.'

Cooper had a lengthy conversation then hung up. 'They're on it. They'll do their best.'

Thom showed Dennis Baker into the town house. 'No other witnesses around the florist's workshop,' the lieutenant reported, pulling off his coat and gratefully accepting a cup of coffee. 'We searched for an hour. Either nobody saw anything or has the guts to admit they did. This guy's got everybody spooked.'

'We need more.' Rhyme looked at the diagram that Sachs had sketched of the scene. 'Where was the SUV parked?' he asked.

'Across the street from the workshop,' Sachs replied.

'And you searched the spot where it was parked.' It wasn't a question. Rhyme knew she would have. 'Any cars in front or behind it?'

'No.'

'Okay, he runs to the car, his partner drives to the closest intersection and turns, hoping to get lost in the traffic. He won't break any laws so he'll make a nice, careful – and sharp – turn, staying in his lane.' Like speed bumps and sudden braking, sharp, slow turns often dislodge important trace from treads of tires. 'If the street's still sealed off, I want a team from Crime Scene to sweep up everything at the intersection. It's a long shot but I think we have to try.' He turned to Baker. 'You just left the scene, right? About ten, fifteen minutes ago?'

'About that,' Baker replied, sitting and stretching as he downed his coffee. He looked exhausted.

'Was the street still sealed?'

'Wasn't paying much attention. I think it was.'

'Find out,' Rhyme said to Sellitto, 'and if so, send a team.'

But the detective's call revealed that the street was now open to traffic. Any trace left by the killer's Explorer would have been obliterated by the first or second vehicle making the same turn.

'Damn,' Rhyme muttered, his eyes returning once again to the evidence chart, thinking it had been a long time since a case had presented so much difficulty.

Thom rapped on the doorjamb and led someone else into the room, a middle-aged woman in an expensive black coat. She was familiar to Rhyme but he couldn't recall the name.

'Hello, Lincoln.'

Then he remembered. 'Inspector.'

Marilyn Flaherty was older than Rhyme but they'd both been captains at the same time and had worked together on a few special commissions. He remembered her as being smart and ambitious – and, out of necessity, just a little bit flintier and more driven than her male counterparts. They spoke for a few minutes about mutual acquaintances and colleagues past and present. She asked about the Watchmaker case and he gave her a synopsis.

The inspector then pulled Sachs aside and asked about the status of the investigation, meaning, of course, the Other Case. Rhyme couldn't help overhearing Sachs tell her that she'd found nothing conclusive. There'd been no major drug thefts from the evidence room of the 118th Precinct. Creeley's partner and his employees confirmed the businessman's depression and reported that he'd been drinking more lately. It turned out that he'd been going to Vegas and/or Atlantic City recently.

'Possible organized crime connection,' Flaherty pointed out.

'That's what I was thinking,' Sachs said. Then she added that there seemed to be no clients with grudges against Creeley but that she and Pulaski were awaiting the client list from Jordan Kessler to check it out themselves.

Suzanne Creeley, though, remained convinced that he'd had nothing to do with drugs or criminal activity and that he hadn't killed himself.

'And,' Sachs said, 'we've got another death.'

'*Another* one?'

'A man who came to the St James a few times. Maybe met with the same people that Creeley did.'

Another death? Rhyme reflected. He had to admit that the Other Case was developing some very interesting angles.

'Who?' Flaherty asked.

'Another businessman. Frank Sarkowski. Lived in Manhattan.'

Flaherty was looking over the lab, the evidence charts, the equipment, frowning. 'Any clue who killed him?'

'I think it was during a robbery. But I won't know until I read the file.'

Rhyme could see the frustration in Flaherty's face.

Sachs too was tense. He soon realized why. As soon as Flaherty said, 'I'm going to hold off on Internal Affairs for the time being,' Sachs relaxed. They weren't going to take the case away from her. Well, Lincoln Rhyme was happy for Sachs, though in his heart he would have preferred that she hand off the Other Case to Internal Affairs and get back to working on His Case.

Flaherty asked, 'That young officer? Ron Pulaski? He's working out okay?'

'He's doing a good job.'

'I'm going to report to Wallace, Detective.' The inspector nodded at Rhyme. 'Lincoln, it was good seeing you again. Take care.'

'So long, Inspector.'

Flaherty walked to the door and let herself out, walking just like a general on a parade ground.

Amelia Sachs was about to call Pulaski and find out what he'd learned about Sarkowski when she heard a voice near her ear. 'The Grand Inquisitor.'

Sachs turned to look at Sellitto, dumping sugar in his coffee. He said, 'Hey, step into my office.' And gestured toward the front hallway of Rhyme's town house.

Leaving the others, the two detectives walked into the low-lit entryway.

'Inquisitor. That's what they call Flaherty?' Sachs asked.

'Yup. Not that she isn't good.'

'I know. I checked her out.'

'Uhm.' The big detective sipped coffee and finished a Danish. 'Look, I'm up to my ass in psycho clockmakers so I don't know what's up with this St James thing. But if you got cops maybe're on the take, how come it's you and not Internal Affairs running the case?'

'Flaherty didn't want to bring them in yet. Wallace agreed.'

'Wallace?'

'Robert Wallace. The deputy mayor.'

'Yeah, I know him. Stand-up guy. And it's the right call, bringing in IAD. Why didn't she want to?'

'She wanted to give it to somebody in her command. She said the One One Eight's too close to the Big Building. Somebody'd find out Internal Affairs was involved and they'd cut and run.'

Sellitto jutted his lower lip out in concession. 'That could be.' Then his voice lowered even further. 'And you didn't argue too much 'cause you wanted the case.'

She looked him in the eye. 'That's right.'

'So you asked and you got.' He gave a cool laugh.

'What?'

'Now you're walking point.'

'What's wrong with that?'

'Just, you gotta know the score. Now, anything goes bad, anything at all – good people get burned, bad guys get away – the fuckup's on your shoulders, even if you do everything right. Flaherty's protected and IAD's smelling like roses. On the other hand, you get righteous collars, they take over and suddenly everybody forgets your name.'

'You're saying I got set up?' Sachs shook her head. 'But Flaherty didn't *want* me to take the case. She was going to hand it off.'

'Amelia, come on. End of a date, a guy says, "Hey, had a great time but it's probably better if I don't ask you upstairs." What's the first thing the girl says?'

'"Let's go upstairs." What he had in mind all along. You're saying Flaherty was playing me?'

'All I'm saying is she *didn't* take the case away from you, right? Which she could've done in, like, five seconds.'

Sachs's nail dug absently into her scalp. Her gut twisted

at the idea of department politics at this high level – largely uncharted territory for her.

'Now, my point is, I wish you weren't lead on a case like this, not now in your career. But you are. So you have to remember – keep your head down. I mean stay fucking invisible.'

'I—'

'Lemme finish. Invisible for two reasons. One, people find out you're after bad cops, rumors're going to start – about this shield taking cash or that shield losing evidence, whatever. Fact they're *not* doesn't mean shit. Rumors're like the flu. You can't wish 'em away. They run their course and they take people's careers with 'em.'

She nodded. 'What's the second reason?'

'Just because you got a shield, don't think you're immune. A bad uniform in the One One Eight, yeah, he's not going to clip you. That doesn't happen. But the civilians he's dealing with won't want to hear his opinion. They won't think twice about tossing your body into the trunk of a car at JFK long-term parking . . . God bless you, kid. Go get 'em. But be careful. I don't want to have to go breaking any bad news to Lincoln. He'd never forgive me.'

Ron Pulaski returned to Rhyme's, and Sachs met him in the front hallway, as she stood, looking into the kitchen, and thinking about what Sellitto had told her.

She briefed him about the latest in the Watchmaker case then asked, 'What's the Sarkowski situation?'

He flipped through his notes. 'I located his spouse and proceeded to interview her. Now, the decedent was a fifty-seven-year-old white male who owned a business in Manhattan. He had no criminal record. He was murdered on November four of this year and was survived by said wife and two teenage children, one male, one female. Death occurred by gunshot. He—'

'Ron?' she asked in a certain tone.

He winced. 'Oh, sorry. Streamline, sure.'

His copspeak was a habit Sachs was determined to break.

Relaxing, the rookie continued. 'He was the owner of a building on the West Side, Manhattan. Lived there too. He also owned a company that did maintenance and trash disposal work for big companies and utilities around the city. His business had a clean record – federal, city and state. No organized crime connections, no investigations ongoing. He himself had no warrants or arrests, except a speeding ticket last year.'

'Any suspects in his death?'

'No.'

'What house ran the case?'

'The One Three One.'

'He was in *Queens* when he died, not Manhattan?'

'That's right.'

'What happened?'

'The perp got his wallet and cash then shot him three times in the chest.'

'The St James? Did she ever hear him say anything about it?'

'Nope.'

'Did he know Creeley?'

'The wife wasn't sure, didn't think so. I showed her the picture and she didn't recognize him.' He grew quiet for a moment and then added, 'One thing. I think I saw it again, the Mercedes.'

'You did?'

'After you dropped me off I crossed the street fast to beat a light and I looked behind me to see if there was traffic. I couldn't get a good look but I thought I saw the Merc. Couldn't see the tag. Just thought I'd mention it.'

Sachs shook her head. 'I had a visitor too.' She told him

about the break-in to her car. And added that she believed she'd seen the Mercedes as well. 'That driver's been a busy boy.' She then looked at his hands, which held only his thick notebook. 'Where's the Sarkowski file?'

'Okay, that's the problem. No file, no evidence. I went through the entire evidence locker in the One Three One. Nothing.'

'Okay, this's getting funky. No evidence?'

'Missing.'

'The file was checked out?'

'Might've been but it's not in the computer log. It should've been there if somebody took it or it got sent somewhere. But I got the name of the case detective. He lives in Queens. Just retired. Art Snyder.' Pulaski handed her a sheet of paper with the man's name and address on it. 'You want me to talk to him?'

'No, I'll go see him. I want you to stay here and write up our notes on a whiteboard. I want to see the big picture. But don't do it in the lab. There's too much traffic.' Crime scene and other officers routinely made deliveries to Rhyme's. With a case involving crooked cops, she didn't want anyone to see what they'd learned. She nodded toward Rhyme's exercise room, where his ergometer and treadmill were located. 'We'll keep it in there.'

'Sure. But that won't take long. When I'm done, you want me to meet you at Snyder's?'

Sachs thought again about the Mercedes. And she heard Sellitto's words looping through her head: . . . *The trunk of a car at JFK long-term parking* . . .

'Naw, when you're through, just stay here and help out Lincoln.' She laughed. 'Maybe it'll improve his mood.'

THE WATCHMAKER

CRIME SCENE ONE

Location:
- Repair pier in Hudson River, 22nd Street.

Victim:
- Identity unknown.
- Male.
- Possibly middle-aged or older, and may have coronary condition (presence of anticoagulants in blood).
- No other drugs, infection or disease in blood.
- Coast Guard and ESU divers checking for body and evidence in New York Harbor.
- Checking missing persons' reports.

Perp:
- See below.

M.O.:
- Perp forced victim to hold on to deck, over water, cut fingers or wrists until he fell.
- Time of attack: Between 6 P.M. Monday and 6 A.M. Tuesday.

Evidence:
- Blood type AB positive.
- Fingernail torn, unpolished, wide.
- Portion of chain-link fence cut with common wire cutters, untraceable.
- Clock. See below.
- Poem. See below.
- Fingernail markings on deck.

- No discernible trace, no fingerprints, no footprints, no tire tread marks.

CRIME SCENE TWO

Location:
- Alley off Cedar Street, near Broadway, behind three commercial buildings (back doors closed at 8:30 to 10 P.M.) and one government administration building (back door closed at 6 P.M.).
- Alley is a cul-de-sac. Fifteen feet wide by one hundred and four feet long, surfaced in cobblestones, body was fifteen feet from Cedar Street.

Victim:
- Theodore Adams.
- Lived in Battery Park.
- Freelance copywriter.
- No known enemies.
- No warrants, state or federal.
- Checking for a connection with buildings around alley. None found.

Perp:
- The Watchmaker.
- Male.
- No database entries for the Watchmaker.

M.O.:
- Dragged from vehicle to alley, where iron bar was suspended over him. Eventually crushed throat.

- Awaiting medical examiner's report to confirm.
- No evidence of sexual activity.
- Time of death: Approximately 10:15 P.M. to 11 P.M. Monday night. Medical examiner to confirm.

Evidence:
- Clock.
  - No explosives, chemical- or bioagents.
  - Identical to clock at pier.
  - No fingerprints, minimal trace.
  - Arnold Products, Framingham, MA.
  - Sold by Hallerstein's Timepieces, Manhattan.
- Poem left by perp at both scenes.
  - Computer printer, generic paper, HP LaserJet ink.
  - Text:
    The full Cold Moon is in the sky,
    shining on the corpse of earth,
    signifying the hour to die and end the journey begun at
    birth.
              – The Watchmaker
  - Not in any poetry databases; probably his own.
  - Cold Moon is lunar month, the month of death.
- $60 in pocket, no serial number leads; prints negative.
- Fine sand used as 'obscuring agent'. Sand was generic.

Because he's returning to the scene?
- Metal bar, 81 pounds, is needle-eye span. Not being used in construction across from the alleyway. No other source found.
- Duct tape, generic, but cut precisely, unusual. Exactly the same lengths.
- Thallium sulfate (rodent poison) found in sand.
- Soil containing fish protein – from perp, not victim.
- Very little trace found.
- Brown fibers, probably automotive carpeting.

Other:
- Vehicle.
  - Probably Ford Explorer, about three years old. Brown carpet.
  - Review of license tags of cars in area Tuesday morning reveals no warrants. No tickets issued Monday night.
- Checking with Vice about prostitutes, re: witness.
  - No leads.

INTERVIEW WITH HALLERSTEIN

Perp:
- EFIT composite picture of the Watchmaker – late forties, early fifties, round face, double chin, thick nose, unusually light blue eyes. Over 6 feet tall, lean, hair black, medium length, no

jewelry, dark clothes. No name.
- Knows great deal about clocks and watches and which timepieces had been sold at recent auctions and were at current horological exhibits in the city.
- Threatened dealer to keep quiet.
- Bought 10 clocks. For 10 victims?
- Paid cash.
- Wanted moon face on clock, wanted loud tick.

Evidence:
- Source of clocks was Hallerstein's Timepieces, Flatiron District.
- No prints on cash paid for clocks, no serial number hits. No trace on money.
- Called from pay phones.

CRIME SCENE THREE

Location:
- 481 Spring Street.

Victim:
- Joanne Harper.
- No apparent motive.
- Didn't know second victim, Adams.

Perp:
- The Watchmaker.
- Assistant.
  - Probably man spotted earlier by victim, at her shop.
  - White, heavyset, in sunglasses, cream-colored parka and cap. Was driving the SUV.

M.O.:
- Picked locks to get inside.
- Intended method of attack unknown. Possibly planning to use florist's wire.

Evidence:
- Fish protein came from Joanne's (orchid fertilizer).
- Thallium sulfate nearby.
- Florist's wire, cut in precise lengths. (To use as murder weapon?)
- Clock.
  - Same as others. No nitrates.
  - No trace.
- No note or poem.
- No footprints, fingerprints, weapons or anything else left behind.
- Black flakes – roofing tar.
  - Checking ASTER thermal images of New York for possible sources.

Other:
- Perp was checking out victim earlier than attack. Targeting her for a purpose. What?
- Have police scanner. Changing frequency.
- Vehicle.
  - Tan SUV.
  - No tag number.
  - Putting out Emergency Vehicle Locator.
  - 423 owners of tan Explorers in area. Cross-reference against criminal warrants. Two found. One owner too old; other is in jail on drug charges.

- 56-year-old Creeley, apparently suicide by hanging. Clothesline. But had broken thumb, couldn't tie noose.
- Computer-written suicide note about depression. But appeared not to be suicidally depressed, no history of mental/emotional problems.
- Around Thanksgiving two men broke into his house and possibly burned evidence. White men, but faces not observed. One bigger than other. They were inside for about an hour.
- Evidence in Westchester house:
  - Broke through lock; skillful job.
  - Leather texture marks on fireplace tools and Creeley's desk.
  - Soil in front of fireplace has higher acid content than soil around house and contains pollutants. From industrial site?
  - Traces of burned cocaine in fireplace.
  - Ash in fireplace.
    - Financial records, spreadsheet, references to millions of dollars.
    - Checking logo on documents, sending entries to forensic accountant.
    - Diary re: getting oil changed, haircut appoint-

  ment and going to St James Tavern.
- St James Tavern
  - Creeley came here several times.
  - Apparently didn't use drugs while here.
  - Not sure whom he met with, but maybe cops from the nearby 118th Precinct of the NYPD.
  - Last time he was here – just before his death – he got into an argument with persons unknown.
  - Checked money from officers at St James – serial numbers are clean, but found coke and heroin. Stolen from precinct?
  - Not much drugs missing, only 6 or 7 oz. of pot, 4 of coke.
- Unusually few organized crime cases at the 118th Precinct but no evidence of intentional stalling by officers.
- Two gangs in the East Village possible but not likely suspects.
- Interview with Jordan Kessler, Creeley's partner, and follow-up with wife.
  - Confirmed no obvious drug use.
  - Didn't appear to associate with criminals.
  - Drinking more than usual, taken up gambling; trips to

Vegas and Atlantic City.
Losses were large, but not
significant to Creeley.
- Not clear why he was
  depressed.
- Kessler didn't recognize

burned records.
- Awaiting list of clients.
- Kessler doesn't appear to
  gain by Creeley's death.
- Sachs and Pulaski followed
  by AMG Mercedes.

FRANK SARKOWSKI HOMICIDE

- Sarkowski was 57 years old,
  no police record, murdered on
  November 4 of this year,
  survived by wife and two
  teenage children.
- Victim owned building and
  business in Manhattan.
  Business was doing maintenance for other companies
  and utilities.
- Art Snyder was case detective.

- No suspects.
- Murder/robbery?
- Business deal went bad?
- Killed in Queens – not sure
  why he was there.
- File and evidence missing.
- No known connection with
  Creeley.
- No criminal record –
  Sarkowski or company.

Chapter
FIFTEEN

The bungalow was in Long Island City, that portion of Queens just over the East River from Manhattan and Roosevelt Island.

Christmas decorations – plenty of them – were perfectly arranged in the yard, the sidewalk perfectly cleared of ice and snow, the Camry in the driveway perfectly clean, despite the recent snow. Window frames were being scraped for a new coat of paint, and a stack of bricks sat destined for a new path or patio.

This was the house of a man with newly acquired free time.

Amelia Sachs hit the doorbell.

The front door opened a few seconds later and a solid man in his late fifties squinted up at her. He was in a green velour running suit.

'Detective Snyder?' Sachs was careful to use his former title. Being polite gets you further than a gun, her father used to say.

'Yeah, come on in. You're Amelia, right?'

Last name versus first name. You always choose which battles you want to fight. She smiled, shook his hand and followed him inside. Cold streetlight bled inside and the living room was unfriendly and chill. Sachs smelled damp smoke from the fireplace, as well as the scent of cat. She pulled off her jacket and sat on a wheezing sofa. It was clear that the Barcalounger, beside which were three remote controls, was the king's throne.

'The wife's out,' he announced. A squint. 'You Herman Sachs's girl?'

Girl . . .

'That's right. Did you work with him?'

'Some, yeah. BK and a couple assignments in Manhattan. Good guy. Heard the retirement party was a blast. Went on all night. You want a soda or water or anything? No booze, sorry.' He said this with a certain tone in his voice, which – along with the cluster of veins in his nose – told her that, like a lot of cops of a certain age, he'd had a problem with the bottle. And was now in recovery. Good for him.

'Nothing for me, thanks . . . just have a few questions. You were case detective on a robbery/homicide just before you retired. Name was Frank Sarkowski.'

Eyes sweeping the carpet. 'Yeah, remember him. Some businessman. Got shot in a mugging or something.'

'I wanted to see the file. But it's gone. The evidence too.'

'No file?' Snyder shrugged, a little surprised. Not too much. 'Records room at the house . . . always a mess.'

'I need to find out what happened.'

'Geez, I don't remember much.' Snyder scratched the back of his muscular hand, flaking with eczema. 'You know, one of *those* cases. No leads at all . . . I mean zip. After a week you kind of forget about 'em. You musta run some of those.'

The question was almost a taunt, a comment on the fact that she obviously hadn't been a detective for long and prob- ably *hadn't* run many of those sorts of cases. Or any other, for that matter.

She didn't respond. 'Tell me what you remember.'

'Found him in this vacant lot, lying by his car. No money, no wallet. The piece was nearby.'

'What was it?'

'A cold Smittie knockoff. Was wiped clean – no prints.'

Interesting. Cold meant no serial numbers. The bad guys bought them on the street when they wanted an untraceable weapon. You could never completely obliterate the numbers of a stamped gun – which was a requirement for all U.S. manufacturers – but some foreign weapon companies didn't put serial numbers on their products. They were what professional killers used and often left behind at crime scenes.

'Snitches hear anything afterward?'

Many homicides were solved because the killer made the mistake of bragging about his prowess at a robbery and exaggerating what he'd stolen. Word often got back to snitches, who'd dime the guy out for a favor from the cops.

'Nothing.'

'Where was the vacant lot?'

'By the canal. You know those big tanks?'

'The natural gas tanks?'

'Yeah.'

'What was he doing there?'

Snyder shrugged. 'No idea. He had this maintenance company. I think one of his clients was out there, and he was checking on them or something.'

'Crime Scene find anything solid? Trace? Fingerprints? Footprints?'

'Nothing jumped out at us.' His rheumy eyes kept examining her. He seemed a little bewildered. He might be thinking, So this is the new generation NYPD. Glad I got out when I did.

'Were you convinced everything was what it seemed to be? A robbery that went bad.'

He hesitated. 'Pretty convinced.'

'But not totally convinced?'

'I guess it coulda been a clip.'

'Pro?'

Snyder shrugged. 'I mean, there's nobody around. You've gotta walk a half mile just to get to a residential street. It's all factories and things. Kids just don't hang there. There's no reason to. I was thinking the shooter took the wallet and money to make it look like a mugging. And leaving the gun behind – that smelled like a hit to me.'

'But no connection to the mob?'

'Not that I found. But one of his employees told me he'd just had some business deal fall through. Lost a lot of money. I followed up but it didn't lead anywhere.'

So Sarkowski – maybe Creeley too – might've been working with some OC crew: drugs or money laundering. It went south and they killed him. That would explain the Mercedes tail – some capos or soldiers were checking up on her investigation – and the cops at the 118 were running interference for the crew.

'The name Benjamin Creeley come up in your investigation?'

He shook his head.

'Did you know that the vic – Sarkowski – used to hang at the St James?'

'The St James . . . Wait, that bar in Alphabet City? Around the corner from . . .' His voice faded.

'That's right. The One One Eight.'

Snyder was troubled. 'I didn't know that. No.'

'Well, he did. Funny that a guy who lived on the West Side and worked in Midtown would hang out in a dive way over there. You know anything about that?'

'Naw. Not a single thing.' He looked around the room sullenly. 'But if you're asking me if anybody at the One One Eight came to me and said bury the Sarkowski case, they didn't. We ran it by the book and got on to other shit.'

She looked him in the eye. 'What do you know about the One One Eight?'

He picked up one of the remotes, played with it, put it back down.

'Did I mention something?' Sachs said.

'What?' he asked glumly. She noticed his eyes flick to an empty break-front. She could see rings on the wood, where the bottles had been.

'I've got a shitty memory,' she told him.

'Memory?'

'I can hardly remember my name.'

Snyder was confused. 'A kid like you?'

'Oh, you bet,' she said with a laugh. 'The minute I walk out your front door I'll forget I was even here. Forget your name, your face. Gone completely. Funny how that works.'

He got the message. Still, he shook his head. 'Why're you doing this?' he asked in a whisper. 'You're young. You gotta learn – about some things it's better just to let sleeping dogs lie.'

'But what if they're not sleeping?' she asked, leaning forward. 'I got two widows and I got kids without their dads.'

'Two?'

'Creeley, that guy I mentioned. Went to the same bar as Sarkowski. Looks like they knew people from the One One Eight. And they're both dead.'

Snyder stared at the flatscreen TV. It was impressive.

She asked, 'So what do you hear?'

He was studying the floor, seemed to notice some stains. Maybe he'd add replacing the carpet to his list of household projects. Finally: 'Rumors. But that's it. I'm being straight with you. I don't know names. I don't know anything specific.'

Sachs nodded reassuringly. 'Rumors'll do.'

'Some scratch was floating around. That's all.'

'Money? How much?'

'Could be tall paper. I mean, serious. Or could be walking-around change.'

'Go on.'

'I don't know any details. It's like you're on the street doing your job and somebody says something to a guy you're standing next to and it doesn't quite, you know, register but then you get the idea.'

'You remember names?'

'No, no. This was a while ago. Just, there might be some money. I don't know how it got paid. Or how much. Or to who. All's I heard was the person putting it together, they had something to do with Maryland. That's where all the money goes.'

'Anywhere specific? Baltimore? The Shore?'

'Nope.'

Sachs considered this, wondering what the scenario might've been. Did Creeley or Sarkowski have a house in Maryland, maybe on the water – Ocean City or Rehobeth? Did some of the cops at the One One Eight? Or was it the Baltimore syndicate? That made sense; it explained why they couldn't find any leads to a Manhattan, Brooklyn or Jersey crew.

She asked, 'I want to see the Sarkowski file. Can you point me in any direction?'

Snyder hesitated. 'I'll make some calls.'

'Thanks.'

Sachs rose.

'Wait,' Snyder said. 'Lemme say one thing. I called you a kid. Okay, shouldn't've said that. You got balls, you don't back down, you're smart. Anybody can see that. But you ain't been around long in this business. You gotta understand that what you're thinking about the One One Eight. They're not going to be clipping anybody. And even if something *is* going down, it's not going to be black-and-white. You gotta ask yourself, What the fuck difference does it make? A few dollars here or there? Sometimes a bad cop saves a baby's life. And sometimes a good cop takes something he shouldn't. That's life on the streets.' He gave her a perplexed frown. 'I mean, Christ, you of all people oughta know that.'

'Me?'

'Well, sure.' He looked her up and down. 'The Sixteenth Avenue Club.'

'I don't know what that is.'

'Oh, I'll bet you do.'

And he told her all about it.

Dennis Baker was saying to Rhyme, 'I hear she's a great shot.'

The lab was male only at the moment; Kathryn Dance had returned to the hotel to check in once again and Amelia was out on the Other Case. Pulaski, Cooper and Sellitto were here, along with Jackson the dog.

Rhyme explained about Sachs's pistol club and the competitions she was in. Proudly he told Baker that she was very close to being the top handgun shot in the metro league. She'd be competing soon and was hoping to make the number-one slot.

Baker nodded. 'Looks like she's in as good shape as most of the rookies just out of the academy.' He patted his belly. 'I should be working out more myself.'

Ironically, wheelchair-bound Rhyme was himself doing more exercising now than before the accident. He used a powered bicycle – an ergometer – and a computerized treadmill daily. He also did aqua therapy several times a week. This regimen served two purposes. It was intended to keep his muscle mass solid for the day when, as he believed, he would walk again. The exercises were also moving him further toward that goal by improving the nerve function in the damaged parts of his body. In the past few years he'd regained functions that doctors had told him he'd never again have.

But Rhyme sensed that Baker wasn't particularly interested in Sachs's Bowflex routines – a deduction confirmed when the man asked his next question. 'I heard that you guys're . . . going out.'

Amelia Sachs was a lantern that attracted many moths and Rhyme wasn't surprised that the detective was checking out the availability of the flame. He laughed at the detective's quaint term. *Going out*. He said, 'You could put it that way.'

'Must be tough.' Then Baker blinked. 'Wait, I didn't mean what you think.'

Rhyme though, had a pretty good idea what the detective was saying. He wasn't referring to a relationship between a crip and somebody who was mobile – Baker seemed hardly to notice Rhyme's condition. No, he was referring to a very different potential conflict. 'Two cops, you meant.'

The Other Case versus His Case.

Baker nodded. 'Dated an FBI agent once. She and I had jurisdictional issues.'

Rhyme laughed. 'That's a good way to put it. Of course, my ex wasn't a cop and we had a pretty rough time too. Blaine had a great fastball. I lost some nice lamps. And a Bausch & Lomb microscope. Probably shouldn't've brought it home . . . Well, having it at home was okay; I shouldn't've had it on the nightstand in the bedroom.'

'I'm not gonna make jokes about microscopes in the bedroom,' Sellitto called from across the room.

'Sounds like you just did, if you ask me,' Rhyme replied.

Deflecting Baker's small talk, Rhyme wheeled over to Pulaski and Cooper, who were trying to lift prints from the spool in the florist shop, on Rhyme's hope that the Watchmaker couldn't undo the green metallic wire with gloves on and had used his bare hands. But they were having no success.

Rhyme heard the door open and a moment later Sachs walked into the lab, pulled off her leather jacket and tossed it distractedly on a chair. She wasn't smiling. She nodded a greeting to the team and then asked Rhyme, 'Any breaks?'

'Nothing yet, no. Some more strikes on the EVL but they didn't play out. No ASTER information either.'

Sachs stared at the chart. But it seemed to Rhyme that she was seeing none of the words. Turning to the rookie, she said, 'Ron, the detective on the Sarkowski case told me he heard rumors about money going to our One One Eight friends at the St James. He thinks there's a Maryland connection. We find it, we find the money and probably the names of some people involved. I'm thinking it's a Baltimore OC hook.'

'Organized crime?'

'Unless you went to a different academy than me, that's what OC means.'

'Sorry.'

'Make some calls. Find out if anybody from a Baltimore crew's been operating in New York. And find out if Creeley, Sarkowski or anybody from the One One Eight has a place there or does a lot of business in Maryland.'

'I'll stop by the precinct and—'

'No, just call. Make it anonymous.'

'Wouldn't it be better to do it in person? I could—'

'The *better* thing,' Sachs said harshly, 'is to do what I'm telling you.'

'Okay.' He raised his hands in surrender.

Sellitto said, 'Hey, some of your good humor's rubbing off on the troops, Linc.'

Sachs's mouth tightened. Then she relented. 'It'll be safer that way, Ron.'

It was a Lincoln Rhyme apology, that is to say, not much of one at all, but Pulaski accepted it. 'Sure.'

She looked away from the whiteboards. 'Need to talk to you, Rhyme. Alone.' A glance at Baker. 'You mind?'

He shook his head. 'Not at all. I've got some other cases to check on.' He pulled on his coat. 'I'll be downtown if you need me.'

'So?' Rhyme asked her in a soft voice.

'Upstairs. Alone.'

Rhyme nodded. 'All right.' What was going on here?

Sachs and Rhyme took the tiny elevator to the second floor and he wheeled into the bedroom, Sachs behind him.

Upstairs, she sat down at a computer terminal, began typing furiously.

'What's up?' Rhyme asked.

'Give me a minute.' She was scrolling through documents.

Rhyme observed two things about her: Her hand had been digging into her scalp and her thumb was bloody from the wounding. The other was that he believed she'd been crying. Which had happened only two or three times in all the time they'd known each other.

She typed harder, pages rolled past, almost too fast to read.

He was impatient. He was concerned. Finally he had to say firmly, 'Tell me, Sachs.'

She was staring at the screen, shaking her head. Then turned to him. 'My father . . . he was crooked.' Her voice choked.

Rhyme wheeled closer, as her eyes returned to the documents on the screen. They were newspaper stories, he could see.

Her legs bounced with tension. 'He was on the take,' she whispered.

'Impossible.' Rhyme hadn't known Herman Sachs, who had died of cancer before he and Sachs met. He'd been a portable, a beat cop, all his life (a fact that had given Sachs her nickname when she was working in Patrol – the 'Portable's Daughter'). Herman had cop blood in his veins – his father,

Heinrich Sachs, had come over from Germany in 1937, immigrating with his fiancée's father, a Berlin police detective. After becoming a citizen, Heinrich joined the NYPD.

The thought that anyone in the Sachs line could be corrupt was unthinkable to Rhyme.

'I just talked to a detective on the St James case. He worked with Dad. There was a scandal in the late seventies. Extortion, bribes, even some assaults. A dozen or so uniforms and detectives got collared. They were known as the Sixteenth Avenue Club.'

'Sure. I read about it.'

'I was a baby then.' Her voice quaked. 'I never heard about it, even after I joined the force. Mother and Pop never mentioned it. But he was with them.'

'Sachs, I just can't believe it. You ask your mother?'

The detective nodded. 'She said it was nothing. Some of the uniforms who got busted just started to name names to cut deals with the prosecutor.'

'That happens in IAD situations. All the time. Everybody dimes out everybody else, even innocents. Then it gets sorted out. That's all there was to it.'

'No, Rhyme. That *isn't* all. I stopped at the Internal Affairs records room and tracked down the file. Pop *was* guilty. Two of the cops who were part of the scam swore out affidavits about seeing him put the finger on shopkeepers and protecting numbers' runners, even losing files and evidence in some big cases against the Brooklyn crews.'

'Hearsay.'

'*Evidence*,' she snapped. 'They had evidence. His prints on the buy money. And on some unregistered guns he was hiding in his garage.' She whispered, 'Ballistics traced one to an attempted hit a year before. My dad was stashing a hot weapon, Rhyme. It's all in the file. I saw the print examiner's report. I saw the *prints*.'

Rhyme fell silent. Finally he asked, 'Then how'd he get off?'

She gave a bitter laugh. 'Here's the joke, Rhyme. Crime Scene fucked up the search. The chain-of-custody cards weren't filled out right, and his lawyer at the hearing excluded the evidence.'

Chain-of-custody cards exist so that evidence can't be doctored or unintentionally altered to increase the chances a suspect will be convicted. But there was no way that tampering had occurred in Herman Sachs's case; it's virtually impossible to get fingerprints on evidence unless the suspect himself actually touches it. Still, the rules have to be applied evenly and if the COC cards aren't filled out or are wrong, the evidence will almost always be excluded.

'Then . . . there were pictures of him with Tony Gallante.'

A senior organized crime capo from Bay Ridge.

'Your father and Gallante?'

'They were having dinner together, Rhyme. I called a cop that Pop used to work with, Joe Knox – he was in the Sixteenth Avenue Club too. Got busted. I asked him about Dad, point-blank. He didn't want to say anything at first. He was pretty shaken up I'd called but finally he admitted it was true. Dad and Knox and a couple others put the finger on store owners and contractors for over a year. They ditched evidence, they even threatened to beat up people who complained.

'They thought Pop was going down big-time but, with the screwup, he got off. They called him the "fish that got away".'

Wiping tears, she continued to scroll through the computer files. She was reviewing official documents too – archives in the NYPD that Rhyme had access to because of the work he did for the department. He wheeled close, so close he could smell her scented soap. 'Twelve officers in the Sixteenth Avenue Club were indicted. Internal Affairs knew about three others but they couldn't make the case because of evidence problems.

He was one of those three,' Sachs said. 'Jesus. The fish that got away . . .'

She slumped in a chair, her finger disappearing into her hair and scraping. She realized she was doing it and dropped her hand into her lap. There was fresh blood on the nail.

'When that thing with Nick happened,' Sachs began. Another deep breath. 'When that happened, all I could think was, there's nothing worse than a crooked cop. Nothing . . . And now I find out my father *was* one.'

'Sachs . . .' Rhyme felt painful frustration at not being able to lift his arm and place his hand on hers, to try to take some of the terrible sting away. He felt a burst of anger at this impotence.

'They took bribes to destroy evidence, Rhyme. You know what that means. How many perps ended up going free because of what they did?' She turned back to the computer. 'How many shooters got off? How many innocent people're dead because of my father? How many?'

Chapter
SIXTEEN

Vincent's hunger was returning, as thick and heavy as a tide, and he couldn't stop staring at the women on the street.

His mental violations made him even hungrier.

Here was a blonde with short hair, carrying a shopping bag. Vincent could imagine his hands cupping her head as he lay on top of her.

And here was a brunette, her hair long like Sally Anne's, dangling from underneath her stocking cap. He could almost feel the quivering of her muscles as his hand pressed into the small of her back.

Here, another blonde, in a suit, carrying a briefcase. He wondered if she'd scream or cry. He bet she was a screamer.

Gerald Duncan was now driving the Band-Aid-mobile, maneuvering it down an alley and then back to a main street, heading north.

'No more transmissions.' The killer nodded at the police scanner, from which was clattering only routine calls and more traffic information. 'They've changed the frequency.'

'Should I try to find the new one?'

'They'll be scrambling it. I'm surprised they weren't from the beginning.'

Vincent saw another brunette – oh, she's nice – walking out of a Starbucks. She was wearing boots. Vincent liked boots.

How long could he wait? he wondered.

Not very long. Maybe until tonight, maybe until tomorrow. When he'd met Duncan, the killer told him he'd have to give up having his heart-to-hearts until they started on their 'project'. Vincent had agreed – why not? The Watchmaker told him there would be five women among his victims. Two were older, middle-aged, but he could have them too if he was interested (it's a chore but somebody's got to do it, Clever Vincent quipped to himself).

So he'd been abstaining.

Duncan shook his head. 'I've been trying to figure out how they knew it was we.'

We? He did talk funny sometimes.

'You have any idea?'

'Nope,' Vincent offered.

Duncan still wasn't angry, which surprised Vincent. Vincent's stepfather had screamed and shouted when he was mad, like after the Sally Anne incident. And Vincent himself would grow enraged when one of his ladies fought back and hurt him. But not Duncan. He said anger was inefficient. You had to look at the great scheme of things, he'd say. There was always a grand plan, and little setbacks were insignificant, not worth wasting your energy on. 'It's like time. The centuries and millennia are what matter. With humans, it's the same thing. A single life is nothing. It's the generations that count.'

Vincent supposed he agreed, though as far as he was concerned, *every* heart-to-heart was important; he didn't want to miss a chance for a single one. And so he asked, 'Are we going to try again? With Joanne?'

'Not now,' the killer replied. 'They might have a guard with her. And even if we're able to get to her they'd realize I wanted her dead for a reason. It's important that they think these are just random victims. What we'll do now is—'

He stopped talking. He was looking in the rearview mirror. 'What?'

'Cops. A police car came out of a side street. It started to turn one way but then turned toward us.'

Vincent looked over his shoulder. He could see the white car with a light bar on top about a block behind them. It seemed to be accelerating quickly.

'I think he's after us.'

Duncan turned quickly down a narrow street and sped up. At the next intersection he turned south. 'What do you see?'

'I don't think . . . Wait. There he is. He's after us. Definitely.'

'That street there – up a block. On the right. You know it? Does it go through to the West Side Highway?'

'Yeah. Take it.' Vincent felt his palms sweating.

Duncan turned and sped down the one-way street, then turned left onto the highway, heading south.

'In front of us? What's that? Flashing lights?'

'Yep.' Vincent could clearly see them. Heading their way. His voice rose. 'What're we going to do?'

'Whatever we have to,' Duncan said, calmly turning the wheel precisely and making an impossible turn seem effortless.

Lincoln Rhyme struggled to tune out the droning of Sellitto on his cell phone. He also tuned out the rookie, Ron Pulaski, making calls about Baltimore mobsters.

Tuning it all out so he could let something else into his thoughts.

He wasn't sure what. A vague memory kept nagging.

A person's name, an incident, a place. He couldn't say. But it was something he *knew* was important, vital.

What?

He closed his eyes and swerved close to the thought. But it got away.

Ephemeral, like the puff balls he would chase when he was a boy in the Midwest, outside of Chicago, running through fields, running, running. Lincoln Rhyme had loved to run, loved to catch puff balls and the whirlygig seeds that spiraled from trees like descending helicopters. Loved to chase dragonflies and moths and bees.

To study them, to learn about them. Lincoln Rhyme was born with a fierce curiosity, a scientist even then.

Running . . . breathless.

And now the immobilized man was also running, trying to grasp a different sort of elusive seed. And even though the pursuit was in his mind only, it was no less strenuous and intense than the footraces of his youth.

There . . . there . . .

Almost have it.

No, not quite.

Hell.

Don't think, don't force. *Let* it in.

His mind sped through memories whole and memories fragmented, the way his feet would pound over fragrant grass and hot earth, through rustling reeds and cornfields, under massive thunderheads boiling up miles high and white in the blue sky.

A thousand images from homicides, and kidnappings and larcenies, crime scene photos, department memos and reports, evidence inventories, the art captured in microscope eyepieces, the mountain peaks and valleys on the screen of a gas chromatograph. Like so many whirlygigs and puff balls and grasshoppers and katydids and robin feathers.

Okay, close . . . close . . .

Then his eyes opened.

'Luponte,' he whispered.

Satisfaction filled the body that could feel no sensation.

Rhyme wasn't sure but he believed there was something significant about the name Luponte.

'I need a file.' Rhyme glanced at Sellitto, who was now sitting at a computer monitor, examining the screen. 'A file!'

The big detective looked over at him. 'Are you talking to me?'

'Yes, I'm talking to you.'

Sellitto chuckled. 'A file? Do I have it?'

'No. I need you to find it.'

'About what? A case?'

'I think so. I don't know when. All I know is the name Luponte figures.' He spelled it. 'Was a while ago.'

'The perp?'

'Maybe. Or maybe a witness, maybe an arresting or a supervisor. Or even brass. I don't know.'

Luponte . . .

Sellitto said, 'You're looking like the cat that got the cream.'

Rhyme frowned. 'Is that an expression?'

'I don't know. I just like the sound of it. Okay, the Luponte file. I'll make some calls. Is it important?'

'With a psychotic killer out there, Lon, do you think I'm going to have you waste time finding me something that's *not* important?'

A fax arrived.

'Our ASTER thermal images?' Rhyme asked eagerly.

'No. It's for Amelia,' Cooper said. 'Where is she?'

'Upstairs.'

Rhyme was about to call her but just then she walked into the lab. Her face was dry and no longer red, her eyes clear. She rarely wore makeup but he wondered if she'd made an exception to hide the fact she'd been crying.

'For you,' Cooper told her, looking over the fax. 'Secondary analysis of the ash from what's-his-name's place.'

'Creeley.'

The tech said, 'The lab finally imaged the logo that was on the spread-sheet. It's from software that's used in corporate accounting. Nothing unusual. It's sold to thousands of CPAs around the country.'

She shrugged, taking the sheet and reading. 'And Queens had a forensic accountant look over the recovered entries. It's just standard payroll and compensation figures for executives in some company. Nothing unusual about it.' She shook her head. 'Doesn't seem important. I'm guessing whoever broke in just burned whatever they could find to make sure they destroyed everything connecting them to Creeley.'

Rhyme looked at her troubled eyes. He said, 'It's also common practice to burn materials that have nothing to do with the case just to lead investigators off.'

Sachs nodded. 'Yeah, sure. Good point, Rhyme. Thanks.'

Her phone rang.

The policewoman listened, frowning. 'Where?' she asked. 'Okay.' She jotted some notes. 'I'll be right there.' She said to Pulaski, 'May have a lead to the Sarkowski file. I'll check it out.'

Uneasily he asked, 'You want me to go with you?'

Calmer now, she smiled, though Rhyme could see it was forced. 'No, you stay here, Ron. Thanks.'

She grabbed her jacket and, without saying anything else, hurried out.

As the front door clicked shut behind her, Sellitto's phone rang. He tensed as he listened. Then he looked up, announced, 'Get this. There was a hit on the EVL. Tan Explorer, two white males inside. Evading an RMP. They're in pursuit.' He listened some more. 'Got it.' He hung up. 'They followed it to that big garage on the river at Houston by the West Side Highway. Exits're sealed. This could be it.'

Rhyme ordered his radio to pick up the scrambled

transmissions, and everyone in the lab stared at the small black plastic speakers. Two patrol officers reported that the Explorer had been spotted on the second floor but was abandoned. There was no sign of the men who'd been inside.

'I know the garage,' Sellitto said. 'It's a sieve. They could've gotten out anywhere.'

Bo Haumann and a lieutenant reported that they had squads combing the streets around the garage, but there was no sign yet of the Watchmaker or his partner.

Sellitto shook his head in frustration. 'At least we've got their wheels. It'll tell us plenty. We should get Amelia back to run the scene.'

Rhyme debated. He'd been anticipating that the conflict between the two cases might come to a head, though he'd never thought it would happen this fast.

Sure, they should get her back.

But the criminalist decided not to. He knew her perhaps even better than he knew himself and he understood that she needed to run with the St James case.

There's nothing worse than a crooked cop . . .

He'd do this for her.

'No. Let her go.'

'But. Linc—'

'We'll find somebody else.'

The tense silence, which seemed to go on forever, was broken with: 'I'll do it, sir.'

Rhyme glanced to his right.

'You, Ron?'

'Yessir. I can handle it.'

'I don't think so.'

The rookie looked him in the eye and recited, '"It's important to note that the location where the victim's corpse is actually found is often the least important of the many crime scenes created when a homicide occurs – since it is there that conscientious perpetrators will cleanse the scene of trace and plant false evidence to lead off investigators. The more important—"'

'That's—'

'Your textbook, sir. I've read it. A couple of times, actually.'

'You memorized it?'

'Just the important parts.'

'What's *not* important?'

'I meant I memorized the specific rules.'

Rhyme debated. He was young, inexperienced. But he at least knew the players and he had a sharp eye. 'All right, Ron. But you don't take a single step into the scene unless we're online with each other.'

'That's fine, sir.'

'Oh, it's *fine*?' Rhyme asked wryly. 'Thanks for your approval, rookie. Now, get going.'

They were out of breath from the run.

Duncan and Vincent, both carrying large canvas bags containing the contents of the Band-Aid-mobile, slowed to a walk at a park near the Hudson River. They were two blocks from the garage where they'd abandoned the SUV in their flight from the cops.

So wearing the gloves – which Vincent had first thought of as way too paranoid – had paid off after all.

Vincent looked back. 'They're not following. They didn't see us.'

Duncan leaned against a sapling, hawked and spit into the grass. Vincent pressed his chest, which ached from the run. Steam flowed from their mouths and noses. The killer still wasn't angry but was even more curious than before. 'The Explorer too. They knew about the car. I don't understand it. How did they know? And who's after us? . . . That red-haired policewoman I saw on Cedar Street – maybe it's she.'

She . . .

Then Duncan looked down at his side and frowned. The canvas bag was open. 'Oh, no,' he whispered.

'What?'

The killer dropped to his knees and began to rummage through it. 'Some things're missing. The book and ammunition are still in the car.'

'Nothing with our names on it. Or fingerprints, right?'

'No. They won't identify us.' He glanced at Vincent. 'All your food wrappers and the cans? You wore gloves, right?'

Vincent lived in terror of disappointing his friend and was always careful. He nodded.

Duncan looked back at the garage. 'But still . . . every bit of evidence they get is like finding another gear from a watch. With enough of them, if you're smart, you can understand how it works. You can even figure out who made it.' He pulled his jacket off, handed it to Vincent. He wore a gray sweatshirt underneath. He took a baseball cap out of the bag and pulled it on.

'Meet me back at the church. Go straight there. Don't stop for anything.'

Vincent whispered, 'What're you going to do?'

'The garage's dark and it's big. They won't have enough cops to cover it all. And that side door we used, it's almost impossible to see from outside. They might not have anybody stationed there . . . If we're lucky they might not've found the Explorer yet. I'll get the things we left.'

He took out the box cutter and slipped it into his sock. Then he reached into his pocket, pulled out his small pistol and checked to make sure it was loaded. He replaced it.

Vincent asked, 'But what if they have? Found it, I mean.'

In his calm voice Duncan answered, 'Depending, I may try to get them anyway.'

Chapter
SEVENTEEN

Ron Pulaski didn't believe he'd ever felt pressure like this, standing in the freezing-cold garage, staring at the tan Explorer, brilliantly lit by spotlights.

He was alone. Lon Sellitto and Bo Haumann – two legends in the NYPD – were at the command post, downstairs from this level. Two crime scene techs had set up the lights, thrust suitcases into his hands and left, wishing him good luck in what seemed like a pretty ominous tone of voice.

He was dressed in a Tyvek suit, without a jacket, and he was shivering.

Come on, Jenny, he said silently to his wife, as he often did in moments of stress, think good thoughts for me. He added, though speaking only to himself, Let me not fuck this up, which is what he'd share with his brother.

Headsets sat on his ears and he was told he was being patched into a secure frequency directly to Lincoln Rhyme, though so far he'd heard nothing but static.

Then abruptly: 'So what've you got?' Lincoln Rhyme's voice snapped through the headsets.

Pulaski jumped. He turned the volume down. 'Well, sir,

there's the SUV in front of me. Approximately twenty feet away. It's parked in a pretty deserted part of the—'

'*Pretty* deserted. That's like being fairly unique or kind of pregnant. Are there cars nearby or not?'

'Yes.'

'How many?'

'Six, sir. They range from ten to twenty feet away from the subject vehicle.'

'Don't need the "*sir*". Save your breath for the important things.'

'Right.'

'Are the cars empty? Anybody hiding in them?'

'ESU cleared them.'

'Are the hoods hot?'

'Uhm, I don't know. I'll check.' Should've thought of that.

He touched them all – with the back of his hand, in case fingerprints might become an issue. 'No. They're all cold. Been here for a while.'

'Okay, so no witnesses. Any sign of recent tread marks heading toward the exit?'

'Nothing looks fresh, no. Other than the Explorer's.'

Rhyme said, 'So they probably didn't have backup wheels. Which means they took off on foot. That's better for us . . . Now, Ron, take in the totality of the scene.'

'Chapter Three.'

'I wrote the fucking book. I don't need to hear it again.'

'Okay, the totality – the car's parked carelessly, across two lines.'

'They bailed out fast, of course,' Rhyme said. 'They knew they were being followed. Any obvious footprints?'

'No. The floor's dry.'

'Where's the closest door?'

'A stairwell exit, twenty-five feet away.'

'Which's been cleared by ESU?'

'That's right.'

'What else about the totality?'

Pulaski stared, looking around him, three-sixty. It's a garage. That's all it is . . . He squinted, willing himself to see something helpful. But there was nothing. Reluctantly he said, 'I don't know.'

'We never *know* in this business,' Rhyme said in an even voice, momentarily a gentle professor. 'It's all about the odds. What *strikes* you? Impressions. Just throw some out.'

Pulaski could think of nothing for a moment. But then something occurred to him. 'Why'd they park here?'

'What?'

'You asked what struck me. Well, it's weird they parked here, this far from the exit. Why not drive right to it? And why not try to hide the Explorer better?'

'Good point, Ron. I should've asked the question myself. What do you think? Why would they park there?'

'Maybe he panicked.'

'Could be. Good for us – nothing like fear to make somebody careless. We'll think about it. Okay, now walk the grid to and from the exit and then around the car. Look underneath and on the roof. You know the grid?'

'Yes.' Swallowing the 'sir'.

For the next twenty minutes Pulaski walked back and forth, examining the garage floor and ceiling around the car. He didn't miss a millimeter. He smelled the air – and drew no conclusion from the exhaust/oil/disinfectant aroma of the garage. Troubled again, he told Rhyme that he hadn't found anything. The criminalist gave no reaction and told Pulaski to search the Explorer itself.

They'd run the VIN and the tag numbers on the SUV and found that it actually *had* belonged to one of the men Sellitto had identified earlier but who'd been dismissed as a suspect because he was serving a year on Rikers Island for possession of cocaine. The Explorer had been confiscated because of the drugs, which meant that the Watchmaker had stolen it from a lot where it was awaiting sheriff's auction – a clever idea, Rhyme reflected, since it often took weeks to log the seizures into DMV and several months before vehicles actually went up for sale. The license plates themselves had been stolen from another tan Explorer parked at Newark Airport.

Now, with a curious, low tone in his voice, Rhyme said, 'I love cars, Ron. They tell us so much. They're like books.'

Pulaski remembered the pages of Rhyme's text that echoed his comments. He didn't quote them but said, 'Sure, the VIN, the tags, bumper stickers, dealer stickers, inspection—'

A laugh. '*If* the owner's the perp. But ours was stolen, so the Jiffy Lube location where he changed the oil or the fact he has an honor student at John Adams Middle School aren't really helpful, now, are they?'

'Guess not.'

'Guess not,' Rhyme repeated. 'What information can a *stolen* car tell us?'

'Well, fingerprints.'

'Very good. There're so many things to touch in a car – the steering wheel, gearshift, heater, radio, hand grips, hundreds of them. And they're such shiny surfaces. Thank you, Detroit . . . Well, Tokyo or Hamburg or wherever. And another point: Most people consider cars their attaché cases and utility drawers – you know, those kitchen drawers that you throw everything into? Effluvia of personal effects. Almost like a diary where no one thinks to lie. Search for that first. The PE.'

Physical evidence, Pulaski recalled.

As the young cop bent forward he heard a scrape of metal from somewhere behind him. He jumped back and looked around, into the gloom of the garage. He knew Rhyme's rule about searching crime scenes alone and so he'd sent all the backup away. The noise was just from a rat, maybe. Ice melting and falling. Then he heard a click. It reminded him of a ticking clock.

Get on with it, Pulaski told himself. Probably just the hot spotlights. Don't be such a wuss. *You* wanted the job, remember?

He studied the front seats. 'We've got crumbs. Lots of them.'

'Crumbs?'

'Junk food, mostly, I'd guess. Look like cookie crumbs, corn chips, potato chips, bits of chocolate. Some sticky stains. Soda, I'd say. Oh, wait, here's something, under the backseat . . . This's good. A box of bullets.'

'What kind?'

'Remington. Thirty-two caliber.'

'What's inside the box?'

'Uhm, well, bullets?'

'You sure?'

'I didn't open it. Should I?'

The silence said yes.

'Yep. Bullets. Thirty-twos. But it's not full.'

'How many're missing?'

'Seven.'

'Ah. That's helpful.'

'Why?'

'Later.'

'And get this—'

'Get *what?*' Rhyme snapped.

'Sorry. Something else. A book on interrogation. But it looks more like it's about torture.'

'Torture?'

'That's right.'

'Purchased? Library?'

'No sticker on it, no receipt inside, no library marks. And whosoever it is, he's been reading it a lot.'

'Well said, Ron. You're not assuming it's the perp's'. Keep an open mind. Always keep an open mind.'

It wasn't much praise but the young man enjoyed it.

Pulaski then rolled up trace from the floor and vacuumed it out from the space between and underneath the seats.

'I think I've got everything.'

'Glove compartment.'

'Checked it. Empty.'

'Pedals?'

'Scraped them. Not much trace.'

Rhyme asked, 'Headrests?'

'Oh, didn't get those.'

'Could be hair or lotion transfer.'

'People wear hats,' Pulaski pointed out.

Rhyme shot back, 'On the *remote* chance that the Watchmaker isn't a Sikh, nun, astronaut, sponge diver or somebody else with a head *completely* covered, humor me and check the headrests.'

'Will do.'

A moment later Pulaski found himself looking at a strand of gray-and-black hair. He confessed this to Rhyme. The criminalist didn't play I-told-you-so. 'Good,' he said. 'Seal it in plastic. Now fingerprints. I'm dying to find out who our Watchmaker really is.'

Pulaski, sweating even in the freezing, damp air, labored for ten minutes with a Magna Brush, powders and sprays, alternative light sources and goggles.

When Rhyme asked impatiently, 'How's it going?' the rookie had to admit, 'Actually, there are none.'

'You mean no whole prints. That's okay. Partials'll do.'

'No, I mean there're *none*, sir. Anywhere. In the entire car.'

'Impossible.'

From Rhyme's book Pulaski remembered that there were three types of prints – plastic, which are three-dimensional impressions, such as those in mud or clay; visible, which you can see with the naked eye; and latent, visible only with special equipment. You rarely find plastic prints, and visible are rare, but latents are common everywhere.

Except in the Watchmaker's Explorer.

'Smears?'

'No.'

'This is crazy. They wouldn't've had time to clean-wipe an entire car in five minutes. Do the outside, everything. Especially near the doors and the gas tank lid.'

With unsteady hands, Pulaski kept searching. Had he handled the Magna Brush clumsily? Had he sprayed the chemicals on the wrong way? Was he wearing the wrong goggles?

The terrible head injury he'd suffered not long ago was having lingering effects, including post-traumatic stress and panic attacks. He also suffered from a condition he'd explained to Jenny as 'this real complicated, technical medical thing – fuzzy thinking.' It haunted him that, after the accident, he just wasn't the same, that he was somehow damaged goods, no longer as smart as his brother, though they'd once had the same IQ. He particularly worried that he wasn't as smart as the perps he was going up against in his jobs for Lincoln Rhyme.

But then he thought to himself: Time-out. You're thinking it's your screwup. Goddamn, you were top 5 percent at the academy. You know what you're doing. You work twice as hard as most cops. He said, 'I'm positive, Detective. Somehow they've managed not to leave any prints . . . Wait, hold on.'

'I'm not going anywhere, Ron.'

Pulaski put on magnifying goggles. 'Okay, got something. I'm looking at cotton fibers. Beige ones. Sort of flesh-colored.'

'Sort of,' Rhyme chided.

'Flesh-colored. From gloves, I'm betting.'

'So he and his assistant are careful *and* smart.' There was an uneasiness in Rhyme's voice that troubled Pulaski. He didn't like the idea that Lincoln Rhyme was uncomfortable. A chill trickled down his spine. He remembered the scraping sound. The clicking.

Tick, tock . . .

'Anything in the tire treads and the grille? On the sideview mirror?'

He searched there. 'Mostly slush and soil.'

'Take samples.'

After he'd done this, Pulaski said, 'Finished.'

'Snapshots and video – you know how?'

He did. Pulaski had been the photographer at his brother's wedding.

'Then process the probable escape routes.'

Pulaski looked around him again. Was that another scraping, a footstep? Water was dripping. It too sounded like the ticking of a clock, which set him even more on edge. He started on the grid again, back and forth as he made his way toward the exit, looking up as well as down, the way Rhyme had written in his book.

A crime scene is three-dimensional . . .

'Nothing so far.'

Another grunt from Rhyme.

Pulaski heard what sounded like a footstep.

His hand strayed to his hip. It was then that he realized his Glock was *inside* his Tyvek overalls, out of reach. Stupid. Should he unzip and strap it around the outside of the suit?

But if he did that, it could contaminate the scene.

Ron Pulaski decided to leave the gun where it was.

It's just an old garage; of course there're going to be noises. Relax.

The inscrutable moon faces on the front of the Watchmaker's calling cards stared at Lincoln Rhyme.

The eerie eyes, giving nothing away.

The ticking was all that he heard; from the radio there was only silence. Then some curious sounds. Scrapes, a clatter. Or was it just static?

'Ron? You copy?'

Nothing but the *tick . . . tick . . . tick.*

'Ron?'

Then a crash, loud. Metal.

Rhyme's head tilted. 'Ron? What's going on?'

Still no response.

He was about to order the unit to change frequency to tell Haumann to check on the rookie when the radio finally crackled to life.

He heard Ron Pulaski's panicked voice. '. . . needs assistance! Ten-thirteen, ten . . . I—'

A 10–13 was the most urgent of all radio codes, an officer in distress call.

Rhyme, shouting, 'Answer me, Ron! Are you there?'

'I can't—'

A grunt.

The radio went dead.

Jesus.

'Mel, call Haumann for me!'

The tech hit some buttons. 'You're on,' Cooper shouted, pointed to Rhyme's headset.

'Bo, Rhyme. Pulaski's in trouble. Called in a ten-thirteen on my line. Did you hear?'

'Negative. But we'll move on it.'

'He was going to run the stairwell closest to the Explorer.'

'Roger.'

Now that he was on the main frequency, Rhyme could hear all the transmissions. Haumann was directing several tactical support teams and calling for a medical unit. He ordered his men to spread out in the garage and cover the exits.

Rhyme pressed his head back into the headrest of his chair, furious.

He was mad at Sachs for abandoning His Case for the Other Case and forcing Pulaski to take the assignment. He was mad at himself for letting an inexperienced rookie search a potentially hot scene alone.

'Linc, we're on the way. We can't see him.' It was Sellitto's voice.

'Well, don't goddamn tell me what you *haven't* found.'

More voices.

'Nothing on this level.'

'There's the SUV.'

'Where is he?'

'Somebody over there, our nine o'clock?'

'Negative. That's a friendly.'

'More lights! We need more lights!'

Moment of silence passed. Hours, it felt.

What was going on?

Goddamn it, somebody let me know!

But there was no response to this tacit demand. He went back to Pulaski's frequency.

'Ron?'

All he heard was a series of clicks, as if somebody whose throat had been cut was trying to communicate, though he no longer had a voice.

Chapter
EIGHTEEN

'Hey, Amie. Gotta talk.'

'Sure.'

Sachs was driving to Hell's Kitchen in Midtown Manhattan, on her quest for the Frank Sarkowski homicide file. But she wasn't thinking about that. She was thinking of the clocks at the crime scenes. Thinking of time moving forward and time standing still. Thinking of the periods when we want time to race ahead and save us from the pain we're experiencing. But it never does. It's at these moments that time slows interminably, sometimes even stops like the heart of a death-row prisoner at the moment of execution.

'Gotta talk.'

Amelia Sachs was recalling a conversation from years earlier.

Nick says, 'It's pretty serious.' The two lovers are in Sachs's Brooklyn apartment. She's a rookie, in her uniform, her shoes polished to black mirrors. (Her father's advice: *'Shined shoes get you more respect than an ironed uniform, honey. Remember that.'* And she had.)

Dark-haired, handsome, bulging-muscle Nick (he too could've been a model) is also a cop. More senior. Even more of a cowboy than Sachs is now. She sits on the coffee table, a nice one, teak, bought a year ago with the last of the fashion modeling money.

Nick was on an undercover assignment tonight. He's in a sleeveless T-shirt and jeans and wearing his little gun – a revolver – on his hip. He needs a shave, though Sachs likes him scruffy. The plans for this evening were: He'd come home and they'd have a late supper. She's got wine, candles, salad and salmon, all laid out, all homey.

On the other hand, Nick hasn't been home nights for a while. So maybe they'll eat dinner later.

Maybe they won't eat at all.

But now something's wrong. Something *pretty serious*.

Well, he's standing in front of her, he's not dead or wounded, shot down on an undercover set – the most dangerous assignment in copdom. He was going after crews jacking trucks. A lot of money was involved and that meant a lot of guns. Three of Nick's close buddies have been with him tonight. She wonders, her heart sinking, if one of them was killed. She knows them all.

Or is it something else?

Is he breaking up with me?

Lousy, lousy . . . but at least it's better than somebody getting capped in a shootout with a crew from East New York.

'Go on,' she says.

'Look, Amie.' It's her father's nickname for her. There are only two men in the world she lets call her by the name. 'The thing is—'

'Just tell me,' she says. Amelia Sachs delivers news straight. She expects the same.

'You're going to hear it soon. I wanted to tell you first. I'm in trouble.'

She believes she understands. Nick's a cowboy, always ready to pull out his MP-5 machine gun and exchange lead with a perp. Sachs, a better shot, at least with a pistol, is slow to squeeze the trigger. (Her father again: *'You can't take back bullets.'*) She supposes that there's been a firefight and that Nick has killed someone – maybe even an innocent. Okay. He'll be suspended until the shooting review board meets to decide if it was justifiable.

Her heart goes out to him and she's about to say that she'd be there for him, no matter what, we'll get through it, when he adds, 'I got busted.'

'You—'

'Sammy and me . . . Frank R too . . . the heists – the truck-jackings. We got nailed. In a big way.' His voice is shaking. She's never known him to cry but it sounds like he's a few seconds away from bawling his eyes out.

'You're on the bag?' she gasps.

He stares at her green carpet. Finally a whisper: 'Yeah . . .' Though now he's started the confession, he doesn't need to pull back. 'But it's worse.'

Worse? What could possibly be worse?

'We were the *doers*. We jacked the trucks ourselves.'

'You mean, tonight, you . . .' Her voice has stopped working.

'Oh, Amie, not just tonight. For a year. The whole fucking year. We had guys in warehouses tell us about shipments. We'd pull the trucks over and . . . Well, you get it. You don't need to know the details.' He rubs his haggard face. 'We just heard – they've issued warrants for us. Somebody dimed us out. They got us cold. Oh, man, did they get us.'

She's thinking back to the nights he was out on a set, working undercover to collar hijackers. At least once a week.

'I got sucked in. I didn't have any choice . . .'

She doesn't need to respond to this, to say, yes, yes, yes, my God, we *always* have choices. Amelia Sachs doesn't offer excuses herself and she's deaf to them from others. He understands this about her, of course, it's part of their love.

It *was* part of their love.

And he stops trying. 'I fucked up, Amie. I fucked up. I just came by to tell you.'

'You going to surrender?'

'I guess. I don't know what I'm going to do. Fuck.'

Numb, there's nothing she can think of to say, not a single thing. She's thinking of their times together – the hours on the range, wasting pounds of ammo; in bars on Broadway, slogging down frozen daiquiris; lying in front of the old fireplace in her Brooklyn apartment.

'They'll look into my life with a microscope, Amie. I'll tell 'em you're clean. I'll try to keep you out of it. But they'll ask you a lot of questions.'

She wants to ask why he did it. What reason could he possibly have? Nick'd grown up in Brooklyn, a typical good-looking, street-smart neighborhood kid. He'd run with a bad crowd for a while but had some sense smacked into him by his father and gave that up. Why had he slipped back? Was it the thrill? Was it the money? (That was something else he'd hidden from her, she realized now; where'd he been socking it away?)

Why?

But she doesn't have the chance.

'I've got to go now. I'll call you later. I love you.'

He kissed the top of her motionless head. Then out the door.

Thinking back to those endless moments, the endless night, time stopped, as she sat staring at the candles burning down to pools of maroon wax.

I'll call you later . . .

But no call ever came.

The double hit – his crime and the death of their relationship – took its toll; she decided to quit Patrol completely. Give it up for a desk job. It was only the chance meeting with Lincoln Rhyme that pulled her back from that decision and kept her in uniform. But the incident sealed within her an abiding repulsion for crooked police. It was something that was more horrific to her than lying politicians and cheating spouses and ruthless perps.

This was why nothing would stop her from finding out if the St James crew was in fact a circle of bad cops from the 118th Precinct. And if so, nothing would stop her from bringing down the crooked officers and the OC crews working with them.

Her Camaro now skidded to the curb. Sachs tossed the NYPD parking identification card onto the Chevy's dash and climbed out, slamming the door fiercely as if she were trying to close a hole that had opened between the present and this hard, hard past.

'Hell, that's gross.'

In the upper floor of the parking garage where the Watchmaker's SUV was found, the patrol officer who made this comment to his colleagues was looking down at the figure, lying on his belly.

'Man, you got that one right,' one of his buddies replied. 'Jesus.'

Another offered the uncoplike declaration, 'Yuck.'

Sellitto and Bo Haumann jogged up to the scene.

'Are you all right? Are you all right?' Sellitto shouted.

He was speaking to Ron Pulaski, who stood over the man on the ground, who was covered with pungent trash. The rookie, decorated with garbage himself, was gasping. Pulaski nodded. 'Scared the hell out of me. But I'm fine. Man, he was pretty strong for a homeless guy.'

A medic ran up and rolled the attacker over on his back. Pulaski'd cuffed him and the metal bracelets jingled on his wrists. His eyes danced madly and his clothing was torn and filthy. The body stench was overwhelming. He'd recently urinated in his pants. (Hence, 'gross' and 'yuck'.)

'What happened?' Haumann asked Pulaski.

'I was searching the scene.' He pointed out the stairwell landing. 'It appeared that the perpetrators made their exit through this locale . . .'

Stop it, he reminded himself.

He tried again. 'The perps ran up those stairs, I'm pretty sure, and I was searching up here, looking for footprints. Then I heard something and turned around. This guy was coming for me.' He pointed to a pipe the homeless guy had been carrying. 'I couldn't get my weapon out in time but I threw that trash can at him. We fought for a minute or two and I finally got him in a chokehold.'

'We don't use those,' Haumann reminded.

'I meant to say I was successfully able to restrain him through self-defense methods.'

The tactical chief nodded. 'Right.'

Pulaski found the headset and plugged it back in. He winced as a voice blasted into his ears: 'For Christ's sake, are you alive or dead? What's going on?'

'Sorry, Detective Rhyme.'

Pulaski explained what had happened.

'You're all right?'

'Yes, I'm fine.'

'Good,' the criminalist said. 'Now, tell me why the fuck your weapon was inside your overalls.'

'An oversight, sir. Won't happen again, sir.'

'Oh, it better not. What's the number-one rule on a hot scene?'

'A hot—'

'A *hot* scene – where the perp might still be around. The rule is: Search well but watch your back. Got it?'

'Yessir.'

'So the escape route's contaminated,' Rhyme grumbled.

'Well, it's just covered with garbage.'

'Garbage,' was Rhyme's exasperated response. 'Then I guess you better start cleaning it up. I want all the evidence here in twenty minutes. Every bit. You think you can do that?'

'Yes, sir. I'll—'

Rhyme disconnected abruptly.

As two ESU officers pulled on latex gloves and carted off the homeless guy, Pulaski bent down and started to remove the trash. He was trying to recall what there was about Rhyme's tone that sounded familiar. Finally it occurred to him. It was the very same mix of anger and relief when Pulaski's father had a 'discussion' with his twin sons after he'd caught them having a footrace on the elevated train tracks near their home.

Like a spy.

Standing on a street corner in Hell's Kitchen, retired detective Art Snyder was in a trench coat and old alpine hat with a small feather in it, looking like a has-been foreign agent from a John le Carré novel.

Amelia Sachs walked up to him.

Snyder acknowledged her with only a brief glance and, after looking around the streets, turned and started walking west, away from the bustling Times Square.

'Thanks for the call.'

Snyder shrugged.

'Where're we going?' she asked.

'I'm meeting a buddy of mine. We play pool up the street here every week. I didn't want to talk on the phone.'

Spies . . .

An emaciated man with slicked-back yellow hair – not blond, but yellow – hit them up for some change. Snyder looked at him closely and then handed over a dollar. The man walked on, saying thanks, but grudgingly, as if he'd been expecting a five.

They were walking through a dim part of the street when

Sachs felt something brush her thigh, twice, and she wondered for a moment if the retiree was coming on to her. Glancing down, though, she saw a folded piece of paper that he was subtly passing to her.

She took it and when they were under a streetlight, she looked it over.

The sheet was a photocopy of a page from a binder or book.

Snyder leaned close, whispered, 'This's a page from the file log. At the One Three One.'

She looked it over. In the middle was an entry:

> File Number: 3453496, Sarkowski, Frank
> Subject: Homicide
> Sent to: 158 Precinct
> Requested by:
> Date Sent: November 28
> Date Returned:

'The patrolman I'm working with,' Sachs said, 'said there was no reference in the log to it being checked out.'

'He must've only looked in the computer. I looked there too. It probably was entered but then it got erased. This is the manual backup.'

'Why'd it go to the One Five Eight?'

'Don't know. There's no reason for it to've.'

'Where'd you get this?'

'A friend found it. Cop I worked with. Stand-up guy. Already forgot I asked.'

'Where would it've gone in the One Five Eight? The file room?'

Snyder shrugged. 'No idea.'

'I'll check it out.'

He clapped his hands together. 'Fucking cold.' He looked behind them. Sachs did too. Was that a black car pausing at the intersection?

Snyder stopped walking. He nodded toward a run-down storefront. *Flannagan's Pool and Billiards. Est. 1954.* 'Where I'm going.'

'Thanks again,' she told him.

Snyder looked inside then glanced at his watch. He said to Sachs, 'Not many of these old places left in Times Square . . . I used to work the Deuce. You know—'

'Forty-second Street. I walked it too.' She looked back again toward Eighth Avenue. The black car was gone.

He was staring into the pool hall, speaking softly. 'I remember the summers most. Some of those August days. Even the gangbangers and chain snatchers were home, it was so hot. I remember the restaurants and bars and movie theaters. Some of 'em had these signs up, I guess from the forties or fifties, saying they were air conditioned. Funny, a place that advertised they had air-conditioning to get people inside. Pretty different nowadays, huh? . . . Times sure change.' Snyder pulled open the door and stepped into the smoky room. 'Times sure as hell change.'

Chapter
NINETEEN

Their new car was a Buick LeSabre.

'Where'd you get it?' Vincent asked Duncan as he climbed into the passenger seat. The car sat idling at the curb in front of the church.

'The Lower East Side.' Duncan glanced at him.

'Nobody saw you?'

'The owner did. Briefly. But he's not going to be saying anything.' He tapped his pocket, where the pistol rested. Duncan nodded toward the corner where he'd slashed the student to death earlier. 'Any police around?'

'No. I mean, I didn't see any.'

'Good. Sanitation probably picked up the Dumpster and the body's halfway out to sea on a barge.'

Slash their eyes . . .

'What happened at the garage?' Vincent asked.

Duncan gave a slight grimace. 'I couldn't get close to the Explorer. There weren't that many cops but some homeless man was there. He was making a lot of noise and then I heard shouting and cops started running into the place. I had to leave.'

They pulled away from the curb. Vincent had no idea where they were going. The Buick was old and smelled of cigarette smoke. He didn't know what to call it. It was dark blue but 'Blue-mobile' wasn't funny. Clever Vincent wasn't feeling very witty at the moment. After a few minutes of silence he asked, 'What's your favorite food?'

'My—?'

'Food. What do you like to eat?'

Duncan squinted slightly. He did this a lot, considered questions seriously and then recited the answers he'd planned out. But this one flummoxed him. He gave a faint laugh. 'You know, I don't eat that much.'

'But you must have some favorite.'

'I've never thought about it. Why're you asking?'

'Oh, just, I was thinking I could make us dinner sometime. I can cook a lot of different things. Pasta – you know, spaghetti. Do you like spaghetti? I make it with meatballs. I can make a cream sauce. They call that Alfredo. Or with tomato.'

The man said, 'Well, I guess tomato. That's what I'd order in a restaurant.'

'Then I'll make that for you. Maybe if my sister's in town, I'll have a dinner party. Well, not a party. Just the three of us.'

'That's . . .' Duncan shook his head. He seemed moved. 'Nobody's made me dinner since . . . Well, nobody's made me dinner for a long time.'

'Next month, maybe.'

'Next month could work. What's your sister like?'

'She's a couple years younger than me. Works in a bank. She's skinny too. I don't mean you're skinny. Just, you know, in good shape.'

'She married, have kids?'

'Oh, no. She's really busy at her job. She's good at it.'

Duncan nodded. 'Next month. Sure, I'll come back to town. We could have dinner. I couldn't help you. I don't cook.'

'Oh, I'd do the cooking. I like to cook. I watch the Food Channel.'

'But I could bring some dessert. Something already made. I know you like your sweets.'

'That'd be great,' said an excited Vincent. He looked around the cold, dark streets. 'Where're we going?'

Duncan was silent for a moment. He eased the car to a stoplight, the front wheels precisely on the dirty, white stop line. He said, 'Let me tell you a story.'

Vincent looked over at his friend.

'In seventeen fourteen the British Parliament offered twenty thousand pounds to anyone who could invent a portable clock accurate enough to be used at sea.'

'That was a lot of money then, right?'

'Huge amount of money. They needed a clock for their ships because every year thousands of sailors died from navigational errors. See, to plot a course you need both longitude and latitude. You can determine latitude astronomically. But longitude needs accurate time. A British clockmaker named John Harrison decided to go for the prize. He started working on the project in seventeen thirty-five and finally created a small clock that you could use on a ship and that lost only a few seconds over the course of an entire transatlantic voyage. When did he finish? In seventeen sixty-one.'

'Took him that long?'

'He had to cope with politics, competition, conniving businessmen and members of Parliament and, of course, the mechanical difficulties – almost impossibilities – of creating the clock. But he never stopped. Twenty-six years.'

The light changed to green and Duncan accelerated slowly. 'In answer to your question, we're going to see about the next girl on our list. We had a setback. But nothing's going to stop us. It's not a big deal—'

'In the great scheme of things.'

A brief smile crossed the killer's face.

*

'First of all, they have security cameras in the garage?' Rhyme asked.

Sellitto's laugh meant 'in your dreams'.

He, Pulaski and Baker were back in Rhyme's apartment, going over what the rookie had collected in the garage. The homeless man who'd attacked Pulaski was in Bellevue. He had no connection to the case and was diagnosed as a paranoid schizophrenic off his meds.

'Wrong time, wrong place,' Pulaski had muttered.

'You or him?' Rhyme'd responded. He now asked, 'Security cameras at the *impound* where he boosted the SUV?'

Another laugh.

A sigh. 'Let's see what Ron found. First, the bullets?'

Cooper brought the box to Rhyme and opened it for him.

A .32-caliber ACP bullet is an uncommon round. The semiautomatic pistol bullet has more range than the smaller .22 but not much stopping power, like the more powerful .38 or 9-millimeter. Thirty-twos have traditionally been called ladies' guns. The market is somewhat limited but is still quite large. Finding a compatible .32 in the possession of a suspect could be circumstantial evidence that he was the Watchmaker but Cooper couldn't just ring up local gun stores and get a shortlist of who'd been buying these rounds lately.

Since seven were missing from the box, and the Autauga MkII pistol holds seven in a full clip, that was Rhyme's best guess for the weapon, but the Beretta Tomcat, the North American Guardian and the LWS-32 were also chambered for those slugs. The killer could be carrying any of them. (If he was armed at all. Bullets, Rhyme pointed out, *suggest* but don't guarantee that the suspect carried or owned a gun.)

Rhyme noted that the slug was a 71-grain, big enough to do very serious damage if it was fired at close range.

'On the board, rookie,' Rhyme commanded. Pulaski wrote as dictated.

The book he'd found in the Explorer was entitled *Extreme Interrogation Techniques* and had been published by a small company in Utah. The paper, printing job and typography – not to mention the style of writing – were third-rate.

Written by an anonymous author who claimed he'd been a Special Forces soldier, the book described using torture techniques that would ultimately result in death if the subject didn't confess – drowning, strangulation, suffocation, freezing in cold water and others. One involved suspending a weight above a subject's throat. Another, cutting his wrists and letting him bleed until he confessed.

'Christ,' Dennis Baker said, wincing. 'It's his blueprint . . . He's going to kill *ten* victims like that? Sick.'

'Trace?' Rhyme asked, concerned more about the forensic implications of the book than the psychological makeup of its purchaser.

Holding the book over a large sheet of clean newsprint, Cooper opened every page and dusted each one to dislodge trace. Nothing fell out.

No fingerprints either, of course.

Cooper learned that the book wasn't sold through the major Web-based or retail bookstore chains – they refused to carry it. But it was readily available through online auction companies and a number of right-wing, paramilitary organizations, which sold everything you needed to protect yourself from the scourge of minorities, the foreign-born and the U.S. government itself. (In recent years Rhyme had consulted on a number of terrorist investigations; many had been linked to al-Qaeda and other fundamentalist Islamic groups but just as many had involved domestic terrorism – a threat he himself felt was being largely ignored by authorities in this country.)

A call to the publisher resulted in no cooperation, which didn't surprise Rhyme. He was told they didn't sell the book directly to readers and if Rhyme wanted to find out what retail outlets bought the book in quantity a court order would be necessary. It would take weeks to get one.

'Do you understand,' Dennis Baker snapped into the speakerphone, 'that somebody's using this as a guidebook to torture and kill people?'

'Well, that's sort of what it's *for*, you know.' The head of the company hung up.

'Goddamn.'

Continuing to look over the evidence, they learned that the grit and leaves and cinders that Pulaski had extracted from the grille, the tire treads and sideview mirrors were not distinctive. The trace in the back bed of the SUV revealed sand that matched what the perp had used as the obscuring agent in the Cedar Street alleyway.

The crumbs were from corn chips, potato chips, pretzels and chocolate candy. Bits of peanut butter crackers too, as well as stains from soda – sugared, not diet. None of this would lead them to a suspect, of course, but it could be another plank in the bridge connecting a perp to the Explorer if they found one.

The short cotton fibers – flesh-colored – were, as Pulaski suggested, similar to those shed by a generic brand of work gloves sold in thousands of drugstores, garden shops and grocery stores. Apparently they'd meticulously wiped the Explorer after they'd stolen it and worn gloves every time they were inside the vehicle.

This was a first. And a reminder of the Watchmaker's deadly brilliance.

The hair from the headrest was nine inches long and was black with some gray in it. Hair is good evidence since it's always falling out or is being pulled out in struggles. Generally it offers only class characteristics, though, meaning that a hair found at a scene will provide a circumstantial connection to a suspect who has similar hair, based on the color, texture, length or presence of dye or other chemicals. But hair generally can't be individuated: that is, it can't be linked conclusively to the suspect unless the follicle's attached, allowing for a DNA profile. The hair that Pulaski found, though, had no follicle.

Rhyme knew it was too long to be the Watchmaker's – the EFIT picture, according to Hallerstein, depicted medium length. It might have been from a wig – the Watchmaker could be using disguises – but Cooper could find no adhesive on the end. His assistant had worn a cap and it could have come from him. Rhyme decided, though, that the hair had probably come from someone else – a passenger riding in the SUV before the Watchmaker stole it. A nine-inch hair could be a man's or a woman's, of course, but Rhyme felt that it was probably a woman's. The gray suggested middle age and nine inches was an odd length for a man of that age to wear his hair – shoulder length or much shorter would be more likely. 'The Watchmaker or his assistant may have a girlfriend or another partner but that doesn't seem likely . . . Well, put it on the board anyway,' Rhyme ordered.

'Because,' Pulaski said, as if reciting something he'd heard, 'you just never know, right?'

Rhyme lifted an eyebrow. Then he asked, 'Shoes?'

The only footprint Pulaski had found was from a smooth-soled, size-thirteen shoe. It was just past a pool of water the wearer had stepped in; he'd left a half dozen prints on the way to the exit before they faded. Pulaski was pretty sure it was the Watchmaker's or his partner's, since it was on the most logical route from the Explorer to the nearest exit. He'd also noted that there was some distance between the prints and only a few of them displayed the heel. 'Means he was running,' Pulaski said. 'That wasn't in your book. But it made sense.'

It was hard to dislike this kid, Rhyme reflected.

But the print was only marginally helpful. There was no way to determine the brand because the leather had no distinctive tread marks. Nor were there any unusual wear patterns, which might indicate podiatric or orthopedic characteristics.

'At least we know he's got big feet,' Pulaski said.

Rhyme muttered, 'I missed that statute where it says someone with size-eight feet is prohibited from wearing size-thirteen shoes.'

The rookie nodded. 'Oops.'

Live and learn, thought Rhyme. He looked over the evidence again. 'That's it?'

Pulaski nodded. 'I did the best I could.'

Rhyme grunted. 'You did fine.'

Probably not very enthusiastic. He wondered if the results would've been different if Sachs had been walking the grid. He couldn't help but think they would be.

The criminalist turned to Sellitto. 'What about the Luponte file?'

'Nothing yet. If you knew more it'd be easier to find.'

'If I knew more, I could find it myself.'

The rookie was staring at the evidence boards. 'All this . . . and it comes down to we hardly know anything about him.'

Not exactly true, Rhyme thought. We know he's one goddamn smart perp.

THE WATCHMAKER

CRIME SCENE ONE

Location:
• Repair pier in Hudson River, 22nd Street.

Victim:
• Identity unknown.
• Male.
• Possibly middle-aged or older, and may have coronary condition (presence of anti-

coagulants in blood).
• No other drugs, infection or disease in blood.
• Coast Guard and ESU divers checking for body and evidence in New York Harbor.
• Checking missing persons' reports.

Perp:
• See below.

M.O.:
- Perp forced victim to hold on to deck, over water, cut fingers or wrists until he fell.
- Time of attack: between 6 P.M. Monday and 6 A.M. Tuesday.

Evidence:
- Blood type AB positive.
- Fingernail torn, unpolished, wide.
- Portion of chain-link fence cut with common wire cutters, untraceable.
- Clock. See below.
- Poem. See below.
- Fingernail markings on deck.
- No discernible trace, no fingerprints, no footprints, no tire tread marks.

CRIME SCENE TWO

Location:
- Alley off Cedar Street, near Broadway, behind three commercial buildings (back doors closed at 8:30 to 10 P.M.) and one government administration building (back door closed at 6 P.M.).
- Alley is a cul-de-sac. Fifteen feet wide by one hundred and four feet long, surfaced in cobblestones, body was fifteen feet from Cedar Street.

Victim:
- Theodore Adams.
- Lived in Battery Park.
- Freelance copywriter.
- No known enemies.
- No warrants, state or federal.

- Checking for a connection with buildings around alley. None found.

Perp:
- The Watchmaker.
- Male.
- No database entries for the Watchmaker.

M.O.:
- Dragged from vehicle to alley, where iron bar was suspended over him. Eventually crushed throat.
- Awaiting medical examiner's report to confirm.
- No evidence of sexual activity.
- Time of death: approximately 10:15 P.M. to 11 P.M. Monday night. Medical examiner to confirm.

Evidence:
- Clock.
  - No explosives, chemical- or bioagents.
  - Identical to clock at pier.
  - No fingerprints, minimal trace.
  - Arnold Products, Framingham, MA.
  - Sold by Hallerstein's Timepieces, Manhattan.
- Poem left by perp at both scenes.
  - Computer printer, generic paper, HP LaserJet ink.
  - Text:
    The full Cold Moon is in the sky,
    shining on the corpse of earth,
    signifying the hour to die

*and end the journey
begun at birth.*
      – The Watchmaker

- Not in any poetry data-
  bases; probably his own.
- Cold Moon is lunar month,
  the month of death.
- $60 in pocket, no serial
  number leads; prints negative.
- Fine sand used as 'obscuring
  agent'. Sand was generic.
  Because he's returning to the
  scene?
- Metal bar, 81 pounds, is
  needle-eye span. Not being
  used in construction across
  from the alleyway. No other
  source found.
- Duct tape, generic, but cut
  precisely, unusual. Exactly the
  same lengths.
- Thallium sulfate (rodent
  poison) found in sand.
- Soil containing fish protein –
  from perp, not victim.
- Very little trace found.
- Brown fibers, probably automotive carpeting.

Other:
- Vehicle.
  - Ford Explorer, about three
    years old. Brown carpet.
    Tan.
  - Review of license tags of
    cars in area Tuesday
    morning reveals no
    warrants. No tickets issued
    Monday night.
- Checking with Vice about
  prostitutes, re: witness.
  - No leads.

INTERVIEW WITH HALLERSTEIN

Perp:
- EFIT composite picture of the
  Watchmaker – late forties,
  early fifties, round face,
  double chin, thick nose,
  unusually light blue eyes. Over
  6 feet tall, lean, hair black,
  medium length, no jewelry,
  dark clothes. No name.
- Knows great deal about
  clocks and watches and
  which timepieces had been
  sold at recent auctions and
  were at current horological
  exhibits in the city.
- Threatened dealer to keep
  quiet.
- Bought 10 clocks. For 10
  victims?
- Paid cash.
- Wanted moon face on clock,
  wanted loud tick.

Evidence:
- Source of clocks was
  Hallerstein's Timepieces,
  Flatiron District.
- No prints on cash paid for
  clocks, no serial number hits.
  No trace on money.
- Called from pay phones.

CRIME SCENE THREE

Location:
- 481 Spring Street.

Victim:
- Joanne Harper.
- No apparent motive.
- Didn't know second victim,
  Adams.

Perp:
- The Watchmaker.
- Assistant.
  - Probably man spotted earlier by victim, at her shop.
  - White, heavyset, in sunglasses, cream-colored parka and cap. Was driving the SUV.

M.O.:
- Picked locks to get inside.
- Intended method of attack unknown. Possibly planning to use florist's wire.

Evidence:
- Fish protein came from Joanne's (orchid fertilizer).
- Thallium sulfate nearby.
- Florist's wire, cut in precise lengths. (To use as murder weapon?)
- Clock.
  - Same as others. No nitrates.
  - No trace.
- No note or poem.
- No footprints, fingerprints, weapons or anything else left behind.
- Black flakes – roofing tar.
  - Checking ASTER thermal images of New York for possible sources.

Other:
- Perp was checking out victim earlier than attack. Targeting her for a purpose. What?
- Have police scanner. Changing frequency.
- Vehicle.
  - Tan.
  - No tag number.

- Putting out Emergency Vehicle Locator.
- 423 owners of tan Explorers in area. Cross-reference against criminal warrants. Two found. One owner too old; other is in jail on drug charges.
  - Owned by the man in jail.

WATCHMAKER'S EXPLORER

Location:
- Found in garage, Hudson River and Houston Street.

Evidence:
- Explorer owned by man in jail. Had been confiscated, and stolen from lot, awaiting auction.
- Parked in open. Not near exit.
- Crumbs from corn chips, potato chips, pretzels, chocolate candy. Bits of peanut butter crackers. Stains from soda, regular, not diet.
- Box of Remington .32-caliber auto pistol ammo, seven rounds missing. Gun is possible Autauga Mk II.
- Book – *Extreme Interrogation Techniques*. Blueprint for his murder methods? No helpful information from publisher.
- Strand of gray-and-black hair, probably woman's.
- No prints at all, throughout entire vehicle.
- Beige cotton fibers from gloves.
- Sand matching that used in alleyway.
- Smooth-soled size-13 shoe print.

Chapter
TWENTY

'I need a case file.'

'Yeah.' The woman was chewing gum. Loudly.

Snap.

Amelia Sachs was in the file room at the 158th Precinct in lower Manhattan, not far from the 118th. She gave the night-duty file clerk at the gray desk the number of the Sarkowski file. The woman typed on a computer keyboard, a staccato sound. A glance at the screen. 'Don't have it.'

'You sure?'

'Don't have it.'

'Hm.' Sachs gave a laugh. 'Where do we think it's run off to?'

'Run off to?'

'It came here on the twenty-eighth or twenty-ninth of November from the One Three One house. It looked like it was requested from somebody here.'

Snap.

'Well, it's, like not logged in. You sure it came here?'

'No, not one thousand percent. But—'

'One thousand?' the woman asked, chewing away. A pack of cigarettes sat next to her, ready to be scooped up in a hurry when she fled downstairs on her break or left for the night.

'Is there any scenario where it wouldn't've been logged?'

'Scenario?'

'Would a file always be logged in?'

'If it's for a specific detective it'd go directly to his office and he'd log it. You've gotta log it. It's a rule.'

'If there was no recipient name on the request?'

'Then it'd come here.' She nodded at a large basket holding a card that said *Pending*. 'And whoever wanted it'd have to come down and pick it up. Then he'd log it in. Has to be logged in.'

'But it wasn't.'

'Has to be. Because otherwise, how do we know where it is?' She pointed to another sign. *Log it!*

Sachs prowled through the large basket.

'Like, you're not supposed to do that.'

'But see my problem?'

A blink. The gum snapped.

'It came here. But you can't find it. So what do I do about that?'

'Submit a request. Somebody'll look for it.'

'Is that really going to happen? Because I'm not sure it would.' Sachs looked toward the file room. 'I'll just take a look, you don't mind.'

'Really, you can't.'

'Just take a few minutes.'

'You can't—'

Sachs walked past her and plunged into the stacks of files. The clerk muttered something Sachs couldn't hear.

All the files were organized by number and color-coded to indicate that they were open or closed or trial pending. Major Cases files had a special border on them. Red. Sachs found the recent files and, going through the numbers one by one, sure enough – the Sarkowski file wasn't there.

She paused, looking up the stacks, hands on her hips.

'Hi,' a man's voice said.

She turned and found herself looking at a tall, gray-haired man in a white shirt and navy slacks. He had a military bearing about him and he was smiling. 'You're—?'

'Detective Sachs.'

'I'm DI Jefferies.' A deputy inspector generally ran the precinct. She'd heard the name but knew nothing about him. Except that he was obviously a hard worker, since he was here still on the job at this late hour.

'What can we do you for, Detective?'

'There was a file delivered here from the One Three One. About two weeks ago. I need it as part of an investigation.'

He glanced at the file clerk who'd just dimed her out. She was standing in the hallway. 'We don't have it, sir. I told her that.'

'Are you sure it was sent here?'

Sachs said, 'The log at the transferring house said it was.'

'Was it logged?' Jefferies asked the clerk.

'No.'

'Well, is it in the pending basket?'

'No.'

'Come on into my office, Detective. I'll see what we can do.'

Sachs ignored the clerk. She didn't want to give her the satisfaction.

Through the nondescript halls, turning corners here and there, not saying a word. Sachs struggling on her arthritic legs to keep up with the man's energetic pace.

Inspector Jefferies strode into his corner office, nodded at the chair across from his desk and closed the door, which had a large brass plaque on it. *Halston P. Jefferies.*

Sachs sat.

Jefferies suddenly leaned down, his face inches from hers. He slammed his fist onto the desk. 'What the fuck do you think you're doing?'

Sachs reared back, feeling his hot, garlicky breath wash over her face: 'I . . . What do you mean?' She swallowed the 'sir' she'd nearly appended to the sentence.

'Where are you out of?'

'Where?'

'You fucking rookie, what's your house?'

Sachs couldn't speak for a moment, she was so shocked by the man's fury. 'Technically I'm working Major Cases—'

'What the hell does "technically" mean? Who're you working for?'

'I'm lead detective on this case. I'm supervised by Lon Sellitto. In MC. I—'

'You haven't been a detective—'

'I—'

'Don't you ever interrupt a superior officer. Ever. You understand me?'

Sachs bristled. She said nothing.

'Do you understand me?' he shouted.

'Perfectly.'

'You haven't been a detective very long, have you?'

'No.'

'I know that, because a real detective would've followed protocol. She would've come to the dep inspector and introduced herself and asked if it was all right to review a file. What you did . . . Were you about to interrupt me again?'

She had been. She said, 'No.'

'What you did was a personal insult to me.' A fleck of spittle arced between them like a mortar round.

He paused. Would it be an interruption to talk now? She didn't care. 'I had no intention of insulting you. I'm just running an investigation. I needed a file that's turned up missing.'

'"Turned up missing." What kind of thing is that to say? Either it's turned up or it's missing. If you're as sloppy with your investigating as you are with your language, I'm wondering if you didn't lose the file yourself and're trying to cover your ass by blaming us.'

'The file was checked out of the One Three One and routed here.'

'By who?' he snapped.

'That's the problem. That part of the log was blank.'

'Were there any other files checked out that came here?' He sat on the edge of his desk and stared down at her.

Sachs frowned.

He continued. 'Any files from *anywhere* else?'

'I don't know what you mean.'

'Do you know what I do here?'

'I'm sorry?'

'What's my job at the One Five Eight?'

'Well, you're in charge of the precinct, I assume.'

'You assume,' he mocked. 'I've known officers dead in the streets because they *assumed*. Shot down dead.'

This was getting tedious. Sachs's eyes went cold and locked onto his. She had no trouble maintaining the gaze.

Jefferies hardly noticed. He snapped, 'In addition to running the precinct – your brilliant deduction – I'm in charge of the manpower allocation committee for the entire department. I review thousands of files a year, I see what the trends are, determine what shifts we need to make in personnel to cover work load. I work hand in glove with the city and state to make sure we get what we need. You probably think that's a waste of time, don't you?'

'I don't—'

'Well, it's not, young lady. Those files are reviewed by me and they're returned . . . Now, what's this particular report you're so goddamn interested in?'

Suddenly she didn't want him to know. This whole scene was off. Logically, if he had something to hide, it was unlikely that he'd behave like such a prick. But, on the other hand, he might be acting this way to divert suspicion. She thought back. She'd given the clerk only the file number, not the name Sarkowski. Most likely the scatterbrain wouldn't remember the lengthy digit.

Sachs said calmly, 'I'd prefer not to say.'

He blinked. 'You—?'

'I'm not going to tell you.'

Jefferies nodded. He seemed calm. Then he leaned forward and slammed his hand down on the desk again. 'You fucking *have* to tell me. I want the case name and I want it now.'

'No.'

'I'll see you're suspended for insubordination.'

'You do what you have to, Inspector.'

'You will tell me the name of the file. And you will tell me now.'

'No, I won't.'

'I'll call your supervisor.' His voice was cracking. He was getting hysterical. Sachs actually wondered if he'd physically hurt her.

'He doesn't know about it.'

'You're all the same,' Jefferies said, a searing voice. 'You think you get a gold shield, you know everything there is to know about being a cop. You're a kid, you're just a kid – and a wiseass one. You come to my precinct, accuse me of stealing files—'

'I didn't—'

'Insubordination – you insult me, you interrupt me. You don't have any idea what it's like to be a cop.'

Sachs gazed at him placidly. She'd slipped into a different place – her personal cyclone cellar. She knew that there might be disastrous implications from this confrontation but at the moment he couldn't touch her. 'I'm leaving now.'

'You're in deep trouble, young lady. I remember your shield. Five eight eight five. Think I didn't? I'll see you busted down to Warrants. How'd you like to shuffle paper all day long? You do not come into a man's precinct and insult him!'

Sachs strode past him, flung the door open and hurried up the hall. Her hands started shaking, her breath was coming fast.

His voice, nearly a scream, followed her down the hall. 'I'll remember your shield. I'll make some calls. If you ever come back to my precinct again, you will regret it. Young lady, did you hear me?'

U.S. Army Sergeant Lucy Richter locked the door of her old Greenwich Village co-op and headed into the bedroom, where she stripped off her dark green uniform, bristling with perfectly aligned bars and campaign ribbons. She wanted to toss the garment on the bed but, of course, she hung it carefully in the closet, the blouse too, and tucked her ID and security badges carefully in the breast pocket, where she always kept them. She then cleaned and polished her shoes before setting them carefully in a rack on the closet door.

A fast shower, then, wrapped in an old pink robe, she curled up on the shag rug on the bedroom floor and gazed out the window. Her eyes took in the buildings across Barrow Street, the lights flickering between the wind-blown trees and the moon, white in the black sky, above lower Manhattan. This was a familiar sight to her, comforting. She used to sit here, just like this, when she was a little girl.

Lucy had been out of the country for some time and was back home on leave. She'd finally gotten over the jet lag and the grogginess from a marathon sleepfest. Now, with her husband still at work, she was content to sit, look out the window and to think about the distant past, and the recent.

The future, too, of course. The hours we have yet to spend seem to obsess us far more than those we've already experienced, Lucy reflected.

She grew up in this very co-op, here in the most congenial of Manhattan neighborhoods. She loved the Village. And when her parents moved across town and became snowbirds they transferred the place to their twenty-two-year-old daughter. Three years later, the night her boyfriend had proposed to her, she'd said yes but with a qualification: They had to live here. He, of course, agreed.

She enjoyed her life in the neighborhood, hanging out with friends, working food service and office jobs (a college dropout, she was nonetheless always the sharpest and hardest worker among her peers). She liked the culture and the quirkiness of the city. Lucy would sit right here, looking out the window, south, at the imposing landscape of this imposing city, think about what she wanted to do with her life or think about nothing at all.

But then came that September day and she watched it all, the flames, the smoke, then the horrible absence.

Lucy continued her routine, more or less content, and waited for the anger and hurt to go away, the emptiness to fill. But they never did. And so the skinny girl who was a Democrat and liked *Seinfeld* and baked her own bread with organic flour walked out the front door of this co-op, took the Broadway train uptown to Times Square and enlisted in the army.

Something, she'd explained to her husband, Bob, she had to do. He'd kissed her forehead, held her hard and didn't try to talk her out of it. (For two reasons. First, a former Navy SEAL, he thought the military experience was important for everyone. And second, he believed Lucy had an unerring sense of doing the right thing.)

Basic training in dusty Texas, then she shipped out and went overseas – Bob went with her for some of the time, his boss at the delivery company being particularly patriotic – while they rented out the co-op for a year. She learned German, how to drive every type of truck that existed, and a fact about herself: that she had an innate gift for organization. She was given the job of managing fuelers, the men and women who got petroleum products and other vital supplies where they were needed.

Gasoline and diesel fuel win wars; empty tanks lose them. That's been the rule of warfare for one hundred years.

Then one day her lieutenant came to her and told her two things. One, she was being promoted from corporal to sergeant. Two, she was being sent to school to learn Arabic.

Bob returned to the States and Lucy lugged her gear to a C130 and flew off to the land of bitter fog.

Be careful what you ask for . . .

Lucy Richter had gone from America – a country with a changed landscape – to a place with none. Her life became desert vistas, searing heat from a hovering sun and a dozen different kinds of sand – some of it abrasive grit that scarred your skin, some fine as talcum that worked its way into every square inch of existence. Her job took on a new gravity. If a truck runs out of fuel on a trip from Berlin to Cologne, you ring up a supply vehicle. If it happens in a combat zone, people die.

And she made sure it *never* happened.

Hours and hours of juggling tankers and ammunition trucks and the occasional oddity – like playing cowgirl to wrangle sheep into transport trucks, part of an impromptu, voluntary mission to get food to a small village that had been without supplies for weeks.

Sheep . . . What a hoot!

And now she was back in a land with a skyline, no live-stock outside of delis or Food Emporium counters, no sand, no burning sun . . . no bitter fog.

Very different from her life overseas.

Lucy Richter, though, was hardly a woman at peace. Which is why she was now staring south, looking for answers in the Great Emptiness of the changed landscape.

Yes or no . . .

The phone rang. She jumped at the sound. She'd been doing this a lot lately – at every sudden noise. Phone, slamming door, backfire.

Chill . . . She picked up the handset. 'Hello?'

'Hey, girl.' It was a good friend of hers from the neighborhood.

'Claire.'

'What's happening?'

'Just chilling.'

'Hey, what time zone're you in?'

'God only knows.'

'Bob home?'

'Nope. Working late.'

'Good, meet me for cheesecake.'

'*Only* cheesecake?' Lucy asked pointedly.

'White Russians?'

'You're in the ballpark. Let's do it.'

They picked a late-night restaurant nearby and hung up.

With a last look at the black empty southern sky, Lucy rose, pulled on sweats, a ski jacket and hat and left the co-op. She clopped down the dim stairway to the first floor.

She stopped, blinking in surprise as a figure startled her.

'Hey, Lucy,' the man said. Smelling of camphor and cigarettes, the superintendent – he'd been old when she grew up here – was carrying bound newspapers out to the sidewalk. Outweighing him by thirty pounds and six inches taller, Lucy grabbed two of the bundles from him.

'No,' he protested.

'Mr Giradello, I have to stay in shape.'

'Ah, in shape? You're stronger than my son.'

Outside, the cold stung her nose and mouth. She loved the sensation.

'I saw you in your uniform tonight. You get that award?'

'This Thursday. It was just the rehearsal today. And it's not an award. A commendation.'

'S'the difference?'

'Good question. I don't really know. I think you *win* an award. A commendation they give you instead of a pay hike.' She piled the trash at the curb.

'Your parents're proud.' A statement, not a question.

'They sure are.'

'Say hi for me.'

'I will. Okay, I'm freezing, Mr Giradello. Gotta go. You take care.'

'Night.'

Lucy started up the sidewalk. She noticed a dark blue Buick parked across the street. Two men were inside. The one in the passenger seat glanced at her and then down. He lifted and drank a soda thirstily. Lucy thought: Who'd be having a cold drink in weather like this? She herself was looking forward to an Irish coffee, boiling hot and with a double dose of Bushmills. Whipped cream too, of course.

She then glanced down at the sidewalk, stopped suddenly and changed course. Amused, Lucy Richter reflected that patches of slick ice were probably the *only* danger she hadn't been exposed to in the past eighteen months.

Chapter
TWENTY-ONE

Kathryn Dance was alone with Rhyme in his town house. Well, Jackson, the Havanese, was present too. Dance was holding the dog.

'That was wonderful,' she told Thom. The three of them had just finished a dinner of the aide's beef bourguignon, rice, salad and a Caymus Cabernet. 'I'd ask for the recipe but I'd never do it justice.'

'Ah, an appreciative audience,' he said, glancing at Rhyme.

'I'm appreciative. Just not excessively.'

Thom nodded at the bowl that had held the main course. 'To him it's "stew". He doesn't even try the French. Tell her what you think of food, Lincoln.'

The criminalist shrugged. 'I'm not fussy about what I eat. That's all.'

'He calls it "fuel",' the aide said and carted the dishes to the kitchen.

'You have dogs at home?' Rhyme asked Dance, nodding at Jackson.

'Two. They're a lot bigger than this guy. The kids and I take 'em to the beach a couple times a week. They chase seagulls and we chase them. Exercise all around. And if that sounds too healthy, don't worry. Afterward we go for waffles at First Watch in Monterey and replace any calories we've lost.'

Rhyme glanced into the kitchen, where Thom was washing dishes and pans. He lowered his voice and asked if she'd engage in a bit of subterfuge.

She frowned.

'I wouldn't mind if a bit of *that*' – he nodded toward a bottle of old Glenmorangie scotch – 'ended up in *there*.' The nod shifted toward his tumbler. 'You might want to keep it quiet, though.'

'Thom?'

A nod. 'He enacts Prohibition from time to time. It's rather irritating.'

Kathryn Dance knew the value of indulging. (Okay, maybe she'd gained six pounds in Tijuana; that had been a long, long week.) She set the dog down and poured him a good healthy dose. She fit the cup into the holder of his wheelchair, arranging the straw near his mouth.

'Thanks.' He took a long sip. 'Whatever you're billing the city for your time, I'll authorize double pay. And help yourself. Thom won't give *you* any grief.'

'Maybe some caffeine.' She poured a black coffee and allowed herself one of the oatmeal cookies that the aide had set out. He'd baked them himself.

Dance glanced at her watch. Three hours earlier in California. 'Excuse me for a minute. Check in at home.'

'Go right ahead.'

She made a call on her mobile. Maggie answered.

'Hey, sweets.'

'Mommy.'

The girl was a talker and Dance got a ten-minute account of a Christmas shopping trip with her nana. Maggie concluded with: 'And then we came back here and I read Harry Potter.'

'The new one?'

'Uh-huh.'

'How many times is that?'

'Six.'

'Wouldn't you like to read something different? Expand your horizons?'

Maggie replied, 'Gee, Mom, like, how many times've you listened to Bob Dylan? That *Blonde on Blonde* album. Or U2?'

Unassailable logic. 'You got me there, sweets, only don't say *like*.'

'Mom. When're you coming home?'

'Tomorrow probably. Love you. Put your brother on.'

Wes came on the phone and they too chatted for a while, the conversation more halting and more serious in tone. He'd been dropping hints about taking karate lessons and now he asked her point-blank if he could. Dance, though, preferred he take up something less combative if he wanted a sport other than soccer and baseball. His muscular body would be perfect for tennis or gymnastics, she thought, but those didn't have much appeal to him.

As an interrogator, Kathryn Dance knew a great deal about the subject of anger; she saw it in the suspects as well as the victims she interviewed following crimes. She believed that Wes's recent interest in martial arts came from the occasional anger that settled like a cloud over him after his father's death. Competition was fine but she didn't think it would be healthy for him to engage in a fighting sport, not at this point in his life. Sanctioned fury can be a very dangerous thing, especially with youngsters.

She talked to him about the decision for some time.

Working on the Watchmaker case with Rhyme and Sachs had made Kathryn Dance very aware of time. She realized how much she used it in her work – and with her children. The passage of time, for instance, diffuses anger quickly (outbursts can rarely be sustained longer than three minutes) and weakens resistance to opposing positions – better than strident argument in most cases. Dance didn't now say no to karate but got him to agree to try a few tennis lessons. (She'd once overheard him say to a friend, 'Yeah, it sucks when your mom's a cop.' Dance had laughed hard to herself at that.)

Then his mood changed abruptly and he was talking happily about a movie he'd seen on HBO. Then his phone was beeping with a text message from a friend. He had to go, bye, Mom, love you, see you soon.

Click.

The millisecond of spontaneous 'love you' made the whole negotiation worth it.

She hung up and glanced at Rhyme. 'Kids?'

'Me? No. I don't know that they'd be my strong suit.'

'They're *nobody's* strong suit until you have them.'

He was looking at her ubiquitous iPod earbuds, which dangled around her neck like a stethoscope on a doctor. 'You like music, I gather . . . How's that for a clever deduction?'

Dance said, 'It's my hobby.'

'Really? You play?'

'I sing some. I used to be a folkie. But now, if I take time off, I throw the kids and the dogs into the back of a camper and go track down songs.'

Rhyme frowned. 'I've heard of that. It's called—'

'Song catching is the popular phrase.'

'Sure. That's it.'

This was a passion for Kathryn Dance. She was part of a long tradition of folklorists, people who would travel to out-of-the-way places to field-record traditional music. Alan Lomax was perhaps the most famous of these, hiking throughout the U.S. and Europe to capture old-time songs. Dance went to the East Coast from time to time but those tunes had been well documented, so most of her recent trips were to inner cities, Nova Scotia, Western Canada, the bayou and places with large Latino populations, like Southern and Central California. She'd record and catalog the songs.

She told this to Rhyme and explained too about a website she and a friend maintained with information on the musicians, the songs and the music itself. They helped the musicians copyright their original songs and distributed to them any fees listeners paid for downloads of the music. Several musicians had been contacted by record companies, which had bought their music for sound tracks of independent films.

Kathryn Dance didn't tell Rhyme, though, that there was more to her relationship with music.

Dance often found herself overloaded. To do her job well, she needed to hard-wire herself to the witnesses and criminals she interviewed. Sitting three feet from a psychotic killer, jousting with him for hours or days or weeks, was an exhilarating process, but exhausting and debilitating too. Dance was so empathic and so closely connected to her subjects that she felt their emotions long after the sessions ended. She heard their voices in her mind, endlessly looping through her thoughts.

Sí, sí, okay, sí, I kill her. I cut her throat . . . Well, her son too, that boy. He there. He see me. I have to kill him, I mean, who wouldn't? But she deserve it, the way she look at me. It no my fault. Can I have that cigarette you talking about?

The music was a miracle cure. If Kathryn Dance was listening to Sonny Terry and Brownie McGhee or U2 or Dylan or David Byrne, she wasn't replaying the memory of an indignant Carlos Allende complaining that the victim's engagement ring cut his palm while he was slitting her throat.

It hurt, what I'm saying. Bad. That bitch . . .

Lincoln Rhyme asked, 'You ever perform professionally?'

She had, some. But those years, in Boston and then Berkeley and North Beach in San Francisco, had left her empty. Performance seems personal but she'd found that it's really about you and the music, not you and the listener. Kathryn

Dance was much more curious about what other people had to say – and to sing – about themselves, about life and love. She realized that with music, as with her job, she preferred the role of professional *audience*.

She told Rhyme, 'Tried it. But in the end I just thought it was better to keep music as a friend.'

'So you became a cop instead. About a hundred-and-eighty-degree change.'

'Go figure.'

'How'd that happen?'

Dance debated. Normally reluctant to talk about herself (listen first, talk last), she nonetheless felt a connection to Rhyme. They were rivals, in a way – forensics versus kinesics – yet ones who shared a common purpose. Also, his drive and his stubbornness reminded her of herself. His clear love of the hunt, as well.

So she said, 'Jonny Ray Hanson . . . Jonny without an *h*.'

'A perp?'

She nodded and told him the story. Six years ago Dance had been hired by prosecutors as a consultant to help pick jurors in the case of the State of California v. Hanson.

A thirty-five-year-old insurance agent, Hanson lived in Contra Costa County, north of Oakland, a half hour from the home of his ex-wife, who had a restraining order against him. One night someone had tried to break into her house. The woman wasn't home and some county sheriff's deputies, who regularly patrolled past her house, spotted and chased him, though the perp got away.

'Doesn't seem all that serious . . . but there was more to it. The sheriff's department was concerned because Hanson kept up the threats and had assaulted her twice. So they picked him up and talked to him for a while. He denied it and they let him go. But finally they thought they could make a case and arrested him.'

Because of the prior offenses, Dance explained, a B-and-E charge would put him away for at least five years – and give his ex-wife and college-age daughter a respite from his harassment.

'I spent some time with them at the prosecutor's office. I felt so bad for them. They'd been living in absolute terror. Hanson would mail them blank sheets of paper, he'd leave weird messages on their phone. He'd stand exactly one block away – that was okay under the restraining order – and stare at them. He'd have food delivered to their house. Nothing illegal but the message was clear: I'll always be watching you.'

To go shopping, mother and daughter had been forced to sneak out of their neighborhood in disguise and go to malls ten or fifteen miles from where they lived.

Dance had picked what she thought was a good jury, stacking it with single women and professional men (liberal but not too liberal), who'd be sympathetic to the victims' situation. As she often did, Dance stayed through trial to give the prosecution team advice – and to critique her choices, as well.

'I watched Hanson in court carefully and I was convinced he was guilty.'

'But something went wrong?'

Dance nodded. 'Witnesses couldn't be located or their testimony fell apart, physical evidence either disappeared or was contaminated, Hanson had a series of alibis that the prosecution couldn't shake: Every key point in the DA's case was countered by the defense; it was as if they'd bugged the prosecutor's office. He was acquitted.'

'That's tough.' Rhyme looked her over. 'But there's more to the story, I sense.'

'I'm afraid there is. Two days after the trial, Hanson tracked down his wife and daughter in a shopping center parking garage and knifed them to death. The daughter's boyfriend was with them. Hanson killed him too. He fled the area and was finally caught – a year later.'

Dance sipped her coffee. 'After the murders, the prosecutor was trying to figure out what went wrong at trial. He asked me to look over the transcript of the initial interview at the sheriff's office.' She gave a bitter laugh. 'When I reviewed it I was floored. Hanson was brilliant – and the sheriff's department deputy who interviewed him was either totally inexperienced or lazy. Hanson played him like a fish. He ended up learning enough about the prosecution's case to completely undermine it – which witnesses to intimidate, what evidence he should dispose of, what kind of alibis he should come up with.'

'And I'm assuming he got one other bit of information,' Rhyme said, shaking his head.

'Oh, yes. The deputy asked if he'd ever been to Mill Valley. And later he asked if he ever frequented shopping centers in Marin County. That gave Hanson enough information to know where his ex and their daughter sometimes shopped. He basically just camped out around the Mill Valley mall until they showed up. That's where he killed them – and they didn't have any police protection there since it was a different county.

'That night I drove back home along Route One – the Pacific Coast Highway – instead of taking the One Oh One, the big freeway. I was thinking, Here I am being paid a hundred and fifty bucks an hour to anybody who needs a jury consultant. That's all fine, nothing immoral about that – it's the way the system works. But I couldn't help but think that if I'd conducted that interview myself, Hanson would've gone to jail and three people wouldn't have died.

'Two days later I signed up for the academy, and the rest, as they say, is history. Now, what's the scoop with you?'

'How'd I decide to become a cop?' He shrugged. 'Nothing

quite so dramatic. Boring, actually . . . just kind of fell into it.'

'Really?'

Rhyme laughed.

Dance frowned.

'You don't believe me.'

'Sorry, was I studying you? I try not to. My daughter says I look at her like she's a lab rat sometimes.'

Rhyme sipped more scotch and said with a coy smile, 'So?'

She lifted an eyebrow. 'So?'

'I'm a tough nut for a kinesics expert, somebody like me. You can't really read me, can you?'

She laughed. 'Oh, I can read you just fine. Body language seeks its own level. You give just as much away with your face and eyes and head as somebody who's got the use of his whole body.'

'Really?'

'That's the way it works. It's actually easier – the messages are more concentrated.'

'I'm an open book, hm?'

'Nobody's an open book. But some books are easier to read than others.'

'I remember you were talking about the response states when you interrogate somebody. Anger, depression, denial, bargaining . . . After the accident I had plenty of therapy. Didn't want to, but when you're flat on your back, what can you do? The shrinks told me about the stages of grief. They're pretty much the same.'

Kathryn Dance knew the stages of grief very well. But, once again, this was not a subject for today. 'Fascinating how the mind deals with adversity – whether it's physical trauma or emotional stress.'

Rhyme looked off. 'I fight with the anger a lot.'

Dance kept her deep green eyes on Rhyme and shook her

head. 'Oh, you're not nearly as angry as you make out you are.'

'I'm a crip,' he said stridently. 'Of course I'm angry.'

'And I'm a woman cop. So we both have a right to get pissed off sometimes. And depressed for all sorts of reasons and we deny things. But anger? No, not you. You've moved on. You're in acceptance.'

'When I'm not tracking down killers' – a nod at the evidence board – 'I'm doing physical therapy. A lot more than I ought to be doing, Thom tells me. Ad nauseam, by the way. That's hardly accepting things.'

'That's not what acceptance is. You accept the condition and you fight back. You're not sitting around all day. Oh, sorry, I guess you are.'

The sorry was not an apology. Rhyme couldn't help but laugh hard and Dance saw that she scored big points with the joke. She'd assessed that Rhyme was a man with no respect for delicacy and political correctness.

'You accept reality. You're trying to change it but you're not lying to yourself. It's a challenge, it's tough, but it doesn't anger you.'

'I think you're wrong.'

'Ah, you just blinked twice. Kinesic stress response. You don't believe what you're saying.'

'You're a tough woman to argue with.' He drained the glass.

'Ah, Lincoln, I've got your baseline down. You can't fool me. But don't worry. Your secret's safe.'

The front door opened. Amelia Sachs walked into the room. She tossed off her jacket and the women greeted each other. It was obvious from her posture and her eyes that something was troubling her. She went to the front window and looked out, then pulled the shade down.

'What's the matter?' Rhyme asked.

'I just got a call from a neighbor. She said that somebody

was at my building today, asking about me. He gave the name Joey Treffano. I used to work with Joey in Patrol. He wanted to know what I was up to, asked a lot of questions, looked over the building. My neighbor thought it seemed funny and gave me a call.'

'And you think somebody was pretending to be Joey? It wasn't him?'

'Positive. He left the force last year and moved to Montana.'

'Maybe he came back to visit, wanted to look you up.'

'If he did, it was his ghost. He was killed in a motorcycle accident last spring . . . And both Ron and I've been tailed. And earlier today somebody went through my purse. It was in my car, locked up. They broke in.'

'Where?'

'At the scene on Spring Street, near the florist's shop.'

It was then that something in the back of Kathryn Dance's mind began to nag. She finally seized the memory. 'There's one thing I ought to say . . . Might be nothing but it's worth mentioning.'

The hour was late but Rhyme had called everyone together. Sellitto, Cooper, Pulaski and Baker. Amelia Sachs was now looking them over.

She said, 'We have a problem I want you to know about. Somebody's been tailing me and Ron. And Kathryn just told me that she thought she'd seen someone too.'

The kinesics expert nodded.

Sachs then glanced at Pulaski. 'You told me you thought you'd seen that Mercedes. Have you seen it again?'

'Nope. Not since this afternoon.'

'How about you, Mel? Anything unusual?'

'I don't think so.' The slim man pushed his glasses higher on his nose. 'But I never pay attention. Lab techs aren't used to being tailed.'

Sellitto said he thought he might've seen someone but wasn't sure.

'When you were in Brooklyn today, Dennis,' Sachs asked Baker, 'you get the feeling that somebody was watching you?'

He paused. 'Me? I wasn't in Brooklyn.'

She frowned. 'But . . . you weren't?'

Baker shook his head. 'No.'

Sachs turned to Dance, who'd been studying Baker. The California agent nodded.

Sachs's hand strayed to her Glock and she turned toward Baker. 'Dennis, keep your hands where we can see them.'

His eyes went wide. 'What?'

'We need to have a little talk.'

None of the others in the room – who'd been briefed beforehand – gave any reaction, though Pulaski kept his hand near his own piece. Lon Sellitto stepped behind Baker.

'Hey, hey, hey,' the man said, frowning and looking over his shoulder at the heavyset detective. 'What *is* this?'

Rhyme said, 'We want to ask you a few questions, Dennis.'

What Kathryn Dance had felt worth mentioning was something very subtle and it wasn't that somebody'd been following her; Sachs had simply said that to keep Dennis Baker at ease. Dance recalled that earlier, when Baker had mentioned that he'd been at the scene in front of the florist's workshop, she'd observed him crossing his legs, avoiding eye contact and sitting in a position that suggested possible deception. His exact comment at that moment was that he'd just left the scene and couldn't recall if Spring Street had been reopened or not. Since he'd have no reason to lie about where he was, she didn't think anything of it at the time.

But when Sachs mentioned that somebody had broken into her car at the scene – where Baker had been – she remembered the lieutenant's possibly deceptive behavior. Sachs had called Nancy Simpson, who'd been at the scene, and asked her what time Baker had left.

'Right after you, Detective,' the officer had said.

But Baker had said he'd stayed for almost an hour.

Simpson added that she believed Baker had gone to Brooklyn. Sachs had asked him about being in the borough now to see if Dance could pick up signs of possible deception.

'You broke into my car and went through my purse,' she said. Her voice was harsh. 'And you asked a neighbor about me – pretending to be a cop I'd worked with.'

Would he deny it? This could blow up in their faces if Dance and Sachs were wrong.

But Baker looked down at the floor. 'Look, this's all a misunderstanding.'

'You talked to my neighbor?' she asked angrily.

'Yes.'

She eased closer to him. They were about the same height but Sachs, in her anger, seemed to tower over him. 'You drive a black Mercedes?'

He frowned. 'On a cop's salary?' This answer seemed genuine.

Rhyme glanced at Cooper, who went to the DMV database. The tech shook his head. 'Not his wheels.'

Well, they got one wrong. But Baker'd clearly been nabbed at something.

'So, what's the story?' Rhyme asked.

Baker looked at Sachs. 'Amelia, I really wanted you on the case. You and Lincoln together, you're an A team. And frankly, you guys get good press. And I wanted to be associated with you. But after I convinced the top floor to bring you on board, I heard there was a problem.'

'What?' she asked firmly.

'In my briefcase, there's a sheet of paper.' He nodded to

Pulaski, who was standing beside the battered attaché case. 'It's folded up. In the top right-hand side.'

The rookie opened the case and found it.

'It's an email,' Baker continued.

Sachs took it from Pulaski. She read it once, frowning. She was motionless for a moment. Then she stepped closer to Rhyme and set it on the wide arm of his wheelchair. He read the brief, confidential note. It was from a senior inspector at Police Plaza. It said that a few years earlier Sachs had been involved with an NYPD detective, Nicholas Carelli, who'd been convicted of various charges, including hijackings, bribes and assault.

Sachs had not been implicated in the incidents but Carelli had been released not long ago and the brass were concerned that she might have had some contact with him. They didn't think she'd done anything illegal but if she was seen with him now, it could be, the email said, 'embarrassing.'

Sachs cleared her throat and said nothing. Rhyme had known all about Nick and Sachs – how they'd talked about getting married, how close they'd been, how shattered she'd been by his secret life as a criminal.

Baker shook his head. 'I'm sorry. I didn't know how else to handle it. I was told to give them a complete report. Details of where I'd observed you, things I learned about you. On the job and off. Any connection with this Carelli or any of his friends.'

'That's why you were pumping me for information about her,' Rhyme said angrily. 'This's bullshit.'

'All respect, Lincoln, I'm putting myself on the line here. They wanted to pull her anyway. They didn't want her on a high-profile case, not with that history. But I said no.'

'I haven't seen Nick in years. I didn't even know he was out.'

'And that's what I'm going to tell them.' He nodded toward

his briefcase again. 'My notes're in there.' Pulaski found some more sheets of paper. He gave them to Sachs and she read through then laid them out for Rhyme to read. They were jottings about the times he'd observed her and questions he'd asked, what he'd seen in her calendar and address book, what people had said about her.

'You broke and entered,' Sellitto said.

'Conceded. Over the line. Sorry.'

'Why the fuck didn't you come to me?' Rhyme snapped.

'Or any of us,' Sellitto said.

'This came from high up. I was told to keep it quiet.' Baker turned to Sachs. 'You're upset. I'm sorry about that. But I really wanted you on the case. It was the only way I could think of. I've already told them my conclusions. The whole thing's gone away. Look, please, can we put this behind us and get on with our job?'

Rhyme glanced at Sachs, and what hurt him the most was to see her reaction to the incident: She wasn't angry any longer. She seemed embarrassed to have been the cause of this controversy and trouble to her fellow officers, distracting them from their mission. It was so unusual – and therefore so hard – to see Amelia Sachs pained and vulnerable.

She handed the email back to Baker. Without a word to anyone she grabbed her jacket and walked calmly out the doorway, pulling her car keys from her pocket.

Chapter
TWENTY-TWO

Vincent Reynolds was studying the woman in the restaurant, a slim brunette, about thirty, in sweats. Her short hair was pulled back and stuck in place with bobby pins. They'd followed her from her old apartment in Greenwich Village, first to a local tavern and now here, a coffeehouse a few blocks away. She and her friend, a blonde in her twenties, were having a great time, laughing and talking nonstop.

Lucy Richter was enjoying her last brief moments on earth.

Duncan was listening to classical music on the Buick's sound system. He was his typically thoughtful, calm self. Sometimes you just couldn't tell what was going on in his mind.

Vincent, on the other hand, felt the hunger unraveling within him. He ate a candy bar, then another.

Fuck the great scheme of things. I need a girl . . .

Duncan took out his gold pocket watch and looked at it, gently wound the stem.

Vincent had seen the watch a few times but he was always impressed with the piece. Duncan had explained that it was made by Breguet, a French watchmaker who lived a long time ago ('in my opinion the finest who ever lived').

The watch was simple. It had a white face, Roman numerals and some small dials that showed the phases of the moon and was a perpetual calendar. It also had a 'parachute', an anti-shock system in it, Duncan explained. Breguet's own invention.

Vincent now asked him, 'How old is it, your watch?'

'It was made in the year twelve.'

'Twelve? Like in Roman times?'

Duncan smiled. 'No, sorry. That's the date on the original bill of sale, so that's what I think of as the year of manufacture. I mean the year twelve in the French revolutionary calendar. After the monarchy fell, the republic declared a new calendar, starting in seventeen ninety-two. It was a curious concept. The weeks had ten days, and each month had thirty. Every six years was a leap year devoted exclusively to sports. For some reason, the government thought the calendar would be more egalitarian than the traditional one. But it was too unwieldy. It only lasted fourteen years. Like a lot of revolutionary ideas – they seem good on paper but they're not very practical.'

Duncan studied the golden disk with affection. 'I like watches from that era. Back then a watch was power. Not many people could afford one. The owner of a watch was a man who controlled time. *You* came to *him* and you waited until the time he'd set for the meeting. Chains and fobs were invented so that even when a man carried a watch in his pocket, you still could see he owned one. Watchmakers were gods in those days.' Duncan paused. 'I was speaking figuratively, but in a way it's true.'

Vincent cocked an eyebrow.

'There was a philosophical movement in the eighteenth century that used the watch as a metaphor. It held that God created the mechanism of the universe, then wound it up and started it running. Sort of a perpetual clock. God was called the 'Great Watchmaker'. Whether you believe it or not, the philosophy had a lot of followers. It gave watchmakers an almost priestlike status.'

Another glance at the Breguet. He put it away. 'We should go,' Duncan said, nodding at the women. 'They'll be leaving soon.'

He put the car in gear, signaled and pulled into the street, leaving behind their victim, about to lose her life to one man and, soon after, her dignity to another. They couldn't take her tonight, though, because Duncan had learned that she had a husband who worked odd hours and could be home at any moment.

Vincent was breathing deeply, trying to keep the hunger at bay. He ate a pack of chips. He asked, 'How are you going to do it? Kill her, I mean.'

Duncan was silent for a few moments. 'You asked me a question earlier. About how long it took the first two victims to die.'

Vincent nodded.

'Well, it's going to take Lucy a *long* time.' Although they'd lost the book on torture, Duncan had apparently memorized much of it. He now described the technique he'd use to murder her. It was called water boarding. You suspend the victim on her back with her feet up. Then you tape her mouth shut and pour water up her nose. You can take as long as you like to kill the person if you give her air from time to time.

'I'm going to try to keep her going for a half hour. Or forty minutes, if I can.'

'She deserves it, hm?' Vincent asked.

Duncan paused. 'The question you're really asking is why am I killing these particular people.'

'Well . . .' It was true.

'I've never told you.'

'No, you haven't.'

Trust is nearly as precious as time . . .

Duncan glanced at Vincent then back to the street. 'You know, we're all on earth for a certain period of time. Maybe only days or months. Many years, we hope.'

'Right.'

'It's as if God – or whatever you believe in – has a huge list of everybody on earth. When the hands of His clock hit a certain time, that's it. They're gone . . . Well, I have my own list.'

'Ten people.'

'Ten people . . . The difference is that God doesn't have any good reason for killing them. I do.'

Vincent was quiet. For a moment he wasn't clever and he wasn't hungry. He was just regular Vincent, listening to a friend sharing something that was important.

'I'm finally comfortable enough telling you what that reason is.'

And he proceeded to do just that.

The moon was a band of white light on the hood of the car, reflecting into her eyes.

Amelia Sachs was now speeding along the East River, the emergency flasher sitting cockeyed on the dash.

She felt a weight crushing her, the consequences from all the events of the past few days: The likelihood that corrupt officers were involved with killers who'd murdered Ben Creeley and Frank Sarkowski. The risk that Inspector Flaherty might take the case away from her at any minute. Dennis Baker's espionage and the vote of no confidence from the brass about Nick. Deputy Inspector Jefferies's tantrum.

And, most of all, the terrible news about her father.

Thinking: What hope is there in doing your job, working hard, giving up your peace of mind, risking your life, if the business of being a cop ultimately spoils the decent core within you?

She slammed the shifter into fourth, nudging the car to seventy. The engine howled like a wolf at midnight.

No cop was better than her father, more solid, more conscientious. And yet look at what had happened to him . . . But then she realized that no, no, she couldn't think of it that way. Nothing had *happened* to him. Turning bad was his own decision.

She remembered Herman Sachs as a calm, humorous man, who enjoyed his afternoons with friends, watching car races, roaming with his daughter through Nassau County junkyards in treasure hunts for elusive carburetors or gaskets or tailpipes. But now she knew that that persona was merely the facade, beneath which was a much darker person, someone she hadn't known at all.

Within Amelia Sachs's soul was an edgy force, something that made her doubt and made her question and compelled her to take risks, however great. She suffered for this. But the reward was the exhilaration when an innocent life was saved or a dangerous perp collared.

That fire drove her in one direction; it had apparently pushed her father in another.

The Chevy fishtailed. She easily brought the skid under control.

Over the Brooklyn Bridge, a skidding turn off the highway. A dozen more turns, this way, that way, heading south.

Finally she found the pier she was looking for and hit the brakes, coming to a stop at the end of ten-foot skid marks. She got out of the car, slamming the door hard. Making her way through a small park, over a concrete barricade. Sachs ignored the warning sign and walked out onto the pier, through a steady, hissing wind.

Man, it was cold.

She stopped at a low wooden railing, gripped it in her gloved hands. Memories assaulted her:

At age ten, a warm summer night, her father boosting her up onto the pylon halfway out on the pier – it was still there – holding her tight. She wasn't afraid because he'd taught her to swim at the community pool and, even if a gust of wind had blown them off the pier into the East River, they'd simply swim back to the ladder, laughing and racing, climb back up – and maybe they'd even jump off again together, holding hands as they plummeted ten feet into the murky, warm water.

At age fourteen, her father with his coffee and she with a soda, looking at the water as he spoke about Rose. 'Your mother, she has her moods, Amie. It doesn't mean she doesn't love you. Remember that. She's just that way. But she's proud of you. Know what she just told me the other day?'

And later, after she'd become a cop, standing here, beside the very same Camaro she'd driven tonight (though painted yellow at the time, a beautiful shade for a muscle car). Sachs in her uniform, Herman in his tweed jacket and cords.

'I've got a problem, Amie.'

'Problem?'

'Sort of a physical thing.'

She'd waited, feeling her fingernail dig into her thumb.

'It's a bit of cancer. Nothing serious. I'll be going through the treatment.' He gave her the details – he'd always talked straight to his daughter – and then he grew uncharacteristically grave, shaking his head. 'But the big problem . . . I just paid five bucks for a haircut and now I'm going to lose it all.' Rubbing his scalp. 'Wish I'd saved the money.'

The tears now rolled down her cheeks. 'Goddamn it,' Sachs muttered to herself. Stop.

But she couldn't. The tears continued and the icy moisture stung her face.

Returning to the car, she fired up the big engine and returned to Rhyme's. When she got home he was upstairs in bed, asleep.

Sachs stepped into the exercise room, where Pulaski had written up the evidence charts on the Creeley/Sarkowski cases. She couldn't help but smile. The diligent rookie had not only stashed the whiteboard here but he'd covered it with a sheet. She pulled the cloth off and looked over his careful writing then added a few notations of her own.

BENJAMIN CREELEY HOMICIDE

- 56-year-old Creeley, apparently suicide by hanging. Clothesline. But had broken thumb, couldn't tie noose.
- Computer-written suicide note about depression. But appeared not to be suicidally depressed, no history of mental/emotional problems.
- Around Thanksgiving two men broke into his house and possibly burned evidence. White men, but faces not observed. One bigger than other. They were inside for about an hour.
- Evidence in Westchester house:
  - Broke through lock; skillful job.
  - Leather texture marks on fireplace tools and Creeley's desk.
  - Soil in front of fireplace has higher acid content than soil around house and contains pollutants. From industrial site?
  - Traces of burned cocaine in fireplace.
    - Ash in fireplace.
- Financial records, spreadsheet, references to millions of dollars.
- Checking logo on documents, sending entries to forensic accountant.
- Diary re: getting oil changed, haircut appointment and going to St James Tavern.
- Analysis of ash from Queens CS lab:
  - Logo of software used in corporate accounting.
  - Forensic accountant: standard executive compensation figures.
  - Burned because of what they revealed, or to lead investigators off?
- St James Tavern
  - Creeley came here several times.
  - Apparently didn't use drugs while here.
  - Not sure whom he met with, but maybe cops from the nearby 118th Precinct of the NYPD.
  - Last time he was here – just

before his death – he got into an argument with persons unknown.

- Checked money from officers at St James – serial numbers are clean, but found coke and heroin. Stolen from precinct?
  - Not much drugs missing, only 6 or 7 oz. of pot, 4 of coke.
- Unusually few organized crime cases at the 118th Precinct but no evidence of intentional stalling by officers.
- Two gangs in the East Village possible but not likely suspects.
- Interview with Jordan Kessler, Creeley's partner, and followup with wife.
- Confirmed no obvious drug use.
- Didn't appear to associate with criminals.
- Drinking more than usual, taken up gambling; trips to Vegas and Atlantic City. Losses were large, but not significant to Creeley.
- Not clear why he was depressed.
- Kessler didn't recognize burned records.
- Awaiting list of clients.
- Kessler doesn't appear to gain by Creeley's death.
- Sachs and Pulaski followed by AMG Mercedes.

FRANK SARKOWSKI HOMICIDE

- Sarkowski was 57 years old, no police record, murdered on November 4 of this year, survived by wife and two teenage children.
- Victim owned building and business in Manhattan. Business was doing maintenance for other companies and utilities.
- Art Snyder was case detective.
- No suspects.
- Murder/robbery?
  - Was shot to death as part of apparent robbery. Weapon recovered on scene – Smith & Wesson knockoff, .38 Special, no prints, cold gun. Case detective believes it could have been a professional hit.
- Business deal went bad?
- Killed in Queens – not sure why he was there.
  - Deserted part of borough, near natural gas tanks.
- File and evidence missing.
  - File went to 158th Precinct on/around November 28. Never returned. No indication of requesting officer.

- No indication where it went in the 158th.
- DI Jefferies not cooperative.
- No known connection with Creeley.
- No criminal record – Sarkowski or company.

- Rumors – money going to cops at the 118th Precinct. Ended up someplace/someone with a Maryland connection. Baltimore mob involved?
- No leads.

Sachs stared at the chart for a half hour until her head began to nod. She returned upstairs, stripped, stepped into the shower and let the hot water pulse down on her, hard, stinging, for a long time. She dried off, pulled on a T-shirt and silk boxers, and returned to the bedroom.

She climbed into bed beside Rhyme and rested her head on his chest.

'You all right?' he asked groggily.

She said nothing but reached up and kissed his cheek. Then she lay back and stared at the bedside clock as the digital numbers flipped forward. The minutes passed slowly, slowly, each one an entire long day passing, until finally, close to three A.M., she slept.

II

9:02 A.M. WEDNESDAY

Time is the fire in which we burn.

— DELMORE SCHWARTZ

Chapter
TWENTY-THREE

Lincoln Rhyme had been awake for more than an hour. A young officer from the Coast Guard had delivered a jacket found floating in New York Harbor, a man's size 44. It was, the captain of the boat deduced, probably the missing victim's; both sleeves were covered in blood, the cuffs slashed.

The jacket was a Macy's house brand and contained no other trace or evidence that could lead back to the owner.

He was now alone in the bedroom with Thom, who'd just finished Rhyme's morning routine – his physical therapy exercises and what the aide delicately called 'hygienic duties'. (Rhyme referred to them as the 'piss 'n' shit detail', though usually only when easy-to-shock visitors were present.)

Amelia Sachs now walked up the stairs and joined him. She dropped her jacket in a chair, walked past him, opened the curtains. She looked out the window, into Central Park.

The slim young man sensed immediately that something was up. 'I'll go make coffee. Or toast. Or something.' He vanished, closing the door behind him.

So what was this? Rhyme wondered unhappily. He'd had more than enough personal issues recently than he wanted to deal with.

Her eyes were still looking over the painful brightness of the park. He asked, 'So what was this errand that was so important?'

'I stopped by Argyle Security.'

Rhyme blinked and looked at her face closely. 'They're the ones that called after you got written up in the *Times*, when we closed that case about the illusionist.'

'Right.'

Argyle was an international company that specialized in safeguarding corporate executives and negotiating the release of kidnapped employees – a popular crime in some foreign countries. They'd offered Sachs a job making twice what she did as a cop. And promised her a carry permit – a license for a concealed weapon – in most jurisdictions, unusual for security companies. That and the promise to send her to exotic and dangerous locations caught her interest, though she'd turned them down immediately.

'What's this all about?'

'I'm quitting, Rhyme.'

'Quitting the force? Are you serious?'

She nodded. 'I've pretty much decided. I want to go in a different direction. I can do good things there too. Protecting families, guarding kids. They do a lot of antiterrorist work.'

Now he too stared out the window at the stark, bald trees of Central Park. He thought about his conversation with Kathryn Dance the previous day, about his early days of therapy. One doctor, a sharp, young man with the NYPD, Terry Dobyns, had told him, 'Nothing lasts forever.' He'd meant this about the depression he'd been experiencing.

Now the sentence meant something very different and he couldn't get the words out of his mind.

Nothing lasts forever . . .

'Ah.'

'I think I have to, Rhyme. I have to.'

'Because of your father?'

She nodded, dug her finger into her hair, scratched. Winced at that pain, or at some other.

'This's crazy, Sachs.'

'I don't think I can do it anymore. Be a cop.'

'It's pretty fast, don't you think?'

'I've thought about it all night. I've never thought about anything so much in my life.'

'Well, keep thinking. You can't make decisions like this after you get some bad news.'

'Bad *news*? Everything I thought about dad was a lie.'

'Not everything,' Rhyme countered. 'One part of his life.'

'But the most important part. That's who he was first, Rhyme. A cop.'

'It was a long time ago. The Sixteenth Avenue Club was closed up when you were a baby.'

'That makes him *less* corrupt?'

Rhyme said nothing.

'You want me to explain it, Rhyme? Like evidence? Add a few drops of reagent and look at the results? I can't. All I know is I have a really bad taste in my mouth. This's affected how I look at the whole job.'

He said kindly, 'It's gotta be tough. But whatever happened to him doesn't touch you. All that matters is you're a good cop, and a lot fewer cases'll be closed if you leave.'

'I'll only close cases if my heart's in it. And it's not. Something's gone.' She added, 'Pulaski's coming along great. He's better now than I was when I started working with you.'

'He's better because *you've* been training him.'

'Don't do that.'

'What?'

'Butter me up, drop those little comments. That's what my mother used to do with my father. You don't want me to leave, I understand, but don't play that kind of card.'

But he had to play the card. And any other he could think of. After the accident Rhyme had wrestled with suicide on a number of occasions. And though he'd come close he always rejected the choice. What Amelia Sachs was now considering was psychic suicide. If she quit the force he knew that she'd be killing her soul.

'But Argyle? It's not for you.' He shook his head. 'Nobody takes corporate security seriously, even – especially – the clients.'

'No, their assignments're good. And they send you back to school. You learn foreign languages . . . They even have a forensics department. And the money's good.'

He laughed. 'Since when has this ever been about money? . . . Give it some time, Sachs. What's the hurry?'

She shook her head. 'I'm going to close the St James case. And I'll do whatever you need to nail the Watchmaker. But after that . . .'

'You know, if you quit, a lot of buttons get pushed. It'll affect you for a long time, if you ever wanted to come back.' He looked away, blood pounding in his temple.

'Rhyme.' She pulled a chair up, sat and closed her hand around his – the right one, the fingers of which had some sensation and movement. She squeezed. 'Whatever I do, it won't affect us, our life.' She smiled.

You and me, Rhyme . . .

You and me, Sachs . . .

He looked off. Lincoln Rhyme was a scientist, a man of the brain, not the heart. Some years ago Rhyme and Sachs had met on a hard case – a series of kidnappings by a killer obsessed with human bones. No one could stop him, except these two misfits – Rhyme, the quadriplegic in retirement, and Sachs, the disillusioned rookie betrayed by her cop lover. Yet, somehow, together, they had forged a wholeness, filling the ragged gaps within each of them, and they'd stopped the killer.

Deny it as much as he wanted to, those words, *you and me*, had been his compass in the precarious world they'd created together. He wasn't at all convinced that she was right that they wouldn't be altered by her decision. Would removing their common purpose change them?

Was he witnessing the transition from Before to After?

'Have you already quit?'

'No.' She pulled a white envelope from her jacket pocket. 'I wrote the resignation letter. But I wanted to tell you first.'

'Give it a couple of days before you decide. You don't owe it to me. But I'm asking. A couple of days.'

She stared at the envelope for a long moment. Finally she said, 'Okay.'

Rhyme was thinking: Here we are working on a case involving a man obsessed with clocks and watches, and the most important thing to me at this moment is buying a little time from Sachs. 'Thanks.' Then: 'Now, let's get to work.'

'I want you to understand . . .'

'There's nothing to understand,' he said with what he felt was miraculous detachment. 'There's a killer to catch. That's all we should be thinking about.'

He left her alone in the bedroom and took the tiny elevator downstairs to the lab, where Mel Cooper was at work.

'Blood on the jacket's AB positive. Matches what was on the pier.'

Rhyme nodded. Then he had the tech call the NASA Jet Propulsion Lab about the ASTER information – the thermal scans to find possible locations of roof tarring.

It was early in California but the tech managed to track down somebody and put some pressure on him to find and upload the images. The pictures arrived soon after. They were striking but not particularly helpful. There were, as Sellitto had suggested, hundreds, possibly thousands of buildings that showed indications of elevated heat, and the system couldn't discriminate between locations that were being reroofed, under construction, being heated with Consolidated Edison steam or simply had particularly hot chimneys.

All Rhyme could think to do was tell Central that any assaults or breakins in or near a building having roofing work done should be patched through to them immediately.

The dispatcher hesitated and said she'd put the notice on the main computer.

The tone of her voice suggested that he was grasping at straws.

What could he say? She was right.

Lucy Richter closed the door to her co-op and flipped the locks.

She hung up her coat and hooded sweatshirt, printed on the front with *4th Infantry Division, Fort Hood*, and on the back the division's slogan: *Steadfast and loyal*.

Her muscles ached. At the gym, she'd done five miles, at a good pace and 9-percent incline, on the treadmill, then a half hour of push-ups and crunches. That was something else military service had done: taught her to appreciate muscle. You can put down physical fitness if you want, make fun of it as vanity and a waste of time but, fact is, it's empowering.

She filled the kettle for tea and pulled a sugared doughnut out of the fridge, thinking about today. There were plenty of things that needed to be done: phone calls to return, emails, baking cookies and making her signature cheesecake for the reception on Thursday. Or maybe she'd just go shopping with friends and buy dessert at a bakery. Or have lunch with her mother.

Or lie in bed and watch the soaps. Pamper herself.

It was the start of heaven – her two weeks away from the land of the bitter fog – and she was going to enjoy every minute of it.

Bitter fog . . .

This was an expression she'd heard from a local policeman outside Baghdad, referring to fumes and smoke following the detonation of an IED – improvised explosive device.

Explosions in movies were just big flares of flaming gasoline. And then were gone, nothing left, except the reaction shot on the characters' faces. In reality what remained after an IED was a thick bluish haze that stank and stung your eyes and burned your lungs. Part dust, part chemical smoke, part vaporized hair and skin, it remained at the scene for hours.

The bitter fog was a symbol of the horror of this new type of war. There were no trusted allies except your fellow soldiers. There were no battle lines. There were no fronts. And you had no clue who the enemy was. It might be your interpreter, a cook, a passer-by, a local businessman, a teenager, an old man. Or somebody five klicks away. And the weapons? Not howitzers and tanks but the tiny parcels that produced the bitter fog, the packet of TNT or C4 or C3 or the shaped charge stolen from your own armory, hidden so inconspicuously that you never saw it until . . . well, the fact was you *never* saw it.

Lucy now rummaged in a cabinet for the tea.

Bitter fog . . .

Then she paused. What was that sound?

Lucy cocked her head and listened.

What was that?

A ticking. She felt her stomach twist at the sound. She and Bob had no wind-up clocks. But that's what it sounded like.

What the hell is it?

She stepped into the small bedroom, which they used mostly as a closet. The light was out. She flicked it on. No, the sound wasn't coming from there.

Her palms sweating, breath coming fast, heart pounding.

I'm imagining the sound . . . I'm going crazy. IED's don't tick. Even timed devices have electronic detonators.

Besides, was she actually thinking that somebody had left a bomb in her co-op in New York City?

Girl, you need some serious help.

Lucy walked to the master bedroom doorway. The closet door was open, blocking her view of the dresser. Maybe it was . . . She stepped forward. But then paused. The ticking was coming from someplace else, not in here. She went up the hall to the dining room and looked inside. Nothing.

She then continued on to the bathroom. She gave a laugh.

Sitting on the vanity, next to the tub, was a clock. It looked like an old one. It was black and on the face was a window with a full moon staring at her. Where had it come from? Had her aunt been cleaning out her basement again? Had Bob bought it when she was away and set it out this morning after she'd left for the health club?

But why the bathroom?

The freaky moon face looked at her with its curious gaze, almost malevolent. It reminded her of the faces of the children along the roadside, their mouths curved into an expression that wasn't quite a smile; you had no idea what was going on in their heads. When they looked at you, were they seeing their saviors? Their enemy? Or creatures from another planet?

Lucy decided she'd call Bob or her mother and ask him about the clock. She went into the kitchen. She made the tea and carried the mug into the bathroom, the phone too, and ran water into the tub.

Wondering if her first bubble bath in months would do anything to wash away the bitter fog.

On the street in front of Lucy's apartment Vincent Reynolds watched two schoolgirls walk past.

He glanced at them but felt no deepening of the hunger already ravaging his body. They were high school kids and too young for him. (Sally Anne had been a teenager, true, but so had he, which made it okay.)

Through his cell phone, Vincent heard Duncan's whispered voice. 'I'm in her bedroom. She's in the bathroom, running a bath . . . That's helpful.'

Water boarding . . .

Because the building had a lot of tenants, and he could easily be spotted picking the lock, Duncan had climbed to the top of a building several doors down and made his way over the roofs to Lucy's, then down the fire escape and into her bedroom. He was real athletic (another difference between the friends).

'Okay, I'm going to do it now.'

Thank you . . .

But then he heard, 'Hold on.'

'What?' Vincent asked. 'Is something wrong?'

'She's on the phone. We'll have to wait.'

Hungry Vincent was sitting forward. Waiting was not something he did well.

A minute passed, two, five.

'What's going on?' Vincent whispered.

'She's still on the phone.'

Vincent was furious.

Goddamn her . . . He wished he could be there with Duncan to help kill her. What the hell was she doing making phone calls now? He wolfed down some food.

Finally the Watchmaker said, 'I'm going to try to get her off the phone. I'll go back up to the roof and come down the stairs into the hallway. I'll get her to open the door.' Vincent heard some rare emotion in the man's next comment. 'I can't wait any longer.'

You don't know the half of it, thought Clever Vincent, who

surfaced momentarily before being sent away by his starving
other half.

Stripping for her bath, Lucy Richter heard another sound. Not
the ticking of the moon clock. From somewhere nearby. Inside?
The hallway? The alley?

A click. Metallic.

What was it?

The life of the soldier is the sound of metal on metal.
Slipping the long rounds of rifle ammo, fragrant with oil, into
the clips, loading and locking the Colts, vehicle door latches,
fueler's belt buckles and vests clinking. The ring of a slug from
an AK-47, dancing off a Bradley or Humvee.

The noise again, *click, click*.

Then silence.

She felt chill air, as if a window was open. Where? The
bedroom, she decided. Half naked, she walked to the bedroom
doorway and glanced in. Yes, the window was open. But when
she'd glanced in earlier, hearing the ticking, hadn't it been
closed? She wasn't sure.

Then Lucy commanded: Don't be so damn paranoid, soldier.
Getting pretty tired of this. There're no IEDs, no suicide
bombers here, no bitter fog.

Get a grip.

One arm covering her breasts – there were apartments
across the alley – she closed and locked the window. Looked
down into the alley. Saw nothing.

It was then that somebody began pounding on the front
door. Lucy spun around, gasping. She pulled on a bathrobe
and hurried to the dark foyer. 'Who's there?'

There was a pause, then a man's voice called, 'I'm a police
officer. Are you all right?'

She called, 'What's wrong?'

'It's an emergency. Please open the door. Are you okay?'

Alarmed, she pulled the robe belt tight and undid the dead-bolts, thinking of the bedroom window and wondering if somebody'd been trying to break it. She unhooked the chain.

Lucy twisted the lock, reflecting only after the door began to push open toward her that she probably should've asked to see an ID or a badge before she unhooked the chain. She'd been caught up in a very different world for so long that she'd forgotten there were still plenty of bad people stateside.

Amelia Sachs and Lon Sellitto arrived at the old apartment building in Greenwich Village, nestled on quaint Barrow Street.

'That's it?'

'Uh-huh,' Sellitto said. His fingers were blue. His ears, red.

They looked into the alley beside the building. Sachs surveyed it carefully.

'What's her name?' she asked.

'Richter. Lucy I think's her first name.'

'Which window's hers?'

'Third floor.'

She glanced up at the fire escape.

They continued on to the front stairs of the apartment building. A crowd of people were watching. Sachs scanned their faces, still convinced that the Watchmaker had swept up at the first scene because he intended to return. Which meant he might have remained here too. But she saw no one that resembled him or his partner.

'We're sure it was the Watchmaker?' Sachs asked Frank Rettig and Nancy Simpson, cold and huddling next to the Crime Scene rapid response van, parked cockeyed in the middle of Barrow.

'Yep, he left one of those clocks,' Rettig explained. 'With the moon faces.'

Sachs and Sellitto started up the stairs.

'One thing,' Nancy Simpson said.

The detectives stopped and turned.

The officer nodded at the building, grimacing. 'It won't be pretty.'

Chapter
TWENTY-FOUR

Sachs and Sellitto ascended the stairs slowly. The air in the dim stairwell smelled of pine cleanser and oil furnace heat.

'How'd he get in?' Sachs mused.

'This guy's a ghost. He gets in however he fucking wants to.'

She looked up the stairwell. They paused outside the door. A nameplate said, *Richter/Dobbs*.

It won't be pretty . . .

'Let's do it.'

Sachs opened the door and walked into Lucy Richter's apartment.

Where they were met by a muscular young woman in sweats, hair pinned up. She turned away from the uniformed officer she'd been talking to. Her face darkened as she glanced at Sachs and Sellitto and noticed the gold badges around their necks.

'You're in charge?' asked Lucy Richter angrily, stepping forward, right in Lon Sellitto's face.

'I'm one of the detectives on the case.' He identified himself. Sachs did too.

Lucy Richter put her hands on her hips. 'What the hell do

you people think you're doing?' the soldier barked. 'You *know* there's some psycho leaving these goddamn clocks when he kills people. And you don't *tell* anybody? I didn't survive all these months of combat in the goddamn desert just to come home and get killed by some motherfucker because you don't bother to share that information with the public.'

It took some time to calm her down.

'Ma'am,' Sachs explained, 'his M.O. isn't that he's delivering these clocks ahead of time to let people know he's on his way. He was *here*. In your apartment. You were lucky.'

Lucy Richter was indeed fortunate.

About a half hour ago a passer-by happened to see a man climb onto her fire escape and head for the roof. He'd called 911 to report it. The Watchmaker had apparently glanced down, realized he'd been spotted and fled.

A search of the neighborhood could find no trace of him and no witnesses had seen anyone matching the Watchmaker's image on the computer composite.

Sachs glanced toward Sellitto, who said, 'We're very sorry for the incident, Ms Richter.'

'Sorry,' she scoffed. 'You need to go public with it.'

The detectives glanced at each other. Sellitto nodded. 'We will. I'll have Public Affairs make an announcement on the local news.'

Sachs said, 'I'd like to search your apartment for evidence he might've left. And ask you a few questions about what happened.'

'In a minute. I have to make some calls. My family'll hear about this on the news. I don't want them to worry.'

'This is pretty important,' Sellitto said.

The soldier opened her cell phone. In a firm voice she added, 'Like I said, in a minute.'

*

'Rhyme, you there?'

'Go ahead, Sachs.' The criminalist was in his laboratory, connected to Sachs via radio. He recalled that in the next month or so they'd planned to try a high-definition video camera mounted to her head or shoulder, broadcasting to Rhyme's lab, which would let him see everything that she saw. They'd joked and called it a James Bond toy. He felt a pang that it would not be Sachs inaugurating this device with him.

Then he forced the sentiment away. What he often told those working for him he now told himself: There's a perp out there; nothing matters but catching him and you can't do that if you're not concentrating 100 percent.

'We showed Lucy the composite of the Watchmaker. She didn't recognize him.'

'How'd he get inside today?'

'Not sure. If he's sticking to his M.O. he picked the front door lock. But then I think he went up to the roof and climbed down the fire escape to the vic's window. He got inside, left the clock and was waiting for her. But for some reason he climbed back outside. That's when the wit outside saw him and the Watchmaker booked on out of here. Went back up the fire escape.'

'Where was he inside her apartment?'

'He left the clock in the bathroom. The fire escape is off the master bedroom so he was in there too.' She paused. Then came on a moment later. 'They've been canvassing for witnesses but nobody saw him or his car. Maybe he and his partner are on foot since we've got his SUV.' A half dozen different subway lines serve Greenwich Village and they could easily have escaped via any of them.

'I don't think so.' Rhyme explained that he felt the Watchmaker and his assistant would prefer wheels. The choice of using vehicles or not when committing a crime is a consistent pattern in a criminal's M.O. It rarely changes.

Sachs searched the bedroom, the fire escape, the bathroom and the routes he would've taken to get to those places. She checked the roof too. It had not been recently tarred, she reported.

'Nothing, Rhyme. It's like he's wearing a Tyvek suit of his own. He's just not leaving anything behind.'

Edmond Locard, the famed French criminalist, developed what he called the exchange principle, which stated that whenever a physical crime occurs, there is some transfer of evidence between the criminal and the location. He leaves something of himself at the scene and he takes some of the scene with him when he departs. The principle is deceptively optimistic, though, because sometimes the trace is so minuscule it's missed and sometimes it's easily located but provides no helpful leads for investigators. Still Locard's principle holds that there would be *some* transfer of materials.

Rhyme often wondered, though, if there existed the rare criminal who was as smart as, or smarter than, Rhyme himself and if such a person could learn enough about forensic science to commit a crime and yet flaunt Locard's principle – leave behind no evidence and pick up none himself. Was the Watchmaker such a person?

'Think, Sachs . . . There's got to be more. Something we're missing. What does the vic say?'

'She's pretty shaken up. Not really concentrating.'

After a pause Rhyme said, 'I'm sending down our secret weapon.'

Kathryn Dance sat across from Lucy Richter in the living room of her apartment.

The soldier was beneath a Jimi Hendrix poster and a wedding photo of herself and her husband, a round-faced, cheerful man in a dress military uniform.

Dance noted the woman was pretty calm, considering the

circumstances, though, as Amelia Sachs had said, something was clearly troubling her. Dance had the impression that it was partly something other than the attack. She didn't exhibit the post-traumatic stress reactions of a near miss; she was troubled in a more fundamental way.

'If you don't mind, could you go through the details again?'

'If it'll help catch that son of a bitch, anything.' Lucy explained that she'd gone to the gym to work out that morning. When she returned she found the clock.

'I was upset. The ticking . . .' Her face now revealed a subtle fear reaction. Fight-or-flight. At Dance's prompting she explained about the bombs overseas. 'I guessed it was a present or something but it kind of freaked me out. Then I felt a breeze and went to look. I found the bedroom window open. That's when the police showed up.'

'Nothing else unusual?'

'No. Not that I can remember.'

Dance asked her a number of other questions. Lucy Richter didn't know Theodore Adams or Joanne Harper. She couldn't think of anyone who'd want to hurt her. She'd been trying to recall something else that could help the police but was drawing a blank.

The woman was outwardly brave ('that son of a bitch') but Dance believed that something in Lucy's mind was preventing her, subconsciously, from focusing on what had just happened. The classic defensive crossing of her arms and legs was a sign, indicating not deception but a barrier against whatever was threatening her.

The agent needed a different approach. She put her notebook down.

'What are you doing in town?' she asked conversationally.

Lucy explained that she was here on leave from her duty in the Middle East. Normally she'd have met her husband, Bob, in Germany, where they had friends, but she was getting a commendation on Thursday.

'Oh, part of that parade, supporting the troops?'

'Right afterward.'

'Congratulations.'

Her smile fluttered. Dance noticed the minuscule reaction.

And she noted one in herself, as well; Kathryn Dance's husband had been recognized for bravery under fire by the Bureau four days before he'd died. But that was a crackle of static that Dance immediately tuned out.

Shaking her head, the agent continued. 'You come back to the States and look what happens – you run into this guy. That's pretty shitty. Especially after being overseas.'

'It's not that bad over there. Sounds worse on the news.'

'Still . . . But it looks like you're coping pretty well.'

Her body was telling a very different story.

'Oh, yeah. You do what you have to. No big deal.' Her fingers were entwined.

'What do you do there?'

'I manage fuelers. Basically it's running supply trucks.'

'Important job.'

A shrug. 'I guess.'

'Good to be here on leave, I'll bet.'

'You ever in the service?'

'No,' Dance answered.

'Well, in the army, remember rule number one: Never pass up R and R. Even if it's just drinking punch with the brass and collecting a wall decoration.'

Dance kept drawing her out. 'How many other soldiers'll be at the ceremony?'

'Eighteen.'

Lucy wasn't comfortable at all. Dance wondered if her underlying uneasiness was because she might have to say a few words in front of the crowd. Public speaking was higher on the fear scale than skydiving. 'And how big's the event going to be?'

'I don't know. A hundred. Maybe two.'

'Is your family going?'

'Oh, yeah. Everybody. We're going to have a reception here afterward.'

'As my daughter says,' Dance offered, 'parties rock. What's on the menu?'

'Forgeddabout it,' Lucy joked. 'We're in the Village. It'll be Italian. Baked ziti, scampi, sausage. My mother and aunt're cooking. I'm making dessert.'

'My downfall,' Dance said. 'Sweets . . . I'm getting hungry.' Then she said, 'Sorry, I got distracted.' Leaving the notebook closed, she looked into the woman's eyes. 'Back to your visitor. You were saying, you made your tea. Running the bath. You feel a breeze. You go into the bedroom. The window's open. What was I asking? Oh, was there anything else you saw that was out of the ordinary?'

'Not really.' She said this quickly, as before, but then she squinted. 'Wait. You know . . . there was one thing.'

'Really?'

Dance had done what's known as 'flooding'. She'd decided that it wasn't only the Watchmaker that was bothering Lucy but rather her duty overseas, as well as the upcoming awards ceremony, for some reason. Dance had gone back to the topics and kept bombarding her with questions, in hopes of numbing her and letting the other memories break through.

Lucy rose and walked to the bedroom. Saying nothing, Dance followed her. Amelia Sachs joined them.

The soldier looked around the room.

Careful, Dance told herself. Lucy was onto something. Dance kept silent. Too many interviewers ruin a session by pouncing. The rule with vague memories is that you can let them surface but you can rarely reel them in.

Watching and listening are the two most important parts of the interview. Talking comes last.

'There *was* something that bothered me, something other than the window being open . . . Oh, you know what? I've got it. When I walked to the bedroom earlier, to see about the ticking, something was different – I couldn't see the dresser.'

'Why was that unusual?'

'Because when I left to go to the health club I glanced at it to see if my sunglasses were there. They were and I picked them up. But then when I looked into the room later, when I heard the ticking, I couldn't see the dresser – because the closet door was partly open.'

Dance asked, 'So after the man left the clock he was probably hiding in the closet or behind the door.'

'Makes sense,' Lucy said.

Dance turned to Sachs, who nodded with a smile and said, 'Good. I better get to work.' And she pulled open the closet door with her latex-gloved hand.

A second time they'd failed.

Duncan was driving even more carefully, *meticulously*, than he usually did.

He was silent and completely calm. Which bothered Vincent even more. If Duncan slammed down his fist and screamed, like Vincent's stepfather, Vincent would have felt better. ('You did *what?*' the man had raged, referring to the rape of Sally Anne. 'You fat pervert!') He was worried that Duncan had had enough and was going to give up the whole thing.

Vincent didn't want his friend to go away.

Duncan merely drove slowly, stayed in his lane, didn't speed, didn't try to beat yellow lights.

And didn't say a word for a long time.

Finally he explained to Vincent what had happened: As he'd started to climb to the roof – planning to get into the building, knock on Lucy's door and get her to hang up the phone, he'd glanced down and seen a man in the alley, staring at him, pulling his cell phone from his pocket, shouting for Duncan to stop. The killer had hurried to the roof, run west several buildings then rapelled into the alley. He'd then sprinted to the Buick.

Duncan was driving meticulously, yes, but without any obvious destination. At first Vincent wondered if this was to lose the police but there didn't seem to be any risk of pursuit. Then he decided that Duncan was on automatic pilot, driving in large circles.

Like the hands of a clock.

Once again the shock of a narrow escape faded and Vincent felt the hunger growing again, hurting his jaw, hurting his head, hurting his groin.

If we don't eat, we die.

He wanted to be back in Michigan, hanging out with his sister, having dinner with her, watching TV. But his sister wasn't here, she was miles and miles away, maybe thinking of him right now – but that didn't give him any comfort . . . The hunger was too intense. Nothing was working out! He felt like screaming. Vincent had better luck cruising strip malls in New Jersey or waiting for a college coed or recep- tionist jogging through a deserted park. What was the point of—

In his quiet voice Duncan said, 'I'm sorry.'

'You . . . ?'

'I'm sorry.'

Vincent was disarmed. His anger diminished and he wasn't sure what to say.

'You've been helping me, working hard. And look what's happened. I've let you down.'

Here was Vincent's mother, explaining to him, when he was ten, that she'd let him down with Gus, then with her second husband, then with Bart, then with Rachel the experiment, then with her third husband.

And every time, young Vincent had said just what he said now. 'It's okay.'

'No, it's not . . . I talk about the great scheme of things. But that doesn't minimize our disappointments. I owe you. And I'll make it up to you.'

Which is something his mother *never* said, much less did, leaving Vincent to find what comfort he could in food, TV shows, spying on girls and having his heart-to-hearts.

No, it was clear that his friend, Duncan, meant what he was saying. He was genuinely remorseful that Vincent hadn't been able to have Lucy. Vincent still felt the urge to cry but now for a different reason. Not from the hunger, not from frustration. He felt filled with an odd sensation. People hardly ever said nice things to him like this. People hardly ever worried about him.

'Look,' Duncan said, 'the one I'm going to do next. You're not going to want her.'

'Is she ugly?'

'Not really. It's just the way she's going to die . . . I'm going to burn her.'

'Oh.'

'In the book, remember the alcohol torture?'

'Not really.'

The pictures in the book were of men being tortured; they hadn't interested Vincent.

'You pour alcohol on the lower half of someone's body and set fire to it. You can put out an alcohol fire quickly if they confess. Of course, I'm not going to be putting it out.'

True, Vincent agreed, he wouldn't want her after that.

'But I have another idea.'

Duncan then explained what he had in mind, Vincent's spirits improving with every word. Duncan asked, 'Don't you think it'll work out for everybody?'

Well, not quite *everybody*, thought Clever Vincent, who was back and in a pretty good mood, all things considered.

Sitting in front of the evidence charts, Rhyme heard Sachs come back on the line.

'Okay, Rhyme. We've found he was hiding in the closet.'

'Which one?'

'In Lucy's bedroom.'

Rhyme closed his eyes. 'Describe it to me.'

Sachs gave him the whole scene – the hallway leading to the bedroom, the layout of the bedroom itself then the furniture, pictures on the wall, the Watchmaker's entrance and exit route and other details. Everything was described in precise, objective detail. Her training and experience shone as sharply as her red hair. If she left the force he wondered how long it would take another cop to walk the grid as well as she did.

Forever, he thought cynically.

Anger flared for a moment. Then he forced the emotion away and concentrated again on her words.

Sachs described the closet. 'Six feet four inches wide. Filled with clothes. Men's on the left, women's on the right, half and half. Shoes on the floor. Fourteen pairs. Four men's, ten women's.

A typical ratio, Rhyme reflected, for a married couple, thinking of his own closet from years ago. 'When he was hiding, was he lying on the floor?'

'No. Too many boxes.'

He heard her ask a question. Then she came back on the line. 'The clothes're ordered now but he must've moved them. I can see some boxes moved on the floor and a few bits of that roofing tar we found earlier.'

'What were the clothes he was hiding between?'

'A suit. And Lucy's army uniform.'

'Good.' Certain garments, like uniforms, are particularly good at collecting evidence, thanks to their prominent epaulettes, buttons and decorations. 'Was he against the front or back?'

'Front.'

'Perfect. Go over every button, medal, bar, decoration.'

'Okay. Give me a few minutes.'

Then silence.

His impatience, laced with anger, was back. He stared at the whiteboards.

Finally she said, 'I found two hairs and some fibers.'

He was about to tell her to check the hairs against samples in the apartment. But of course he didn't need to do this. 'I compared the hairs to hers. They don't match.' He began to tell her to find a sample of the woman's husband's hair when Sachs said, 'But I found her husband's brush. I'm ninety-nine percent sure they're his.'

Good, Sachs. Good.

'But the fibers . . . they don't seem to match anything else here.' Sachs paused. 'They look like wool, light-colored. Maybe a sweater . . . but they were caught on a pocket button at about shoulder level for a man of the Watchmaker's height. Could be a shearling collar.'

A reasonable deduction, though they'd have to examine the fibers more carefully in the lab.

After a few minutes she said, 'That's about it, Rhyme. Not much but it's something.'

'Okay, bring everything in. We'll go over it here.' He disconnected the line.

Thom wrote down the information Sachs gave them. After the aide left the room Lincoln Rhyme stared again at the charts. He wondered if the notes he was looking at weren't simply clues in a homicide case, but evidence of a different sort of murder: the corpse of the last crime scene he and Amelia Sachs would ever work together.

Lon Sellitto was gone and, inside Lucy Richter's apartment, Sachs was just finishing packing up the evidence. She turned to Kathryn Dance and thanked her.

'Hope it's helpful.'

'That's the thing about crime scene work. Only a couple of fibers, but they could be enough for a conviction. We'll just have to see.' Sachs added, 'I'm heading back to Rhyme's. Listen, I don't know if you'd be willing but could you do some canvassing in the neighborhood? You've sure got the touch when it comes to wits.'

'You bet.'

Sachs gave her some printouts with the Watchmaker's composite picture and left, to head back to Rhyme's.

Dance nodded at Lucy Richter. 'You're doing okay?'

'Fine,' the solider replied and offered a stoic smile. She walked into the kitchen and put the kettle on the stove. 'You want some tea? Or coffee?'

'No. I'm going to be outside looking for witnesses.'

Lucy was staring down at the floor, a good semaphore signal to a kinesics expert. Dance said nothing.

The soldier said, 'You said you were from California. You going back soon?'

'Tomorrow, probably.'

'Just wondering if you'd have time for coffee or something.' Lucy played with a potholder. On it were the words *4th Infantry Division. Steadfast and loyal.*

'Sure. We'll work it out.' Dance found a card in her purse and wrote her hotel name on it, then circled her mobile on the front.

Lucy took it.

'Call me,' Dance said.

'I will.'

'Everything okay?'

'Oh, sure. Just fine.'

Dance shook the woman's hand, then left the apartment, reminding herself of an important rule in kinesic analysis: Sometimes you don't need to uncover the truth behind every deception you're told.

Chapter

TWENTY-FIVE

Amelia Sachs returned to Rhyme's with a small carton of evidence.

'What do we have?' he asked.

Sachs went over again what she'd found at the scene, then added details on the boards.

According to the NYPD crime scene database on fibers, what Sachs had discovered on Lucy's uniform *was* from a shearling coat, the sort of collar found on leather jackets that used to be worn by pilots – bomber jackets. Sachs had field-tested the clock for nitrates – this one wasn't explosive either – and it was identical to the other three, yielding no trace except a recent stain of what turned out to be wood alcohol, the sort used as an antiseptic and for cleaning. As with the florist, the Watchmaker hadn't had time to leave another poem or had chosen not to.

Rhyme agreed to go public with the announcement about the calling card of the clock, though he predicted that all the announcement would do would be to guarantee that the killer didn't leave a clock until he was sure the victim was unable to call for help.

The trace that Sachs had found along the route where the killer had most likely escaped revealed nothing helpful.

'There wasn't anything else,' she explained.

'Nothing?' Rhyme asked. He shook his head.

Locard's principle . . .

Ron Pulaski arrived, pulling off his coat and hanging it up. Rhyme noticed that Sachs's eyes turned at once to the rookie.

The *Other* Case . . .

Sachs asked, 'Any luck with the Maryland connection?'

The rookie replied, 'Three ongoing federal investigations into corruption at the Baltimore waterfront. One of them has a link to the New York metro area but it was only the Jersey docks. And it's not about drugs. They're looking into kickbacks and falsified shipping documents. I'm waiting to hear back from Baltimore PD about state investigations. Neither Creeley or Sarkowski had any property in Maryland and neither of them ever went there on business that I could find. The closest Creeley got was regular business meetings in Pennsylvania to meet some client. And Sarkowski didn't travel at all. Oh, and still no client list from Jordan Kessler. I left a message again but he hasn't returned the call.'

He continued. 'I found a couple of people assigned to the One One Eight who were born in Maryland but they don't have any connection there now. I ran a roster of names of everybody who's assigned to the house against property tax databases in Maryland—'

'Wait,' Sachs said. 'You did that?'

'Was that wrong?'

'Uhm, no, Ron. It was right. Good thinking.' Sachs shared a smile with Rhyme. He lifted an eyebrow, impressed.

'Maybe. But nothing panned out.'

'Well, keep digging.'

'Sure thing.'

Sachs then walked over to Sellitto and asked, 'Got a question. You know Halston Jefferies?'

'Dep inspector at the One Five Eight?'

'Right. What's with him? Got a real short fuse.'

Sellitto laughed. 'Yeah, yeah, he's a rageaholic.'

'So I'm not the only one he acts that way with?'

'Nup. Reams you out for no reason. How'd you cross paths?' He glanced at Rhyme.

'Nope,' the criminalist replied cheerfully. 'That'd have to be *her* case. Not *my* case.'

Her exasperated look didn't faze him. Pettiness could, in some circumstances, be quite exhilarating, Rhyme reflected.

'I needed a file and I went to the source. He thought I should've gotten his okay.'

'But you needed to keep the brass in the dark about what's going on at the One One Eight.'

'Exactly.'

'It's just the way he is. Had some problems in the past. His wife was a socialite—'

'That's a great word,' Pulaski interrupted, '"socialite", like "socialist". Only they're opposites. In a way.'

When Sellitto shot him a cool look the rookie fell silent.

The detective continued. 'I heard they lost some serious money, Jefferies and his wife. I mean *big* money. Money you and me, we can't even find where the decimal point goes. Some business thing his wife was into. He was hoping to run for office – Albany, I think. But you can't go there without big bucks. And she left him after the business fell through. Though with a temper like that, he had to've had issues beforehand.'

She was nodding at this information when her phone rang. She answered. 'That's right, that's me . . . Oh, no. Where? . . . I'll be there in ten minutes.'

Her face pale and grave, she hurried out the door, saying, 'Problem. I'll be back in a half hour.'

'Sachs,' Rhyme began. But he heard only the slamming front door in response.

The Camaro eased up over the curb on West Forty-fourth Street, not far from the West Side Highway.

A big man in an overcoat and a fur hat squinted at Sachs as she climbed out of the car. She didn't know him, or he her, but the all-business parking job and the NYPD placard on the dash made it clear she was the one he was waiting for.

The young man's ears and nose were bright red and steam curled from his nose. He stamped his feet to keep the circulation going. 'Whoa, this's cold. I'm sicka winter already. You Detective Sachs?'

'Yeah. You're Coyle?'

They shook hands. He had a powerful grip.

'What's the story?' she asked.

'Come on. I'll show you.'

'Where?'

'The van. In the lot up the street.'

As they walked, briskly in the cold, Sachs asked, 'What house you from?' Coyle had identified himself as a cop when he called.

The traffic was loud. He didn't hear.

She repeated her question. 'What house you from? Midtown South?'

He blinked at her. 'Yeah.' Then blew his nose.

'I was there for a while,' Sachs told him.

'Hmm.' Coyle said nothing else. He directed her through the large parking lot. At the far end Coyle stopped, next to a Windstar van, the windows dark, the motor running.

He glanced around. Then opened the door.

Canvassing apartments and stores in Greenwich Village, near Lucy Richter's, Kathryn Dance was reflecting on the symbiotic relationship between kinesic and forensic sciences.

A practitioner of kinesics requires a human being – a witness, a suspect – the same way a forensic scientist requires evidence.

Yet this case was distinguished by a surprising absence of both people and physical clues.

It frustrated her. She'd never been involved in an investigation quite like this one.

Excuse me, sir, madam, hey there, young man, there was some police activity near here earlier today, did you hear about it, ah, good, I wonder if you happened to see anyone in that area, leaving quickly. Or did you see anything suspicious, anything out of the ordinary? Take a look at this picture . . .

But, nothing.

Dance didn't even recognize chronic witnessitis, the malady where people clearly know something but claim they don't, out of fear for themselves or their families. No, after forty freezing minutes on the street, she'd found the problem was simply that nobody'd seen squat.

Excuse me, sir, yes, it's a California ID but I'm working with the New York Police Department, you can call this number to verify that, now have you seen . . .

Zero.

Dance was taken aback once, shocked actually, when she approached a man coming out of an apartment. She'd blinked and her thoughts froze as she stared up at him – he was identical to her late husband. She'd controlled herself and run through her litany. He'd sensed something was up, though, and frowned, asking if she was all right.

How unprofessional can we be? Dance thought angrily. 'Fine,' she'd said with a fake smile.

Like his neighbors, though, the businessman hadn't seen anything unusual and headed up the street. With a long look back at him, Dance continued her search.

She wanted a lead, wanted to help nail this perp. Like any cop, of course, she wanted to take a sick, dangerous man off the streets. But she also wanted to spend time interviewing him after he'd been collared. The Watchmaker was different from any other perp she'd ever come up against. Kathryn Dance wanted badly to find out what made him tick – and laughed to herself at the unintended choice of words.

She continued stopping people for another block but found no one who could help.

Until she met the shopper.

On the sidewalk a block from Lucy's apartment she stopped a man wheeling a handcart filled with groceries. He glanced at the composite picture of the Watchmaker and said impulsively, 'Oh, yeah, I think I saw somebody who looked like him . . .' Then he hesitated. 'But I didn't really pay any attention.' He started to leave.

Kathryn Dance, though, knew instantly he'd seen more.

Witnessitis.

'This's really important.'

'All I saw was somebody running up the street. That's it.'

'Listen, got an idea. Anything perishable in there?' She nodded at the grocery cart.

He hesitated again, trying to anticipate her. 'Not really.'

'How 'bout if we get some coffee and I ask you a few more questions. You mind?'

She could tell he did mind but just then a blast of icy wind rocked them and he looked like he wouldn't mind getting out of the cold. 'I guess. But I really can't tell you anything else.'

Oh, we'll see about that.

Amelia Sachs sat in the back of the van.

With Coyle's help, she was struggling to get retired detective Art Snyder into a sitting position on the backseat of the van. He was half conscious, muttering words she couldn't hear.

When Coyle had first opened the door, Snyder had been sprawled out, head back, unconscious, and she thought – to her horror – that he'd killed himself. She soon learned that he was simply drunk, though extremely so. She'd shaken him gently. 'Art?' He'd opened his eyes, frowning and disoriented.

Now, the two officers got him on a seat.

'No, just wanna sleep. Leave me alone. Wanna sleep.'

'This's his van?'

'Yeah,' Coyle answered.

'What happened? How'd he get here?'

'He was up the street at Harry's. They wouldn't serve him – he was drunk already – and he wandered outside. I came in to buy some ciggies just after. The bartender knew I was a cop and told me about him. Didn't want him to drive off and kill himself or somebody else. I found him here, halfway inside. Your card was in his pocket.'

Art Snyder shifted groggily. 'Leave me alone.' His eyes closed.

She glanced at Coyle. 'I'll take over from here.'

'You sure?'

'Yeah. Only, could you flag down a cab, send it over here?'

'Sure.'

The cop climbed out of the van and walked away. Sachs crouched down, touched his arm. 'Art?'

He opened his eyes, squinting as he recognized her. 'You . . .'

'Art, we're going to get you home.'

'Leave me alone. Leave me the fuck alone.'

There was a cut on his forehead and his sleeve was torn from a fall. He'd vomited not long ago.

He snapped, 'Haven't you done enough? Haven't you fucking done enough to me?' His eyes bulged. 'Go away. I want to be alone. Leave me alone!' He rolled to his knees, tried crawling to the driver's seat. 'Go . . . away!'

Sachs pulled him back. He wasn't a small man but the alcohol had weakened him. He tried to stand but fell back on the seat.

'You were doing great.' She nodded at a pint bottle on the floor. It was empty.

'What's it to you? What the fuck is it to you?'

'What happened?' she persisted.

'Don't you get it? You happened. *You.*'

'Me?'

'Why did I think it'd keep quiet? There're no fucking secrets in the department. I ask a few questions for you, where's the fucking file, what happened to it . . . next thing, my buddy I was meeting to play pool I told you about? He never shows. And doesn't return my calls . . .' He wiped his mouth on his sleeve. 'Then I get a call – this guy was my partner for three years, him and me and our wives were going on a cruise. Guess who can't fucking make it? . . . All because I was asking questions. A retired cop asking questions . . . I should've told you to go fuck yourself the minute you walked through the door.'

'Art, I—'

'Oh, don't worry, lady. I didn't mention your name. Didn't mention anything.' He groped for the bottle. He saw it was empty. And flung it to the floor.

'Look, I know a good counselor. You can—'

'Counselor? What's he gonna *counsel* me on? How I fucked up my life?'

She glanced toward the bottle. 'You stumbled. Everybody stumbles.'

'Not what I'm talking about. This's *because* I fucked everything up.'

'What do you mean, Art?'

'Because I was a cop. I wasted everything. I wasted my life.'

She felt a chill; his words echoed her feelings. He was expressing exactly the reason she wanted to leave the force. She said, 'Art, how 'bout we get you home?'

'I could've done a hundred other things. My brother's a plumber. My sister went to grad school and works for an ad agency now. She did that butterfly commercial for those feminine things. She's famous. I could've done something.'

'You're just feeling—'

'Don't,' he snapped, pointing a finger at her. 'You don't know me good enough to talk to me that way. You got no right.'

Sachs fell silent. True. She didn't have the right.

'Whatever happens 'causa what you're looking into, I'm fucked. Good or bad, I'm fucked.'

Her heart chilled to see his anger and pain; she put her arm around him, 'Art, listen—'

'Get your hands off me.' His head lolled against the window.

Coyle walked up a moment later, directing a Yellow Cab toward the van. Together Coyle and Sachs helped Snyder to the cab and got him inside. She gave the driver Snyder's address, then emptied her wallet, handing him close to fifty dollars and the detective's car keys. 'I'll call his wife, let her know he's coming,' she told the cabbie. The taxi eased into thick Midtown traffic.

'Thanks,' she said to Coyle, who nodded and walked off. She was grateful he didn't ask any questions.

After he was gone, Sachs reached into her pocket and extracted Snyder's pistol, which she'd lifted from his rear belt holster when she'd put her arm around him. Maybe he had another piece at home but at least he wouldn't be using this one to kill himself. She unloaded it, kept the bullets and hid the weapon in the springs under the front passenger seat. She then locked the door and returned to her car.

Her index finger dug into her thumb. Her skin itched. Her anger steamed as she realized that apart from the extortion and the stolen evidence there was a broader crime that her father – and all crooked cops – committe ' Her simple effort to get to the truth had turned into s ething flinty and dangerous, affecting even the innocent. Snyder's future life as a retiree, which he'd looked forward to for years, was dissolving. All because of whatever happened at the 118th Precinct.

Just like the families of the convicted cops in the Sixteenth Avenue Club had their lives changed forever by what her father and his buddies had done. Wives and children had been forced to give up their homes to banks and quit school to get jobs; they'd been ostracized, forever tainted by the scandal.

She still had time to get out – leave police work, and get out. Get into Argyle, get away from the bullshit and the politics, make a new life for herself. She still had time. But for Art Snyder, it was too late.

Why, Dad? Why'd you do it?

Amelia Sachs would never know.

Time had passed and taken with it any chance she might find answers to that question.

All she could do was speculate, which does nothing but leave a wound in the soul that feels like it will never heal.

Turning back the clock was the only answer and that, of course, was no answer at all.

Tony Parsons was sitting across from Kathryn Dance in a coffee shop, his shopping cart of groceries beside them.

He squinted and shook his head. 'I've been trying to remember but I really can't think of anything else.' He grinned. 'Think you wasted your money.' He lifted his coffee cup.

'Well, we'll give it a shot.' Dance knew he had more information. Her guess was that he'd spoken without thinking – oh, how interrogators love impulsive subjects – and then realized that the man he'd seen might be a killer, maybe even the one who'd committed those horrible murders at the pier and in the alleyway the previous day. Dance knew that people who are happy to give statements about cheating neighbors and shoplifting teens grow forgetful when the crimes turn capital.

Maybe a tough nut, Dance reflected, but that didn't bother her. She loved challenges (the exhilaration she often felt when a subject finally confessed was always dulled by the thought that the signature on his statement marked the end of another verbal battle).

She poured milk into her coffee and looked longingly at a piece of apple pie sitting in a display case at the counter. Four hundred and fifty calories. Oh, well. She turned back to Parsons.

He poured some extra sugar into his coffee and stirred it. 'You know, maybe if we just talked about it for a bit I *could* remember something else.'

'That's a great idea.'

He nodded. 'Now, then, let's have us a good old heart-to-heart.'

And gave her a big smile.

Chapter
TWENTY-SIX

She was his consolation prize.

She was his present from Gerald Duncan.

She was the killer's way of saying he was sorry and meaning it, not like Vincent's mother.

It was also a good way to slow down the police – raping and killing one of their own. Duncan had mentioned the redheaded policewoman working at the site of the second murder and suggested Vincent take her (oh, yes, please . . . red hair, like Sally Anne's). But, watching the police at Lucy Richter's apartment in Greenwich Village from the Buick, he and Duncan had realized there was no way to get to the redhead; she was never by herself. Yet the other woman, a plainclothed detective or something, started up the street by herself, looking for witnesses, it seemed.

Duncan and Vincent had gone into a discount store and bought the handcart, a new winter jacket, and fifty dollars' worth of soap, junk food and soda to fill the cart with. (Somebody wheeling around groceries isn't suspicious – his friend, always, always thinking.) The plan was for Vincent to start trolling the streets of Greenwich Village until he found the second cop, or she found him, then he'd lead her to an abandoned building a block from Lucy Richter's place.

Vincent would take her to the basement and he could have her for as long as he wanted, while Duncan would take care of the next victim.

Duncan had then studied Vincent's face. 'Would you have a problem killing her, the policewoman?'

Afraid he'd disappoint his friend, who was doing him such a wonderful favor, Vincent had said, 'No.'

But Duncan obviously knew it wasn't true. 'Tell you what – just leave her in the basement. Tie her up. After I'm through in Midtown, I'll drive down there and take care of her myself.'

Vincent had felt a lot better, hearing that.

The hunger raged through him now as he looked over Kathryn Dance, sitting only a few feet from him. Her braid, her smooth throat, her long fingers. She wasn't heavy but she had a good figure, not like those skinny model sorts you saw a lot of in the city. Who'd want somebody like *that*?

Her figure made him hungry.

Her green eyes made him hungry.

Even her name, Kathryn, made him hungry. For some reason it seemed to fall into the same category of name as Sally Anne. He couldn't say why. Maybe it was old-fashioned. Also, he liked the way she looked hungrily at the desserts. She's just like me! He could hardly wait to get her face-down in the building up the street.

He sipped the coffee. 'So, you were saying you're from California?' Vincent – well, Helpful Tony Parsons – asked.

'That's right.'

'Pretty, I'll bet.'

'Is, yes. Parts of it. Now think back to what you saw exactly. That man running? Tell me about him.'

Vincent knew he'd have to stay focused – at least until they were alone at the abandoned building. 'Be careful,' the killer had said, briefing him. 'Be coy. Pretend that you know something about me but you don't want to talk. Be hesitant. That's how a real witness would be.'

Now he told her – coyly and hesitantly – a few more things about the man running up the street and added to the vague description of Gerald Duncan, though it was pretty much what the police knew anyway, since they had that computer picture of him (he'd have to tell Duncan about that). She jotted some notes.

'Any unusual characteristics?'

'Hmm. Don't remember any. Like I said, I wasn't very close.'

'Any weapons?'

'Don't think so. What exactly did he do?'

'There was an attempted assault.'

'Oh, no. Anybody hurt?'

'No, fortunately.'

Or *un-*, thought Clever Vincent/Tony.

'Was he carrying anything?' Agent Dance asked.

Keep it simple, he reminded himself. Don't let her trip you up.

He frowned thoughtfully and hesitated. Then he said, 'You know, he might've been. Carrying something, I mean. A bag, I think. I couldn't really see. He was going pretty fast . . .' He stopped speaking.

Kathryn cocked her head. 'You were going to say something else?'

'I'm sorry I'm not more help. I know it's important.'

'That's okay,' the woman said reassuringly, and for a moment Vincent had a pang of guilt about what was going to happen to her in a few minutes.

Then the hunger told him not to feel guilty. It was normal to have the urge.

If we don't eat, we die . . .

Don't you agree, Agent Dance?

They sipped coffee. Vincent told her a few other tidbits about the suspect.

She was chatting like a friend. Finally he decided the time was right. He said, 'Look, there *is* something else . . . I was kind of scared before. You know, I'm around here every day. What if he comes back? He might figure out I said something about him.'

'We can keep it anonymous. And we'll protect you. I promise.'

A clever hesitation. 'Really?'

'You bet. We'll have a policeman guarding you.'

Now, *there's* an interesting idea. Can I have the redhead?

He said to Dance, 'Okay, I saw where he ran to. It was the back door of a building up the street. He ran inside.'

'The door was unlocked? Or did he have a key?'

'Unlocked, I think. I'll show you if you want.'

'That'd be very helpful. Are you through?' She nodded at the cup.

He drained the coffee. 'Am now.'

She flipped closed her notebook, which he'd have to remember to get from her after he was finished.

'Thanks, Agent Dance.'

'You're very welcome.'

As he wheeled the groceries outside, the agent paid the check. She joined him and they started up the sidewalk where he directed.

'Is it always this cold in New York in December?'

'A lot of times, yep.'

'I'm freezing.'

Really? You look plenty hot to me.

'Where are we going?' she asked, slowing down and looking at the street signs. She squinted against the glare. She paused and jotted in her notebook, reciting as she wrote. 'The perp was recently in this location, Sherman Street in Greenwich

Village.' She looked around. 'Went up alley between Sherman and Barrow . . .' A glance at Vincent. 'What side of the street's the alley on? North, south? I need to be accurate.'

Ah, *she's* meticulous too.

He thought for a moment, disoriented by the hunger more than the bitter cold. 'That'd be southeast.'

She looked at her notebook, laughing. 'Can hardly read it – the shivering. This cold is too much. I can't wait to get back to California.'

And you'll be waiting a purty long time, missy . . .

They resumed walking.

'You have a family?' she asked.

'Yep. A wife and two kids.'

'I have two children. Son and daughter.'

Vincent nodded, wondering: How old is the daughter?

'So this's the alley?' she asked.

'Yep. There's where he ran to.' Pulling the grocery cart behind him, he started into the alley that would lead to their love nest, the abandoned building. He felt a painful erection.

Vincent reached into his pocket and gripped the handle of his knife. No, he couldn't kill her. But if she fought back, he'd have to protect himself.

Slash the eyes . . .

It'd be gross but her bloody face wouldn't be a problem for Vincent; he preferred them on their bellies anyway.

They were walking deeper into the passageway now. Vincent looked around and saw the building, forty or fifty feet away.

Dance paused again, opened the notebook. She recited what she wrote: 'The alley runs behind six, no, seven residential buildings. There are four Dumpsters here. The surface of the alley is asphalt. The perpetrator ran this way, going south.' Gloves back on, over her quivering, fingers which ended in deliciously red nails.

The hunger was consuming Vincent. He felt himself

withering away. He gripped the knife in a tense hand, breathing quickly.

She paused once more.

Now! Take her.

He started to pull the knife from his pocket.

But the bark of a siren cut through the air, coming from the other end of the alley. He glanced at it in shock.

And then he felt the gun muzzle touch the back of his head.

Agent Dance was shouting, 'Raise your hands. Now!' Gripping his shoulder.

'But—'

'Now.'

She shoved the gun harder into his skull.

No, no, no! He let go of the knife and lifted his arms.

What was going on?

The police car skidded to a stop in front of them, another right behind it. Four huge cops jumped out.

No . . . Oh, no . . .

'On your face,' one of them ordered. 'Do it!'

But he couldn't move, he was so shocked.

Then Dance was stepping back as police officers surrounded him, pulling him to the ground.

'I didn't do anything! I didn't!'

'You!' one of the men cried. 'On your belly – *now*.'

'But it's cold, it's dirty! And I haven't *done* anything!'

They flung him to the hard ground. He grunted as the breath was knocked from his body.

It was just like with Sally Anne, all over again.

You, fat boy, don't fucking move! Pervert! . . .

No, no, no!

Hands were all over him, grappling. He felt the pain as his arms were pulled taut behind him and cuffs were ratcheted on. He was searched, pockets turned inside out.

'Got an ID, got a knife.'

It was now, it was thirteen years ago, Vincent could hardly tell.

'I didn't do anything! What's this all about?'

One of the officers said to Agent Dance, 'We heard you loud and clear. You didn't need to go into the alley with him.'

'I was afraid he'd bolt. I wanted to stay with him as long as I could.'

What was going on? Vincent wondered. What did she mean?

Agent Dance glanced at the officer and nodded toward Vincent. 'He was doing a good job until we got into the diner. Once we sat down I knew he was faking.'

'No, you're crazy. I—'

She turned to Vincent.

'Your accent and expressions were inconsistent and your body language told me you weren't really having a conversation with me at all. You had another agenda, trying to manipulate me for some reason . . . Which turned out to be getting me alone in the alley.'

She explained that when she'd paid the check she'd slipped her phone out of her pocket and hit REDIAL, calling an NYPD detective she'd been working with. She'd whispered briefly what she'd concluded and had him send officers to the area. She'd kept the phone line open, hidden under her notebook.

That's why she was reciting the names of the streets out loud; she was giving them directions.

Vincent then looked at her hands. She caught his eye. And held up the pen she'd been writing with. 'Yep. That's my gun.'

He looked back at the other cops. 'I don't know what's going on here. This is bullshit.'

One of them said, 'Listen, why don't you save your breath. Just before she called we got a report that the getaway driver in the attack earlier was back in the neighborhood with a cart of groceries. He was a fat, white guy.'

Her name's Sally Anne, fat boy. She escaped and called the police and told us all about you . . .

'That's not me! I haven't done anything. You're wrong. You're so wrong.'

'Yeah,' one of the uniformed cops said with an amused expression, 'we hear that a lot. Let's go.'

They gripped him by the upper arms and hauled him roughly to the squad car. He heard Gerald Duncan's voice in his mind.

I'm sorry. I've let you down. I'll make it up to you . . .

And something hardened within pudgy Vincent Reynolds. He decided that nothing they could do to him would ever make him betray his friend.

The large, pear-shaped man sat next to the front window of Lincoln Rhyme's laboratory, hands cuffed behind him.

His driver's license and DMV records revealed that he wasn't Tony Parsons but Vincent Reynolds, a twenty-eight-year-old word-processing operator who lived in New Jersey and worked for a half dozen temp agencies, none of which knew much about him, other than what the basic employment checks and résumé verification had revealed; he was a model, if unmemorable, employee.

With a mix of anger and uneasiness, Vincent alternated glances between the floor and the officers around him – Rhyme, Sachs, Dance, Baker and Sellitto.

There were no priors or warrants out on him and a search of his shabby apartment in New Jersey revealed no obvious connection to the Watchmaker. Nor evidence of a lover, close friends or parents. The officers found a letter he was writing to his sister in Detroit. Sellitto got her number from Michigan State Police and called. He left a message for her to call them.

He was working Monday night, at the time of the pier and Cedar Street killings, but he'd taken time off since then.

Mel Cooper had emailed a digital picture of him to Joanne

Harper at the florist shop. The woman reported that he did resemble the man staring in her window, but she couldn't be certain, because of the glare, the dirty glass in the front windows of her workshop and his sunglasses.

Though they suspected him of being the Watchmaker's accomplice, the evidence linking him to the scenes was sketchy. The shoe print from the garage where the SUV had been abandoned was the same size as his shoes, thirteen, but there were no distinguishing marks to make a clear match. Among the groceries – which Rhyme suspected he'd bought as a cover to get close to Dance or another investigator – were chips, cookies and other junk food. But these packages were unopened and a search of his clothes revealed no crumbs that might specifically match what had been recovered in the SUV.

They were holding him only for possession of an illegal knife and interfering with a police operation – the usual charge when a phony witness comes forward.

Still, a good portion of City Hall and Police Plaza wanted to pull an Abu Ghraib on Vincent and browbeat or threaten him until he squealed. This was Dennis Baker's preference; the lieutenant had been getting pressure from City Hall to find the perp.

But Kathryn Dance said, 'Doesn't work. They curl up like rolly bugs and give you garbage.' She added, 'For the record, torture's very inefficient at getting accurate information.'

And so Rhyme and Baker had asked her to handle Vincent's interview. They needed to find the Watchmaker as fast as possible and, if rubber hoses were out, they wanted an expert.

The California special agent now drew the curtains closed and sat down across from Vincent, nothing between them. She scooted the chair forward until she was about three feet away. Rhyme supposed this was to get into his space and help break down his resistance. But he also realized that if Vincent flipped out he could lunge forward and injure her severely with his head or teeth.

She was undoubtedly aware of this too but gave no indication of feeling in danger. She offered a reserved smile and said calmly, 'Hello, Vincent. I know you've been informed of your rights and you've agreed to talk to us. We appreciate that.'

'Absolutely. Anything I can do. This is a big . . .' he shrugged . . . 'misunderstanding, you know.'

'Then we'll get everything straightened out. I just need some basic information first.' She asked his full name, address, age, where he worked, if he'd ever been arrested.

He frowned. 'I already told him this.' A look at Sellitto.

'I'm sorry. Left hand, right hand, you know. If you wouldn't mind going over it again.'

'Oh, all right.'

Rhyme figured that since he was giving her verified facts, she'd be creating a baseline kinesic reading. Now that Kathryn Dance had altered the criminalist's opinion about interviewing and witnesses, he was intrigued by the process.

Dance nodded pleasantly as she jotted down Vincent's responses and thanked him from time to time for his cooperation. Her politeness confused Rhyme. He himself would be a hell of a lot tougher.

Vincent grimaced. 'Look, I can, you know, talk to you for as long as you want. But I hope you sent somebody to look for that man I saw. You don't want him to get away. I'm worried about that. I try to help, and look what happens – this's the story of my life.'

Though what he'd told Dance and the officers on the scene about the suspect wasn't helpful. The building he claimed the killer disappeared into showed no signs that anyone had been inside recently.

'Now if you could go through the facts once more. Tell me

what happened. Only, if you wouldn't mind, I'd like you to tell it to me in reverse order.'

'What?'

'Reverse chronological order. It's a good way to jump-start memories. Start with the last event first and go back in time from there. The suspect – he's going through the doorway of that old building in the alley . . . Let's begin with some specifics. The color of the door.'

Vincent shifted in his chair, frowned. After a moment he gave his account, starting with the man pushing through the doorway (he couldn't remember the color). Vincent then explained what happened just before that – the man running down the alley. Then entering it. And before that he was running down the street. Finally Vincent told them about spotting a man on Barrow, looking around uneasily, then breaking into a run.

'Okay,' Dance said, jotting notes. 'Thank you, Vincent.' She gave a faint frown. 'But why did you tell me your name was Tony Parsons?'

'Because I was scared. I did a good deed, I told you what I saw, but I was afraid the killer would murder me if he found out my name.' His jaw trembled. 'I wished I hadn't said anything about what I'd seen. But I did and got scared. I *told* you I was afraid.'

The man's whining irritated Rhyme. Grill him, he silently urged Kathryn Dance.

But she asked pleasantly, 'Tell me about the knife.'

'Okay, I shouldn't've had it. But I was mugged a few years ago. It was terrible. I'm so stupid. I should've just left it at home. I usually do that. I just don't think. And then it gets me in trouble.'

Then she slipped her jacket off and set it on the chair next to her.

He continued. 'Everybody else is smart enough not to get

involved. I say something and look what happens.' Gazing at the floor, disgust twitching at the corners of his mouth.

Dance asked details of how he learned about the Watchmaker's killings and where he was at the times of the other attacks.

The questions were curious to Rhyme. Superficial. She wasn't probing the way he would have, demanding alibis and pulling apart his story. What seemed to be some good leads, she let drop. Dance never once asked if there was another reason he'd been leading her into the alley, which they all suspected was to murder her – perhaps even to torture her into telling what the police might know about the Watchmaker.

The agent gave no reaction to his answers but merely jotted notes. Finally the agent looked behind Vincent at Sachs. 'Amelia, could you do me a favor?'

'Sure.'

'Could you show Vincent the footprint we found?'

Sachs rose and got the electrostatic image. She held it up for Vincent to look at.

'What about it?' he asked.

'That's your size shoe, isn't it?'

'About.'

She continued to stare at him, saying nothing. Rhyme sensed she was setting up a brilliant trap. He watched them both closely . . .

'Thanks,' Dance said to Sachs, who sat down again.

The agent eased forward, slightly more into the suspect's personal space. 'Vincent, I'm curious. Where'd you get the groceries?'

A brief hesitation. 'Well, at the Food Emporium.'

Rhyme finally understood. She was going to draw him out about the groceries and then ask him why he'd bought them in Manhattan if he lived in New Jersey – since everything in the cart would be available closer to home and probably cheaper. She leaned forward, pulling off her glasses.

Now – she was going to snare him.

Kathryn Dance smiled and said, 'Thank you, Vincent. I think that'll be it. Hey, you thirsty?' the agent added. 'Want a soda?'

Vincent nodded. 'Yeah. Thanks.'

Dance glanced at Rhyme. 'Could we get him something?'

Rhyme blinked and shot a perplexed look at Sachs, who was frowning. What the hell was Dance thinking? She hadn't gotten a single bit of information out of him. The criminalist was thinking, A waste of time. That's all she's going to ask him? And now she's playing hostess? Reluctantly Rhyme called Thom, who brought Dance a Coke.

Dance put a straw in and held it up for the handcuffed man to drink from. He drained the glass in seconds.

'Vincent, just give us a few minutes alone, if you don't mind, and I think we'll get this all straightened out.'

'Okay. Sure.'

The patrol officers escorted him out. Dance shut the door behind him.

Dennis Baker shook his head, staring unhappily at the agent. Sellitto muttered, 'Worthless.'

Dance frowned. 'No, no, we're doing fine.'

'We are?' Rhyme asked.

'Right on track . . . Now, here's the situation. I got his base-line readings and then asked him about the reverse order of events – it's a good way to catch up deceptive subjects who've been improvising. People can describe an *actual* series of past events in any order – from start to finish or backward – without a problem. But people fabricate events in only one direction, start to finish. When they try to reconstruct it back-ward, they don't have the cues that they used in creating the scenario and they trip up. So, I learned right up front that he's the Watchmaker's assistant.'

'You did?' Sellitto laughed.

'Oh, that was obvious. His recognition responses were off the charts. And he's not afraid for his personal safety, like he claimed. No, he knows the Watchmaker and he's been involved in the crimes but in a way that I can't figure out. More than just a getaway driver.'

'But you didn't ask him about any of that,' Baker pointed out. 'Shouldn't we be picking apart where he said he was at the times of the attacks at the florist shop and the apartment in Greenwich Village?'

Rhyme's observation, too.

'Oh, no. Worst thing to do. If I did, those are the subjects he'd stonewall on instantly.' She continued. 'He's a complicated person, there's a lot of conflict going on inside him, and my feeling is that he's in the second state of stress response, depression. That's essentially anger turned inward. And it's very difficult to break through. Given his personality type, I'd need to create a sympathetic bond between us and it would take days, maybe weeks, to get to the truth with traditional interrogation methods. But we don't have days. Our only chance is to try something radical.'

'What?'

Dance nodded at the straw Vincent had used. 'Can you order a DNA test?' she asked Rhyme.

'Yes. But it'll take some time.'

'That's okay, as long as we can say truthfully it's been ordered.' She smiled. 'Never lie. But you don't have to tell a suspect everything.'

Rhyme wheeled around to the main portion of the lab, where Mel Cooper and Pulaski were still working on the evidence. He explained what they needed and Cooper packaged the straw in plastic and filled out a DNA analysis request. 'There. Technically it's been ordered. The lab just doesn't know it yet.' He laughed.

Dance explained: 'There's something big he's keeping from me. He's very nervous about it. His response to my question about being arrested was deceptive but it's also very rehearsed. I think he was collared but it was a while ago. There're no prints on file so he fell through the cracks – maybe a lab screwup, maybe he was a juvenile. But I know he's run into the law before. And I finally got a sense of what it might be. That's why I took my jacket off and had Amelia walk around in front of him. He's eating up the two of us with his eyes. Trying not to but he can't help it. That makes me think there's a sexual assault or two in his past. I want to bluff and use that against him.

'The problem is,' she continued, 'that he could call me on it. Then we lose our bargaining power and it'll take a long time to grind him down and get anything helpful.'

Sellitto said to Rhyme, 'I know where you come down on it.'

Hell, yes, Rhyme thought. 'Take the chance.'

Sellitto asked, 'And you, Dennis?'

'I oughta call downtown. But we'd be kicking ourselves if they say no. Go ahead and do it.'

The agent said, 'One other thing I need to do. I have to take myself out of the equation. Whatever he had planned with me in the alley, we have to let it go. If I bring it up it'll move the relationship to a different place and he's going to stop talking to me; we'll have to start over again.'

'But you know what he was going to do to you?' Sachs asked.

'Oh, I know exactly what he had in mind. But we have to stay focused on our goal – finding the Watchmaker. Sometimes you just have to let other things slide.'

Sellitto looked at Baker and nodded.

The agent walked to the closest computer and typed some commands, then a user name and pass code. She squinted when the website appeared and typed in some more commands. A page of some suspect's DNA rolled onto the screen.

Dance opened her purse and replaced the sheep glasses with the wolf ones. 'Now it's time for the fun part.' She walked to the door and opened it, asked that Vincent be brought back.

The big man, sweat stains under his arms, lumbered back into the room and sat down in the chair, which groaned under his weight. He was cautious.

Dance broke the silence with, 'I'm afraid we've got a problem, Vincent.'

His eyes narrowed.

Dance held up the plastic evidence bag containing the straw he'd drunk from. 'You know about DNA, don't you?'

'What're you talking about?'

Rhyme wondering. Is it going to work? Will he fall for it?

Was Vincent going to end the interview, clam up and insist on an attorney? He had every right to do that. The bluff would end in disaster and they might never get any information from him until after the Watchmaker had killed his next victim.

Calmly Dance asked, 'You ever seen your DNA analysis, Vincent?'

Dance turned the computer monitor toward Vincent. 'I don't know if you're aware of the FBI's Combined DNA Index System. We call it CODIS. Whenever there's a rape or sexual assault and the perp isn't caught, his fluids, skin and hair are collected. Even with a condom, there's usually some material left on or near the victim with DNA in it. The profile is stored and when police get a suspect, his profile is matched against what's in the forensic index. Take a look.'

Beneath the heading *CODIS* were dozens of lines of numbers, letters, grids and fuzzy bars virtually incomprehensible to anyone unfamiliar with the system.

The man was completely still, though his breathing was heavy. His eyes, to Rhyme, seemed defiant. 'This's bullshit.'

'You know, Vincent, that nobody ever beats a case built on solid DNA. And we've gotten convictions years after the assaults.'

'You can't . . . I didn't say it was okay to do that.' He stared at the bagged straw.

'Vincent,' Kathryn Dance said softly, 'you're in trouble.'

Technically true, Rhyme reflected. He was in possession of a deadly weapon.

Never lie . . .

'But you've got something we want.' A pause, then Dance continued. 'I don't know about New York procedures but in California our district attorneys have a lot of latitude to work with cooperative suspects.'

She looked at Sellitto, who took over. 'Yeah, Vincent, same thing here. The DA'll listen to our recommendations.'

Lost in the bars on the computer screen, his teeth set, Vincent said nothing.

Baker continued. 'Here's the deal: If you help us get the Watchmaker and if you confess to the prior sexual assaults, we'll get you immunity on the murder and assault counts for the two victims the other day. We'll make sure you have access to a treatment center. And you'll be isolated from the general population.'

Dance said firmly, 'But you have to help us. Right now, Vincent. What do you say?'

The man glanced at the screen that contained a DNA analysis that had nothing whatsoever to do with him. His leg was bouncing slightly – a sign that a debate was raging within him.

He turned his defiant eyes to Kathryn Dance.

Yes or no? What would it be?

A full minute passed. Rhyme heard only the ticking of the Watchmaker's clocks.

Vincent grimaced. He looked up at them with cold eyes. 'He's a businessman from the Midwest. His name's Gerald Duncan. He's staying in a church in Manhattan. Can I have another Coke?'

Chapter
TWENTY-SEVEN

'Where is he now?' Dennis Baker barked.

'There was somebody else he was going to . . .' Vincent's voice faded.

'Kill?'

The suspect nodded.

'Where?'

'I don't know exactly. He said Midtown, I think. He didn't tell me. Really.'

They glanced at Kathryn Dance, who apparently sensed no deception and nodded.

'I don't know whether he's there now or the church.'

He gave the address.

Sachs said, 'I know it. Closed a while ago.'

Sellitto called ESU and had Haumann put together some tactical teams.

'He was going to meet me back in the Village in an hour or so. Near that building in the alley.'

Where, Rhyme reflected, Vincent had been going to rape and kill Kathryn Dance. Sellitto ordered unmarked cars stationed near the building.

'Who's the next victim?' Baker asked.

'I don't know. I really don't. He didn't tell me anything about her because . . .'

'Why?' Dance asked.

'I wasn't going to have anything to do with her.'

Do with her . . .

Rhyme understood. 'So you were helping him out and in exchange he'd let you have the victims.'

'Only the women,' Vincent said quickly, shaking his head in disgust. 'Not men. I'm not weird or anything . . . And only after they were dead, so it wasn't really rape. It's *not*. Gerald told me that. He looked it up.'

Dance and Sellitto seemed unmoved by this but Baker blinked. Sachs was trying to control her temper.

Baker asked, 'Why weren't you going to *do* anything with the next one?'

'Because . . . he was going to burn her to death.'

'Jesus,' Baker muttered.

'Is he armed?' Rhyme asked.

Vincent nodded. 'He's got a gun. A pistol.'

'A thirty-two?'

'I don't know.'

'What's he driving?' Sellitto asked.

'It's a dark blue Buick. It's stolen. A couple years old.'

'License plates?'

'I don't know. Really. He just stole it.'

'Put out an EVL,' Rhyme ordered. Sellitto called it in.

Dance leapt in with, 'And what else?' She sensed something.

'What do you mean?'

'What about the car upsets you?'

He looked down. 'I think he killed the owner. I didn't know he was going to. I really didn't.'

'Where?'

'He didn't tell me.'

Cooper sent out a request for any reports of recent carjackings, homicides or missing persons.

'And . . .' Vincent swallowed. His leg was bouncing faintly again.

'What?' Baker asked.

'He killed somebody else too. This college student, I think, a kid. In an alley around the corner from the church, near Tenth Avenue.'

'Why?'

'He saw us coming out of the church. Duncan stabbed him and put the body in a Dumpster.'

Cooper phoned the local precinct house to check this out.

'Let's have him call Duncan,' Sellitto said, nodding at Vincent. 'We could trace his mobile.'

'His phone won't work. He takes the battery and SIM chip out when we're not actually . . . you know, working.'

Working . . .

'He said you can't trace it that way.'

'Is the phone in his name?'

'No. It's one of those prepaid ones. He buys a new one every few days and throws out the old one.'

'Get the number,' Rhyme ordered. 'Run it with the service providers.'

Mel Cooper called the major mobile companies in the area and had several brief conversations. He hung up and reported, 'East Coast Communications. Prepaid, like he said. Cash purchase. No way to trace it if the battery's out.'

'Hell,' Rhyme muttered.

Sellitto's phone rang. Bo Haumann's Emergency Service Unit teams were on their way. They'd be at the church in a few minutes.

'Sounds like that's our only hope,' Baker said.

He, Sachs and Pulaski hurried out the door to join the tactical operation.

Rhyme, Dance and Sellitto remained in his lab, to try to learn more about Gerald Duncan from Vincent, while Cooper searched databases for any information on him.

'What's his interest in clocks and time and the lunar calendar?' Rhyme asked.

'He collects old clocks and watches. He really was a watchmaker – a hobby, you know. It's not like he has a shop or anything.'

Rhyme said, 'But he might've worked for one at some point. Find out the professional organization of watchmakers. Collectors too.'

Cooper typed on his keyboard. He asked, 'America only?'

Dance asked Vincent, 'What's his nationality?'

'He's American, I guess. He doesn't have an accent or anything.'

After browsing a number of websites Cooper shook his head. 'It's a popular business. The big groups seem to be the Geneva Association of Watchmakers, Jewelers and Goldsmiths, the Association Interprofessionnelle de la Haute Horlogerie in Switzerland; the American Watchmakers' Institute; the Swiss Association of Watch and Jewelry Retailers, also in Switzerland; the British Association of Watch and Clock Collectors; the British Horological Institute; the Employers' Association of the Swiss Watch Industry; and the Federation of the Swiss Watch Industries . . . but there're dozens more.'

'Send them emails,' Sellitto said. 'Ask about Duncan. As a watchmaker or collector.'

'And Interpol,' Rhyme said. Then to Vincent: 'How did you meet?'

The man gave a rambling account about a coincidental, innocent meeting. Kathryn Dance listened and in her calm voice asked a few questions and announced that he was being deceptive. 'The deal is you play straight with us,' she said, leaning forward. Her gaze was cool through her predator glasses.

'Okay, I was just, like, summarizing, you know.'

'We don't want summaries,' Rhyme growled. 'We want to know how the fuck you met him.'

The rapist admitted while it *was* a coincidence, the meeting wasn't so innocent. He gave the details of their initial contact at a restaurant near where Vincent worked. Duncan was checking out one of the men who'd been killed the previous day and Vincent had his eye on a waitress.

What a pair, these two, Rhyme reflected.

Mel Cooper looked up from the computer screen. 'Getting some hits here . . . We've got sixty-eight Gerald Duncans in fifteen midwestern states. I'm running warrants and VICAP first then cross-referencing approximate ages and professions. You can't narrow down the location any more?'

'I would if I could. He never talked about himself.'

Dance nodded. She believed him.

Lon Sellitto asked the question that Rhyme had been about to. 'We know he's targeting specific victims, checking 'em out ahead of time. Why? What's he up to?'

The rapist answered, 'His wife.'

'He's married?'

'Was.'

'Tell us.'

'His wife and him came to New York on vacation a couple years ago. He was at a business dinner somewhere and his wife went to a concert by herself. She was walking back to the hotel on this deserted street and she got hit by a car or truck. The driver took off. She screamed for help but nobody came to save her, nobody even called the police or fire department. The doctor said that she probably lived for ten, fifteen minutes after she was hit. And even somebody who wasn't a doctor could've stopped the bleeding, he said. Just a pressure point or something like that. But nobody helped.'

'Run all the hospitals for admissions under the name Duncan, eighteen to thirty-six months ago,' Rhyme ordered.

But Vincent said, 'Don't bother. Last year he broke into the hospital and stole her chart. The police report too. Bribed a clerk or something. He's been planning this ever since.'

'But why's he picking *these* victims?'

'When the police investigated they got the names of ten people who were nearby when she died. Whether they could have saved her or not, I don't know. But Gerald, he convinced himself they could have. He's spent the past year finding out where they live and what their schedules are. He needed to get them alone so they could die slowly. That's the important thing to him. Like his wife died slowly.'

'The man on the pier Tuesday? Is he dead?'

'He's gotta be. Duncan made him hold on and then cut his arms and just stood there watching him until he fell into the river. He said he tried to swim for a while but then he just stopped moving and floated under the pier.'

'What was his name?'

'I don't remember. Walter somebody. I didn't help him with the first two. I didn't, really.' He glanced at Dance with fear in his eyes.

'What else do you know about Duncan?' she asked.

'That's about it. The only thing he really liked to talk about was time.'

'Time? What about it?'

'Anything, everything. The history of time, how clocks work, about calendars, how people sense time differently. He'd tell me, like, the term "speed up" comes from pendulum clocks. You'd move the weight up on the pendulum to make the clock run faster. "Slow down" – you moved the weight down to slow it . . . With anybody else it would've been just boring. But the way he talked about it, well, you kind of got caught up in what he was saying.'

Cooper looked up from his computer screen. 'We've got a couple of replies from the watchmaker associations. No record of a Gerald Duncan . . . Wait, here's Interpol . . . Nothing there either. And I can't find anything in VICAP.'

Sellitto's phone rang. He took the call and spoke for a few minutes. He eyed the rapist coolly as he talked. Then he disconnected.

'That was your sister's husband,' he said to Vincent.

The man frowned. 'Who?'

'Your sister's husband.'

Vincent shook his head. 'No, you must've talked to the wrong person. My sister's not married.'

'Yes, she is.'

The rapist's eyes were wide. 'Sally Anne's married?'

With a disgusted glance at Vincent, Sellitto said to Rhyme and Dance, 'She was too upset to return the call herself. Her husband did. Thirteen years ago he locked her in the basement of their house for a week while their mother and stepfather were on their honeymoon. His own sister . . . He tied her down and sexually assaulted her repeatedly. He was fifteen, she was thirteen. He did juvie time and was released after counseling. Records were sealed. That's why we had no hits on IAFIS.'

'Married,' Vincent whispered, ashen-faced.

'She's been treated for depression and eating disorders ever since. He was caught stalking her a dozen times, so she got a restraining order. The only contact between them in the past three years is letters he's been sending.'

'He's been threatening her?' Dance asked.

Sellitto muttered, 'Nope. They're love letters. He wanted her to move here and live with him.'

'Oh, man,' muttered the unflappable Mel Cooper.

'Sometimes he'd write recipes in the margins. Sometimes he'd draw porn cartoons. The brother-in-law said if there's anything they can do to make sure he stays in jail forever, they'll do it.' Sellitto looked at the two patrol officers standing behind Vincent. 'Get him out of here.'

The officers helped the big man to his feet and they started out the door. Vincent Reynolds could hardly walk, he was so shaken. 'How could Sally Anne get married? How could she do this to me? We were going to be together forever . . . How could she?'

Chapter
TWENTY-EIGHT

Like assaulting a medieval castle.

Sachs, Baker and Pulaski joined Bo Haumann around the corner from the church in the nondescript Chelsea section of town. The ESU troops had deployed quietly up and down the streets surrounding the place, keeping a low profile.

The church had only enough doors to satisfy the fire code, and steel bars on most of the windows. This would make it difficult for Gerald Duncan to escape, of course, but it also meant that ESU had few options for access. That, in turn, increased the likelihood that the killer had booby-trapped the entrances or would wait for them with a weapon. And the stone walls, two feet thick, also made the risk greater than it might otherwise have been because the Search and Surveillance team's thermal- and sound-sensing equipment was largely useless; they simply couldn't tell if he was inside.

'What's the plan?' asked Amelia Sachs, standing next to Bo Haumann in the alley behind the church. Dennis Baker was beside her, his hand close to his pistol. His eyes danced around the streets and sidewalk, which told Sachs that he hadn't been on a tactical entry for a long time – if ever. She was still pissed about the spying; she wasn't very sympathetic that he was sweating.

Ron Pulaski was nearby, his hand resting on the grip of his Glock. He too rocked nervously on his feet as he gazed at the imposing, sooty structure.

Haumann explained that the teams would do a simple dynamic entry through all doors, after taking them out with explosive charges. There was no choice – the doors were too thick for a battering ram – but charges would clearly announce their presence and give Duncan a chance to prepare at least some defense within the building. What would he do when he heard the explosions and the footsteps of the cops charging inside?

Give up?

A lot of perps do.

But some don't. They either panic or cling to some crazy idea that they can fight their way though a dozen armed officers. Rhyme had told her about Duncan's mission of revenge; she didn't figure somebody that obsessed would be the surrendering type.

Sachs took her position with a side-door entry team while Baker and Pulaski remained at the command post with Haumann.

Through her headset she heard the ESU commander say, 'Entry devices are armed . . . Teams, report, K.'

The A, B and C teams called in that they were ready.

In his raspy voice, Haumann called, 'On my count . . . Five, four, three, two, one.'

Three sharp cracks resounded as the doors blew open simultaneously, setting off car alarms and shaking nearby windows. Officers poured inside.

It turned out that their concern about fortified positions and booby traps had been unfounded. The bad news, though, was that a search of the place made it clear that the

Watchmaker was either one of the luckiest men on earth or had anticipated them yet again. He wasn't here.

'Check this out, Ron.'

Amelia Sachs stood in a doorway of a small, upstairs store-room in the church.

'Freaky,' the young officer offered.

That worked.

They were looking at a number of moon-faced clocks stacked against a stone wall. The faces stared out with their cryptic look, not quite a smile, not quite a leer, as if they knew exactly how much time was allotted for your life and were pleased to be counting down to the final second.

All of them were ticking, a sound that Sachs found unnerving.

She counted five of them. Which meant he had one with him.

Burn her to death . . .

Pulaski was zipping up his Tyvek crime scene suit and strapping his Glock outside the overalls. Sachs told him that she'd walk the grid up here, where Vincent had said the men had been staying. The rookie would take the ground floor of the church.

He nodded, looking uneasily at the dark corridors, the shadows. The blow to his skull the previous year had been severe and a supervisor had wanted to sideline him, put him behind a desk. He'd struggled to come back from the head injury and simply would not let the brass take him off the street. She knew he got spooked sometimes. She could see in his eyes that he was constantly making the decision whether or not to step up to the task in front of him. Even though he always chose to do so, there were some cops, she knew, who wouldn't want to work with him because of this. Sachs, though, would far rather work with somebody who confronted his ghosts every time he went out on the street. That was guts.

She'd never hesitate to have him as a partner.

Then she realized what she'd thought and qualified it: *If* I were going to stay on the force.

Pulaski wiped his palms, which Sachs could see were sweaty, despite the chill, and pulled on latex gloves.

As they divided up the evidence collection equipment she said, 'Hey, heard you got jumped in the garage, running the Explorer scene.'

'Yeah.'

'Hate it when that happens.'

He gave a laugh that meant he understood this was her way of saying it's okay to be nervous. He started for the door.

'Hey, Ron.'

He stopped.

'By the way, Rhyme said you did a great job.'

'He did?'

Not in so many words. But that was Rhyme. Sachs said, 'He sure did. Now, go search the shit out of that scene. I want to nail this bastard.'

He gave a grin. 'You bet.'

Sachs said, 'It's not a Christmas present. It's a job.'

And nodded him downstairs.

She found nothing that suggested who the next victim was but at least there was a significant amount of evidence in the church.

From Vincent Reynolds's room Sachs recovered samples of a dozen different junk foods and sodas, as well as proof of his darker appetites: condoms, duct tape and rags, presumably to use as gags. The place was a mess. It smelled of unwashed clothes.

In Duncan's room Sachs found horological magazines

(without subscription labels), watchmaker's and other tools (including the wire cutters that were probably used to cut the chain-link fence at the first scene) and clothes. Unlike Vincent's this room was eerily pristine and ordered. The bed was so tautly made that a drill instructor would have approved. The clothes hung perfectly in the closet (all the labels removed, she noticed), the space between the hangers exactly the same. Items on the desk were aligned at exact angles to one another. He was careful to leave next to nothing about himself personally; two museum programs, from Boston and Tampa, were hidden up under a trash container, but while they suggested he'd been to those cities, they weren't, of course, where Vincent said he lived, the Midwest. There was also a pet hair roller.

It's like he's wearing a Tyvek suit of his own . . .

She also found some clues that were possibly from the prior crime scenes – a roll of duct tape that would probably match the tape at the alley and that, presumably, was used to gag the victim on the pier. She found an old broom with dirt, fine sand and bits of salt on it. She guessed it was what he'd used to sweep the scene around where Teddy Adams had been killed.

There was also evidence that she hoped might reveal his present location or that related in some way to the next victims. In a small plastic Tupperware container were some coins, three Bic pens, receipts from a parking garage down-town and a drugstore on the Upper West Side, and a book of matches (missing three of them) from a restaurant on the Upper East Side. There were no fingerprints on any of these items. She also found a pair of shoes whose treads were dotted with gaudy green paint, and an empty gallon jug that had contained wood alcohol.

There were no fingerprints but she did find plenty of cotton fibers the same color as those in the Explorer. She then found a plastic bag containing a dozen pairs of the gloves themselves, no store labels or receipts. The bag had no prints on it.

In his search downstairs Ron Pulaski didn't find much but he made a curious discovery: a coating of white powder in a toilet. Tests would tell for certain but he believed it was from a fire extinguisher since he also found a trash bag near the back door, inside of which was the empty carton an extinguisher had been sold in. The rookie had looked over the box carefully but there were no store labels to indicate where it had been purchased.

Why the extinguisher had been discharged was unclear. There was no evidence that anything in the bathroom had been burning.

She had a call patched through to Vincent Reynolds, in the lockup, and he told her that Duncan had recently bought a fire extinguisher. He didn't know why it had been discharged.

After chain-of-custody cards were filled out, Sachs and Pulaski joined Baker, Haumann and the others just inside the front door of the church, where they'd been waiting while the two officers walked the grid. Sachs called Rhyme on the radio and told him and Sellitto what they'd found.

As she recited the evidence, she could hear Rhyme instructing Thom to include it on the charts.

'Boston and Tampa?' the criminalist asked, referring to the museum programs. 'Vincent might be wrong. Hold on.' He had Cooper check with Vital Statistics and DMV for any Gerald Duncans in those cities but, while there were residents with that name, their ages didn't match the perp's.

The criminalist was silent for a moment. Then he said, 'The fire extinguisher . . . I'm betting he made an incendiary device out of it. He used alcohol as the accelerant. There was some on the clock at Lucy Richter's apartment too. That's how he's going to burn the next victim to death.

And what's the one thing about fire extinguishers?'

'Give up,' Sachs replied.

'They're invisible. One could be sitting right next to some-body and they'd never think twice about it.'

Baker said, 'I say we take whatever clues we've found here and divide them up, hope one of them leads us to the next victim. We've got receipts, those matches, the shoes.'

Rhyme's voice crackled over the radio, 'Whatever you do, make it fast. According to Vincent, if he's not at the church, he's on his way to the next victim. He might already be there by now.'

THE WATCHMAKER

CRIME SCENE ONE

Location:
- Repair pier in Hudson River, 22nd Street.

Victim:
- Identity unknown.
- Male.
- Possibly middle-aged or older, and may have coronary condition (presence of anticoagulants in blood).
- No other drugs, infection or disease in blood.
- Coast Guard and ESU divers checking for body and evidence in New York Harbor.
- Checking missing persons' reports.
- Recovered jacket in New York Harbor. Bloody sleeves. Macy's, size 44. No other clues, no sign of body.

Perp:
- See below.

M.O.:
- Perp forced victim to hold on to deck, over water, cut fingers or wrists until he fell.
- Time of attack: between 6 P.M. Monday and 6 A.M. Tuesday.

Evidence:
- Blood type AB positive.
- Fingernail torn, unpolished, wide.
- Portion of chain-link fence cut with common wire cutters, untraceable.
- Clock. See below.
- Poem. See below.
- Fingernail markings on deck.
- No discernible trace, no fingerprints, no footprints, no tire tread marks.

CRIME SCENE TWO

Location:
- Alley off Cedar Street, near

Broadway, behind three commercial buildings (back doors closed at 8:30 to 10 P.M.) and one government administration building (back door closed at 6 P.M.).
- Alley is a cul-de-sac. Fifteen feet wide by one hundred and four feet long, surfaced in cobblestones, body was fifteen feet from Cedar Street.

Victim:
- Theodore Adams.
- Lived in Battery Park.
- Freelance copywriter.
- No known enemies.
- No warrants, state or federal.
- Checking for a connection with buildings around alley. None found.

Perp:
- The Watchmaker.
- Male.
- No database entries for the Watchmaker.

M.O.:
- Dragged from vehicle to alley, where iron bar was suspended over him. Eventually crushed throat.
- Awaiting medical examiner's report to confirm.
- No evidence of sexual activity.
- Time of death: approximately 10:15 P.M. to 11 P.M. Monday night. Medical examiner to confirm.

Evidence:
- Clock.
  - No explosives, chemical—or bioagents.
  - Identical to clock at pier.
  - No fingerprints, minimal trace.
  - Arnold Products, Framingham, MA.
  - Sold by Hallerstein's Timepieces, Manhattan.
- Poem left by perp at both scenes.
  - Computer printer, generic paper, HP LaserJet ink.
  - Text:
    *The full Cold Moon is in the sky,
    shining on the corpse of earth,
    signifying the hour to die
    and end the journey begun at   birth.*
        – The Watchmaker
  - Not in any poetry data-bases; probably his own.
  - Cold Moon is lunar month, the month of death.
- $60 in pocket, no serial number leads; prints nega-tive.
- Fine sand used as 'obscuring agent'. Sand was generic. Because he's returning to the scene?
- Metal bar, 81 pounds, is needle-eye span. Not being used in construction across from the alleyway. No other source found.
- Duct tape, generic, but cut precisely, unusual. Exactly the same lengths.
- Thallium sulfate (rodent poison) found in sand.

- Soil containing fish protein – from perp, not victim.
- Very little trace found.
- Brown fibers, probably automotive carpeting.

Other:
- Vehicle.
  - Ford Explorer, about three years old. Brown carpet. Tan.
  - Review of license tags of cars in area Tuesday morning reveals no warrants. No tickets issued Monday night.
- Checking with Vice about prostitutes, re: witness.
  - No leads.

INTERVIEW WITH HALLERSTEIN

Perp:
- EFIT composite picture of the Watchmaker – late forties, early fifties, round face, double chin, thick nose, unusually light blue eyes. Over 6 feet tall, lean, hair black, medium length, no jewelry, dark clothes. No name.
- Knows great deal about clocks and watches and which timepieces had been sold at recent auctions and were at current horological exhibits in the city.
- Threatened dealer to keep quiet.
- Bought 10 clocks. For 10 victims?
- Paid cash.

- Wanted moon face on clock, wanted loud tick.

Evidence:
- Source of clocks was Hallerstein's Timepieces, Flatiron District.
- No prints on cash paid for clocks, no serial number hits. No trace on money.
- Called from pay phones.

CRIME SCENE THREE

Location:
- 481 Spring Street.

Victim:
- Joanne Harper.
- No apparent motive.
- Didn't know second victim, Adams.

Perp:
- The Watchmaker.
- Assistant.
  - Probably man spotted earlier by victim, at her shop.
  - White, heavyset, in sunglasses, cream-colored parka and cap. Was driving the SUV.

M.O.:
- Picked locks to get inside.
- Intended method of attack unknown. Possibly planning to use florist's wire.

Evidence:
- Fish protein came from Joanne's (orchid fertilizer).
- Thallium sulfate nearby.
- Florist's wire, cut in precise

lengths. (To use as murder weapon?)
- Clock.
  - Same as others. No nitrates.
  - No trace.
- No note or poem.
- No footprints, fingerprints, weapons or anything else left behind.
- Black flakes – roofing tar.
  - Checking ASTER thermal images of New York for possible sources.
    - Results inconclusive.

Other:
- Perp was checking out victim earlier than attack. Targeting her for a purpose. What?
- Have police scanner. Changing frequency.
- Vehicle.
  - Tan SUV.
  - No tag number.
  - Putting out Emergency Vehicle Locator.
  - 423 owners of tan Explorers in area. Cross-reference against criminal warrants. Two found. One owner too old; other is in jail on drug charges.
    - Owned by the man in jail.

WATCHMAKER'S EXPLORER

Location:
- Found in garage, Hudson River and Houston Street.

Evidence:
- Explorer owned by man in jail. Had been confiscated, and

stolen from lot, awaiting auction.
- Parked in open. Not near exit.
- Crumbs from corn chips, potato chips, pretzels, chocolate candy. Bits of peanut butter crackers. Stains from soda, regular, not diet.
- Box of Remington .32-caliber auto pistol ammo, seven rounds missing. Gun is possible Autauga Mk II.
- Book – *Extreme Interrogation Techniques*. Blueprint for his murder methods? No helpful information from publisher.
- Strand of gray-and-black hair, probably woman's.
- No prints at all, throughout entire vehicle.
- Beige cotton fibers from gloves.
- Sand matching that used in alleyway.
- Smooth-soled size-13 shoe print.

CRIME SCENE FOUR

Location:
- Barrow Street, Greenwich Village.

Victim:
- Lucy Richter.

Perp:
- The Watchmaker.
- Assistant.

M.O.:
- Planned means of death unknown.
- Entry/exit routes not determined.

Evidence:
- Clock.
  - Same as others.
  - Left in bathroom.
  - No explosives.
  - Wood alcohol stain, no other trace.
- No note or poem.
- No recent roof tarring.
- No fingerprints or shoe prints.
- No distinctive trace.
- Wool fibers from shearling jacket or coat.

INTERVIEW WITH VINCENT REYNOLDS AND SEARCH OF CHURCH

Location:
- 10th Avenue and 24th Street.

Perp:
- The Watchmaker:
  - Name is Gerald Duncan.
  - Businessman from 'the Midwest', specifics unknown.
  - Wife died in NY; he's murdering for revenge.
  - Armed with pistol and box cutter.
  - His phone can't be traced.
  - Collects old clocks and watches.
  - Searching watchmakers and horological organizations.
    - No immediate hits.
  - No info from Interpol or criminal information databases.
- Assistant:
  - Vincent Reynolds.
  - Temp employee.
  - Lives in New Jersey.
  - History of sexual assaults.

Evidence:
- Five additional clocks, identical to others. One missing.
- In Vincent's room:
  - Junk food, sodas.
  - Condoms.
  - Duct tape.
  - Rags (gags?).
- In Duncan's room:
  - Horological magazines.
  - Tools.
  - Clothes.
  - Programs from Tampa and Boston art museums.
  - Additional duct tape.
  - Old broom with dirt, sand and salt.
  - Three Bic pens.
  - Coins.
  - Receipt from parking garage, downtown.
  - Receipt from drugstore on Upper West Side.
  - Book of matches from restaurant on Upper East Side.
  - Shoes with bright green paint.
  - Empty gallon jug of alcohol.
  - Pet hair roller.
  - Beige gloves.
- No fingerprints.
- Fire extinguisher residue.
- Empty box that contained fire extinguisher.
- Extinguisher to be alcohol incendiary device?

Other:
- Murdered a student near the church, was a witness.
  - Local precinct is checking.
- Vehicle is a stolen, dark blue Buick.

- Murdered driver.
- Searching – carjackings, homicides, missing persons.
- Emergency Vehicle Locator ordered; no hits yet.

Sarah Stanton walked quickly over the frozen sidewalk back to the Midtown office building where she worked, clutching her Starbucks latte and a chocolate chip cookie – a guilty pleasure, but a reward for what would be a long day at the office.

Not that she needed a tasty incentive to get back to her workstation; she loved her job. Sarah was an estimator for a large flooring and interior design company. The mother of an eight-year-old, she'd gone back to work a few years earlier than planned, thanks to a tough divorce. She'd started as a receptionist and moved her way up quickly to become the head estimator for the company.

The work was demanding, a lot of numbers – but the company was good and she liked the people she worked with (well, most of them). And she had flexibility with her hours, since she was in the field a lot, meeting with clients. This was important because she had to get her son dressed and ready for school, then escort him all the way to Ninety-fifth Street by nine A.M. and then head back to Midtown for her job, the timetable subject always to the whims of the Metropolitan Transit Authority. Today she would work more than ten hours; tomorrow, she was taking off entirely to go Christmas shopping with her boy.

Sarah swiped her entry card and pushed through the back door of the building, then performed her afternoon workout routine – walking up the stairs to her office rather than use the elevator. The company took up all of the third floor but her workstation was in a smaller office, which occupied only a portion of the second floor. This office was quiet, housing only four employees, but Sarah preferred that. The bosses rarely came down here and she could get her work done without interruption.

She climbed to the landing and paused. She reached for the door handle, thinking as she nearly always did: Why did these doors open without any kind of lock from the stairwell side? It'd be pretty easy for somebody—

She jumped, hearing a faint tap of metal. Spinning around, Sarah saw no one.

And . . . was that the sound of breathing?

Was somebody hurt?

Should she go see? Or call security?

'Is anyone there? Hello?'

Only silence.

Probably nothing, she thought. And stepped into the corridor that led to the back door of her office. Sarah unlocked the door and walked down the long corridor of the company.

Shedding her coat and setting the coffee and cookie on her desk, she sat down at her workstation, glancing at her computer.

Odd, she thought. On the screen was the window that read, 'Date and Time Properties'.

This was the utility in the Windows XP operating system that you used to set the date and time and time zone of your computer. It showed a calendar with the day's date indicated and, to the right, both an analog clock with sweep hands and below it a digital clock, both ticking off the seconds.

The screen hadn't been there before she'd made the run to Starbucks.

Had it popped up by itself? she wondered. Why? Maybe somebody'd used her computer while she was away, though she had no idea who it might be or why.

No matter. She closed the window on the screen and scooted forward.

She glanced down. What was that?

Sarah saw a fire extinguisher under her desk. It hadn't been there earlier either. The company was always doing weird things like this. Putting in new lighting, coming up with evacuation plans, rearranging furniture, for no apparent reason.

Now, fire extinguishers.

Probably something else we have the terrorists to thank for.

Taking a fast look at her son's picture, feeling comfort in seeing his smile, she set her purse under her desk and unwrapped her cookie.

Lieutenant Dennis Baker walked slowly down the deserted street. He was south of Hell's Kitchen in a largely industrial area on the west side.

As he'd suggested, the officers had divided up the clues found at the church in their hunt for the Watchmaker. He'd told Sachs and Haumann that he'd remembered a warehouse that was being painted with that same shade of sickly green paint found on the shoes in the Watchmaker's room. While the rest of the team were tracking down other leads, he'd come here.

The massive building stretched along the street, dark, abandoned, bleak even in the sharp sunlight. The lower six or seven feet of the grimy brick walls were covered with graffiti and half the windows were broken – some even shot out, it seemed. On the roof was a faded sign, *Preston Moving and Storage*, in an old-style typeface.

The front doors, painted that green color, were locked and chained shut but Baker found a side entrance, half hidden behind a Dumpster. It was open. He looked up and down the street then pulled the door open and stepped inside. Baker started through the dim place, lit only by slanting shafts of light. The smell was of rotting cardboard and mildew and heating oil. He drew his pistol. It felt awkward in his hand. He'd never fired a single shot in the line of duty.

Walking silently along the corridor, Baker approached the facility's main storage area, a massive open space whose floor was dotted with pools of greasy standing water and trash. Plenty of condoms too, he noticed in disgust. This was probably the least romantic site for a liaison you could imagine.

A flash of light from the offices lining the wall caught his attention. His eyes were growing accustomed to the dimness and as he walked closer he noticed a burning desk lamp inside a small room. There was one other thing he could see, as well.

One of the black, moon-faced clocks – the Watchmaker's calling cards.

Baker started forward.

Which is when he stepped on a large patch of grease he hadn't been able to see in the darkness and went down hard on his side, gasping. He dropped his pistol, which slid away across the filthy concrete floor. He winced in pain.

It was at this moment that a man jogged up fast behind him from one of the side corridors.

Baker glanced up into the eyes of Gerald Duncan, the Watchmaker.

The killer bent down.

And he offered his hand, helping Baker up. 'You all right?'

'Just got the wind knocked out of me. Careless. Thanks, Gerry.'

Duncan stepped away, retrieved Baker's pistol and handed it to him. 'You didn't really need that.' He laughed.

Baker put the gun back in his holster. 'Wasn't sure who else I might run into, other than you. Spooky place.'

The Watchmaker gestured toward the office. 'Come on inside. I'll tell you exactly what's going to happen to her.'

What was going to happen meant how the men were going to commit murder.

And the 'her' he was referring to was an NYPD detective named Amelia Sachs.

Chapter
TWENTY-NINE

Sitting on one of the chairs in the warehouse office, Dennis Baker brushed at his slacks, now stained from the fall.

Italian, expensive. Shit.

He said to Duncan, 'We've got Vincent Reynolds in custody and we took the church.'

Duncan would know this, of course, since he himself had made the call alerting the police that the Watchmaker's partner was wheeling a grocery cart around the West Village (Baker had been surprised, and impressed, that Kathryn Dance had tipped to Vincent even before Duncan dimed out his supposed partner).

And Duncan had known too that the rapist would give up the church under pressure.

'Took a little longer than I thought,' said Baker, 'but he caved.'

'Of course he did,' Duncan said. 'He's a worm.'

Duncan had planned the sick fuck's capture all along; it was necessary to feed the cops the information to make them believe that the Watchmaker was a vengeful psychopath, not the hired murderer he actually was. And Vincent was key to pointing the police in the right direction for the completion of Duncan's plan.

And that plan was as elaborate and elegant as the finest timepiece. Its purpose was to halt Amelia Sachs's investigation threatening to unearth an extortion ring that Baker had been running from the 118th Precinct.

Dennis Baker came from a family of law enforcers. His father had been a transit cop, who retired early after he took a spill down a subway station stairwell. An older brother worked for the Department of Corrections and Baker's uncle was a cop in a small town in Suffolk County, where the family was from. Initially he'd had no interest in the profession – the handsome, well-built young man wanted big bucks. But after losing every penny in a failed recycling business, Baker decided to join up. He moved from Long Island to New York City and tried to reinvent himself as a policeman.

But coming to the job later in life – and the cocky, TV-cop style he adopted – worked against him, alienating brass and fellow officers. Even his family history in law enforcement didn't help (his relatives fell low in the blue hierarchy). Baker could make a living as a cop but he wasn't destined for a corner office in the Big Building.

So he decided to go for the bucks after all. But not via business. He'd use his badge.

When he first started shaking down businessmen he wondered if he'd feel guilty about it.

Uh-uh. Not a bit.

The only problem was that to support his lifestyle – which included a taste for wine, food and beautiful women – he needed more than just a thousand or so a week from Korean wholesalers and fat men who owned pizza parlors in Queens. So Baker, a former partner and some cops from the 118th came up with a plan for a lucrative extortion ring. Baker's cohorts would steal a small amount of drugs from the evidence lockers or would score some coke or smack on the street. They'd target the children of rich businessmen in Manhattan clubs and plant the drugs on them. Baker would talk to the parents, who'd be told that for a six-figure payment, the arrest reports would disappear. If they didn't pay, the kids'd go to jail. He'd also occasionally plant drugs on businessmen themselves.

Rather than just taking the money, though, they'd arrange for the victims to lose it in sham business deals, like with Frank Sarkowski, or in fake poker games in Vegas or Atlantic City – the approach they took with Ben Creeley. This would provide the marks with a reasonable explanation as to why they were suddenly two or three hundred thousand dollars poorer.

But then Dennis Baker made a mistake. He got lazy. It wasn't easy finding the right marks for the scam and he decided to go back to some of the earlier targets for a second installment of extortion money.

Some paid the second time. But two of them – Sarkowski and Creeley – were businessmen with pretty tough hides, and while they were willing to pay once to get Baker out of their hair, they drew the line at a second payment. One threatened to go to the police, and one to the press. In early November Baker and a cop from the 118th had kidnapped Sarkowski and driven him to an industrial section of Queens, near where a client of his company had a factory. He'd been shot, the crime staged to look like a mugging. Several weeks later Baker and the same cop had later broken into Creeley's high-rise, strung a rope around the businessman's neck and tossed him off the balcony.

They'd stolen or destroyed the men's personal files, books and diaries – anything that might've led back to Baker and his scam. As for the police reports, there was virtually nothing in Creeley's that was incriminating but the Sarkowski file contained references to evidence that a sharp investigator might draw some troubling conclusions from. So one of the people involved in the plan had engineered its disappearance.

Baker thought the deaths would go unnoticed and they continued with their scam – until a young policewoman showed up. Detective Third-Grade Amelia Sachs didn't believe that Benjamin Creeley had committed suicide and started looking into the death.

There was no stopping the woman. They had no choice but to kill her. With Sachs dead or incapacitated Baker doubted that anyone else would follow up on the cases as fervently as she was. The problem, of course, was that if she *were* to die, Lincoln Rhyme would deduce immediately that her death was related to the St James investigation and then *nothing* would stop him and Sellitto from pursuing the killers.

So Baker needed Sachs to die for a reason unrelated to the 118th Precinct crimes.

Baker put some feelers out to a few organized crime wise guys he knew and soon he heard from Gerald Duncan, a professional killer who could manipulate crime scenes and set up fake motives to steer suspicion completely away from the man or woman hiring him to kill. 'Motive is the one sure way to get yourself caught,' Duncan had explained. 'Eliminate the motive, you eliminate suspicion.'

They'd agreed on a price – brother, the man wasn't cheap – and Duncan had gone to work planning the job.

Duncan tracked down some loser he could use to feed information about the Watchmaker to the police. Vincent Reynolds turned out to be a perfect patsy, soaking up the story Duncan fed him – about going psycho because of a dead wife and killing apathetic citizens.

Then, the previous day, Duncan had put the plan into operation. The Watchmaker killed the first two of the victims, picked at random – some guy he'd kidnapped from West Street in the Village and murdered on the pier and the one in the alley a few hours later. Baker had made sure Sachs was assigned to the case. There were two more attempted murders by the killer – the fact they didn't succeed was irrelevant; the Watchmaker was still one spooky doer, who needed to be stopped fast.

Then Duncan made his next moves: sending Vincent to attack Kathryn Dance, so that the police would believe that the Watchmaker was willing to kill police officers, and setting up Vincent to be captured and dime the Watchmaker out to the police.

It was now time for the final step: The Watchmaker would kill yet another cop, Amelia Sachs, her death entirely the work of a vengeful killer, unrelated to the 118th Precinct investigation.

Duncan now asked, 'She found out you were spying on her?'

Baker nodded. 'You called that right. She's one smart bitch. But I did what you suggested.'

Duncan anticipated that she'd be suspicious of everyone except people she knew personally. He'd explained that when people suspect you, you have to give them another – harmless – reason for your behavior. You simply confess to the lesser crime, act contrite and they're satisfied; you're off the suspect list.

At Duncan's suggestion, Baker asked some officers about Sachs. He heard rumors that she'd been involved with a crooked cop and he'd ginned up an email from someone in the Big Building and used that as a reason to be spying on her. She wasn't happy, but she didn't suspect him of anything worse.

'Here's the plan,' Duncan now explained, showing him a diagram of an office building in Midtown. 'This's where the last victim works. Her name's Sarah Stanton. She's got a cubicle on the second floor. I picked the place because of the layout.

It'll be perfect. I couldn't put one of the clocks there because the police announced the killer was using them – but I pulled up the time and date window on her computer.'

'Good touch.'

Duncan smiled. 'I thought so.' The killer's voice was soft, his words precise, but the tone was filled with the modest pleasure of an artisan showing off a finished piece of furniture or a musical instrument . . . or a watch, Baker reflected.

Duncan explained that he'd dressed like a workman, waited until Sarah went out then planted a fire extinguisher, filled with flammable alcohol. In a few minutes Baker was to call Rhyme or Sellitto and report that he'd found evidence of where the extinguisher bomb was planted. The ESU and bomb squad would then speed to the office, Amelia Sachs too.

'I set the device up so that if she moves the extinguisher a certain way, it'll spray her with alcohol and ignite. Alcohol burns really fast. It'll kill or injure her but won't set fire to the whole office.' The police, he continued, might even disarm the device and save the woman. It wouldn't matter; all that Duncan cared about was getting Amelia Sachs into the office to search the scene.

Sarah's cubicle was at the end of a narrow corridor. Sachs would be searching it alone, as she always did. When she turned her back, Baker, waiting nearby, would shoot her and anybody else present. The weapon he'd use was Duncan's .32 automatic, loaded with bullets from the same box he'd intentionally left in the SUV for the police to find. After shooting Sachs, Baker would break a nearby window, which was fifteen feet above an alleyway. He'd throw the gun out, making it seem as if the Watchmaker had leapt out the window and escaped, dropping the gun. The unusual murder weapon, linked to the rounds found in the Explorer, would leave no doubt that the Watchmaker was the killer.

Sachs would be dead and the investigation into the corruption at the 118th Precinct would grind to a halt.

Duncan said, 'Let some other officers get to her body first but it'd be a nice touch if you pushed them aside and tried to resuscitate her.'

Baker said, 'You think of everything, don't you?'

'What's so miraculous about timepieces,' Duncan said, gazing at the moon-faced clock, 'is that none of them ever has more or fewer parts than is needed to do what the watchmaker intends. Nothing missing, but nothing superfluous.' He added in a soft voice, 'It's pure perfection, wouldn't you say?'

Amelia Sachs and Ron Pulaski were slogging through the cold streets of lower Manhattan, and she was reflecting that sometimes the biggest hurdles in a case weren't from the perps but from bystanders, witnesses and victims.

They were following up on one of the clues that had been uncovered in the church, receipts from a parking garage not far from the pier where the first victim had died. But the attendant was unhelpful. *Lady, no, he no familiar. Nobody look like him I remember. Ahmed – maybe he saw him . . . Oh, but he not here today. No, I don't know his phone number . . .*

And so it went.

Frustrated, Sachs nodded toward a restaurant adjacent to the parking garage. She said, 'Maybe he stopped in there. Let's give it a try.'

Just then her radio crackled. She recognized Sellitto's voice. 'Amelia, you copy?'

She grabbed Pulaski's arm and turned up the volume, so they both could hear. 'Go ahead, K.'

'Where are you?'

'Downtown. The parking garage didn't pan out. We're going to canvass a couple of restaurants.'

'Forget it. Get up to Three Two Street and Seven Avenue.

Fast. Dennis Baker's found a lead. Looks like the next vic's in an office building there.'

'Who is she?'

'We're not sure exactly. We'll probably have to sweep the whole place. We've got Arson and the bomb squad on the way – she's the one he's going to burn to death. Man, I hope we're in time. Anyway, get up there now.'

'We'll be there in fifteen minutes.'

The fire department was sending two dozen men and women into the twenty-seven-story Midtown building. And Bo Haumann was assembling five ESU entry teams – expanded ones, six cops each, rather than the typical four – to do a floor-by-floor search.

Sachs's drive here had taken closer to a half hour, thanks to holiday traffic. Not a huge delay but the extra fifteen minutes made a big difference: She'd missed a spot on an entry team. Amelia Sachs was officially a crime scene detective but her heart was also with tactical teams, the ones who went through the perps' doors first.

If they found the Watchmaker here, it would've been her last chance for a takedown before she quit the force. She supposed she'd see some excitement in her new job as security specialist at Argyle, but the local law enforcers would surely get most of the tactical fun.

Sachs and Pulaski now ran from the car to the command post at the back door of the office building.

'Any sign of him?' she asked Haumann.

The grizzled man shook his head. 'Not yet. We had a sequence on a video camera in the lobby of somebody who kind of looked like the composite, carrying a bag. But we don't know if he left or not. There're two back and two side door exits that aren't alarmed and aren't scanned by cameras.'

'You evacuating?' a man's voice asked.

Sachs turned around. It was Detective Dennis Baker.

'Just started,' Haumann explained.

'How'd you find him?' Sachs asked.

Baker said, 'That warehouse with the green paint – he used it as a staging area. I found some notes and a map of this building.'

The policewoman was still angry about Baker's spying on her but solid police work deserves credit and she nodded to him and said, 'Good job.'

'Nothing inspired,' he replied with a smile. 'Just pounding the pavement. And a little bit of luck.' Baker's eyes rose to the building as he pulled his gloves on.

Chapter
THIRTY

Sitting in her cubicle, Sarah Stanton heard another squawk over the building's public address system above her head.

It was a running joke in the office that the company put some kind of filter on the speakers that made the transmissions completely unintelligible. She turned back to her computer, calling, 'What're they saying? I can't make heads or tails of it.'

'Some announcement,' one of her coworkers called.

Duh.

'They keep *doing* that. Pisses me off. Is it a fire drill?'

'No idea.'

A moment later she heard the whoop of the fire alarm.

Guess it is.

After 9/11 the alarm had gone off every month or so. The first couple times she'd played along and trooped downstairs like everybody else. But today the temperature was in the low twenties and she had way too much work to do. Besides, if it really was a fire and the exits were blocked she could just jump out the window. Her office was only on the second floor.

She returned to her screen.

But then Sarah heard voices at the far end of the corridor

that led to her cubicle. There was an urgency about the sound. And something else – the jangling of metal. Firemen's equipment? she wondered.

Maybe something really was happening.

Heavy footsteps behind her, approaching. She turned around and saw policemen in dark outfits, with guns. Police? Oh, God, was it a terrorist attack? All she thought about was getting to her son's school, picking him up.

'We're evacuating the building,' the cop announced.

'Is it terrorists?' somebody called. 'Has there been another attack?'

'No.' He didn't explain further. 'Everybody move out in an orderly fashion. Take your coats, leave everything else.'

Sarah relaxed. She wouldn't have to worry about her son.

Another of the officers called, 'We're looking for fire extinguishers. Are there any in this area? Don't touch them. Just let us know. I repeat, do not touch them!'

So there *is* a fire, she thought, pulling on her coat.

Then she reflected that it was curious that the fire department would use the company's extinguishers on a fire. Didn't they have their own? And why should they be so concerned that we'd use one? Not like you need special training.

I repeat, do not touch them! . . .

The policeman looked into an office near Sarah's workstation.

'Oh, Officer? You want an extinguisher?' she asked. 'I've got one right here.'

And she pulled the heavy red cylinder off the floor.

'No!' cried the man and he leaped toward her.

Sachs winced as the transmission crackled loudly through her earpiece. 'Fire and containment team, second floor, southeast corner office. K. Lanam Flooring and Interiors. Now! Move, move, move!'

A dozen firefighters and officers from the bomb squad shouldered their equipment and sprinted fast toward the rear door.

'Status?' Haumann shouted into his microphone.

All they could hear were harried voices over the raw howl of the fire alarm.

'Do you have detonation?' the head of ESU repeated urgently.

'I don't see smoke,' Pulaski said.

Dennis Baker stared up at the second floor. He shook his head.

'If it's alcohol,' one of the fire chiefs said, 'there won't be smoke until the secondary materials ignite.' He added evenly, 'Or her hair and skin.'

Sachs continued to scan the windows, clenching her fists. Was the woman dying in agony now? With police officers or firemen alongside her?

'Come on,' Baker whispered.

Then a voice clattered through the radio: 'We've got the device . . . We've . . . Yeah, we've got it. It didn't detonate.'

Sachs closed her eyes.

'Thank God,' Baker said.

People were streaming out of the office building now, under the gaze of ESU and patrol officers who were looking for Duncan, comparing the composite pictures with the faces of workers.

An officer led a woman up to Sachs, Baker and Pulaski, just as Sellitto joined them.

The potential victim, Sarah Stanton, explained that she'd found a fire extinguisher under her desk; it hadn't been there earlier and she hadn't seen who'd left it. Somebody in the office remembered seeing a workman in a uniform nearby but couldn't remember details and didn't recognize the composite or recall where he'd gone.

'Status of the device?' Haumann called.

An officer radioed, 'Didn't see a timer but the pressure gauge on the top was blank. That could be the detonator. And I can smell alcohol. Bomb squad's got it in a containment vessel. They're taking it up to Rodman's Neck. We're still sweeping for the perp.'

'Any sign of him?' Baker asked.

'Negative. There're two fire stairwells and the elevators. He could've gotten out that way. And we've got four or five other companies on that floor. He might've gotten into one of them. We'll search 'em in a minute or two, as soon as we get an all-clear for devices.'

Ten minutes later officers reported that there were no other bombs in the building.

Sachs interviewed Sarah, then called Rhyme and told him the status of the case so far. The woman didn't know the other victims and had never heard of Gerald Duncan. She was very upset that the man's wife might've been killed outside her apartment, though she remembered nothing of any fatal accidents in the area.

Finally Haumann told them that all of his officers had finished the sweep; the Watchmaker had escaped.

'Hell,' Dennis Baker muttered. 'We were so close.'

Discouraged, Rhyme said, 'Well, walk the grid and tell me what you find.'

They signed off. Haumann sent two teams to stake out the warehouse that Duncan had used as a staging site in case the killer returned there and Sachs dressed in the white Tyvek bodysuit and grabbed a metal suitcase containing basic evidence collection and preservation equipment.

'I'll help,' Pulaski said, also dressing in the white overalls.

She handed him the suitcase and she picked up another one.

On the second floor, she paused and surveyed the hallway. After photographing it Sachs entered Lanam Flooring and proceeded to Sarah Stanton's workstation.

She and Pulaski set up the suitcases and extracted the basic evidence collection equipment: bags, tubes, swabs, adhesive rollers for trace, electrostatic footprint sheets and latent-print chemicals and equipment.

'What can I do?' Pulaski asked. 'You want me to search the stairwells?'

She debated. They'd have to be searched eventually but she decided that it would be better to run them herself; they were the most logical entry and exit routes for the Watchmaker and she wanted to make certain that no evidence was missed. Sachs surveyed the layout of Sarah's cubicle and then noticed an empty workstation next to it. It was possible that the Watchmaker had waited there until he had a chance to plant the bomb. Sachs told the rookie, 'Run that cubicle.'

'You got it.' He stepped into the cubicle, pulled out his flashlight and began walking a perfect grid. She caught him sniffing the air too, another of Lincoln Rhyme's dictates for crime scene officers searching. This boy was going to go places, she reflected.

Sachs stepped into the cubicle where they'd found the device. She heard a noise and glanced back. It was only Dennis Baker. He came up the corridor and stopped about twenty feet from the cubicles, far enough away so there was no risk of contaminating the scene.

She wasn't sure exactly why he was here but, since they still weren't sure where the Watchmaker was, she was grateful for his presence.

Search well but watch your back . . .

This was the difference:

Detective Dennis Baker – along with a cop from the 118th – had murdered Benjamin Creeley and Frank Sarkowski. It had been tough but they'd done it without hesitation. And he was prepared to kill any other civilians who threatened their extortion scheme. No problem at all. Five million dollars in cash – their haul to date – buries a lot of guilt.

But Baker had never killed a fellow cop.

Frowning, fidgeting, he was watching Amelia Sachs and the kid, Pulaski, who also presented an easy target.

A big difference.

This was killing family members, fellow officers.

But the sad truth was that Sachs and, by association, Pulaski, could destroy his life.

And so there was no debate.

He now studied the scene. Yes, Duncan had it planned perfectly. There was the window. He glanced out. The alley, fifteen feet below, was deserted. And next to him was the gray metal chair the killer had told him about, the one he'd pitch through the window after killing the officers. There was the large air-conditioning intake vent, whose grate he'd remove after the shots, to make it appear that the Watchmaker had been hiding inside.

A deep breath.

Okay, it's time. He had to act fast, before anyone else came onto the scene. Amelia Sachs had sent the other officers into the main hallway but someone could return here at any minute.

He took the .32 and quietly pulled back the slide to make certain a bullet was in the chamber. Holding the gun behind his back, he eased closer. He was staring at Sachs, who moved around the crime scene almost like a dancer. Precise, fluid, lost in concentration, as she searched. It was beautiful to watch.

Baker tore himself out of this reverie.

Who first? he debated.

Pulaski was ten feet from him, Sachs twenty, both facing away.

Logically, Pulaski should be the first one, being closer. But Baker had learned from Lincoln Rhyme about Sachs's skill as a marksman. She could draw and fire in seconds. The kid had probably never even fired his weapon in combat. He might get his hand on his pistol after Baker killed Sachs, but the rookie would die before he could draw.

A few breaths.

Amelia Sachs unwittingly cooperated. She stood up from where she'd been crouching. Her back presented a perfect target. Baker pointed his gun high on her spine and squeezed the trigger.

Chapter
THIRTY-ONE

To most people the sound would be a simple metallic click, lost in the dozen other ambient noises of a big-city office building.

To Amelia Sachs, though, it was clearly the spring-activated firing pin of an automatic weapon striking the primer cap of a malfunctioning bullet, or someone dry-firing a gun. She'd heard the distinctive sound a hundred times – from her own pistols and her fellow officers'.

This click was followed with what usually came next – the shooter working the slide to eject the bad round and chamber the next one in the clip. In many cases – like now – the maneuver was particularly frantic, the shooter needed to clear the weapon instantly and get a new bullet ready fast. It could be a matter of life and death.

This all registered in a fraction of a second. Sachs dropped the roller she was using to collect trace. Her right hand slammed to her hip – she always knew the exact place where her holster rested – and an instant later she spun around, hunched in a combat shooting position, her Glock in her hand, facing where the sound had come from.

She saw in her periphery, to her right, Ron Pulaski, standing up in the next office, looking at her weapon, alarmed, wondering what she was doing.

Twenty feet away was Dennis Baker, his eyes wide. In his gloved hand was a tiny pistol, a .32, she thought, pointed her way, as he worked the slide. She noted that it was an Autauga MK II, the type of gun that Rhyme speculated the Watchmaker might have.

Baker blinked. Couldn't speak for a moment. 'I heard something,' he said quickly. 'I thought he'd come back, the Watchmaker.'

'You pulled the trigger.'

'No, I was just chambering a round.'

She glanced at the floor, where the bum shell lay. The only reason for it to be there was if he'd tried to shoot, then ejected the defective bullet.

Taking the tiny .32 in his left hand, Baker lowered his right. It strayed to his side. 'We have to be careful. I think he's back.'

Sachs centered the sights directly on Baker's chest.

'Don't do it, Dennis,' she said, nodding toward his hip, where his regulation pistol rested. 'I *will* fire. I'm assuming you've got armor under your suit. My first slug'll be on your chest but two and three'll go higher. It won't be nice.'

'I . . . You don't understand.' His eyes were wide, panicked. 'You have to believe me.'

Wasn't that one of the key phrases that signaled deception, according to Kathryn Dance?

'What's going on?' Pulaski asked.

'Stay there, Ron,' Sachs ordered. 'Don't pay attention to a thing he says. Draw your weapon.'

'Pulaski,' Baker said, 'she's going nuts. Something's wrong.'

But from the corner of her eye she saw the rookie pull his weapon and aim it in Baker's direction.

'Dennis, set the thirty-two on the table. Then with your left hand take your service piece by the grip – thumb and index finger only. Set it down too then move back five steps. Lie face-down. Okay. You clear on that?'

'You don't understand.'

She said calmly, 'I don't need to understand. I need you to do what I'm telling you.'

'But—'

'And I need you to do it now.'

'You're crazy,' Baker snapped. 'You've had it in for me ever since you found out I was checking into you and your old boyfriend. You're trying to discredit me . . . Pulaski, she's going to kill me. She's gone rogue. Don't let her bring you down too.'

Pulaski said, 'You've been apprised of Detective Sachs's instructions. I'll disarm you if it's necessary. Now, sir, what's it going to be?'

Several seconds passed. It seemed like hours. Nobody moved.

'Fuck.' Baker set the pistols where he'd been told and lowered himself to the floor. 'You're both in deep shit.'

'Cuff him,' Sachs told Pulaski.

She covered Baker while the bewildered rookie got the man's hands behind him and ratcheted on the cuffs.

'Search him.'

Sachs grabbed her Motorola. 'Detective Five Eight Eight Five to Haumann. Respond, K.'

'Go ahead, K.'

'We've got a new development here. I've got somebody in cuffs I need escorted downstairs.'

'What's going on?' the ESU head asked. 'Is it the perp?'

'That's a good question,' she replied, holstering her pistol.

With this latest twist in the case, a new person was present in front of the Midtown office building where Detective Dennis Baker had apparently just attempted to kill Amelia Sachs and Ron Pulaski.

Using the touch-pad controller, Lincoln Rhyme maneuvered the red Storm Arrow wheelchair along the sidewalk to the building's entrance. Baker sat in the back of a nearby squad car, cuffed and shackled. His face was white. He stared straight ahead.

At first he'd claimed that Sachs was targeting him because of the Nick Carelli situation. Then Rhyme decided to check with the brass. He asked the senior NYPD official who'd sent the email about it. It turned out that it was *Baker* who'd brought up a concern about Sachs's possible connection with a crooked cop and the brass had never sent the email at all; Baker'd written it himself. He'd created the whole thing as cover in case Sachs caught him following or checking up on her.

Using the touch pad, Rhyme eased closer to the building, where Sellitto and Haumann had set up their command post. He parked and Sellitto explained what had happened upstairs. But added, 'I don't get it. Just don't get it.' The heavy detective rubbed his bare hands together. He glanced up at the clear, windy sky as if he'd just realized it was one of the chilliest months on record. When he was on a case, hot and cold didn't really register.

'You find anything on him?' Rhyme asked.

'Just the thirty-two and latex gloves,' Pulaski said. 'And some personal effects.'

A moment later Amelia Sachs joined them, holding a carton containing a dozen plastic evidence bags. She'd been searching Baker's car. 'It's getting better by the minute, Rhyme. Check this out.' She showed Rhyme and Sellitto the bags one by one. They contained cocaine, fifty thousand in cash, some old clothing, receipts from clubs and bars in Manhattan, including the St James. She lifted one bag that seemed to contain nothing. On closer examination, though, he could see fine fibers.

'Carpeting?' he asked.

'Yep. Brown.'

'Bet they match the Explorer's.'

'That's what I'm thinking.'

Another link to the Watchmaker.

Rhyme nodded, staring at the plastic bag, which rippled in the chill wind. He felt that burst of satisfaction that occurred when the pieces of the puzzle started to come together. He turned to the squad car where Baker sat and called through the half-open window. 'When were you assigned to the One One Eight?'

The man stared back at the criminalist. 'Fuck you. You think I'm saying anything to you pricks? This is bullshit. Somebody planted all that on me.'

Rhyme said to Sellitto, 'Call Personnel. I want to know his prior assignments.'

Sellitto did and, after a brief conversation, looked up and said, 'Bingo. He was at the One One Eight for two years. Narcotics and Homicide. Promoted out to the Big Building three years ago.'

'How did you meet Duncan?'

Baker hunkered down in the backseat and returned to his job of staring straight ahead.

'Well, isn't this a tidy little confluence of our cases,' Rhyme said, in good humor.

'A what?' Sellitto barked.

'Confluence. A coming together, Lon. A merger. Don't you do crosswords.'

Sellitto grunted. 'What cases?'

'Obviously, Sachs's case at the One One Eight and the Watchmaker situation. They weren't separate at all. Opposite sides of the same knife blade, you could say.' He was pleased with the metaphor.

His Case and the Other Case . . .

'You want to explain?'

Did he really need to?

Amelia Sachs said, 'Baker was a player in the corruption at the One One Eight. He hired the Watchmaker – well, Duncan – to take me out 'cause I was getting close to him.'

'Which pretty much proves there is indeed something rotten in Denmark.'

Now it was Pulaski's chance not to get it. 'Denmark? The one in Europe?'

'The one in Shakespeare, Ron,' the criminalist said impatiently. And when the young officer grinned blankly Rhyme gave up.

Sachs took over again. 'He means it's proof there was *major* corruption at the One One Eight. Obviously they're doing more than just sitting on investigations for some crew out of Baltimore or Bay Ridge.'

Looking up absently at the office building, Rhyme nodded, oblivious to the cold and the wind. There were some unanswered questions, of course. For instance, Rhyme wasn't sure if Vincent Reynolds really was a partner or was just being set up.

Then there was the matter of where the extortion money was, and Rhyme now asked, 'Who's the one in Maryland? Who're you working with? Was it OC or something else?'

'Are you deaf?' Baker snapped. 'Not a fucking word.'

'Take him to CB,' Sellitto said to the patrol officers standing beside the car. 'Book him on assault with intent for the time being. We'll add some other ornaments later.' As they watched the RMP drive away, Sellitto shook his head. 'Jesus,' the detective muttered. 'Were we lucky.'

'Lucky?' Rhyme grumbled, recalling that he'd said something similar earlier.

'Yeah, that Duncan didn't kill any more vics. And here too – Amelia was a sitting duck. If that piece hadn't misfired . . .' His voice faded before he described the tragedy that had nearly occurred.

Lincoln Rhyme believed in luck about as much as he believed in ghosts and flying saucers. He started to ask what the hell did luck have to do with anything, but the words never came out of his mouth.

Luck . . .

Suddenly a dozen thoughts, like bees escaping from a jostled hive, zipped around him. He was frowning. 'That's odd . . .' His voice faded. Finally he whispered, 'Duncan.'

'Something wrong, Linc? You okay?'

'Rhyme?' Sachs asked.

'Shhhhh.'

Using the touch-pad controller he turned slowly in a circle, glanced in a nearby alleyway, then at the bags and boxes of evidence Sachs had collected. He gave a faint laugh. He ordered, 'I want Baker's gun.'

'His service piece?' Pulaski asked.

'Of *course* not. The other one. The thirty-two. Where is it? Now, hurry!'

Pulaski found the weapon in a plastic bag. He returned with it.

'Field-strip it.'

'Me?' the rookie asked.

'Her.' Rhyme nodded at Sachs.

Sachs spread out a piece of plastic on the sidewalk, replaced her leather gloves with latex ones and in a few seconds had the gun dismantled, the parts laid out on the ground.

'Hold up the pieces one by one.'

Sachs did this. Their eyes met. She said, 'Interesting.'

'Okay. Rookie?'

'Yessir?'

'I've got to talk to the medical examiner. Track him down for me.'

'Well, sure. I should call?'

Rhyme's sigh was accompanied by a stream of breath flowing

from his mouth. 'You *could* try a telegram, you *could* go knock, knock, knockin' on his door. But I'll bet the best approach is to use . . . your . . . *phone*. And don't take no for an answer. I *need* him.'

The young man gripped his cell phone and started punching numbers into the keypad.

'Linc,' Sellitto said, 'what's this—'

'And I need you to do something too, Lon.'

'Yeah, what?'

'There's a man across the street watching us. In the mouth of the alley.'

Sellitto turned. 'Got him.' The guy was lean, wearing sunglasses despite the dusk, a hat and jeans and a leather jacket. 'Looks familiar.'

'Invite him to come over here. I'd like to ask him a few questions.'

Sellitto laughed. 'Kathryn Dance's really having an effect on you, Linc. I thought you didn't trust witnesses.'

'Oh, I think in this case it'd be good to make an exception.'

Shrugging, the big detective asked, 'Who is he?'

'I could be wrong,' Rhyme said with the tone of a man who believed he rarely was, 'but I have a feeling he's the Watchmaker.'

Chapter
THIRTY-TWO

Gerald Duncan sat on the curb, beside Sachs and Sellitto. He was handcuffed, stripped of his hat, sunglasses, several pairs of beige gloves, wallet and a bloody box cutter.

Unlike Dennis Baker's, his attitude was pleasant and co-operative – despite his being pulled to the ground, frisked and cuffed by three officers, Sachs among them, a woman not noted for her delicate touch on takedowns, particularly when it came to perps like this one.

His Missouri driver's license confirmed his identity and showed an address in St Louis.

'Christ,' Sellitto said, 'how the hell'd you spot him?'

Rhyme's conclusion about the onlooker's identity wasn't as miraculous as it seemed. His belief that the Watchmaker might not have fled the scene arose before he'd noticed the man in the alley.

Pulaski said, 'I've got him. The ME.'

Rhyme leaned toward the phone that the rookie held out in a gloved hand and had a brief conversation with the doctor. The medical examiner delivered some very interesting information. Rhyme thanked him and nodded; Pulaski disconnected. The criminalist maneuvered the Storm Arrow wheelchair closer to Duncan.

'You're Lincoln Rhyme,' the prisoner said, as if he was honored to meet the criminalist.

'That's right. And you're the *quote* Watchmaker.'

The man gave a knowing laugh.

Rhyme looked him over. He appeared tired but gave off a sense of satisfaction – even peace.

With a rare smile Rhyme asked the suspect, 'So. Who was he really? The victim in the alleyway. We can search public records for Theodore Adams, but that'd be a waste of time, wouldn't it?'

Duncan tipped his head. 'You figured that out too?'

'What about Adams?' Sellitto asked. Then realized that there were broader questions that should be asked. 'What's going on here, Linc?'

'I'm asking our suspect about the man we found in the alley yesterday morning, with his neck crushed. I want to know who he was and how he died.'

'This asshole murdered him,' Sellitto said.

'No, he didn't. I just talked to the medical examiner. He hadn't gotten back to us with the final autopsy but he just gave me the preliminary. The victim died about five or six P.M. on Monday, not at eleven. And he died instantly of massive internal injuries consistent with an automobile accident or fall. The crushed throat had nothing to do with it. The body was frozen solid when we found it the next morning, so the tour doc couldn't do an accurate field test for cause or time of death.' Rhyme cocked his eyebrow. 'So, Mr Duncan. Who and how?'

Duncan explained, 'Just some poor guy killed in a car crash up in Westchester. His name's James Pickering.'

Rhyme urged, 'Keep going. And remember, we're eager for answers.'

'I heard about the accident on a police scanner. The ambulance took the body to the morgue in the county hospital in Yonkers. I stole the corpse from there.'

Rhyme said to Sachs, 'Call the hospital.'

She did. After a brief conversation she reported, 'A thirty-one-year-old male ran off the Bronx River Parkway about five Monday night. Lost control on a patch of ice. Died instantly, internal injuries. Name of James Pickering. The body went to the hospital but then it disappeared. They thought it might've been transferred to another hospital by mistake but they couldn't find it. The next of kin aren't taking it too well, as you can imagine.'

'I'm sorry about that,' Duncan said, and he did look troubled. 'But I didn't have any choice. I have all his personal effects and I'll return them. And I'll pay for the funeral expenses myself.'

'The ID and things in the wallet that we found on the body?' Sachs asked.

'Forgeries.' Duncan nodded. 'Wouldn't pass close scrutiny but I just needed people fooled for a few days.'

'You stole the body, drove him to the alley and set him up with an iron bar on his neck to make it look like he'd died slowly.'

A nod.

'Then you left the clock and note too.'

'That's right.'

Lon Sellitto asked, 'But the pier, at Twenty-second Street? What about the guy you killed there?'

Rhyme glanced at Duncan. 'Is your blood type AB positive?'

Duncan laughed. 'You're good.'

'There never was a victim on the pier, Lon. It was his own blood.' Looking over the suspect, Rhyme said, 'You set the note and clock on the pier, and poured your blood around it and on the jacket – which you tossed into the river. You made the fingernail scrapings yourself. Where'd you get your blood? You collect it yourself?'

'No, I got it at a hospital in New Jersey. I told them I wanted to stock-pile it before some surgery I was planning.'

'That's why the anticoagulants.' Stored blood usually has a thinning agent included to prevent it from clotting.

Duncan nodded. 'I wondered if you'd check for that.'

Rhyme asked, 'And the fingernail?'

Duncan held up his ring finger. The end of the nail was missing. He himself had torn it off. He added, 'And I'm sure Vincent told you about a young man I supposedly killed near the church. I never touched him. The blood on the box cutter and on some newspaper in the trash nearby – if it's still there – is mine.'

'How did that happen?' Rhyme asked.

'It was an awkward moment. Vincent thought the kid saw his knife. So I had to pretend that I killed him. Otherwise Vincent might suspect me. I followed him around the corner, then ducked into an alley, cut my own arm with the knife and smeared some of my own blood on the box cutter.' He showed a recent wound on his forearm. 'You can do a DNA test.'

'Oh, don't worry. We will . . .' Another thought. 'And the carjacking – you never killed anybody to steal the Buick, did you?' They'd had no reports either of missing students in Chelsea or of drivers murdered during the commission of a carjacking anywhere in the city.

Lon Sellitto was compelled to chime in again with, 'What the hell's going on?'

'He's not a serial killer,' Rhyme said. 'He's not any kind of killer. He set this whole thing up to make it look like he was.'

Sellitto asked, 'No wife killed in an accident?'

'Never been married.'

'How'd you figure it out?' Pulaski asked Rhyme.

'A couple things you said made me wonder, Lon.'

'Me?'

'For one thing, you mentioned his name, Duncan.'

'So? We knew it.'

'Exactly. Because Vincent Reynolds told us. But Mr Duncan is someone who wears gloves twenty-four/seven so he won't leave prints. He's way too careful to give his name to a person like Vincent – unless he didn't care if we found out who he was.

'Then you said it was lucky he didn't kill the recent victims and Amelia. Pissed me off at first, hearing that. But I got to thinking about it. You were right. We didn't really save any victims at all. The florist? Joanne? I figured out he was targeting her, sure, but she's the one who called nine-one-one after she heard a noise in the workshop – a noise he probably made intentionally.'

'That's right,' Duncan agreed. 'And I left a spool of wire on the floor to warn her that somebody'd broken in.'

Sachs said, 'Lucy, the soldier in Greenwich Village – we got an anonymous phone call from a witness about a break-in. But it wasn't a witness at all, right? It was you making that call.'

'I told Vincent that somebody in the street called nine-one-one. But, no, I called from a pay phone and reported myself.'

Rhyme nodded at the office building behind them. 'And here – the fire extinguisher was a dud, I assume.'

'Harmless. I poured a little alcohol on the outside but it's filled with water.'

Sellitto was on the phone, calling the Sixth Precinct, the NYPD Bomb Squad headquarters. A moment later he hung up. 'Tap water.'

'Just like the gun you gave Baker, the one he was going to use to kill my Sachs here.' Rhyme glanced at the dismantled .32. 'I just checked it out – the firing pin's been broken off.'

Duncan said to Sachs, 'I plugged the barrel too. You can check. And I knew he couldn't use his own gun to shoot you because that would tie him to your death.'

'Okay,' Sellitto barked. 'That's it. Somebody, talk to me.'

Rhyme shrugged. 'All I can do is get us to this station, Lon. It's up to Mr Duncan to complete the train ride. I suspect he's planned to enlighten us all along. Which is why he was enjoying the show from the grandstand across the street.'

Duncan nodded and said to Rhyme, 'You hit it on the head, Detective Rhyme.'

'I'm decommissioned,' the criminalist corrected.

'The whole point of what I've done is what just happened – and, yes, I was enjoying it very much: watching that son of a bitch Dennis Baker get arrested and dragged off to jail.'

'Keep going.'

Duncan's face grew still. 'A year ago I came here on business – I own a company that does lease financing of industrial equipment. I was working with a friend – my best friend. He saved my life when we were in the army twenty years ago. We were working all day drafting documents then went back to our hotels to clean up before dinner. But he never showed. I found out he'd been shot to death. The police said it was a mugging. But something didn't seem right. I mean, how often do muggers shoot their victims point-blank in the forehead – twice?'

'Oh, shooting fatalities during the commission of robberies are extremely rare, according to recent . . .' Pulaski's voice trailed off, under Rhyme's cool glance.

Duncan continued. 'Now, the last time I saw him my friend told me something odd. He said that the night before, he'd been in a club downtown. When he came out, two policemen pulled him aside and said they'd seen him buying drugs. Which was bullshit. He didn't do drugs. I know that for a fact. He knew he was being shaken down and demanded to see a police supervisor. He was going to call somebody at headquarters and complain. But just then some people came out of the club and the police let him go. The next day he was shot and killed.

'Too much of a coincidence. I kept going back to the club and asking questions. Cost me five thousand bucks but finally I found somebody willing to tell me that Dennis Baker and some of his fellow cops ran shakedown scams in the city.'

Duncan explained about a scheme of planting drugs on businessmen or their children and then dropping the charges for huge extortion payments.

'The missing drugs from the One One Eight,' Pulaski said.

Sachs nodded. 'Not enough to sell but enough to plant as evidence, sure.'

Duncan added, 'They were based out of some bar in lower Manhattan, I heard.'

'The St James?'

'That's it. They'd all meet there after their shifts at the station house were over.'

Rhyme asked, 'Your friend. The one who was killed. What was his name?'

Duncan gave them the name and Sellitto called Homicide. It was true. The man had been shot during an apparent mugging and no perp was ever collared.

'I used my connection I'd made at the club – paid him a lot of money – to get introduced to some people who knew Baker. I pretended I was a professional killer and offered my services. I didn't hear anything for a while. I thought he'd gotten busted or gone straight and I'd never hear from him. It was frustrating. But finally Baker called me and we met. It turns out he'd been checking me out to see if I was trustworthy. Apparently he was satisfied. He wouldn't give me too many details but said he had a business arrangement that was in jeopardy. He and another cop had taken care of some 'problems' they'd been having.'

Sachs asked, 'Creeley or Sarkowski? Did he mention them?'

'He didn't give me any names but it was obvious that he was talking about killing people.'

Sachs shook her head, eyes troubled. 'I was upset enough thinking that some of the cops from the One One Eight were taking kickbacks from mobsters. And all along *they* were the actual killers.'

Rhyme glanced at her. He knew she'd be thinking of Nick Carelli. Thinking of her father too.

Duncan continued. 'Then Baker said there was a new problem. He needed someone else eliminated, a woman detective. But they couldn't kill her themselves – if she died everyone'd know it was because of her investigation and they'd follow up on the case even more intensely. I came up with this idea of pretending to be a serial killer. And I made up a name – the Watchmaker.'

Sellitto said, 'That's why there were no hits in the watchmaker trade associations.' They'd all come back negative on a Gerald Duncan.

'Right. The character was all a creation of mine. And I needed someone to feed you information and make you think there really was a psycho, so I found Vincent Reynolds. Then we started the supposed attacks. The first two I faked, when Vincent wasn't around. The others – when he was with me – I bungled them on purpose.

'I had to make sure you found the box of bullets that'd connect the Watchmaker to Baker. I was going to drop them somewhere so you'd find them. But' – Duncan gave a laugh – 'as it turned out, I didn't have to. You found out about the SUV and nearly got us.'

'So that's why you left the ammunition inside.'

'Yep. The book too.'

Another thought occurred to Rhyme. 'And the officer who searched the garage said it was curious you parked out in the open, not at the doorway. That was because you had to make sure we found the Explorer.'

'Exactly. And all the other supposed crimes were just leading up to this one – so you could catch Baker in the act of trying to kill her. That'd give you probable cause, I figured, to search his car and house and find evidence to put him away.'

'What about the poem? "The full Cold Moon . . ."'

'I wrote it myself.' Duncan smiled. 'I'm a better businessman than a poet. But it seemed sufficiently scary to suit my needs.'

'Why'd you pick these particular people as victims?'

'I didn't. I picked the *locations* because they'd allow us to get away quickly. This last one, the woman here, was because I needed a good layout to flush out Baker.'

'Revenge for your friend?' Sachs asked. 'A lot of other people would just've had him killed outright.'

Duncan said sincerely, 'I'd never hurt anybody. I couldn't do that. I might bend the law a bit – I admit I committed some crimes here. But they were victimless. I didn't even steal the cars; Baker got them himself – from a police pound.'

'The woman who was the first victim's supposed sister?' Sachs asked. 'Who was she?'

'A friend I asked to help. I lent her a lot of money a few years ago but there was no way she could repay it. So she agreed to help me out.'

'And the girl in the car with her?' Sachs asked.

'Her real daughter.'

'What's the woman's name?'

A rueful smile. 'I'll keep that to myself. Promised her I would. Just like the guy in the club who set me up with Baker. That was part of the deal and I'm sticking to it.'

'Who else is involved in the shakedowns at the One One Eight, other than Baker?'

Duncan shook his head regretfully. 'I wish I could tell you. I want them put away as much as Baker. I tried to find out. He wouldn't talk about his scheme. But I got the impression there's somebody involved other than the officers from the precinct.'

'Somebody else?'

'That's right. High up.'

'From Maryland or with a place there?' Sachs asked.

'I never heard him mention that. He trusted me but only up to a point. I don't think he was worried about my turning him in; it seemed like he was afraid I'd get greedy and go after the money myself. It sounded like there was a lot of it.'

A dark-colored city car pulled up to the police tape and a slim, balding man in a thin overcoat climbed out. He joined Rhyme and the others. He was a senior assistant district attorney. Rhyme had testified at several of the trials the man had prosecuted. The criminalist nodded a greeting and Sellitto explained the latest developments.

The prosecutor listened to the bizarre turn the case had taken. Most of the perps he put away were stupid Tony Soprano sorts or even more stupid crackheads and punks. He seemed amused to find himself with a brilliant criminal – whose crimes, as it turned out, were not nearly as serious as it seemed. What excited him far more than a serial killer was the career-making prosecution of a deadly corruption scam in the police department.

'Any of this going through IAD?' he asked Sachs.

'No. I've been running it myself.'

'Who cleared that?'

'Flaherty.'

'The inspector? Running Op Div?'

'Right.'

He began asking questions and jotting notes. After doing so, in precise handwriting for five minutes, he paused. 'Okay, we've got B and E, criminal trespass . . . but no burglary.'

Burglary is breaking and entering for the purpose of committing a felony, like larceny or murder. Duncan had no purpose other than trespassing.

The prosecutor continued. 'Theft of human remains—'

'Borrowing. I never intended to keep the corpse,' Duncan reminded him.

'Well, it's up to Westchester to decide that one. But here we've also got obstruction of justice, interference with police procedures—'

Duncan frowned. 'Though you could say that since there were no murders in the first place, the police procedures weren't necessary, so interference with them is moot.'

Rhyme chuckled.

The assistant district attorney, however, ignored the comment. 'Possession of a firearm—'

'Barrel was plugged,' Duncan countered. 'It was inoperable.'

'What about the stolen motor vehicles? Where'd they come from?'

Duncan explained about Baker's theft from the police impound lot in Queens. He nodded to the pile of his personal effects, which included a set of car keys. 'The Buick's parked up the street. On Thirty-first. Baker got it from the same place as the SUV.'

'How'd you take delivery of the cars? Anybody else involved?'

'Baker and I went together to pick them up. They were parked in a restaurant lot. Baker knew some of the people there, he said.'

'You get their names?'

'No.'

'What was the restaurant?'

'Some Greek diner. I don't remember the name. We took the four-ninety-five to get out there. I don't remember the exit but we were only on the freeway for about ten minutes after we got out of the Midtown Tunnel and turned left at the exit.'

'North,' Sellitto said. 'We'll have somebody check it out. Maybe Baker's been dealing in confiscated wheels too.'

The prosecutor shook his head. 'I hope you understand the consequences of this. Not just the crimes – you'll have civil fines for the diversion of emergency vehicles and city employees. I'm talking tens, hundreds of thousands of dollars.'

'I have no problem with that. I checked the laws and sentencing guidelines before I started this. I decided the risk of a prison sentence was worth exposing Baker. But I wouldn't have done this if there was any chance somebody innocent would get hurt.'

'You still put people at risk,' Sellitto muttered. 'Pulaski was attacked in the parking garage where you left the SUV. He could've been killed.'

Duncan laughed. 'No, no, *I'm* the one who saved him. After we abandoned the Explorer and were running out of the garage I spotted that homeless guy. I didn't like the looks of him. He had a club or tire iron or something in his hand. After Vincent and I split up, I went back to the garage to make sure he didn't hurt anybody. When he started toward you' – Duncan glanced at Pulaski – 'I found a wheel cover in the trash and pitched it into the wall so you'd turn around and see him coming.'

The rookie nodded. 'That's what happened. I thought the guy stumbled and made the noise himself. But whatever, I was ready for him when he came at me. And there *was* a wheel cover nearby.'

'And Vincent?' Duncan continued. 'I made sure he never got close enough to any women to hurt them. *I'm* the one who turned him in. I called nine-one-one and reported him. I can prove it.' He gave details about where and when the rapist was caught – which confirmed that he'd been the one who called the police.

The prosecutor looked like he needed a time-out. He glanced at his notes, then at Duncan, and rubbed his shiny head. His ears were bright red from the cold. 'I've gotta talk to the attorney general about this one.' He turned to two detectives from Police Plaza who'd met him here. The prosecutor nodded at Duncan and said, 'Take him downtown. And keep somebody on him close – remember, he's diming out crooked cops. People could be gunning for him.'

Duncan was helped to his feet.

Amelia Sachs asked, 'Why didn't you just come to us and tell us what happened? Or make a tape of Baker admitting what he'd done? You could've avoided this whole charade.'

Duncan gave a harsh laugh. 'And who could I trust? Who could I send a tape to? How did I know who was honest and who was working with Baker? . . . It's a fact of life, you know.'

'What's that?'

'Corrupt cops.'

Rhyme noticed Sachs gave absolutely no reaction to this comment, as two uniformed officers led their perp, such as he was, to a squad car. They were, at least temporarily, once again a team.

You and me, Sachs . . .

Lincoln Rhyme's case had become Amelia Sachs's and if the Watchmaker had turned out to be toothless there was still a lot of work left to do. The corruption scandal at the 118th house was now 'front-burnered', as Sellitto said (prompting Rhyme's sardonic comment, 'Now *there's* a verb you don't hear every day'). Benjamin Creeley's and Frank Sarkowski's killer or killers had yet to be identified specifically from among the cops who were suspected of complicity. And the case against Baker had to be cobbled together and the Maryland connection – and the extortion money – unearthed.

Kathryn Dance volunteered to interview Baker but he was refusing to say a word so the team had to rely on traditional crime scene and investigative work.

On Rhyme's instruction, Pulaski was cross-referencing Baker's phone calls and poring over his records and Palm Pilot, trying to find out whom he spent the most time with at the 118th and elsewhere but wasn't coming up with anything helpful. Mel Cooper and Sachs were analyzing evidence from Baker's car, house on Long Island and office at One Police Plaza, as well as the houses or apartments of several girlfriends he'd been dating recently (none of whom knew about the others, it turned out). Sachs had searched with her typical diligence and had returned to Rhyme's with cartons of clothes, tools, checkbooks, documents, photos, weapons and trace from his tire treads.

After an hour of looking over all of this, Cooper announced, 'Ah. Got something.'

'What?' Rhyme asked.

Sachs told him, 'Found some ash in the clothes that were in the trunk of Baker's car.'

'And?' Sellitto asked.

Cooper added, 'Identical to the ash found in the fireplace at Creeley's. Places him at that scene.'

They also found a fiber from Baker's garage that matched the rope used in Benjamin Creeley's 'suicide'.

'I want to link Baker to Sarkowski's death too,' Rhyme said. 'Get Nancy Simpson and Frank Rettig out to Queens, that place where his body was found. Take some soil samples. We might be able to place Baker or one of his buddies there too.'

'The soil I found at Creeley's, in front of the fireplace,' Sachs pointed out, 'had chemicals in it – like from a factory site. It might match.'

'Good.'

Sellitto called Crime Scene in Queens and ordered the collection.

Sachs and Cooper also found samples of sand and some vegetation that turned out to be seaweed. These substances were found in Baker's car. And there were similar samples in his garage at home.

'Sand and seaweed,' Rhyme commented. 'Could be a summer house – Maryland, again. Maybe Baker's got one, or a girlfriend of his.'

But a check of the real estate databases showed that this wasn't the case.

Sachs wheeled in the other whiteboard from Rhyme's exercise room and she jotted the latest evidence. Clearly frustrated, she stood back and stared at the notations.

'The Maryland connection,' she said. 'We've *got* to find it. If they killed two people, and nearly Ron and me, they're willing to kill more. They know we're closing them up and they won't want any witnesses. And they're probably destroying evidence right now.'

Sachs was silent. She looked flustered.

It's hard when your lover is also your professional partner. But Lincoln Rhyme couldn't hold back, even – especially – with Amelia Sachs. He said in a low, even voice, 'This's *your* case, Sachs. You've been living it. I haven't. Where does it all point?'

'I don't know.' She dug a thumbnail into her finger. Her mouth tight, she shook her head, staring at the evidence chart. Loose ends. 'There's not enough evidence.'

'There's *never* enough evidence,' Rhyme reminded. 'But that's not an excuse. That's what we're here for, Sachs. We're the ones who examine a few dirty bricks and figure out what the entire castle looked like.'

'I don't know.'

'I can't help you, Sachs. You've got to figure this one out on your own. Think about what you've got. Somebody with a connection to Maryland . . . somebody following you in a Mercedes . . . saltwater and seaweed . . . cash, a lot of cash. Crooked cops.'

'I don't *know*,' she repeated stridently.

But he wasn't giving an inch. 'That's not an option. You *have* to know.'

She glared at him – and at the hard message beneath the

words, which was: You can walk out that door tomorrow and throw away your career if you want. But for now you're still a cop with a job to do.

Her fingernails worried her scalp.

'There's something more, something you're missing,' Rhyme muttered as he too gazed at the evidence charts.

'So, you're saying we have to think outside the box,' said Ron Pulaski.

'Ah, clichés,' Rhyme snapped. 'Well, okay, if you're in a box, maybe you're there for a reason. *I* say don't think outside it; I say look more closely at what's inside with you . . . So, Sachs, what do *you* see in there?'

She stared at the charts for some moments.

Then she smiled and whispered, 'Maryland.'

BENJAMIN CREELEY HOMICIDE

- 56-year-old Creeley, apparently suicide by hanging. Clothesline. But had broken thumb, couldn't tie noose.
- Computer-written suicide note about depression. But appeared not to be suicidally depressed, no history of mental/emotional problems.
- Around Thanksgiving two men broke into his house and possibly burned evidence. White men, but faces not observed. One bigger than other. They were inside for about an hour.
- Evidence in Westchester house:
  - Broke through lock; skillful job.
  - Leather texture marks on

fireplace tools and Creeley's desk.
- Soil in front of fireplace has higher acid content than soil around house and contains pollutants. From industrial site?
- Traces of burned cocaine in fireplace.
- Ash in fireplace.
  - Financial records, spreadsheet, references to millions of dollars.
  - Checking logo on documents, sending entries to forensic accountant.
  - Diary re: getting oil changed, haircut appointment and going to St James Tavern.
  - Analysis of ash from

Queens CS lab:
- Logo of software used in corporate accounting.
- Forensic accountant: standard executive compensation figures.
- Burned because of what they revealed, or to lead investigators off?

- St James Tavern
  - Creeley came here several times.
  - Apparently didn't use drugs while here.
  - Not sure whom he met with, but maybe cops from the nearby 118th Precinct of the NYPD.
  - Last time he was here – just before his death – he got into an argument with persons unknown.
  - Checked money from officers at St James – serial numbers are clean, but found coke and heroin. Stolen from precinct?
    - Not much drugs missing, only 6 or 7 oz. of pot, 4 of coke.
- Unusually few organized crime cases at the 118th Precinct but no evidence of intentional stalling by officers.
- Two gangs in the East Village possible but not likely suspects.
- Interview with Jordan Kessler, Creeley's partner, and follow-up with wife.
  - Confirmed no obvious drug use.
  - Didn't appear to associate with criminals.
  - Drinking more than usual, taken up gambling; trips to Vegas and Atlantic City. Losses were large, but not significant to Creeley.
  - Not clear why he was depressed.
  - Kessler didn't recognize burned records.
  - Awaiting list of clients.
  - Kessler doesn't appear to gain by Creeley's death.
  - Sachs and Pulaski followed by AMG Mercedes.

FRANK SARKOWSKI HOMICIDE

- Sarkowski was 57 years old, no police record, murdered on November 4 of this year, survived by wife and two teenage children.
- Victim owned building and business in Manhattan. Business was doing maintenance for other companies and utilities.
- Art Snyder was case detective.
- No suspects.
- Murder/robbery?
  - Was shot to death as part of apparent robbery. Weapon recovered on scene – Smith & Wesson knockoff, .38 Special, no prints, cold gun.

Case detective believes it could have been a professional hit.
- Business deal went bad?
- Killed in Queens – not sure why he was there.
  - Deserted part of borough, near natural gas tanks.
- File and evidence missing.
  - File went to 158th Precinct on/around November 28. Never returned. No indication of requesting officer.
  - No indication where it went in the 158th.

- DI Jefferies not cooperative.
- No known connection with Creeley.
- No criminal record – Sarkowski or company.
- Rumors – money going to cops at the 118th Precinct. Ended up someplace/someone with a Maryland connection. Baltimore mob involved?
- No leads.
- No indications of mob involvement.
- No other Maryland connections found.

THE WATCHMAKER

CRIME SCENE FIVE

Location:
- Office building. Thirty-second Street and Seventh Ave.

Victims:
- Amelia Sachs/Ron Pulaski.

Perp:
- Dennis Baker, NYPD

M.O.:
- Gunshot (attempt).

Evidence:
- 32 Autauga Mk II pistol.
- Latex gloves.
- Recovered from Baker's car, home, office:
  - Cocaine.
  - $50,000 cash.
  - Clothing.
  - Receipts from clubs and bars, incl. the St James.
  - Carpeting fibers from Explorer.
- Fiber that matched the rope used in Creeley's death.
- Ash found at Baker's same as ash in Creeley's fireplace.
- Presently taking soil samples from site where Sarkowski was murdered.
- Sand and seaweed. Oceanfront Maryland connection?

Other:
- Gerald Duncan set up entire scheme to implicate Dennis Baker and others who killed Duncan's friend. Eight or ten other officers from the 118th are involved, not sure who. Someone else, other than cops from the 118th, is involved. Duncan no longer homicide suspect.

Chapter
THIRTY-THREE

Amelia Sachs walked into a tiny, deserted grocery store in Little Italy, south of Greenwich Village. The windows were painted over and a single bare bulb burned inside. The door to the darkened back room was ajar, revealing a large heap of trash, old shelves and dusty cans of tomato sauce.

The place resembled a former social club of a small-time organized crime crew, which in fact it had been until it was raided and closed up a year ago. The landlord was temporarily the city, which was trying to dump the place, but so far, no takers. Sellitto had said it'd be a good, secure place for a sensitive meeting of this sort.

Seated at a rickety table were Deputy Mayor Robert Wallace and a clean-cut young cop, an Internal Affairs detective. The IAD officer, Toby Henson, greeted Sachs with a firm handshake and a look in his eyes that suggested if she offered any positive response to an invitation to go out with him, he'd give her the evening of her life.

She nodded grimly, focussed only on doing the hard job that lay ahead. Her rethinking of the facts, looking *within* the box, as Rhyme urged, had produced results, which turned out to be extremely unpleasant.

'You said there was a situation?' Wallace asked. 'You didn't want to talk about it over the phone.'

She briefed the men about Gerald Duncan and Dennis Baker. Wallace had heard the basics but Henson laughed in surprise. 'This Duncan, he was just a citizen? And he wanted to bring down a crooked cop? That's why he did this?'

'Yep.'

'He have names?'

'Only Baker's. There're about eight or ten others from the One One Eight but there's someone else, a main player.'

'Someone else?' Wallace asked.

'Yep. All along we were looking for somebody with a connection to Maryland . . . Did we get *that* one wrong.'

'Maryland?' the IAD man asked.

Sachs gave a grim laugh. 'You know that game of Telephone?'

'You mean at a kids' party? You whisper something to the person next to you and by the time it goes around, it's all different?'

'Yep. My source heard "Maryland". I think it was "Marilyn".'

'A person's name?' When she nodded, Wallace's eyes narrowed. 'Wait, you don't mean . . . ?'

'Inspector Marilyn Flaherty.'

'Impossible.'

Detective Henson shook his head. 'No way.'

'I wish I was wrong. But we've got some evidence. We found sand and saltwater trace in Baker's car. She's got a house in Connecticut, near the beach. And I've been followed by somebody in a Mercedes AMG. At first I thought it was a crew from Jersey or Baltimore. But it turns out that that's what Flaherty owns.'

'A cop owns an AMG?' the Internal Affairs officer asked in disbelief.

'Don't forget Flaherty's a cop making a couple hundred thousand a year illegally,' Sachs said stiffly. 'And we found a black-and-gray hair about the length of hers in the Explorer that Baker had stolen from the pound. Oh, and remember: She definitely didn't want IAD to handle the case.'

'Yeah, that was strange,' Wallace agreed.

'Because she was going to bury the whole thing. Give it to one of her people to "handle". But it would've disappeared.'

'Holy shit, an inspector,' whispered the IAD pretty boy.

'She's in custody?' Wallace asked.

Sachs shook her head. 'The problem is we can't find the money. We don't have probable cause to subpoena her bank records or get paper to search her house. That's why I need you.'

Wallace said, 'What can I do?'

'I've asked her to meet us here. I'm going to brief her on what happened – only a watered-down version. I want you to tell her that we've discovered Baker has a partner. The mayor's called a special commission and he's going to pull out all the stops to track them down. Tell her that Internal Affairs is totally on board.'

'You're thinking she'll panic, head for the money and you'll nail her.'

'That's what we hope. My partner's going to put a tracker on her car while she's in here tonight. After she leaves, we're going to tail her . . . Now, are you okay lying to her?'

'No, I'm not.' Wallace looked down at the rough tabletop, marred with graffiti. 'But I'll do it.'

Detective Toby Henson had apparently lost all interest in his romantic future with Sachs. He sighed and gave an assessment that she couldn't help but agree with. 'This's going to be bad.'

Now, what've we learned?

Ron Pulaski, accustomed to thinking *we* because of the twin thing, asked himself this question.

Meaning: What've *I* learned in working on this case with Rhyme and Sachs?

He was determined to be the best cop he could and he spent a lot of time evaluating what he'd done right and what he'd done wrong on the job. Walking down the street now toward the old grocery store where Sachs was meeting with Wallace, he couldn't really see that he'd messed up anything too bad on the case. Oh, sure, he could've run the Explorer scene better. And he was damn sure going to keep his weapon *outside* the Tyvek jumpsuit from now on – and not use choke holds, unless he really had to.

But on the whole? He'd done pretty good.

Still, he wasn't satisfied. He supposed this feeling came from working for Detective Sachs. That woman set a high bar. There was always something else to check out, one more clue to find, another hour to spend on the scene.

Could drive you crazy.

Could also teach you to be one hell of a cop.

He'd really have to step up now, with her leaving. Pulaski'd heard that rumor, of course, and he wasn't very happy about it. But he'd do what was necessary. He didn't know, though, that he'd ever have her drive. After all, at the moment, hurrying down the freezing street, he was thinking of his family. He really wanted just to head home. Talk to Jenny about her day – not his, no, no – and then play with the kids. That was so fun, just watching the look in his boy's eyes. It changed so fast and so completely – when his son noticed something he'd never seen before, when he made connections, when he laughed. He and Jenny would sit on the floor with Brad in between them, crawling back and forth, his tiny fingers gripping Pulaski's thumb.

And their newborn daughter? She was round and wrinkled as an old grapefruit and she'd lie nearby in the SpongeBob bassinet and be happy and perfect.

But the pleasure of his family would have to wait. After what was about to happen, it was going to be a long night.

He checked street numbers. He was two blocks from the storefront where he'd be meeting Amelia Sachs. Thinking: What else've I learned?

One thing: You damn well better have learned to steer clear of alleys.

A year ago he'd nearly been beaten to death because he'd been walking too close to a wall, with a perp hiding around the corner of a building. The man had stepped out and walloped him in the head with a billy club.

Careless and stupid.

As Detective Sachs had said, 'You didn't know. Now you do.'

Approaching another alley now, Pulaski veered to the left to walk along the curb – in the unlikely event that somebody, a mugger or junkie, was hiding in the alley.

He turned and looked down it, saw the empty stretch of cobblestones. But at least he was being smart. That's the way it was, being a cop, learning these small lessons and making them a part of—

The hand got him from behind.

'Jesus,' he gasped as he was pulled through the open door of the van at the curb, which he hadn't seen because he was staring into the alley. He gasped and started to call out for help.

But his assailant – Deputy Inspector Halston Jefferies, his eyes cold as the moon overhead – slapped his hand over the rookie's mouth. Somebody else grabbed Pulaski's gun hand and in two seconds flat he'd disappeared into the back of the van.

The door slammed shut.

*

The front door of the old grocery store opened and Marilyn Flaherty walked inside, closed the door behind her and latched it.

Unsmiling, she looked around the bleak store, nodded at the other officers and Wallace. Sachs thought she looked even more tense than usual.

The deputy mayor, playing it cool, introduced her to the IAD detective. She shook his hand and sat at the battered table, next to Sachs.

'Top secret, hm?'

Sachs said, 'This's turned into a hornets' nest.' She watched the woman's face carefully as she laid out the details. The inspector kept up the great stone face, giving nothing away. Sachs wondered what Kathryn Dance would see in her stiff-backed posture, the tight lips, the quick, cold eyes. The woman was virtually motionless.

The detective told her about Baker's partner. Then added, 'I know how you feel about Internal Affairs but, with all respect, I've decided we need to bring them in.'

'I—'

'I'm sorry, Inspector.' Sachs turned toward Wallace.

But the deputy mayor said nothing. He simply shook his head, sighed, then glanced at the IAD man. The young officer pulled out his weapon.

Sachs blinked. 'What . . . Hey, what're you doing?'

He trained the gun on the space midway between her and Flaherty.

'What is this?' the inspector gasped.

'It's a mess,' Wallace said, sounding almost regretful. 'It's a real mess. Both of you, keep your hands on the table.'

The deputy mayor looked them over, while Toby Henson handed his own gun to Wallace, who covered the women.

Henson wasn't IAD at all, he was a detective out of the 118th part of the inner circle of the extortion ring, and the man who'd helped Dennis Baker murder Sarkowski and Creeley. He now pulled on leather gloves and took Sachs's Glock from her holster. He patted her down for a backup piece. There was none. He searched the inspector's purse and removed her small service revolver.

'You called it right, Detective,' Wallace said to Sachs, who stared at him in shock. 'We've got a situation . . . a situation.' He pulled out his cell phone and made a call to one of the officers in front, also part of the extortion scheme. 'All clear?'

'Yep.'

Wallace disconnected the phone.

Sachs said, 'You? It was you? But . . .' Her head swivelled toward Flaherty.

The inspector asked, 'What's this all about?'

The deputy mayor nodded at the inspector and said to Sachs, 'Wrong in a big way. She had nothing to do with it. Dennis Baker and I were partners – but *business* partners. On Long Island. We grew up there. Had a recycling company together. It went bust and he went to the academy, became a cop. I got another business up and running. Then I got involved in city politics and we stayed in touch. I became police liaison and ombudsman and got a feel for what kind of scams worked and what didn't. Dennis and I came up with one that did.'

'Robert!' Flaherty snapped. 'No, no . . .'

'Ah, Marilyn . . .' was all the silver-haired man could muster.

'So,' Amelia Sachs said, her shoulders sagging, 'what's the scenario here?' She gave a grim laugh. 'The inspector kills me and then kills herself. You plant some money in her house. And . . .'

'And Dennis Baker dies in jail – he messes with the wrong inmate, falls down the stairs, who knows? Too bad. But he should've been more careful. No witnesses, that's the end of the case.'

'You think anybody's going to buy it? Somebody at the One One Eight'll turn. They'll get you sooner or later.'

'Well, excuse me, Detective, but we have to put out the fires we've got, don't you think? And you're the biggest fucking fire I've got at the moment.'

'Listen, Robert,' Flaherty said, her voice brittle, 'you're in trouble but it's not too late.'

Wallace pulled on gloves. 'Check the street again, tell them to get the car ready.' The deputy mayor picked up Sachs's Glock.

The man walked to the door.

Wallace's eyes turned cold as he looked over Sachs and took a firm grip on the pistol.

Sachs stared into his eyes. 'Wait.'

Wallace frowned.

She looked him over, eerily calm under the circumstances, he thought. Then she said, 'ESU One, move in.'

Wallace blinked. 'What?'

To the deputy mayor's shock, a man's voice shouted from the darkened back room, 'Nobody move! Or I will fire!'

What was this?

Gasping, Wallace looked into the doorway, where an ESU officer was standing, his H&K machine gun's muzzle moving from the politician to Henson at the front door.

Sachs reached down and grabbed something under the table. Her hand emerged with another Glock. She must've clipped it there earlier! She spun to the front door, training the pistol on Henson. 'Drop the weapon! Get down on the floor!' The ESU officer shifted his gun back to the deputy mayor.

Wallace, thinking in panic: Oh, Christ, it's a sting . . . All a setup.

'Now!' Sachs shouted again.

Henson muttered, 'Shit.' He did as he was told.

Wallace continued to grip Sachs's Glock. He looked down at it.

Her eyes on Henson, Sachs turned slightly toward Wallace. 'That piece you're holding's unloaded. You'd die for no reason.'

Disgusted, he dropped the gun on the table, held his hands up.

Mystified, Inspector Flaherty was scooting back in her chair, standing up.

Sachs said into her lapel, 'Entry teams, go.'

The front door crashed open and a half dozen cops pushed inside – ESU officers. Following them were Deputy Inspector Halston Jefferies and the head of Internal Affairs Division, Captain Ron Scott. A young blond patrolman entered too.

The ESU officers muscled Wallace to the floor. He felt the pain in his hip and joints. Henson was cuffed as well. The deputy mayor looked outside and saw the two other officers from the One One Eight, the ones who'd been standing guard in front. They were lying on the cold sidewalk, in restraints.

'Hell of a way to find out,' Amelia Sachs said to no one as she reloaded her own Glock and slipped it back in her holster. 'But it sure answers our question.'

The query she'd referred to wasn't about Robert Wallace's guilt – they'd learned beforehand that he was one of Baker's partners; it was about whether Marilyn Flaherty had been involved too.

They'd set up the whole thing to find out, as well as get a taped admission from Wallace.

Lon Sellitto, Ron Scott and Halston Jefferies had established a command post in a van up the street and hidden the ESU sniper in the back room to make sure Wallace and the cop with him didn't start shooting before Sachs had a chance to tape the conversation. Pulaski was supposed to take the front door with one team, and another one would take the back. But at the last minute they learned that Wallace had other officers with him, cops from the 118, who might or might not be crooked, so they'd had to change plans a bit.

Pulaski, in fact, nearly walked right into Wallace's cops outside the storefront and ruined the whole thing.

The rookie said, 'Inspector Jefferies pulled me into the command van just before those guys outside saw me.'

Jefferies snapped, 'Walking down the street like a Boy Scout on a fucking hike. You want to stay alive on the streets, kid, keep your goddamn eyes open.' The inspector's rage seemed tame in comparison with yesterday's tantrum, Sachs noted. At least he wasn't spitting.

'Yessir. I'll be more careful in the future, sir.'

'Jesus Christ, they let anybody into the academy these days.'

Sachs tried to repress a smile. She turned to Flaherty. 'Sorry, Inspector. We just had to make sure you weren't a player.' She explained her suspicions and the clues that had led her to believe that the inspector might've been working with Baker.

'The Mercedes?' Flaherty asked. 'Sure, it was mine. And, sure, you were being tailed. I had an officer from Op Div keeping an eye on you and Pulaski. You were both young, you were inexperienced and you might've been way out of your league. I gave him my own car to use because you would've noticed a pool vehicle right away.'

The expensive car had indeed thrown her off and actually started her thinking in another direction. If the mob wasn't involved, she was beginning to wonder that maybe Pulaski had called it wrong about Creeley's partner, Jordan Kessler, and that the businessman might somehow be involved in the deaths. Maybe, she'd speculated, Creeley and Sarkowski had gotten caught up in one of the Enron-style investigations currently under way and were killed because of something they'd learned about corporate fraud at   client's company.

Kessler seemed to be the only player in the game who could afford a vehicle like an AMG Merc.

But now she realized that the case was all about corrupt cops, and the ash in Creeley's fireplace wasn't from doctored accounting records but simply evidence that they'd burned to make sure they destroyed any records of the extortion money, as she'd originally speculated.

Now the inspector's attention turned to Robert Wallace. She asked Sachs, 'How'd you find him?'

'Tell him, Ron,' she instructed Pulaski.

The rookie began. 'Detective Sachs here ascertained . . .' He paused. 'Detective Sachs found a bunch of trace in Baker's vehicle and house that gave us the idea, well, gave Detectives Sachs and Rhyme the idea that maybe the other person involved lived near a beach or marina.'

Sachs took it up, 'I didn't think that DI Jefferies was involved because he wouldn't request a file to be sent to his own precinct if he wanted to destroy it. Somebody else had it routed there and intercepted it before it was logged in. I went back to him and asked if anybody had been in the file room lately, somebody who might have a connection to the case. Somebody had. You.' A glance at Wallace. 'Then I asked the next logical question. Did you have a Maryland connection? And you sure did. Just not an obvious one.'

Thinking inside the box . . .

'Oh, Jesus Christ,' he muttered. 'Baker told me you'd mentioned Maryland. But I never thought you'd find it.'

Ron Scott, the IAD head, said to Flaherty, 'Wallace has a boat docked at his place on the South Shore of Long Island. Registered in New York but built in Annapolis. She's *The Maryland Monroe*.' Scott looked him over and gave a cold laugh. 'You boat people really love your puns.'

Sachs said, 'The sand, seaweed and saltwater trace in Baker's car and house match those at his marina. We got a warrant and searched the boat. Got some good evidence. Phone numbers, documents, trace. Over four million in cash – oh, and a lot of drugs too. Plenty of liquor, probably perped. But I'd say the booze's the least of your problems.'

Ron Scott nodded to two ESU officers. 'Get him downtown. Central Booking.'

As he was led out, Wallace called back, 'I'm not saying anything. If you think I'm going to name names, you can forget about it. I'm not confessing.'

Flaherty gave the first laugh Sachs had ever heard from her. 'Are you mad, Robert? Sounds like they've got enough evidence to put you away forever. You don't need to say a word. Actually, I'd just as soon you didn't open your goddamn mouth ever again.'

III

8:32 A.M. THURSDAY

Time is a great teacher, but unfortunately it
kills all its pupils.

— LOUIS-HECTOR BERLIOZ

8:32 A.M., THURSDAY

Chapter
THIRTY-FOUR

Alone now, Rhyme and Sachs looked over the tables containing the evidence that had been collected in both the St James corruption scandal and the Watchmaker case.

Sachs was concentrating hard, but Rhyme knew she was distracted. They'd stayed up late and talked about what had happened. The corruption was bad enough but that officers themselves had actually tried to kill other cops shook her even more.

Sachs claimed she was still undecided about quitting the force but one look at her face told Rhyme that she was going to leave. He also knew she'd had a couple of phone calls with Argyle Security.

There was no doubt.

Rhyme now glanced at the small rectangle of white paper sitting in her briefcase open in his lab: the envelope containing Sachs's letter of resignation. Like the glaring light of the full moon in a dark sky, the whiteness of the letter was blinding. It was hard to see it clearly, it was hard to see anything else.

He forced himself not to think about it and looked back at the evidence.

Gerald Duncan – dubbed 'Perp Lite' by witty Thom – was

awaiting arraignment on the infractions he had committed, all minor ones (the DNA analysis revealed that the blood on the box cutter, on the jacket fished out of the harbor and pooled on the pier was Duncan's own, and the fingernail crescent was a perfect match).

The 118th Precinct corruption case was moving slowly.

There was sufficient evidence to indict Baker and Wallace, as well as Toby Henson. Soil at the Sarkowski crime scene and the samples Sachs had collected at Creeley's Westchester house matched trace found in Baker's and Henson's homes. Of course, they had a rope fiber implicating Baker in Creeley's death, but similar fibers were found on Wallace's boat. Henson owned leather gloves whose texture patterns matched those found in Westchester.

But this trio wasn't cooperating. They were rejecting any plea bargains, and no evidence implicated anyone else, including the two officers who'd been outside the East Village social club, who claimed they were innocent. Rhyme had tried to unleash Kathryn Dance on them but they were refusing to say anything.

Eventually, Rhyme was confident, he could find all the perps from the 118th and build cases against them. But he didn't want eventually; he wanted now. As Sachs had pointed out, the other cops from the St James might be planning to kill more witnesses – maybe even make another attempt on her or Pulaski. It was also possible that one or more of them were forcing Baker, Henson and Wallace to remain silent by threatening their families.

Besides, Rhyme was needed on other cases. Earlier he'd gotten a call about another incident – FBI Agent Fred Dellray (temporarily sprung from financial crimes hell) explained that there'd been a break-in and arson at the federal National Institute of Standards and Technology operation in Brooklyn. The damage was minor but the perp had breached a very sophisticated security system and, with terrorism on everyone's mind, any burglary of a government facility got attention; the Feds wanted Rhyme to assist in the forensic side of the investigation. He wanted to help but he needed to get the Baker–Wallace extortion case wrapped up first.

A messenger arrived with the file on the murder of Duncan's businessman friend, engineered by Baker when the man refused to be extorted. The case was still open – there's no statute of limitations on murder – but there'd been no entries for a year. Rhyme was hoping to find some leads in the older case that might help them identify perps from the 118th Precinct.

Rhyme first went into the *New York Times* archive and read the short account of the death of the victim, Andrew Culbert. It reported nothing other than that he was a businessman from Duluth and had been killed during an apparent mugging in Midtown. No suspects were found. There was no follow-up to the story.

Rhyme had Thom mount the investigation report on his page-turning frame and the criminalist read through the sheets. As often, in a cold case, the notes were in several different handwritings, since the investigation had been passed on – with progressively less energy – as time passed. According to the crime scene report, there'd been little trace, no fingerprints or footprints, no shell casings (death was from two shots to the forehead, the slugs ubiquitous .38 Specials; a test of the weapons they'd collected from Baker and the other cops at the 118th revealed no ballistics matches).

'You have the crime scene inventory?' he asked Sachs.

'Let's see. Right here,' she said, lifting the sheet. 'I'll read it.'

He closed his eyes so he'd have a better image of the items.

'Wallet,' Sachs read, 'one hotel room key to the St Regis, one minibar key, one Cross pen, one PDA, one packet of gum, a small pad of paper with the words "Men's room" on the top. The second sheet said "Chardonnay". That's it. The lead detective from Homicide was John Repetti.'

Rhyme was looking off, his mind stuck on something. He looked at her. 'What?'

'I was saying, Repetti, he ran the case out of Midtown North. You want me to call him?'

After a moment Lincoln Rhyme replied, 'No, I need you to do something else.'

It's possessed.

Listening to the scratchy recording of the bluesman Blind Lemon Jefferson singing, 'See That My Grave Is Kept Clean', through her iPod, Kathryn Dance stared at her suitcase, bulging open, refusing to close.

All I bought was two pairs of shoes, a few Christmas presents . . . okay, *three* pairs of shoes, but one was pumps. They don't count. Oh, but then the sweater. The sweater was the problem.

She pulled it out. And tried again. The clasps got to within a few inches of each other and stopped.

Possessed . . .

I'll go for the elegant look. She found the plastic valet laundry bag and offloaded jeans, a suit, hair curlers, stockings and the offending, and bulky, sweater. She tried the suitcase again.

Click.

No exorcist was necessary.

Her hotel room phone rang and the front desk announced she had a visitor.

Right on time.

'Send 'em up,' Dance said and five minutes later Lucy Richter was sitting on the small couch in Dance's room.

'You want something to drink?'

'No, thanks. I can't stay long.'

Dance nodded at a small fridge. 'Whoever thought up mini-bars is evil. Candy bars and chips. My downfall. Well, everything's pretty much my downfall. And to add insult to injury the salsa costs ten dollars.'

Lucy, who looked like she'd never had to count a calorie or gram of fat in her life, laughed. Then she said, 'I heard they caught him. The officer guarding my house told me. But he didn't have any details.'

The agent explained about Gerald Duncan, how he was innocent all along, and about the corruption scandal at an NYPD precinct.

Lucy shook her head at the news. Then she was looking around the small room. She made some pointless comments about framed prints and the view out the window. Soot, snow and an air shaft were the essential elements of the landscape. 'I just came by to say thanks.'

No, you didn't, thought Dance. But she said, 'You don't need to thank me. It's our job.'

She observed that Lucy's arms were uncrossed and the woman was sitting comfortably now, slightly back, shoulders relaxed, but not slumped. A confession, of some sort, was coming.

Dance let the silence unravel. Lucy said, 'Are you a counselor?'

'No. Just a cop.'

During her interviews, though, it wasn't unusual for suspects to keep right on going after the confession, sharing stories of other moral lapses, hated parents, jealousy of siblings, cheating wives and husbands, anger, joy, hopes. Confiding, seeking advice. No, she wasn't a counselor. But she was a cop and a mother and a kinesics expert, and all three of those roles required her to be an expert at the largely forgotten art of listening.

'Well, you're real easy to talk to. I thought maybe I could ask your opinion about something.'

'Go on,' Dance encouraged.

The soldier said, 'I don't know what to do. I'm getting this commendation today, the one I was telling you about. But there's a problem.' She explained more about her job overseas, running fuel and supply trucks.

Dance opened the minibar, extracted two $6 bottles of Perrier. Lifted an eyebrow.

The soldier hesitated. 'Oh, sure.'

She opened them and handed one to Lucy. Keeping hands busy frees up the mind to think and the voice to speak.

'Okay, this corporal was on my team, Pete. A reservist from South Dakota. Funny guy. Very funny. Coached soccer back home, worked in construction. He was a big help when I first got there. One day, about a month ago, he and I had to do an inventory of damaged vehicles. Some of them get shipped back to Fort Hood for repairs, some we can fix ourselves, some are just scrapped.

'I was in the office and he'd gone to the mess hall. I was going to pick him up at thirteen hundred hours and we were going to drive to the bone lot. I went to get him in a Humvee. I saw Petey there, waiting for me. Just then an IED went off. That's a bomb.'

Dance knew this, of course.

'I was about thirty, forty feet away when it blew. Petey was waving and then there was this flash and the whole scene changed. It was like you blinked and the square became a different place.' She looked out the window. 'The front of the mess hall was gone, palm trees – they just vanished. Some soldiers and a couple of civilians who'd been standing there . . . One instant there, then they were gone.'

Her voice was eerily calm. Dance recognized the tone; she heard it often in witnesses who'd lost loved ones in crimes.

(The hardest interviews to do, worse than sitting across from the most amoral killer.)

'Petey's body was shattered. That's the only way to describe it.' Her voice caught. 'He was all red and black, broken . . . I've seen a lot over there. But this was so terrible.' She sipped the water and then clutched the bottle like a child with a doll.

Dance offered no words of sympathy – they'd be useless. She nodded for the woman to continue. A deep breath. Lucy's fingers intertwined tightly. In her work, Dance characterized this gesture – a common one – of trying to strangle the unbearable tension arising from guilt or pain or shame.

'The thing is . . . I was late. I was in the office. I looked up at the clock. It was about twelve fifty-five but I had a half cup of soda left. I thought about throwing it out and leaving – it'd take five minutes to get to the mess hall – but I wanted to finish the soda. I just wanted to sit and finish it. I was late getting to the mess hall. If I'd been on time he wouldn't've died. I would've picked him up and we'd have been a half mile away when the IED blew.'

'Were you injured?'

'A little.' She pulled up her sleeve and displayed a large leathery scar on her forearm. 'Nothing serious.' She stared at the scar and then drank more water. Her eyes were hollow. 'Even if I'd been just *one* minute late at least he'd've been in the vehicle. He probably would have survived. Sixty seconds . . . That would've made the difference between him living and dying. And all because of a soda. All I wanted was to finish my goddamn soda.' A sad laugh escaped her dry lips. 'And then who shows up and tries to kill me? Somebody calling himself the Watchmaker, leaving a big-ass clock in my bathroom. For months all I can think about is how a single minute, one way or the other, makes the difference between life and death. And here's this freak throwing it in my face.'

Dance asked, 'What else? There's something more, isn't there?'

A faint laugh. 'Yep, here's the problem. See, my tour was scheduled to be up next month. But I felt so guilty about Pete that I told my CO I'd reenlist.'

Dance was nodding.

'That's what this ceremony's about. It's not about getting wounded. We're wounded every day. It's about reenlisting. The army's having a tough time getting new recruits. They're going to use the reenlisters as poster children for the new army. We like it so much we want to go back. That sort of thing.'

'And you're having second thoughts?'

She nodded. 'It's driving me crazy. I can't sleep. I can't make love to my husband. I can't do anything . . . I'm lonely, I'm afraid. I miss my family. But I also know we're doing something important over there, something good for a lot of people. I can't decide. I simply can't decide.'

'What would happen if you told them you changed your mind?'

'I don't know. They'd be pissed probably. But we're not talking court-martial. It's more *my* problem. I'd be disappointing people. I'd be backing down from something. Which I've never done in my life. I'd be breaking a promise.'

Dance thought for a moment, sipping the soda. 'I can't tell you what to do. But I will say one thing: My job is finding the truth. Most everybody I deal with are perps – criminals. They know the truth and they're lying to save their butts. But there're also a lot of people I come across who lie to themselves. And usually they don't even know it.

'But whether you're deceptive to the cops or your mother or husband or friends or yourself, the symptoms're always the same. You're stressed, angry, depressed. Lies turn people ugly. The truth does the opposite . . . Of course, sometimes it seems like the truth is the last thing we want. But I can't tell you how many times I've gotten a suspect to confess and he gives me this look, it's like pure relief in his face. The weirdest thing: Sometimes they even say thanks.'

'You're saying *I* know the truth?'

'Oh, yeah. You do. It's there. Covered up real good. And you might not like it when you find it. But it's there.'

'How do I find it? Interrogate myself?'

'You know, that's a great way to put it. Sure, what you do is look for the same things I look for: anger, depression, denial, excuses, rationalization. When do you feel that way and why? What's behind this feeling or that one? And don't let yourself get away with anything. Keep at it. You'll find out what you really want.'

Lucy Richter leaned forward and hugged Dance – something very few subjects ever did.

The soldier smiled. 'Hey, got an idea. Let's write a self-help book. *The Girl's Guide to Self-Interrogation*. It'll be a best seller.'

'In all our free time.' Dance laughed.

They tapped the water bottles together with a ring.

Fifteen minutes later they were halfway through the blueberry muffins and coffee that they'd ordered from room service when the agent's mobile phone chirped. She looked at the number on caller ID. Kathryn Dance shook her head and gave a laugh.

The doorbell of Rhyme's town house rang. Thom arrived in the lab a moment later, accompanying Kathryn Dance. Her hair was loose, not in the taut braid of earlier, and the iPod earbuds dangled around her neck. She took off a thin overcoat and greeted Sachs and Mel Cooper, who'd just arrived.

Dance bent down and petted Jackson, the dog.

Thom said, 'Hmm, how'd you like a going-away present?' nodding at the Havanese.

She laughed. 'He's adorable but I'm about at my livestock limit at home – both the two- and four-legged variety.'

It had been Rhyme on the phone, asking her, please, could she help them out once more?

'I promise it's the last time,' he now said as she sat beside him.

She asked, 'So what's up?'

'There's a glitch in the case. And I need your help.'

'What can I do?'

'I remember you told me about the Hanson case in California – looking over the transcript of his statement gave you some insights into what he was up to.'

She nodded.

'I'd like you to do the same thing for us.'

Rhyme now explained to her about the murder of Gerald Duncan's friend, Andrew Culbert, which set Duncan on the path of bringing down Baker and Wallace.

'But we found some curious things in the file. Culbert had a PDA but no cell phone. That was odd. Everybody in business nowadays has a cell phone. And he had a pad of paper with two notes on it. One was "Chardonnay". Which might mean that he'd written it to remind himself to buy some wine. But the other was "Men's room". Why would somebody write that? I thought about it for a bit and it occurred to me that it was the sort of thing that somebody'd write if they had a speech or hearing problem. Ordering wine in a restaurant, then asking where the rest rooms were. And no cell phone, either. I wondered if maybe he was deaf.'

'So,' Dance said, 'Duncan's friend was killed because the mugger lost his temper when the victim couldn't understand him or didn't hand over the wallet fast enough. He *thought* that Baker killed his friend but it was just a coincidence.'

Sachs said, 'It gets trickier.'

Rhyme said, 'I tracked down Culbert's widow in Duluth. She told me he'd been deaf and mute since birth.'

Sachs added, 'But Duncan said that Culbert had saved his life in the army. If he was deaf he wouldn't've been in the service.'

Rhyme said, 'I think Duncan just read about a mugging victim and claimed he was his friend – to give some credibility to his plan to implicate Baker.' The criminalist shrugged. 'It might not be a problem. After all, we collared a corrupt cop. But it leaves a few questions. Can you look at Duncan's interview tape and tell us what you think?'

'Of course.'

Cooper typed on his keyboard.

A moment later a wide-angle video of Gerald Duncan came on the monitor. He was sitting comfortably in an interview room downtown as Lon Sellitto's voice was giving the details: who he was, the date and the case. Then the statement proper began. Duncan recited essentially the same facts that he'd told Rhyme while sitting on the curb outside the last 'serial killer' scene.

Dance watched, nodding slowly as she listened to the details of his plan.

When it was finished Cooper hit PAUSE, freeze-framing Duncan's face.

Dance turned to Rhyme. 'That's all of it?'

'Yes.' He noticed her face had gone still. The criminalist asked, 'What do you think?'

She hesitated and then said, 'I have to say . . . My feeling is that it's not just the story about his friend getting killed that's a problem. I think virtually everything he's telling you on that tape is a complete lie.'

Silence in Rhyme's town house.

Total silence.

Finally Rhyme looked up from the image of Gerald Duncan, motionless on the screen, and said, 'Go on.'

'I got his baseline when he was mentioning the details of his plan to get Baker arrested. We know certain aspects of that are true. So when the stress levels change I assume he's being deceptive. I saw major deviations when he's talking about the supposed friend. And I don't think his name's Duncan. Or he lives in the Midwest. Oh, and he couldn't care less about Dennis Baker. He has no emotional interest in the man's arrest. And there's something else.'

She glanced at the screen. 'Can you cue to the middle? There's a place where he touches his cheek.'

Cooper ran the video in reverse.

'There. Play that.'

I'd never hurt anybody. I couldn't do that. I might bend the law a bit . . .

Dance shook her head, frowning.

'What?' Sachs asked.

'His eyes . . .' Dance whispered, 'Oh, this's a problem.'

'Why?'

'I'm thinking he's dangerous, very dangerous. I spent months studying the interview tapes of Ted Bundy, the serial killer. He was a pure sociopath, meaning he could deceive with virtually no outward signs whatsoever. But the one thing I could detect in Bundy was a faint reaction in his eyes when he claimed he'd never killed anyone. The reaction wasn't a typical deception response; it revealed disappointment and betrayal. He was denying something central to his being.' She nodded to the screen. 'Exactly what Duncan just did.'

'Are you sure?' Sachs asked.

'Not positive, no. But I think we've got to ask him some more questions.'

'Whatever he's up to, we better have him moved to level-three detention until we can figure it out.'

Since he'd been arrested for only minor, nonviolent crimes Gerald Duncan would be in a low-security holding tank down on Centre Street. Escape from there was unlikely but not impossible. Rhyme ordered his phone to call the supervisor of Detention in downtown Manhattan.

He identified himself and gave instructions to move Duncan to a more secure cell.

The jailer said nothing. Rhyme assumed this was because he didn't want to take orders from a civilian.

The tedium of politics . . .

He grimaced then glanced at Sachs, meaning that she should authorize the transfer. It was then that the real reason the supervisor's silence became clear. 'Well, Detective Rhyme,' the man said uneasily, 'he was only here for a few minutes. We never even booked him.'

'What?'

'The prosecutor, he cut some deal or another, and released Duncan last night. I thought you knew.'

Chapter
THIRTY-FIVE

Lon Sellitto was back in Rhyme's lab, pacing angrily.

Duncan's lawyer, it seemed, had met with the assistant district attorney and in exchange for an affidavit admitting guilt, the payment of $100,000 for misuse of police and fire resources, and a written guarantee to testify against Baker, all the criminal charges were dropped, subject to being reinstated if he reneged on the appearance in court as a witness against Baker. He'd never even been printed or booked.

The big, rumpled detective stared at the speakerphone, glowering, hands on his hips, as if the unit itself were the incompetent fool who'd released a potential killer.

The defensiveness in the prosecutor's voice was clear. 'It was the only way he'd cooperate,' the man said. 'He was represented by a lawyer from Reed, Prince. He surrendered his passport. It was all legit. He's agreed not to leave the jurisdiction until Baker's trial. I've got him in a hotel in the city, with an officer guarding him. He's not going anywhere. What's the big deal? I've done this a hundred times.'

'What about Westchester?' Rhyme called into the speakerphone. 'The stolen corpse?'

'They agreed not to prosecute. I said we'd help them out on a few other cases they needed our cooperation for.'

The prosecutor would see this as a gold ring in his career; bringing down a gang of corrupt cops would catapult him to stardom.

Rhyme shook his head, livid. Incompetence and selfish ambition infuriated him. It's hard enough to do this job without interference from politicians. Why the hell hadn't anybody called him first, before releasing Duncan? Even before Kathryn Dance's opinion about the interview tape, there were too many unanswered questions to release the man.

Sellitto barked, 'Where is he?'

'Anyway, what proof—?'

'Where the fuck is he?' Sellitto raged.

The prosecutor hesitated and gave them the name of a hotel in Midtown and the mobile number of the officer guarding him.

'I'm on it.' Cooper dialed the number.

Sellitto continued. 'And who was his lawyer?'

The assistant district attorney gave them this name too. The nervous voice said, 'I really don't see what all the fuss—'

Sellitto hung up. He looked at Dance. 'I'm about to push some serious buttons. You know what I'm saying?'

She nodded. 'We've got fan-hitting shit out in California too. But I'm comfortable with my opinion. Do whatever you can to find him. I mean, everything. I'll give that same opinion to whoever you want me to. Chief of department, mayor, governor.'

Rhyme said to Sachs, 'See what the lawyer knows about him.' She took the name, flipped open her phone. Rhyme knew of Reed, Prince, of course. It was a large, respected firm on lower Broadway. The attorneys there were known for handling high-profile, white-collar criminal defense.

In a grim voice Cooper said, 'We've got a problem. That was the officer at the hotel suite, guarding Duncan. He just checked his room. He's gone, Lincoln.'

'What?'

'The officer said he went to bed early last night, saying he wasn't feeling well and he wanted to sleep in today. Looks like he picked the lock to the adjacent room. The officer has no idea when it happened. Could've been last night.'

Sachs pinched her phone closed. 'Reed, Prince doesn't have a lawyer on staff with the name he gave the prosecutor. And Duncan isn't a client.'

'Oh, goddamn,' Rhyme snapped.

'All right,' Sellitto said, 'time for the cavalry.' He called Bo Haumann at ESU and told them they needed to arrest their suspect yet again. 'Only we aren't exactly sure where he is.'

He gave the tactical officer the few details they had. Haumann's reaction, which Rhyme didn't hear, could nonetheless be inferred from Sellitto's expression. 'You don't need to tell *me*, Bo.'

Sellitto left a message with the attorney general himself and then called the Big Building to inform the brass about the problem.

'I want more on him,' Rhyme said to Cooper. 'We were too fucking complacent. We didn't ask enough questions.' He glanced at Dance. 'Kathryn, I really hate to ask this . . .'

She was putting away her cell phone. 'I've already canceled my flight.'

'I'm sorry. It's not really your case.'

'It's been my case since I interviewed Cobb on Tuesday,' Dance said, her green eyes cold, her lips drawn.

Cooper was scrolling through the information they'd learned about Gerald Duncan. He made a list of phone numbers and started calling. After several conversations he said, 'Listen to this. He's not Duncan. The Missouri State Police sent a car out to the address on the license. It's owned by a Gerald Duncan, yeah, but not our Gerald Duncan. The guy who lived there was transferred to Anchorage for his job for six months. The house's empty and up for rent. Here's his picture.'

The image was a driver's license shot of a man very different from the one they'd arrested yesterday.

Rhyme nodded. 'Brilliant. He checked the paper for rental listings, found one that'd been on the market for a while and figured it wasn't going to rent for the next few weeks because of Christmas. Same as the church. And he forged the driver's license we saw. Passport too. We've been underestimating this guy from the beginning.'

Cooper, staring at his computer, called out, 'The owner – the real Duncan – had some credit card problems. Identity theft.'

Lincoln Rhyme felt a chill in the center of his being, a place where in theory he could feel nothing. He had a sense that an unseen disaster was unfolding quickly.

Dance was staring at the still image of Duncan's face as intently as Rhyme stared at his evidence charts. She mused, 'What's he really up to?'

A question they couldn't begin to answer.

Riding the subway, Charles Vespasian Hale, the man who'd been masquerading as Gerald Duncan, the Watchmaker, checked his wristwatch (his Breguet pocket watch, which he'd grown fond of, wouldn't fit the role he was about to assume).

Everything was right on schedule. He was taking the train from the Brooklyn neighborhood where he had his primary safe house, feeling anticipation and an edginess too, but nonetheless he was as close to harmony as he'd ever been in his life.

Very little of what he'd told Vincent Reynolds about his personal past had been true, of course. It couldn't be. He planned a long career at his profession and he knew that the mealy rapist would spill everything to the cops at the first threat.

Born in Chicago, Hale was the son of a high school Latin teacher (hence the middle name, after a noble Roman emperor) and a woman who was the manager of the petites department at a suburban Sears store. The couple never talked much, didn't do much. Every night after a quiet supper his father would gravitate to his books, his mother to her sewing machine. For familial activity they might settle in two separate chairs in front of the small television set and watch bad sitcoms and predictable cop dramas, which allowed them a unique medium of communication – by commenting on the shows, they expressed to each other the desires and resentments that they'd never have the courage to say directly.

Quiet . . .

The boy had been a loner for much of his life. He was a surprise child and his parents treated him with formal manners and apathy and a quizzical air, as if he were a species of plant whose watering and fertilizing schedule they were unsure of. The hours of boredom and solitude grew to be an open sore, and Charles felt a desperation to occupy his time, for fear the excruciating stillness in the household would strangle him.

He spent hours and hours outside – hiking and climbing trees. For some reason it was better to be alone when you were outside. There was always something to distract you, something you might find over the next hill, on the next branch up in the maple tree. He was in the field biology club at school. He went on Outward Bound expeditions and was always the first to cross the rope bridge, dive off the cliff, rappel down a mountainside.

If he was condemned to be inside, Charles developed a habit of filling his time by putting things in order. Arranging office supplies and books and toys could endlessly fill the painful hours. He wasn't lonely when he did that, he didn't ache with boredom, he wasn't afraid of the silence.

Did you know, Vincent, that the word 'meticulous' comes from the Latin meticulosus, *meaning fearful?*

When things weren't precise and ordered, he'd grow frantic, even when the glitch was something as silly as a misaligned train track or a bent bicycle spoke. Anything not running smoothly would set him on edge the way a fingernail screech on a blackboard caused other people to cringe.

Like his parents' marriage, for instance. After the divorce, he never spoke to either of them again. Life should be tidy and perfect. When it wasn't, you should be free to eliminate the disorderly elements altogether. He didn't pray (no empirical evidence that you could put your life in order or achieve your goals via divine communication) but if he had, Charles would have prayed for them to die.

Hale went into the army for two years, where he flourished in the atmosphere of order. He went to Officer Candidate School and caught the attention of his professors, who, after he was commissioned, tapped him to teach military history and tactical and strategic planning, at which he excelled.

After he was discharged he spent a year hiking and mountain climbing in Europe then he returned to America and went into business as an investment banker and venture capitalist, studying law at night.

He worked as an attorney for a time and was brilliant at structuring business deals. He made very good money but there was an underlying loneliness about his life. He shunned relationships because they required improvisation and were full of illogical behavior. More and more his passion for planning and order took on the role of lover. And like anyone who substitutes an obsession for a real relationship, Hale found himself looking for more intense ways to satisfy himself.

He found a perfect solution six years ago. He killed his first man.

Living in San Diego, Hale learned that a business associate had been badly injured. Some drunk driver had plowed into the man's car. The accident shattered the businessman's hip and snapped both legs – one of which had to be amputated. The driver expressed no remorse whatsoever and continued to deny he'd done anything wrong, even blaming the accident on the victim himself. The punk was convicted but, a first-time offender, he got off with a light sentence. Then he began harassing Hale's associate for money.

Hale decided that enough was enough. He came up with an elaborate plan to terrify the kid into stopping. But as he looked over the scheme he realized it made him feel uncomfortable, edgy. There was something clumsy about it. The plan wasn't as precisely ordered as he wanted. Finally he realized what the trouble was. His scheme left the victim scared but alive. If the kid died, then it would work perfectly and there'd be nothing to trace back to Hale or his injured associate.

But could he actually kill a human being? The idea sounded preposterous.

Yes or no?

On a rainy October night he made his decision.

The murder went perfectly and the police never suspected the man's death was anything but an unfortunate home electrocution accident.

Hale was prepared to feel remorse. But there was none. Instead he was ecstatic. The plan had been so perfectly executed, the fact that he'd killed someone was irrelevant.

The addict wanted more of his drug.

A short time later Hale was involved in a joint venture in Mexico City – building a development of upscale haciendas. But a corrupt politician managed to throw up enough stumbling blocks so the deal was going to collapse. Hale's Mexican counterpart explained that the petty politician had done this a number of times.

'It's a shame he can't be removed,' Hale had said coyly.

'Oh, he can never be *removed*,' the Mexican said. 'He is, you would say, invulnerable.'

This caught Hale's attention. 'Why?'

The crooked *Distrito Federal* commissioner, the Mexican explained, was obsessed with security. He drove in a huge armored SUV, a Cadillac custom-made for him, and was always with armed guards. His security company constantly planned different routes for him to get to and from his homes and offices and meetings. He moved his family from house to house randomly and often didn't even stay in houses that he owned, but in friends' or rentals. And he often traveled with his young son – the rumors were that he kept the boy near as a shield. The commissioner also had the protection of a senior federal interior minister.

'So, you could say he's invulnerable,' the Mexican explained, pouring two glasses of very expensive Patrón tequila.

'Invulnerable,' mused Charles Hale in a whisper. He nodded.

Not long after this meeting, five apparently unrelated articles appeared in the October 23 edition of *El Heraldo de México*.

- A fire in the office of Mexicana Seguridad Privado, a security services company, resulted in the evacuation of all employees. No injuries were reported and the damage was minor.
- A hacker shut down the main computer of a mobile phone provider, resulting in a disruption of service in a portion of Mexico City and its southern suburbs for about two hours.
- A truck caught fire in the middle of Highway 160, south of Mexico City, near Chalco, completely blocking northbound traffic.
- Henri Porfirio, the head of the *Distrito Federal* commercial real estate licensing commission, died when his SUV crashed through a one-lane bridge and plunged forty feet, struck a propane truck parked there and exploded. The incident occurred when drivers were following directions from a flagman to pull off the highway and take

a side road to avoid a major traffic jam. Other vehicles had made it successfully over the bridge earlier but the commissioner's vehicle, being armor plated, was too heavy for the old structure, despite a sign that stated it could support the SUV's weight. Porfirio's security chief knew about the traffic jam and had been trying to contact him about a safer route but was unable to because the commissioner's mobile phone was not working. His was the only vehicle that fell.

Porfirio's son was not in the SUV, which he otherwise would have been, because the child came down with a minor case of food poisoning the day before and remained at home with his mother.

- Erasmo Saleno, a senior interior official in the Mexican federal government, was arrested after a tip led police to his summer home, where they found a stash of weapons and cocaine (curiously reporters had been alerted too, including a photographer connected with the Los Angeles Times).

All in a day's news.

A month later Hale's real estate project broke ground and he received from his fellow investors in Mexico a bonus of $500,000 U.S. in cash.

He was pleased with the money. He was more pleased, though, with the connections he'd made through the Mexican businessman. It wasn't long before the man put him in touch with someone in America who needed similar services.

Now, several times a year, between his business projects, he would take on an assignment like this. Usually it was murder, though he'd also engaged in financial scams, insurance fraud and elaborate thefts. Hale would work for anyone, whatever the motive, which was irrelevant to him. He had no interest in why somebody wanted a crime committed. Twice he'd murdered abusive husbands. He killed a child molester one week before he'd murdered a businesswoman who was a major contributor to the United Way.

Good and bad were words whose definitions were different for Charles Vespasian Hale. Good was mental stimulation. Bad was boredom. Good was an elegant plan well executed. Bad was either a sloppy plan or one carelessly carried out.

But his current plot – certainly his most elaborate and far-reaching – was humming along perfectly.

God created the complex mechanism of the universe, then wound it up and started it running . . .

Hale got off the subway and climbed to the street, his nose stinging from the cold, his eyes watering, and started along the sidewalk. He was about to push the button that would set the hands of his real chronograph in motion.

Lon Sellitto's phone rang and he took the call. Frowning, he had a brief conversation. 'I'll look into it.'

Rhyme glanced up expectantly.

'That was Haumann. He just got a call from the manager of a delivery service on the same floor as the company that the Watchmaker broke into in Midtown. He said a customer just called. A package they were supposed to deliver yesterday never showed up. Looks like somebody broke in and stole it around the time that we were sweeping the offices looking for the perp. The manager asked if we knew anything about it.'

Rhyme's eyes slipped to the photographs that Sachs had taken of the hallway. Bless her, she'd taken pictures of the entire floor. Below the name of the delivery service were the words *High Security – Valuable Deliveries Guaranteed. Licensed and Bonded.*

Rhyme heard the white noise of people talking around him. But he didn't hear the words themselves. He stared at the photograph and then at the other evidence.

'Access,' he whispered.

'What?' Sellitto asked, frowning.

'We were so focused on the Watchmaker and the fake killings – and then on his scheme to flush out Baker – we never looked at what else was going on.'

'Which was?' Sachs asked.

'Breaking and entering. The crime he *actually* committed was trespass. All of the offices on that floor were unguarded for a time. When they evacuated the building, they left the doors unlocked?'

'Well, yeah, I suppose,' the big detective said.

Sachs said, 'So while we were focused on the flooring company the Watchmaker might've put on a uniform or just hung a badge over his neck then strolled right inside the delivery service and helped himself to that package.'

Access . . .

'Call the service. Find out what was in the package, who sent it and where it was going. Now.'

Chapter
THIRTY-SIX

A taxicab pulled up in front of the Metropolitan Museum of
Art, on Fifth Avenue. The huge building was decorated for
Christmas, dolled up in the tasteful Victorian regalia that
you'd expect on the Upper East Side. Subdued festive.

Out of this cab climbed Charles Vespasian Hale, who looked
around carefully on the remote chance that the police were
following him. It would have been exceedingly unlikely that
he'd be under surveillance. Still, Hale took his time, looked
everywhere for anyone showing him the least attention. He
saw nothing troubling.

He leaned down to the open taxi window and paid the
driver – tendering the cash in gloved hands – and, hooking a
black canvas bag over his shoulder, he climbed the stairs into
the large cathedral-like lobby, which echoed with the sound
of voices, most of them young; the place was lousy with kids
freed from school. Evergreens and gold and ornaments and
tulle were everywhere. Bach two-part inventions plucked away
cheerily on a recorded harpsichord, echoing in the cavernous
entryway.

'Tis the season . . .

Hale left the black bag at the coat check, though he kept

his coat and hat. The clerk looked inside the bag, noted the four art books, then zipped it back up and told Hale to have a nice day. He took the claim check and paid admission. He nodded a smile at the guards at the entrance and walked past them into the museum itself.

'The Delphic Mechanism?' Rhyme was talking to the director of the Metropolitan Museum of Art via speakerphone. 'It's still on display there?'

'Yes, Detective,' the man replied uncertainly. 'We've had it here for two weeks. It's part of a multi-city tour—'

'Fine, fine, fine. Is it guarded?'

'Yes, of course. I—'

'There's a possibility that a thief's trying to steal it.'

'Steal it? Are you sure? It's a one-of-a-kind *object*. Whoever took possession could never show it in public.'

'He doesn't intend to sell it,' Rhyme said. 'I think he wants it for himself.'

The criminalist explained: The package stolen from the delivery service in the building on Thirty-second Street was from a wealthy patron of the arts and was destined for the Metropolitan Museum. It contained a large portfolio of some antiques being offered to the museum's furniture collection.

The Metropolitan Museum? Rhyme had wondered. He'd then recalled the museum programs found in the church. He'd asked Vincent Reynolds and the clock dealer, Victor Hallerstein, if Duncan had mentioned anything about the Met. He had, apparently – spending considerable time there – and he'd expressed particular interest in the Delphic Mechanism.

Rhyme now told the director, 'We think he may have stolen the package to smuggle something into the museum. Maybe tools, maybe software to disable alarms. We don't know. I can't figure it out at this point. But I think we have to be cautious.'

'My God . . . All right. What do we do?'

Rhyme looked up at Cooper, who typed on his keyboard and gave a thumbs-up. Into the microphone the criminalist said, 'We've just emailed you his picture. Could you print it out and get a copy to all the employees, the security surveillance room and the coat check? See if they recognize him.'

'I'll do it right now. Can you hold for a few minutes?'

'Sure.'

Soon the director came on the line. 'Detective Rhyme?' His voice was breathless. 'He's here! He checked a bag about ten minutes ago. The clerk recognized the picture.'

'The bag's still there?'

'Yes. He hasn't left.'

Rhyme nodded at Sellitto, who picked up the phone and called Bo Haumann at ESU, whose teams were on their way to the museum, and told him this latest news.

'The guard at the Mechanism,' Rhyme asked, 'is he armed?'

'No. Do you think the thief is? We don't have metal detectors at the entrance. He could've brought a gun in.'

'It's possible.' Rhyme looked at Sellitto with a lifted eyebrow. The detective asked, 'Move a team in slow? Undercover?'

'He checked a bag . . . and he knows clocks.' He asked the museum director, 'Did anybody look in the bag?'

'I'll check. Hold on.' A moment later he came back. 'Books. He has art books inside. But the coat-check clerk didn't examine them.'

'Bomb for diversion?' Sellitto asked.

'Could be. Maybe it's only smoke but even then people'll panic. Could be fatalities either way.'

Haumann called in on his radio. His crackling voice: 'Okay, we've got teams approaching all the entrances, public and service.'

Rhyme asked Dance, 'You're convinced he's willing to take lives?'

'Yes.'

He was considering the man's astonishing plot-making skills. Was there some other deadly plan he'd put into play if he realized he was about to be arrested at the museum? Rhyme made a decision. 'Evacuate.'

Sellitto asked, 'The entire museum?'

'I think we have to. First priority – save lives. Clear the coatroom and front lobby and then move everybody else out. Have Haumann's men check out everybody who leaves. Make sure the teams have his picture.'

The museum director had heard. 'You think that's necessary?'

'Yes. Do it now.'

'Okay, but I just don't see how anyone could steal it,' the director said. 'The Mechanism's behind inch-thick bullet-proof glass. And the case can't be opened until the day the exhibit closes, next Tuesday.'

'What do you mean?' Rhyme asked.

'It's in one of our special display cases.'

'But why won't it open until Tuesday?'

'Because the case has a computerized time lock, with a satellite link to some government clock. They tell me nobody can break into it. We put the most valuable exhibits in there.'

The man continued speaking but Rhyme looked away. Something was nagging him. Then he recalled, 'That arson earlier, the one that Fred Dellray wanted us to help out on. Where was it again?'

Sachs frowned. 'A government office. The Institute of Standards and Technology or something like that. Why?'

'Look it up, Mel.'

The tech went online. Reading from the website, he said, 'NIST is the new name for the National Bureau of Standards and—'

'Bureau of Standards?' Rhyme interrupted. 'They maintain the country's atomic clock . . . Is *that* what he's up to? The time lock at the Met has an uplink to the NIST. Somehow he's going to change the time, convince the lock that it's next Tuesday. The vault'll open automatically.'

'Can he do that?' Dance asked.

'I don't know. But if it's possible, he'll find a way. The fire at NIST was to cover up the break-in, I'll bet . . .' Then Rhyme stopped talking, as the full implications of the Watchmaker's plan became clear. 'Oh, no . . .'

'What?'

Rhyme was thinking about Kathryn Dance's observation: That to the Watchmaker, human life was negligible. He said, 'Time everywhere in the country is governed by the U.S. atomic clock. Airlines, trains, national defense, power grids, computers . . . everything. Do you have any idea what's going to happen if he resets it?'

In a cheap Midtown hotel, a middle-aged man and woman sat on a small couch that smelled of mildew and old food. They were staring at a television set.

Charlotte Allerton was the stocky woman who'd pretended to be the sister of Theodore Adams, the first 'victim' in the alley on Tuesday. The man beside her, Bud Allerton, her husband, was the man masquerading as the lawyer who'd secured Gerald Duncan's release from jail by promising that his client would be a spectacular witness in the crooked cop scandal.

Bud really was a lawyer, though he hadn't practiced for some years. He'd resurrected some of his old skills for the sake of Duncan's plan, which called for Bud's pretending to be a criminal attorney from the big, prestigious law firm of Reed, Prince. The assistant district attorney had bought the entire charade, not even bothering to call the firm to check up on the man. Gerald Duncan had believed, correctly, that the prosecutor would be so eager to make a name for himself on a police corruption case that he'd believe what he wanted to. Besides, whoever asks for a lawyer's ID?

The Allertons' attention was almost exclusively on the TV screen, showing local news. A program about Christmas tree safety. Yadda, yadda, yadda . . . For a moment Charlotte's gaze slipped to the master bedroom in the suite, where her pretty, thin daughter sat reading a book. The girl looked through the doorway at her mother and stepfather with the same dark, sullen eyes that had typified her expression in recent months.

That girl . . .

Frowning, Charlotte looked back to the TV screen. 'Isn't it taking too long?'

Bud said nothing. His thick fingers were intertwined and he sat forward, hunched, elbows on knees. She wondered if he was praying.

A moment later the reporter whose mission was to save families from the scourge of burning Christmas trees disappeared and on the screen came the words *Special News Bulletin*.

Chapter
THIRTY-SEVEN

In doing his research into watchmaking, so that he could be a credible revenge killer, Charles Hale had learned of the concept of 'complications'.

A complication is a function in a watch or clock other than telling the time of day. For instance, those small dials that dot the front of expensive timepieces, giving information like day of the week and date, and time zones in different locations, and repeater functions (chimes sounding at certain intervals). Watchmakers have always enjoyed the challenge of getting as many complications into their watches as possible. A typical one is the Patek Philippe Star Calibre 2000, a watch featuring more than one thousand parts. Its complications offer the owner such information as the times of sunrise and sunset, a perpetual calendar, the day, date and month, the season, moon phases, lunar orbit and power reserve indicators for both the watch's movement and the several chimes inside.

The trouble with complications, though, is that they're just that. They tend to distract from the ultimate purpose of a watch: telling time. Breitling makes superb timepieces but some of the Professional and Navitimer models have so many dials, hands and side functions, like chronographs (the technical term for stopwatches) and logarithmic slide rules, that it's easy to miss the big hand and the little hand.

But complications were exactly what Charles Hale needed for his plan here in New York City, distractions to lead the police away from what he was really about. Because there was a good chance that Lincoln Rhyme and his team would find out that he was no longer in custody and that he wasn't really Gerald Duncan, they'd realize he had something else in mind other than getting even with a crooked cop.

So he needed yet another complication to keep the police focused elsewhere.

Hale's cell phone vibrated. He glanced at the text message, which was from Charlotte Allerton. *Special Report on TV: Museum closed. Police searching for you there.*

He put the phone back in his pocket.

And enjoyed a moment of keen, almost sexual, satisfaction.

The message told him that while Rhyme *had* tipped to the fact that he wasn't who he seemed to be, the police were still missing the time of day and focusing on the complication of the Metropolitan Museum. He was pointing the police toward what appeared to be a plan to steal the famous Delphic Mechanism. At the church he'd planted brochures on the horological exhibits in Boston and Tampa. He'd rhapsodized on the device to Vincent Reynolds. He'd hinted to the antiques dealer about his obsession with old timepieces, mentioning the Mechanism specifically, and that he was aware of the exhibit at the Met. The small fire he'd set at the National Institute of Standards and Technology in Brooklyn would make them think he was going to somehow reset the country's cesium clock, disabling the Met's time-security system, and steal the Mechanism.

A plot to steal the device seemed to be just the clever, subtle deduction for the cops to seize as Hale's real motive. Officers would spend hours scouring the museum and nearby

Central Park looking for him and examining the canvas bag he'd left. It contained four hollowed-out books, inside of which were two bags of baking soda, a small scanner and, of course, a clock – a cheap digital alarm. None of them meant anything but each was sure to keep the police busy for hours.

The complications in his plan were as elegant, if not as numerous, as those in what was reportedly the world's most elaborate wristwatch, one made by Gerald Genta.

But at the moment Hale was nowhere near the museum, which he'd left a half hour ago. Not long after he'd entered and checked the bag, he'd walked into a restroom stall, then taken off his coat, revealing an army uniform, rank of major. He'd donned glasses and a military-style hat – hidden in a false pocket in his coat – and had left the museum quickly. He was presently in downtown Manhattan, slowly making his way through the security line leading into the New York office of the Department of Housing and Urban Development.

In a short time a number of soldiers and their families would attend a ceremony in their honor, hosted by the city and the U.S. Departments of Defense and State, in the HUD building. Officials would be greeting soldiers recently returned from foreign conflicts and their families, giving them letters of commendation for their service in recent world conflicts and thanking them for reenlisting. Following the ceremonies, and the requisite photo ops and trite statements to the press, the guests would leave and the generals and other government officials would reconvene to discuss future efforts to spread democracy to other places in the world.

These government officials, as well as the soldiers, their families and any members of the press who happened to be present, were the real point of Charles Hale's mission in New York.

He had been hired for the simple purpose of killing as many of them as he could.

With husky, ever-smiling Bob driving, Lucy Richter sat in the car as they made their way past the reviewing stand outside the Housing and Urban Development building where the parade was just winding down.

Her hand on her husband's muscular thigh, Lucy was silent.

The Honda nosed through the heavy traffic, Bob making casual conversation, talking about the party tonight. Lucy responded halfheartedly. She'd grown troubled once again about the Big Conflict – what she'd confessed to Kathryn Dance. Should she go through with the reenlistment or not?

Self-interrogation . . .

When she'd agreed a month earlier; was she being honest or being deceptive with herself?

Looking for the things Agent Dance told her: anger, depression . . . Am I lying?

She tried to put the debate out of her head.

They were close to the HUD building now and across the street she saw protesters. They were against the various foreign conflicts America was involved in. Her friends and fellow soldiers overseas were pissed off at anybody who protested but, curiously, Lucy didn't see it that way. She believed the very fact that these people were free to demonstrate and were not in jail validated what she was doing.

The couple drew closer to the checkpoint at the intersection near the HUD building. Two soldiers stepped forward to check their IDs and to look in the trunk.

Lucy stiffened.

'What?' her husband asked.

'Look,' she said.

He glanced down. Her right hand was on her hip, where she wore her sidearm when on duty.

'Going for the fast draw?' Bob joked.

'Instinct. At checkpoints.' She laughed. But it was a humorless sound.

Bitter fog . . .

Bob nodded at the soldiers and smiled to his wife. 'I think we're pretty safe. Not like we're in Baghdad or Kabul.'

Lucy squeezed his hand and they proceeded to the parking lot reserved for the honorees.

Charles Hale was not completely apolitical. He had some general opinions about democracy versus theocracy versus communism versus fascism. But he knew his views amounted to the same pedestrian positions offered by listeners calling in to Rush Limbaugh or NPR radio, nothing particularly radical or articulate. So last October when Charlotte and Bud Allerton hired him for the job of 'sending a message' about big government and wrong-minded American intervention in 'heathen' foreign nations, Hale had yawned mentally.

But he was intrigued by the challenge.

'We've talked to six people and nobody'll take the job,' Bud Allerton told him. 'It's next to impossible.'

Charles Vespasian Hale liked that word. One wasn't bored when taking on the impossible. It was like 'invulnerable'.

Charlotte and Bud – her second husband – were part of a right-wing militia fringe group that had been attacking federal government employees and buildings and UN facilities for years. They'd gone underground a while ago but recently, enraged at the government's meddling forays into world affairs, she and the others in her nameless organization decided it was time to go after something big.

This attack would not only send their precious message but would cause some real harm to the enemy: killing generals and government officials who'd betrayed principles America was founded on and sent our boys and – God help us – girls to die on foreign soil for the benefit of people who were backward and cruel and non-Christian.

Hale had managed to extract himself from his rhetoric-addicted clients and got to work. On Halloween he'd come to New York, moved into the safe house in Brooklyn, and spent the next month and a half engrossed in the construction of his timepiece – acquiring supplies, finding unwitting associates to help him (Dennis Baker and Vincent Reynolds), learning everything he could about the Watchmaker's supposed victims and surveilling the HUD building.

Which he was now approaching through the bitterly cold morning air.

This building had been chosen for the ceremonies and meetings not because of the department's mission, which had nothing to do with the military, of course, but because it offered the best security of any federal building in lower Manhattan. The walls were thick limestone; if a terrorist were somehow to negotiate the barricades surrounding the place and detonate a car bomb, the resulting explosion would cause less damage than it would to a modern, glass-facaded structure. HUD was also lower than most offices downtown, which made it a difficult target for missiles or suicide airplanes. It had a limited number of entrances and exits, thus making access control easier, and the room where the awards ceremony and later the strategic meetings would take place faced the windowless wall of the building across the alleyway so no sniper could shoot into the room.

With another two dozen soldiers and police armed with automatic weapons on the surrounding streets and tops of buildings, HUD was virtually impregnable.

From the exterior, that is.

But no one realized that the threat wouldn't be coming from outside.

Charles Hale displayed his three military-issue IDs, two of

them unique to this event and delivered to attendees just two days ago. He was nodded through the metal detector, then physically patted down.

A final guard, a corporal, checked his IDs a second time then saluted him. Hale returned the gesture and stepped inside.

The HUD building was labyrinthine but Hale now made his way quickly to the basement. He knew the layout of the place perfectly because the fifth supposed victim of the psycho Watchmaker, Sarah Stanton, was the estimator of the flooring company that had supplied carpeting and linoleum tile to the building, a fact he'd learned from public filings regarding government contractors. In Sarah's file cabinets he found precise drawings of every room and hallway in HUD. (The company was also across the hall from a delivery service – which he'd called earlier to complain about a package to the Metropolitan Museum that had never been delivered, lending credence to the apparent plot to steal the Delphic Mechanism.)

In fact, all of the Watchmaker's 'assaults' this week, with the exception of the attention-getting blood bath at the pier, were vital steps in his mission today: the flooring company, Lucy Richter's apartment, the Cedar Street alleyway and the florist shop.

He'd broken into Lucy's to photograph, and later forge, the special all-access passes that were required for soldiers attending the awards ceremony (he'd learned her name from a newspaper story about the event). He'd also copied and later memorized a classified Defense Department memo she'd been given about the event and security procedures that would be in effect at HUD today.

The apparent murder of the fictional Teddy Adams had served a purpose, as well. It was in the alley behind this very building that Hale had placed the body of the Westchester car wreck victim. When Charlotte Allerton – playing the man's distraught sister – had arrived, the guards had let the hysterical woman through the back door of HUD and allowed her to use the restroom downstairs without searching her. Once inside, she'd planted what Hale was now retrieving from the bottom of the in-wall trash bin: a silenced .22-caliber pistol and two metal disks. There'd been no other way to get these items into a building protected by a series of metal detectors and pat-downs. He now hid these in his pockets and headed to the sixth-floor conference room.

Once there, Hale spotted what he thought of as the main-spring of his plan: the two large flower arrangements that Joanne Harper had created for the ceremony, one in the front of the room and one in the back. Hale had learned from the Government Service Administration vendor liaison office that she had the contract to supply flower arrangements and plants to the HUD facility. He'd broken into her Spring Street work-shop to hide something in the vases, which would pass through security with, he hoped, only a brief look, since Joanne had been a trusted vendor for several years. When Hale had broken in to her workshop he'd taken with him, in his shoulder bag, something in addition to the moon-faced clock and his tools: two jars of an explosive known as Astrolite. More powerful than TNT or nitroglycerin, Astrolite was a clear liquid that remained explosive even when absorbed into another substance. Hale found which arrangements were going to HUD and poured the Astrolite into the bottom of the vases.

Hale, of course, might have simply broken into the four locations without the fiction of the Watchmaker, but if anyone had seen a burglar or noticed anything missing or out of order, the question would have arisen: What was he really up to? So he'd created layers of motives for the break-ins. His orig-inal plan was simply to pretend to be a serial killer to get access to the four locations he needed to, sacrificing his unfor-tunate assistant, Vincent Reynolds, in order to convince the police that the Watchmaker was just who he seemed to be.

But then in mid November, an organized crime contact in the area called and told him that an NYPD cop named Dennis Baker was looking for a hit man to kill an NYPD detective. The mob wouldn't touch killing a cop, but was Hale interested? He wasn't but he immediately realized that he could use Baker as a second complication to the plan: a citizen getting revenge against a crooked cop. Finally, he added the wonderful flourish of the Delphic Mechanism theft.

Motive is the one sure way to get yourself caught. Eliminate the motive, you eliminate suspicion . . .

Hale now stepped to the front flower arrangement in the conference room and adjusted it the way any diligent soldier would do – a soldier proud to be part of this important occasion. When no one was looking he pushed one of the metal disks he'd just retrieved from downstairs – computerized detonators – into the explosive, pushed the button to arm it and fluffed up the moss, obscuring the device. He did the same to the arrangement in the back, which would detonate via a radio signal from the first detonator.

These two lovely arrangements were now lethal bombs, containing enough explosive to obliterate the entire room.

The tone in Rhyme's lab was electric.

Everyone, except Pulaski, on a mission at Rhyme's request, was staring at the criminalist, who was in turn gazing at the evidence charts that surrounded him like battalions of soldiers awaiting his orders.

'There'll still be too many questions,' Sellitto said. 'You know what's going to happen if we push *that* button.'

Rhyme glanced at Amelia Sachs. 'What do you think?' he asked.

Her ample lips tightened. 'I don't think we have any choice. I say yes.'

'Oh, man,' Sellitto said.

Rhyme said to the rumpled lieutenant, 'Make the call.'

Lon Sellitto dialed a little-known number that connected him immediately to the scrambled phone sitting on the desk of the mayor of New York City.

Standing in the conference room in HUD, which was filling up with soldiers and their guests, Charles Hale felt his phone vibrate. He pulled it from his pocket and glanced down at the text message, another one from Charlotte Allerton. *FAA grounding all flights. Trains stopped. Special team at NIST office checking U.S. clock. It's a go. God bless.*

Perfect, Charles thought. The police believed the complication about the Delphic Mechanism and his apparent plan to hack into the computer controlling the nation's cesium clock.

Hale stepped back, looked over the room and plastered a satisfied look on his face. He left and took the elevator down to the main lobby. He walked outside, where limos were arriving, under heavy security. He eased into the crowd that was gathered on the other side of the concrete barriers, some waving flags, some applauding.

He noted the protesters too, scruffy young people, aging hippies and activist professors and their spouses, he assessed. They carried placards and were chanting things that Hale couldn't hear. The gist, though, was displeasure at U.S. foreign policy.

Hang around, he told them silently.

Sometimes you get what you ask for.

Chapter
THIRTY-EIGHT

Entering the sixth-floor conference room with seventeen other soldiers from all branches of the armed services, United States Army Sergeant Lucy Richter gave a brief smile to her husband. A wink too to her family – her parents and her aunt – who were sitting across the room.

The acknowledgment was perhaps a little abrupt, a little distant. But she was not here as Bob's wife or as a daughter or niece. She was here as a decorated soldier, in the company of her superior officers and her fellow men and women at arms.

The soldiers had assembled downstairs in the building, while their families and friends had come to the conference room. Waiting for their grand entrance, Lucy had chatted with the young man, an air force corpsman from Texas who'd come back to the States for medical treatment (one of those fucking rocket-propelled grenades had ricocheted off his chest pack before exploding several yards away). He was eager to get back home, he'd said.

'Home?' she'd asked. 'I thought we were reenlisting.'

He'd blinked. 'I am. I mean my unit. That *is* home.'

Standing uneasily in front of her chair, she glanced at the

reporters. The way they looked around them, searching hungrily for story opportunities like snipers seeking targets, made her nervous. Then she put them out of her mind and gazed at the pictures that had been mounted for the ceremony. Patriotic images. She was moved by the sight of the American flag, the photo of the Trade Center towers, the military banners and emblems, the officers with their decorations and rows of breast bars, revealing how long and where they'd served.

And all the while the debate raged. Thinking back to what Kathryn Dance had said, she asked herself: And what's the truth for me?

Go back to the land of bitter fog?

Or stay here?

Yes, no?

The side doors opened and in walked two quick-eyed men – Secret Service – followed by a half dozen men and women in suits or uniforms with senior staff insignias and ribbons and medals covering their chests. Lucy recognized a few of the bigwigs from Washington and New York City, though she was more stirred by the presence of the brass from the Pentagon, since they'd come up through the world that she'd made a part of her life.

The wearisome debate continued within her.

Yes, no . . .

The truth . . . What's the truth?

When the officials were seated, a general from New Jersey made a few comments and introduced a poised, handsome man in a dark blue uniform. General Roger Poulin, chairman of the Joint Chiefs of Staff, rose and walked to the microphone.

Poulin nodded to his presenter and then to those in the room. In a deep voice he said, 'Generals, distinguished officials from the Departments of Defense and State and the City of New York, fellow servicemen and women and guests . . .

I'm delighted to welcome you here today to this celebration honoring eighteen brave individuals, people who have risked their lives and displayed their willingness to make the ultimate sacrifice to preserve the freedom of our country and carry the cause of democracy throughout the globe.'

Applause erupted and the guests rose to their feet.

The noise died down and General Poulin began his speech. Lucy Richter listened at first but her attention soon faded. She was looking at the civilians in the room – the family members and guests of the soldiers. People like her father and mother and husband and aunt, the spouses, the children, the parents and grandparents, the friends.

These people would leave after the ceremony, go to their jobs or their homes. They'd get back to the simple business of making their way in the world one day, one hour, one minute at a time.

Her military demeanor would not, of course, let her smile but Lucy Richter could feel her face relaxing and the tension in her shoulders vanish like the bitter fog carried away on a hot wind. The anger, the depression, the denial – everything that Kathryn Dance had told her to look for – suddenly were gone.

She closed her eyes momentarily and then turned her attention back to the man who was, after the president of the United States, her senior commander, understanding clearly now that, whatever else happened in her life, her decision had been made and she was content.

Charles Hale was in the men's room of a small coffee shop not far from the HUD building. In a filthy stall he extracted a trash bag from beneath his undershirt. He stripped off the military uniform and put on jeans, sweats, gloves and a jacket, which he'd just bought. He stuffed the uniform, coat and hat inside, keeping the gun. He took the battery and chip out of his phone and added them to the bag. Then, waiting until the restroom was empty, he stuffed it into the trash, left the coffee shop and walked outside.

On the street again, he bought a prepaid mobile phone with cash and wandered along the shadowy sidewalk until he was three blocks from HUD. From this vantage point he had a narrow view of the back of the building and the alley where the first 'victim' of the Watchmaker had been found. He could just make out a sliver of the sixth-floor window of the conference room where the ceremonies were going on.

The jacket was thin and he supposed he should be cold, but in the excitement of the moment he felt no discomfort. He looked at his digital wristwatch, which was synchronized to the timers in the bomb detonators.

The time was 12:14:19. The ceremony had been under way since noon. With bombs, he'd learned in his exhaustive research, you always gave people the chance to settle in, for stragglers to arrive, for guards to grow lax.

12:14:29.

One nice aspect of these particular bombs, he reflected, something fortuitous, was that Joanne the florist had filled the vases with hundreds of tiny glass marbles. Anybody not killed or badly injured by the explosives themselves would be riddled with these glass pellets.

12:14:44.

Hale found himself leaning forward, his weight on the balls of his feet. There was always the possibility that something would go wrong – that security would make a last-minute sweep for explosives or that somebody had seen him on the video camera entering the building then leaving suspiciously after a short period of time.

12:14:52.

Still, the risk of failure made the victory against boredom that much sweeter. His eyes were riveted on the alleyway behind the HUD building.

12:14:55.

12:14:56.

12:14:57.

12:14:58.

12:14:59.

12:15:00—

Silently a huge fist of flame and debris shot out of the conference room window. A half second later came the stunning sound of the explosion itself.

Voices around him. 'Oh, my God. What—?'

Screams.

'Look, there! What's that?'

'God, no!'

'Call nine-one-one! Somebody . . .'

Pedestrians were clustering on the sidewalk, staring.

'A bomb? An airplane?'

Concern on his face, Hale shook his head, lingering for a moment to savor the success. The explosion seemed bigger than he'd anticipated; the fatalities would be greater than Charlotte and Bud had hoped. It was hard to see how anybody could have survived.

He turned slowly and continued up the street, where he descended once more into the subway station and took the next train uptown. He emerged at the station and headed toward the Allertons' hotel, where he'd pick up the rest of his payment.

Charles Hale was satisfied. He'd staved off boredom and had earned some good money.

Most important, though, was the breathtaking elegance of what he'd done. He'd created a plan that had worked perfectly – like clockwork, he thought, enjoying the self-conscious simile.

Chapter
THIRTY-NINE

'Oh, thank you,' Charlotte whispered, speaking both to Jesus and to the man who'd made their mission a success.

She was sitting forward, staring at the TV. The special news report about the evacuation of the Metropolitan Museum and the halting of public transportation in the area had been replaced by a different story – the bombing at the HUD building. Charlotte squeezed her husband's hand. Bud leaned over and kissed her. He smiled like a young boy.

The news anchorwoman was grim – despite her restrained pleasure at being on duty when such a big story broke – as she gave what details there were: A bomb had gone off within the Housing and Urban Development building in lower Manhattan, where a number of senior government and military officials had been attending a ceremony. An undersecretary of state and the head of the Joint Chiefs were present. The cameras showed smoke pouring from the windows of a conference room. The important detail – the casualty count – had not come in yet, though at least fifty people were in the room where the bomb detonated.

A talking head popped up on the screen; his complete

lack of knowledge of the event didn't stop him from drawing the conclusion that this was the job of fundamentalist Islamic terrorists.

They'd soon know differently.

'Look, honey, we did it!' Charlotte called to her daughter, who had remained in the bedroom, lost in a book. (That satanic Harry Potter. Charlotte had thrown out two of them. Where on earth had the girl gotten another copy?)

The girl gave an exasperated sigh and returned to the book.

Charlotte was momentarily furious. She wanted to storm into the bedroom and slap the girl's face as hard as she could. They'd just won a spectacular victory and the girl was showing nothing but disrespect. Bud had asked several times if he could take a hickory stick to the girl's bare butt. Charlotte had demurred but she was now wondering if maybe it wasn't such a bad idea.

Still, her anger faded when she thought of their victory today. She stood up. 'We better leave.' She shut the TV off and continued packing a suitcase. Bud walked into the bedroom to do the same. They were going to drive to Philadelphia, where they'd get a plane back to St Louis – Duncan had told them to avoid the New York airports afterward. They'd then return to the backwoods of Missouri and go underground again – waiting for the next opportunity to further their cause.

Gerald Duncan would be here soon. He'd collect the rest of his money and leave town too. She wondered if she could convert him to their cause. She'd spoken to him about the idea but he wasn't interested, though he said he'd be more than happy to help them out again if they had any particularly difficult targets and if the money was right.

A knock on the door.

Duncan was right on time.

Laughing, Charlotte strode to the door and flung it open. 'You did it! I—'

But her words stopped short, the smile vanished. The policeman, in black helmet and combat outfit, pushed inside. With him was Amelia Sachs, a large black pistol in her hand, her face furious, eyes squinting as she scanned the room.

A half dozen other cops streamed in behind them. 'Police! Freeze, freeze!'

'No!' Charlotte wailed. She twisted away but got only one step before they tackled her hard.

In the bedroom, Bud Allerton gasped in shock as he heard his wife scream, the harsh voices and the stomping of feet. He slammed the door shut and pulled an automatic pistol from his suitcase, worked the slide to put a round in the chamber.

'No!' his stepdaughter cried, dropping her book and scrabbling for the door.

'Quiet,' he whispered viciously. He grabbed her by the arm. She screamed as he flung her onto the bed. Her head hit the wall and she lay stunned. Bud had never liked the girl, didn't like her attitude, didn't like her sarcasm and her rebelliousness. Children were put on earth to obey – girls especially – or suffer the consequences if they didn't.

He listened at the door. It sounded like a dozen officers were in the living room of the suite. Bud didn't have much time for a prayer but those through whom God speaks can be moved to communicate with Him as circumstances allow.

My dear Lord and Savior Jesus Christ, thank you for the glory you've bestowed upon us, the true believers. Please give me the strength to end my life and hasten my journey to you. And let me send to hell as many of those as I can who have come here to transgress against you.

There were fifteen bullets in the clip of his pistol. He

could take plenty of the police with him, if he remained steady and if God gave him the strength to ignore the wounds he'd receive. But still they'd have a lot of firepower. He needed some advantage.

Bud turned toward his sobbing stepdaughter, who was clutching her bleeding head. He added a coda to the prayer, with a kindness that he thought was particularly generous under the circumstances.

And when you receive this child into heaven, please forgive her her sins against you. She knew not what she did.

He rose, walked over to his stepdaughter and grabbed her by the hair.

'Is Allerton in there?' Amelia Sachs shouted to Charlotte, nodding at the closed bedroom door.

She said nothing.

'The girl?'

Downstairs, the desk manager explained what suite Charlotte and Bud Allerton, along with their daughter, were staying in and the layout of the place. He was pretty sure they were upstairs now. The clerk recognized the picture of the Watchmaker and said that the man had been here several times but hadn't been back today, as far as he knew.

'Where's Allerton?' Sachs now snapped. She wanted to grab the woman and shake her.

Charlotte remained silent, glaring up at the detective.

'Bathroom clear,' one ESU officer called.

'Second bedroom clear.'

'Closet clear,' called Ron Pulaski, the slim officer looking nearly comical in the bulky flak jacket and helmet.

Only the bedroom with the closed door remained. Sachs approached it, stood to the side and motioned the other officers out of the line of fire. 'You, inside the bedroom, listen! I'm a police officer. Open the door!'

No response.

Sachs tested the knob. The door was unlocked. A deep breath, gun up.

She opened the door fast and dropped into a combat shooting position. Sachs saw the girl – the same one who'd been in Charlotte's car at the Watchmaker's first crime scene. The girl's hands were tied together and adhesive tape was over her mouth and nose. Her skin was blue and she thrashed on the bed, desperate for oxygen. It was a matter of seconds until she suffocated.

Ron Pulaski shouted, 'Look, the window's open.' Nodding toward the bedroom window. 'Guy's getting away.'

He started forward.

Sachs grabbed him by the flak jacket.

'What?' he asked.

'It's not secure yet,' she snapped. She nodded to the living room. 'Check the fire escape from there. See if he's outside. And be careful. He might be targeting the window.'

The rookie ran to the front of the room and looked out fast. He called, 'Nope. Might've gotten away.' He radioed ESU outside to check the alley behind the hotel.

Sachs debated. But she couldn't wait any longer. She had to save the girl. She started forward.

But then stopped fast. Despite the horrifying suffocation, Charlotte's daughter was sending her a message. She was shaking her head no, which Sachs took to mean that this was an ambush. The daughter looked to her right, indicating where Allerton, or somebody, was hiding, probably waiting to shoot.

Sachs dropped into a crouch. 'Whoever's in the bedroom, drop your weapon! Lie down, face forward in the middle of the room! Now.'

Silence.

The poor girl thrashed, eyes bulging.

'Drop the weapon now!'

Nothing.

Several ESU officers had come up. One hefted a flash-bang grenade, designed to disorient attackers. But people can still shoot if they're deafened and blinded. Sachs was worried that he'd hit the girl if he started pumping bullets indiscriminately. She shook her head to the ESU officer and aimed into the bedroom through the door. She had to get him and now; the child had no time left.

But the girl was shaking her head again. She struggled to control the convulsions and looked to Sachs's right, then down.

Even though she was dying, she was directing Sachs's fire.

Sachs adjusted her aim – it was much farther to the right than she would have guessed. If she'd fired at the place she'd been inclined to, a shooter would've known her position and possibly hit her with return fire.

The girl nodded.

Still, Sachs hesitated. Was the girl really sending her this message? The child was revealing discipline that few adults could muster, and Sachs didn't dare misinterpret it; the risk of hurting an innocent was too great.

But then she recalled the look in the girl's eyes the first time she'd seen her, in the car near the alley by Cedar Street. There, she'd seen hope. Here, she saw courage.

Sachs gripped her pistol firmly and fired six rounds in a circular pattern where the girl was indicating. Without waiting to see what she'd hit she leapt into the room, ESU officers behind her.

'Get the girl!' she shouted, sweeping the area to her right – the bathroom and closet – with her Glock. One ESU trooper covered the room with his MP-5 machine gun as the other officers pulled the girl to safety on the floor and ripped the tape off her face. Sachs heard the rasp of her desperate inhalation, then sobbing.

Sachs flung open the closet door and stepped aside as the man's corpse – hit four times – tumbled out. She kicked aside his weapon and cleared the closet and the bathroom, then – not taking any chances – the shower stall, the space under the bed and the fire escape too.

A minute later the entire suite was clear. Charlotte, red-faced with fury and sobbing, was sitting handcuffed on the couch and the girl was in the hallway being given oxygen by medics; she'd suffered no serious injuries, they reported.

Charlotte would say nothing about the Watchmaker, and a preliminary search of the rooms gave no indication where he might be. Sachs found an envelope containing $250,000 cash, which suggested that he'd be coming here to collect a fee. She radioed Sellitto downstairs and had him clear the street of all emergency vehicles and set up hidden takedown teams.

Rhyme was on his way in his van and Sachs called to tell him to take the back entrance. She then went into the hallway to check on the girl.

'How you doing?'

'Okay, I guess. My face hurts.'

'They took the tape off pretty fast, I'll bet.'

'Yeah, kinda.'

'Thanks for what you did. You saved lives. You saved *my* life.' The girl gazed at Sachs with a curious look then glanced down. The detective handed her the Harry Potter book she'd found in the bedroom and Sachs asked if the girl knew anything about the man calling himself Gerald Duncan.

'He was creepy. Like, way weird. He'd just look at you like you were a rock or a car or a table. Not a person.'

'You have any idea where he is?'

She shook her head. 'All I know is I heard Mom say he was renting a place in Brooklyn somewhere. I don't know where. He wouldn't say. But he's coming by later to pick up some money.'

Sachs pulled Pulaski aside and asked him to check all the calls to and from Charlotte's and Bud's mobile phones, as well as the calls from the hotel room phone.

'How 'bout the lobby phone too? The pay phone, I mean. And the ones on the street nearby.'

She lifted an eyebrow. 'Good idea.'

The rookie headed off on his mission. Sachs got a soda and gave it to the girl. She opened the can and drank down half of it fast. She was looking at Sachs in a strange way. Then she gave a laugh.

Sachs asked, 'What?'

'You really don't remember me, do you? I met you before.'

'Near the alley on Tuesday. Sure.'

'No, no. Like, a long time before that.'

Sachs squinted. She recalled that she *had* felt some sense of familiarity when she'd seen the girl in the car at the first crime scene in the alley. And she felt it even more strongly now. But she couldn't place where she might've seen the girl prior to Tuesday. 'I'm afraid I don't remember.'

'You saved my life. I was a little girl.'

'A long time . . .' Then Amelia Sachs squinted, turned toward the mother and studied Charlotte more closely. 'Oh, my God,' she gasped.

Chapter
FORTY

Inside the shabby hotel room, Lincoln Rhyme shook his head in disbelief as Sachs told him what she'd just learned: that they had known Charlotte some years ago when she'd come to New York using the pseudonym Carol Ganz. She and her daughter, whose name was Pammy, had been victims in the first case Sachs and Rhyme had worked together – the very one he'd been thinking of earlier, the kidnapper obsessed with human bones, a perp as clever and ruthless as the Watchmaker.

To pursue him, Rhyme had recruited Sachs to be his eyes and ears and legs at the crime scenes and together they'd managed to rescue both the woman and her daughter – only to learn that Carol was really Charlotte Willoughby. She was part of a right-wing militia movement, which abhorred the federal government and its involvement in world affairs. After their rescue and reunion, the woman managed to slip a bomb into the United Nations headquarters in Manhattan. The explosion killed six people.

Rhyme and Sachs had taken up the case but Charlotte and the girl disappeared into the movement's underground, probably in the Midwest or West, and eventually the trail went cold.

From time to time they would check out FBI, VICAP and local police reports with a militia or right-wing political angle but no leads to Charlotte or Pammy panned out. Sachs's concern for the little girl never diminished, though, and sometimes, lying in bed with Rhyme at night, she'd wonder out loud how the girl was doing, if it was too late to save her. Sachs, who'd always wanted children, was horrified at the kind of life her mother was presumably forcing the girl to live – hiding out, having few friends her age, never going to a regular school – all in the name of some hateful cause.

And now Charlotte – with her new husband, Bud Allerton – had returned to the city on yet another mission of terrorism, and Rhyme and Sachs had become entwined in their lives once again.

Charlotte now glared at Rhyme, her eyes filled with both tears and hatred. 'You murdered Bud! You goddamn fascists! You killed him.' The prisoner then gave a cold laugh. 'But we won! How many did we kill tonight? Fifty people. Seventy-five? And how many senior people in the Pentagon?'

Sachs leaned close to her face. 'Did you know there'd be children in that conference room? Husbands and wives of the soldiers? Their parents? Grandparents? Did you *know* that?'

'Of course we knew it,' Charlotte said.

'They were just sacrifices too, is that right?'

'For the greater good,' Charlotte replied.

Which was maybe a slogan she and her group recited at the beginning of their rallies, or whatever meetings they had.

Rhyme caught Sachs's eye. He said, 'Maybe we should show her the carnage.'

Sachs nodded and clicked on the TV.

An anchorwoman was on the screen. '. . . one minor injury. A bomb squad officer who was driving a remote-control robot in an attempt to diffuse the bombs was wounded slightly by shrapnel. He's been treated and released. Property damage was estimated at five hundred thousand dollars. Despite initial reports, neither al-Qaeda nor any other Islamic terrorist group has been implicated in the bombing. According to a New York Police Department spokeswoman, a domestic terrorist organization was responsible. Again, if you're just joining us, two bombs exploded around noon today in the office of Housing and Urban Development in lower Manhattan but there were no fatalities and only one minor injury. An undersecretary of state and the head of the Joint Chiefs of Staff were among the intended victims . . .'

Sachs muted the volume and turned a smug gaze toward Charlotte.

'No,' the woman gasped. 'Oh, no . . . What—?'

Rhyme said, 'Obviously – we figured it out *before* the bomb went off and evacuated the room.'

Charlotte was appalled. 'But . . . impossible. No . . . The airports were shut down, the trains—'

'Oh, *that*,' Rhyme said dismissively. 'We just needed to buy some time. At first, sure, I thought he was stealing the Delphic Mechanism but then I decided it was just a feint. But that didn't mean he *hadn't* done something to the NIST clock. So while we were figuring out what he was really up to, we called the mayor and had him order flights and public transportation in the area suspended.'

You know what's going to happen if we push that button . . .

She glanced into the bedroom where her husband had died such a pointless death. Then the ideologue within her kicked in and she said in a flat voice, 'You'll never beat us. You may win a battle or two. But we'll take our country back. We'll—'

'Yo, hold that rhetoric, wouldja?' The speaker was a tall, lanky black man, stepping into the room. This was FBI Special Agent Fred Dellray. When he'd heard about the domestic terrorist angle he'd handed off the accounting fraud case that he'd been assisting on ('Was a yawner anyway') and announced that he was going to be the federal liaison on the HUD bombing.

Dellray was wearing a powder blue suit and a shocking green shirt underneath a brown herringbone overcoat, circa 1975; the agent's taste in couture was as brash as his manner. He looked Charlotte over. 'Well, well, well, lookit what we caught ou'selves.' The woman gazed back defiantly. He laughed. 'A shame you're going to jail for . . . well, *forever*, and you didn't even do whatcha'll had your heart set on. How's it feel t'be swimmin' laps in the loser pool?'

Dellray's approach to interviewing suspects was a lot different from Kathryn Dance's; Rhyme suspected she wouldn't approve.

Charlotte had been arrested by Sachs on state charges and it was now Dellray's turn to arrest her for the federal crimes – both for this incident and for the UN bombing years ago, her involvement in a federal courthouse shooting in San Francisco and some miscellaneous charges.

Charlotte said she understood her rights and then started another lecture.

Dellray wagged a finger at her. 'Gimme a minute, sweet-heart.' The lean man turned to Rhyme. 'So how'd you figure this one out, Lincoln? We heard X, we heard Y, all 'bout some boys in blue taking money they shouldn'ta been doin' and then some bizarre fella leavin' clocks as callin' cards – then next thing we know the airports're closed and there's a priority-one security alert at HUD innerupting my nap.'

Rhyme detailed the frantic process of kinesic and forensic work that led them to figure out the Watchmaker's real plan. Kathryn Dance had suggested that he was lying about his mission in New York. So they'd looked into the evidence again. Some of it pointed to the possible theft of a rare artifact in the Metropolitan Museum.

But the more he thought about that, the less likely that seemed. Rhyme figured Duncan had made up the story about the undelivered package to the Met just to get them focused on the museum. Somebody as careful as the Watchmaker wouldn't leave the trail he did. He turned in Vincent, knowing the rapist would give up the church, where he'd left other museum programs referring to the Mechanism. He mentioned it to Hallerstein and to Vincent as well. No, he was up to something else. But what? Kathryn Dance reviewed the interview tape again, several times, and decided that he might have been lying when he said he picked the supposed victims simply because their locations meant easy getaways.

'Which meant,' Rhyme told Dellray, 'that he picked them for some other purpose. So, did they have anything in common?'

Rhyme had remembered something Dance learned about the first crime scene. Ari Cobb had said that the SUV was originally parked in the back of the alley but then the Watchmaker returned to the front to leave the body. 'Why? One reason was that he needed to put the victim in a particular place. What was it near? The back door to the Housing and Urban Development building.'

Rhyme had then gotten the client list from the flooring company where he'd planted the fake fire extinguisher bomb and learned that they'd provided carpeting and tile for the HUD offices.

'I sent our rookie downtown to look around. He found a building across Cedar Street that was being renovated. The crews had tarred the roof a week ago, just before the cold spell. Flakes of tar matched those found on our perp's shoes. The roof was a perfect place to check out HUD.'

This also explained why he'd poured sand on the ground at the crime scene and swept it up – to make absolutely certain they didn't find trace that'd help anyone identify him later when he came back to assemble and arm the bombs.

Rhyme also found that the other victims had a connection to the building. Lucy Richter was being recognized there today, and she'd had the specially issued passes and IDs to get into all parts of the building. She also had a classified memo on security and evacuation procedures.

As for Joanne Harper, it turned out that she'd done the flower arrangements for the ceremony – a good way to smuggle something into the building.

'A bomb, I guessed. We got the mayor involved and he called the press, had them hold off on the story that we were evacuating HUD so the perps wouldn't rabbit. But the device blew before the bomb squad could disarm it.' Rhyme shook his head. 'Just *hate* it when good evidence blows up. You know how hard it is to lift prints off pieces of metal that've been flying through the air at thirty thousand feet a second?'

'How'dja get Miss Congeniality here?' Dellray asked, nodding at Charlotte.

Rhyme said dismissively, 'That was easy. She was careless. If Duncan was fake, then the woman helping him at the first scene in the alley had to be fake too. Our rookie got all the tag numbers of cars in the vicinity of the alley off Cedar. The car the supposed sister was driving was an Avis, rented to Charlotte Allerton. We checked all the hotels in the city until we found her.'

Dellray shook his head. 'An' what about yo' perp? Mr Clockmaker?'

'It's "Watchmaker",' the criminalist grumbled. 'And that's a different story.' He explained that Charlotte's daughter, Pam, had heard that he had a place in Brooklyn but she didn't know where it was. 'No other leads.'

Dellray bent down. 'Where in Brooklyn? Need to know. And now.'

Charlotte replied defiantly, 'You're pathetic! All of you! You're just lackeys for the bureaucracy in Washington. You're selling out the heart of our country and—'

Dellray leaned forward, right into her face. He clicked his tongue. 'Uh-uh. No politics, no phi*lo*sophy . . . All we want're answers to the questions. We all together on that?'

'Fuck you,' was Charlotte's response.

Dellray blew air through his cheeks like a trumpet player. He moaned, 'I am *no* match for this intellect.'

Rhyme wished Kathryn Dance was here to interrogate the woman, though he guessed it would take a long time to pry information from her. He eased forward in the wheelchair and said in a whisper, so Pam couldn't hear, 'If you help us out I can make sure you see your daughter from time to time when you're in prison. If you don't cooperate, I will guarantee that you never see her again as long as you live.'

Charlotte glanced into the hallway, where Pam sat on a chair, defiantly clutching her Harry Potter. The dark-haired girl was pretty, with fragile features, but very slim. She wore faded jeans and a dark blue sweatshirt. The skin around her eyes was dark. She clicked her fingernails together compulsively. The girl seemed needy in a hundred different ways.

Charlotte turned back to Rhyme. 'Then I'll never see her again,' she said calmly.

Dellray blinked at this, his usually unrevealing face tightening in revulsion.

Rhyme himself could think of nothing more to say to the woman.

It was then that Ron Pulaski came running into the room. He paused to catch his breath.

'What?' Rhyme asked.

It took a moment for him to be able to answer. Finally, he said, 'The phones . . . The Watchmaker . . .'

'Out with it, Ron.'

'Sorry . . .' A deep breath. 'We couldn't trace his mobile

but a hotel clerk saw her, Charlotte, making calls around midnight every night over the past four or five days. I called the phone company. I got the number she called. They traced it. It's to a pay phone in Brooklyn. At this intersection.' He handed the slip of paper to Sellitto, who relayed it to Bo Haumann and ESU.

'Good job,' Sellitto said to Pulaski. He called the deputy inspector of the precinct where the phone was located. Officers would start a canvass of the neighborhood as soon as Mel Cooper emailed pictures of the composite to the DI.

Rhyme supposed that the Watchmaker might not live near the phone – it wouldn't have surprised the criminalist – but a mere thirty minutes later they had a positive identification from a patrol officer, who found several neighbors who recognized the man.

Sellitto took the number and alerted Bo Haumann.

Sachs announced, 'I'll call in from the scene.'

'Hold on,' Rhyme said, glancing at her. 'Why don't you sit this one out. Let Bo handle it.'

'What?'

'They'll have a full tactical force.'

Rhyme was thinking of the superstition that cops on short time were more likely to get killed or injured than others. Rhyme didn't believe in superstitions. That didn't matter. He didn't want her to go.

Amelia Sachs would be thinking the same thing, perhaps; she was debating, it seemed. Then he saw her looking into the hallway at Pam Willoughby. She turned back to the criminalist. Their eyes met. He gave a faint smile and nodded.

She grabbed her leather jacket and headed for the door.

In a quiet neighborhood in Brooklyn a dozen tactical officers moved slowly along the sidewalk, another six creeping through an alley behind a shabby detached house.

This was a neighborhood of modest houses, in small yards, presently filled with Christmas decorations. The minuscule size of the lots had no effect on the owners' ability to populate the land with as many Santas, reindeer and elves as possible.

Sachs was walking down the sidewalk slowly at the head of the takedown team. She was on the radio with Rhyme. 'We're here,' she said softly.

'What's the story?'

'We've cleared the houses on either side and behind. There's nobody opposite.' A community vegetable garden was across the street. A ragged scarecrow sat in the middle of the tiny lot. Across his chest was a swirl of graffiti.

'Pretty good site for a takedown. We're – hold on, Rhyme.' A light had gone on in one of the front rooms. The cops around her stopped and crouched. She whispered, 'He's still here . . . I'm signing off.'

'Go get him, Sachs.' She heard an unusual determination in his voice. She knew he was upset that the man had escaped. Saving the people at the HUD building and capturing Charlotte were fine. But Rhyme wasn't happy unless all the perps ended up in cuffs.

But he wasn't as determined as Amelia Sachs. She wanted to give Rhyme the Watchmaker – as a present to mark their last case together.

She changed radio frequencies and said into her stalk mike, 'Detective Five Eight Eight Five to ESU One.'

Bo Haumann, at a staging area a block away, came on the radio. 'Go ahead, K.'

'He's here. Just saw a light go on in the front room.'

'Roger, B Team, you copy?'

These were the officers behind the bungalow. 'B Team leader to ESU One. Roger that. We're – hold on. Okay, he's upstairs now. Just saw the light go on up there. Looks like the back bedroom.'

'Don't assume he's alone,' Sachs said. 'There could be some-body else from Charlotte's outfit with him. Or he might've picked up another partner.'

'Roger that, Detective,' Haumann said in his gravelly voice. 'S and S, what can you tell us?'

The Search and Surveillance Teams were just getting into position on the roof of the apartment building behind and in the garden across the street from the Watchmaker's safe house, on which they were training their instruments.

'S and S One to ESU One. All the shades're drawn. Can't get a look at all. We've got heat in the back of the house. But he's not walking around. There's a light on in the attic but we can't see in – no windows, just louvers, K.'

'Same here – S and S Two. No visual. Heat upstairs, nothing on the ground floor. Heard a click or two a second ago, K.'

'Weapon?'

'Could be. Or maybe just appliances or the furnace, K.'

The ESU officer next to Sachs deployed his officers with hand signals. He, Sachs and two others clustered at the front door, another team of four right behind them. One held the battering ram. The other three covered the windows on the ground and the second floors.

'B Team to One. We're in position. Got a ladder next to the lit room in the back, K.'

'A Team, in position,' another ESU officer radioed in a whisper.

'We're no-knock,' Haumann told the teams. 'On my count of three, flashbangs into the rooms that have the lights on. Throw 'em hard to get through the shades. On one, simultan-eous dynamic entry front and back. B Team, split up, cover the ground floor and basement. A Team, go straight upstairs. Remember, this guy knows how to make IEDs. Look for devices.'

'B Team, copy.'

'A, copy.'

Despite the freezing air Sachs's palms were sweating inside the tight Nomex gloves. She pulled the right one away and blew into it. Did the same with the left. Then she cinched up the body armor and unsnapped the cover of her spare ammo clip carrier. The other officers had machine guns but Sachs never went for that. She preferred the elegance of a single well-placed round to a spray of lead.

Sachs and the three officers on the primary entry team nodded at one another.

Haumann's raspy voice began the count. 'Six . . . five . . . four . . . three . . .'

The sound of breaking glass filled the crisp air as officers flung the grenades through the windows.

Haumann, continuing calmly: 'Two . . . one.'

The sharp crack of the flashbangs shook the windows and bursts of white light filled the house momentarily. The burly officer with the battering ram slammed it into the front door. It crashed open without resistance and in a few seconds the officers were spreading out in the sparsely furnished house.

Flashlight in one hand, gun in the other, Sachs stayed with her team as they worked their way up the stairs.

She began hearing the voices of the other officers calling in as they cleared the basement and the rooms on the ground floor.

One upstairs bedroom was empty, the second, as well.

Then all the rooms were declared clear.

'Where the hell is he?' Sachs muttered.

'Always an adventure, huh?' somebody asked.

'Invisible fucking perp,' came another voice.

Then in her earpiece she heard: 'S and S One. Light in the attic just went out. He's up there.'

In the small bedroom toward the back they found a trap-door in the ceiling, a thick string hanging from it. A pull-down stair. An officer shut out the light in this room so it would be harder to target them. They stood back and pointed their guns at the door as Sachs gripped the string and pulled hard. It creaked downward, revealing a folding ladder.

The team leader shouted, 'You, in the attic. Come down now . . . Do you hear me? This is your last chance.'

Nothing.

He said, 'Flashbang.'

An officer pulled one off his belt and nodded.

The team leader put his hand on the ladder but Sachs shook her head. 'I'll take him.'

'Are you sure you want to?'

Sachs nodded. 'Only, let me borrow a helmet.'

She took one and strapped it on.

'We're set, Detective.'

'Let's do it.' Sachs climbed up near the top – then took the flashbang. She pulled the pin and closed her eyes so the flash from the grenade wouldn't blind her and also to acclimate her eyes to the darkness of the attic.

Okay, here we go.

She pitched the grenade into the attic and lowered her head.

Three seconds later it detonated and Sachs, opening her eyes, charged the rest of the way up the ladder into the small area, filled with a haze of smoke and the smell of explosive residue from the flashbang. She rolled away from the opening, clicking on her flashlight and sweeping it in a circle as she moved to a post, the only cover she could find.

Nothing to the right, nothing center, nothing—

It was then that she fell off the face of the earth.

The floor wasn't wood at all, like it seemed, but cardboard over insulating crud. Her right leg crashed through the Sheetrock of the bedroom ceiling, gripping her, immobile. She cried out in pain.

'Detective!' somebody called.

Sachs lifted the light and the gun in the only direction she could see — straight in front of her. The killer wasn't there.

Which meant he was behind her.

It was at that moment that the overhead light clicked on, almost directly above her, making her a perfect target.

She struggled to turn around, awaiting the sharp crack of a gun, the numb slam of the bullet into her head or neck or back.

Sachs thought of her father.

She thought of Lincoln Rhyme.

You and me, Sachs . . .

Then she decided no way was she going out without getting a piece of him. She took the pistol in her teeth and used both hands to wrench herself around and find a target.

She heard boots on the ladder as an ESU officer charged up to help her. Of course, *that's* what the Watchmaker was waiting for — a chance to kill more of the officers. He was using her as bait to draw other cops to their deaths and hoped to escape in the chaos.

'Look out!' she called, gripping her pistol in her hand. 'He's—'

'Where is he?' the A Team leader asked. The man was crouching at the top of the stairs. He hadn't heard her — or hadn't listened — and had sped up the ladder, followed by two other officers. They were scanning the room — including the area behind Sachs.

Her heart pounding furiously, she struggled to look over her shoulder. She asked, 'You don't see him? He's gotta be there.'

'Zip.'

He and another officer bent down, gripped her body armor and pulled her out of the Sheetrock. Crouching, she spun around.

The room was empty.

'How'd he get out?' the ESU officer muttered. 'No doors or windows.'

Sachs noticed something across the room. She gave a sour laugh. 'He was never here at all. Not up here, not downstairs. He probably took off hours ago.'

'But the lights. *Somebody* was turning them on and off.'

'Nope. Take a look.' She pointed to a small beige box connected to the fusebox. 'He wanted to make us think he was still here. Give him a better chance to get away.'

'What is it?'

'What else? It's a timer.'

Chapter
FORTY-ONE

Sachs finished searching the scene at the house in Brooklyn and sent what little evidence she could find to Rhyme's.

She stripped off her Tyvek outfit and pulled her jacket on, then hurried through the cutting chill to Sellitto's car. In the back sat Pam Willoughby, clutching her Harry Potter book and sipping hot chocolate, which the big detective had scrounged for her. He was still in the perp's safe house, finishing up the paperwork. Sachs climbed in, sat beside her. At Kathryn Dance's suggestion, they'd brought the girl here to examine the place and the Watchmaker's possessions, in hopes that something might trigger a memory. But the man hadn't left much behind and in any event nothing Pammy saw gave her any more insights about him.

Smiling, Sachs looked the girl over, remembering that strange expression of hope when she'd seen her in the rental car at the first scene. The policewoman said, 'I've thought about you a lot over the years.'

'Me too,' the girl said, looking down into her cup.

'Where did you go after New York?'

'We went back to Missouri and hid out in the woods. Mom left me with other people a lot. Mostly I just stayed by myself and read. I didn't get along very good with anybody. They were crappy to me. If you didn't think the way they did – which was pretty messed up – they totally dissed you.

'A lot of them were home-schooling people. But I really wanted to go to public school and I made a big deal out of it. Bud didn't want me to but Mom finally agreed. But she said if I told anybody about her, what she'd done, I'd go to jail too as an assistant . . . no, an accomplice. And men would do stuff to me there. You know what I'm talking about.'

'Oh, honey.' Sachs squeezed her hand. Amelia Sachs wanted children badly and knew that, one way or another, they were in her future. She was appalled that a mother had put her child through this.

'And sometimes, when it got real bad, I'd think about you and pretend you were my mother. I didn't know your name. Maybe I heard it back then but I couldn't remember. So I gave you another one: Artemis. From this book I read about mythology. She was the goddess of the hunt. Because you killed that mad dog – the one that was attacking me.' She looked down. 'It's a stupid name.'

'No, no, it's a wonderful name. I love it . . . You recognized me in the alleyway Tuesday, didn't you? When you were in the car?'

'Yeah. I think you were meant to be there – to save me again. Don't you think things like that happen?'

No, Sachs didn't. But she said, 'Life works in funny ways sometimes.'

A city car pulled up and a social worker Sachs knew climbed out and joined them.

'Whoa.' The woman, a pretty African-American, rubbed her hands together in front of the heater vent. 'It's not even winter yet officially. This isn't fair.' She'd been making arrangements for the girl and she now explained, 'We've found a couple real nice foster families. There's one in Riverdale I've known for years. You'll stay there for the next few days while we see if we can track down some of your relatives.'

Pammy was frowning. 'Can I get a new name?'

'A new—?'

'I don't want to be me anymore. And I don't want my mother to talk to me again. And I don't want any of those people she's with to find me.'

Sachs preempted whatever the social worker was going to say. 'We'll make sure nothing happens to you. That's a promise.'

Pammy hugged her.

'So I can see you again?' Sachs asked.

Trying to contain her excitement at this, the girl said, 'I guess. If you want.'

'How 'bout shopping tomorrow?'

'Okay. Sure.'

'Good. It's a date.' Sachs had an idea. 'Hey, you like dogs?'

'Yeah, some folks I stayed with in Missouri had one. I liked him better than the people.'

She called Thom at Rhyme's town house. 'Got a question.'

'Go ahead.'

'Any takers on Jackson yet?'

'Nope. He's still up for adoption.'

'Take him off the market,' Sachs said. She hung up and looked at Pam. 'I've got an early Christmas present for you.'

Sometimes even the best-designed watches simply don't work.

The devices really are quite fragile, when you think about it. Five hundred, a thousand minuscule moving parts, nearly microscopic screws and springs and jewels, all precisely assembled, dozens of separate movements working in unison . . . A hundred things can go wrong. Sometimes the watchmaker miscalculates, sometimes a tiny piece of metal is defective, sometimes the owner winds the mechanism too tight. Sometimes he drops it. Moisture gets under the crystal.

Then again the watch might work perfectly in one environment but not in another. Even the famed Rolex Oyster Perpetual, revolutionary for being the first luxury divers' watch, can't withstand unlimited pressure underwater.

Now, near Central Park, Charles Vespasian Hale sat in his own car, which he'd driven here from San Diego – no trail at all, if you pay cash for gas and avoid toll roads – and wondered what had gone wrong with his plan.

He supposed the answer was the police, specifically Lincoln Rhyme. Hale had done everything he could think of to anticipate his moves. But the former cop managed to end up just a bit ahead of him. Rhyme had done exactly what Hale had been worried about – he'd looked at a few gears and levers and extrapolated from them how Hale's entire timepiece had been constructed.

He'd have plenty of time to consider what went wrong and to try to avoid the same problems in the future. He'd be driving back to California, leaving immediately. He glanced at his face in the rearview mirror. He'd dyed his hair back to its natural color and the pale blue contact lenses were gone, but the collagen, which gave him the thick nose and puffy cheeks and double chin, hadn't bled from his skin yet. And it would take months before he regained the forty pounds he'd lost for the job and became himself again. He felt pasty and sluggish after all this time in the city and needed to get back to his wilderness and mountains once again.

Yes, he'd failed. But, as he told Vincent Reynolds, that wasn't significant in the great scheme of things. He wasn't concerned about the arrest of Charlotte Allerton. They knew nothing of his real identity (they'd believed all along his real name was Duncan) and their initial contacts had been through extremely discreet individuals.

Moreover, there was actually a positive side to the failure here – Hale had learned something that had changed his life. He'd created the persona of the Watchmaker simply because the character seemed spooky and would snag the attention of a populace and police turned on by made-for-TV criminals.

But as he got into the role, Hale found to his surprise that this character was the embodiment of his true personality. Playing the part was like coming home. He had indeed grown fascinated with watches and clocks and time. (He'd also developed an abiding interest in the Delphic Mechanism; stealing it at some point in the future was a distinct possibility.)

The Watchmaker . . .

Charles Hale was himself simply a timepiece. You could use a watch for something joyous like checking contractions for the birth of a baby. Or heinous: coordinating the time of a raid to slaughter women and children.

Time transcends morality.

He now looked down at what sat on the seat next to him, the gold Breguet pocket watch. In his gloved hands, he picked it up, wound it slowly – always better to underwind than over – and carefully slipped it between the sheets of bubble wrap in a large white envelope.

Hale sealed the self-adhesive flap and started the car.

There were no clear leads.

Rhyme, Sellitto, Cooper and Pulaski were sitting in the lab on Central Park West, going over the few things found in the perp's Brooklyn safe house.

Amelia Sachs was not present at the moment. She hadn't announced where she was going. But she didn't need to. She'd mentioned to Thom that she'd be nearby, if they needed her: at a meeting on Fifty-seventh and Sixth. Rhyme had checked the phone directory. That was the location of the Argyle Security headquarters.

Rhyme simply couldn't think about that, and he was

concentrating on how to continue the search for the Watchmaker, whoever he might be.

Working backward, Rhyme constructed a rough scenario of the events. The ceremony had been announced on October 15, so Charlotte and Bud had contacted the Watchmaker sometime around then. He'd come to New York around November 1, the date of the lease on the Brooklyn safe house. A few weeks later, Amelia Sachs had taken over the Creeley case and soon after, Baker and Wallace decided to have her killed.

'Then they hooked up with the Watchmaker. What'd he tell us, when we thought he was Duncan? About their meeting?'

Sellitto said, 'Just that somebody at the club put them together – the club where Baker put the touch on his friend.'

'But he was lying. There was no club . . .' Rhyme shook his head. 'Somebody put them together, somebody who knows the Watchmaker – probably somebody in the area. If we can find them, there could be some solid leads. Is Baker talking?'

'Nope, not a word. Nobody is.'

The rookie was shaking his head. 'That's going to be a tough one. I mean, how many OC crews are there in the metro area? Take forever to track down the right one. Not like they're going to be volunteering to help us out.'

The criminalist frowned. 'What're you talking about? What's an organized crime posse got to do with anything?'

'Well, I just assumed somebody with an OC connection was the one who'd put them together.'

'Why?'

'Baker wants to have a cop killed, right? But he can't do it in a way that'll make him look suspicious so he has to hire somebody. He goes to some mob connection he has. The mob's not going to clip a cop so he puts Baker in touch with somebody who might: the Watchmaker.'

When nobody said anything, Pulaski blushed and looked down. 'I don't know. Just a thought.'

'And a fucking good one, kid,' Sellitto said.

'Really?'

Rhyme nodded. 'Not bad . . . Let's call the OC task force downtown and see if their snitches can tell us anything. Call Dellray too . . . Now, let's get back to the evidence.'

They'd located some friction ridges in the safe house in Brooklyn but none of the fingerprints came back positive from the Bureau's IAFIS system and none matched prints from prior scenes. The lease for the house had been executed under yet another fake name and the man had given a phony prior address. It had been a cash transaction. An exhaustive search of Internet activity in the neighborhood revealed that the man had apparently logged on occasionally through several nearby wireless networks. There were no records of emails, only Web browsing. The site he'd visited most often was a bookstore that sold continuing-education course texts for certain medical specialties.

Sellitto said, 'Shit, maybe somebody else's hired him.'

You bet, Rhyme thought, nodding. 'He'll be targeting another victim – or victims. Probably coming up with his plan right now. Think of the damage he could do pretending to be a doctor.'

And I let him get away.

An examination of the trace evidence Sachs had collected revealed little more than shearling fibers and a few bits of a green vegetative material containing evaporated seawater – which didn't, it turned out, match the seaweed and ocean water found around Robert Wallace's boat on Long Island.

The deputy inspector at the Brooklyn precinct called to report that further canvassing of the neighborhood had been useless. A half dozen people remembered seeing the Watchmaker but nobody knew anything about him.

As for Charlotte and her late husband, Bud Allerton, the investigative efforts were much more successful. The couple had not been nearly as careful as the Watchmaker. Sachs had found a great deal of evidence about the underground militia groups they'd been harbored by, including a large one in Missouri and the infamous Patriot Assembly in upstate New York, which Rhyme and Sachs had tangled with in the past. Phone calls, fingerprints and emails would give the FBI and local police plenty of leads to pursue.

The doorbell rang and Thom left the room to answer it. A moment later he returned with a woman in a military uniform. This would be Lucy Richter, the Watchmaker's fourth 'victim'. Rhyme noted that she was more surprised at the forensic lab in his town house than his disability. Then it occurred to him that this was a woman involved in a type of combat where bombs were the weapon of choice; she'd undoubtedly seen missing limbs and para- and quadriplegia of all sorts. Rhyme's condition didn't faze her.

She explained that she'd called Kathryn Dance not long ago to say she wanted to speak to the investigators; the California detective had suggested she call or stop by Rhyme's.

Thom zipped in and offered her coffee or tea. Normally piqued about visitors and reluctant to give anyone an incentive to linger, Rhyme now, to the contrary, glared at the aide. 'She might be hungry, Thom. Or might want something more substantial. Scotch, for instance.'

'There's just no figuring you out,' Thom said. 'Didn't know there was an armed forces hospitality rule in the Lincoln Rhyme edition of Emily Post.'

'Thanks, but nothing for me,' Lucy said. 'I can't stay long. First, I want to thank you. For saving my life – twice.'

'Actually,' Sellitto pointed out, 'you weren't in any danger the first time. He was never going to hurt you – or any of the victims. The second time? Well, okay, accepted – since he wanted to blow the conference room to smithereens.'

'My family was there too,' she said. 'I can't thank you enough.'

Rhyme was, as always, uneasy with the gratitude, though he nodded with what he thought was an appropriate acknowledgment.

'The other reason is that I found out something that might be helpful. I've been talking to my neighbors about when he broke in. One man, he lives three buildings down the street, told me something. He said that yesterday he was getting a delivery at the back of the building and he found a rope dangling into the alley from the roof. You can get there from my roof pretty easily. I was thinking that maybe that was how he escaped.'

'Interesting,' Rhyme said.

'But there's something else. My husband took a look. Bob was a Navy SEAL for two years—'

'Navy? And you're army?' Pulaski asked, laughing.

She smiled. 'We have some . . . interesting discussions from time to time. Especially during football season. Anyway, he looked at the rope and said whoever tied it knew what he was doing. It was a rare knot used in abseiling – you know, rappelling. It's called a dead man's knot. You don't see it much in this country, mostly in Europe. He must've had some experience rock climbing or mountaineering overseas.'

'Ah, some hard information.' Rhyme glanced darkly at Pulaski. 'A shame the *victim* had to find the evidence, don't you think? That really is in *our* job description.' He turned toward Lucy. 'The rope's still there?'

'Yes.'

'Good . . . You in town for a while?' Rhyme asked. 'If we catch him, we might need you to testify at his trial.'

'I'm going back overseas soon. But I'm sure I can come back for a trial. I could get a special leave for that.'

'How long will you be there?'

'I reenlisted for two years.'

'You did?' Sellitto asked.

'I wasn't going to. It's tough over there. But I decided to go back.'

'Because of the bomb at the ceremony?'

'No, it was just before that. I was looking at the families and the other soldiers there and thinking it's funny how life puts you in places you never thought you'd be. But there you are and you're doing something good and important and, basically, it just feels right. So.' She pulled on her jacket. 'If you need me, I'll get a leave home.'

They said goodbye and Thom saw her out the door.

When he returned Rhyme told the aide, 'Add that to the profile. A rock climber or mountaineer, possibly European trained.' To Pulaski, Rhyme said, 'And have somebody from the CS Unit go collect the rope that you missed in the first place—'

'Actually, I wasn't really the one who searched—'

'—and then find a climbing expert. I want to know where he might've trained. And run the rope too. Where'd he buy it and when?'

'Yessir.'

Fifteen minutes later the doorbell rang again and Thom returned with Kathryn Dance. The white iPod earbuds dangling over her shoulders, she greeted everyone. She was holding a white, eight-and-a-half-by-eleven envelope.

'Hi,' said Pulaski.

Rhyme lifted an eyebrow in greeting.

'I'm on my way to the airport,' Dance explained. 'Just wanted to say goodbye. Oh, this was on the doorstep.'

She handed the envelope to Thom.

The aide glanced at it. 'No return address.' Frowning.

'Let's be safe,' Rhyme said. 'The basket.'

Sellitto took the envelope and walked to a large bin that was made out of woven steel strips – like a wicker laundry hamper. He set the envelope inside and clamped the lid shut.

As a matter of course, any unidentified packages went into the bomb basket, which was designed to diffuse the force of a small-to-medium-sized improvised explosive device. It contained sensors that would pick up any trace of nitrates and other common explosives.

The computer sniffed the vapors emanating from the envelope and reported that it wasn't a bomb.

Wearing latex gloves, Cooper retrieved and examined it. The envelope bore a computer-generated label, reading only, *Lincoln Rhyme*.

'Self-sticking,' the tech added with a resigned grimace. Criminalists preferred old-style envelopes that perps had to lick; the adhesive was a good source of DNA. Cooper added that he was familiar with the brand of envelope; it was sold in stores all over the country and virtually untraceable.

Rhyme wheeled closer and, with Dance beside him, watched the tech extract a pocket watch and a note, also the product of a computer printer. 'It's from him,' Cooper announced.

The envelope had been there for no more than a quarter of an hour – the time between Lucy Richter's departure and Dance's arrival. Sellitto called Central to have some cars from the nearby Twentieth Precinct sweep the neighborhood. Cooper emailed the Watchmaker's composite to the house.

The timepiece was ticking and showed the accurate time. It was gold and there were several small dials set in the face.

'Heavy,' Cooper said. He pulled on magnifying goggles and examined it closely. 'Looks old, signs of wear . . . no personalized engravings.' He took a camel hair brush and dusted the watch over a piece of newsprint. The envelope too. No trace was dislodged.

'Here's the note, Lincoln.' He mounted it on an overhead projector.

Dear Mr Rhyme:

I will be gone by the time you receive this. I have by now, of course, learned that none of the attendees at the conference was injured. I concluded you had anticipated my plans. I then anticipated yours and delayed my trip to Charlotte's hotel, which gave me the chance to spot your officers. I assume you saved her daughter. I am pleased about that. She deserves better than that pair.

So congratulations. I thought the plan was perfect. But I was apparently wrong.

The pocket watch is a Breguet. It is the favorite of the many timepieces I have come across. It was made in the early 1800s and features a ruby cylinder escapement, perpetual calendar and parachute antishock device. I hope you appreciate the phases-of-the-moon window, in light of our recent adventures. There are few specimens like this watch in the world. I give it to you as a present, out of respect. No one has ever stopped me from finishing a job; you're as good as they get. (I would say you're as good as I, but that is not quite true. You did not, after all, catch me.) Keep the Breguet wound (but gently); it will be counting the time until we meet again.

Some advice: If I were you, I would make every one of those seconds count.

– The Watchmaker

Sellitto grimaced.

'What?' Rhyme asked.

'You get classier threats than me, Linc. Usually my perps just say, "I'm gonna kill you." And what the hell is that?' He pointed to the note. 'A semicolon? He's threatening you and he's using semicolons. That's fucked up.'

Rhyme didn't laugh. He was still furious about the man's escape – and furious too that he apparently had no desire to retire. 'When you get tired of making bad jokes, Lon, you might want to notice that his grammar and syntax are perfect. That tells us something else about him. Good education. Private school? Classically trained? Scholarships? Valedictorian? Put those on the chart, Thom.'

Sellitto was unfazed. 'Fucking semicolons.'

'Got something here,' Cooper said, looking up from the computer. 'The green material from his place in Brooklyn? I'm pretty sure it's *Caulerpa taxifolia*. A noxious weed.'

'A *what*?'

'It's a seaweed that spreads uncontrollably. Causes all kinds of problems. It's been banned in the U.S.'

'And presumably, if it spreads, you can find it everywhere,' Rhyme said sourly. 'Useless as evidence.'

'Actually, no,' Cooper explained. 'So far, it's been found only on the Pacific Coast of North America.'

'Mexico to Canada?'

'Pretty much.'

Rhyme added sarcastically, 'That's virtually a street address. Call out the SWAT team.'

It was then that Kathryn Dance frowned. 'The West Coast?' She considered something for a moment. Then she asked, 'Where's the interview with him?'

Mel Cooper found the file. He hit PLAY and for the dozenth time they watched the killer look into the camera and lie to them all. Dance leaned forward intently. She reminded Rhyme of himself gazing at evidence.

He'd been through the interview so often he was numb to the words; it provided nothing helpful now that he could tell. But Dance gave a sudden laugh. 'Got a thought.'

'What?'

'Well, I can't give you an address but I can give you a state. My guess is that he comes from California. Or lived there for some time.'

'Why do you think that?'

She backed up with the rewind command. Then played part of the interview again, the portion where he talked about driving to Long Island to take delivery of the confiscated SUV.

Dance stopped the tape and said, 'I've studied regional expressions. People in California usually refer to their inter-state highways with the article 'the'. *The* four-oh-five in L.A., for instance. In the interview he referred to 'the four ninety-five' here in New York. And did you hear him say *freeway*? That's common in California too, more so than *expressway* or *interstate*. Which is what you hear on the East Coast.'

Possibly helpful, Rhyme thought. Another brick in the wall of evidence. 'On the chart,' he said.

'When I get back I'll open a formal investigation in my office,' she said. 'I'll put out everything we've got statewide. We'll see what happens. Okay, I better be going . . . Oh, I'll be expecting you both out in California sometime soon.'

The aide glanced at Rhyme. 'He needs to travel more. He pretends he doesn't like to but the fact is, once he gets some-place he enjoys it. As long as there's scotch and some good crime to keep him interested.'

'It's Northern California,' Dance said. 'Wine country, mostly, but not to worry, we have plenty of crime.'

'We'll see,' Rhyme said noncommittally. Then he added, 'But one thing – do me a favor?'

'Sure.'

'Shut your cell phone off. I'll probably be tempted to call you again on the way to the airport if something else comes up.'

'If I didn't have the children to get back to I might just pick up.'

Sellitto thanked her again and Thom saw her out the door.

Rhyme said, 'Ron, make yourself useful.'

The rookie looked at the evidence tables. 'I already called about the rope, if that's what you mean.'

'No, that's *not* what I mean,' Rhyme muttered. 'I said *useful*.' He nodded at the bottle of scotch sitting on a shelf across the room.

'Oh, sure.'

'Make it two,' Sellitto grumbled. 'And don't be stingy.'

Pulaski poured the whiskey and handed out two glasses – Cooper declined. Rhyme said to the rookie, 'Don't neglect yourself.'

'Oh, I'm in uniform.'

Sellitto choked a laugh.

'Okay. Maybe just a little.' He poured and then sipped the potent – and extremely expensive – liquor. 'I like it,' he said, though his eyes were telling a different story. 'Say, you ever mix in a little ginger ale or Sprite?'

Chapter
FORTY-TWO

Before and After.

People move on.

For one reason or another, they move on, and Before becomes After.

Lincoln Rhyme heard these words floating through his head, over and over. Broken record. People move on.

He'd actually used the phrase himself – when he'd told his wife he wanted a divorce, not long after his accident. Their relationship had been rocky for some time and he had decided that whether or not he survived the broken neck, he was going to go forward on his own and not tie her down to the difficult life of a gimp's wife.

But back then 'moving on' meant something very different from what Rhyme was facing now. The life he'd constructed over the past few years, a precarious life, was about to change in a big way. The problem, of course, was that by going to Argyle Security, Sachs wasn't really moving on. She was moving back.

Sellitto and Cooper were gone and Rhyme and Pulaski were alone in the downstairs lab, parked in front of an examination table, organizing evidence in the 118th Precinct scandal cases. Finally confronted with the evidence – and the fact they'd unwittingly hired a domestic terrorist – Baker, Wallace and Henson copped pleas and were diming out everybody involved at the 118th. (Though nobody would say a word about who'd hooked the Watchmaker up with Baker. Understandable. You simply don't give up the name of a senior member of an OC crew when you're headed off to the same prison he might end up in, thanks to your testimony.)

Preparing himself for Sachs's departure, Rhyme had concluded that Ron Pulaski would eventually be a fine crime scene cop. He had ingenuity and intelligence and was as dogged as Lon Sellitto. Rhyme could wear the rough edges off him in eight months or a year. Together, he and the rookie would run scenes, analyze evidence and find perps, who'd go to jail or die trying not to. The system would keep going. The process of policing was bigger than just one man or woman; it had to be.

Yes, the system would keep going . . . But it was impossibly hard to imagine that system without Amelia Sachs.

Well, fuck the goddamn sentiment, Rhyme said to himself, and get back to work. He glanced at the evidence board. The Watchmaker's out there somewhere; I'm going to find him. He is . . . not . . . getting . . . away.

'What?' Pulaski asked.

'I didn't say anything,' Rhyme snapped.

'Yeah, you did. I just . . .' He fell silent under Rhyme's withering glare.

Returning to his tasks, Pulaski asked, 'The notes I found in Baker's office? They're on cheap paper. Should I use ninhydrin to raise the latents?'

Rhyme started to respond.

A woman's voice said, 'No. First you try iodine fuming.

Then ninhydrin, *then* silver nitrate. You have to do it in that order.'

Rhyme looked up to see Sachs in the doorway. He slapped a benign look on his face. Putting on a good front, he praised himself. Being *generous*. Being *mature*.

She continued, 'If not, the chemicals can react and you can ruin the prints.'

Well, *this* is awkward, the criminalist thought angrily. He stared at the evidence boards as the silence between them roared like the December wind outside.

She said, 'I'm sorry.'

Unusual to hear those words from her; the woman apologized about as often as Lincoln Rhyme did. Which was close to never.

Rhyme didn't respond. He kept his eyes on the charts.

'Really, I'm sorry.'

Irritated at the greeting card sentiment, he glanced sideways, frowning, barely able to control his anger.

But he saw that she wasn't speaking to him.

Her eyes were fixed on Pulaski. 'I'll make it up to you somehow. You can run the next scene. I'll be copilot. Or the next couple of scenes.'

'How's that?' the rookie asked.

'I know you heard I was leaving.'

He nodded.

'But I've changed my mind.'

'You're not quitting?' Pulaski asked.

'No.'

'Hey, not a problem,' Pulaski said. 'Wouldn't mind sharing the job for a little while more, you know.' His relief at not being the only ant under Lincoln Rhyme's magnifying glass clearly outweighed any disappointment at getting busted back down to assistant.

Sachs tugged a chair around to face Rhyme.

He said, 'I thought you were at Argyle.'

'I was. To turn them down.'

'Can I ask why?'

'I got a call. From Suzanne Creeley. Ben Creeley's wife. She thanked me for believing her, for finding out who'd really killed her husband. She was crying. She told me that she just couldn't bear the thought that her husband had killed himself. Murder was terrible but a suicide – that would've undermined everything they'd had together over the years.'

Sachs shook her head. 'A knot in a rope and a broken thumb . . . I realized that that's what this job is all about, Rhyme. Not the crap I got caught up in, the politics, my father, Baker and Wallace . . . You can't make it too complicated. Being a cop is about finding the truth behind a knot and a broken thumb. Nothing more than that.'

You and me, Sachs . . .

'So,' she asked, matter-of-fact, as she nodded toward the boards, 'our bad boy – anything new on him?'

Rhyme told her about his present, the Breguet, then summarized: 'A rock or mountain climber, possibly trained in Europe. He's spent time in California, near the shore. And he's been there recently. May live there now. Good education. Uses proper grammar, syntax and punctuation. And I want to go over every gear in the watch again. He's a watch*maker*, right? That means he's probably taken the back off to poke around inside. If there's a molecule of trace, I want it.' Rhyme nodded at the man's note and added, 'He admits he was watching Charlotte's hotel around the time we collared her. I want every vantage point where he might've been standing searched. You're recruited for that one, Ron.'

'Got it.'

'And don't forget what we know about him. Maybe he's

gone and maybe he isn't. Make sure your weapon's in reach. *Outside* the Tyvek. Remember—'

'Search well but watch my back?' Pulaski asked.

'An A for retention,' the criminalist said. 'Now get to work.'

IV

12:48 P.M. MONDAY

What then is time? If no one asks me, I know what it is. If I wish to explain it to him who asks, I do not know.

— SAINT AUGUSTINE

Chapter
FORTY-THREE

The December day wasn't particularly cold but the ancient furnace in Rhyme's town house was on the fritz and everyone in his ground floor lab huddled in thick jackets. Clouds of steam blew from their mouths with every exhalation, and extremities were bright red. Amelia Sachs wore two sweaters and Pulaski was in a padded green jacket from which dangled Killington ski lift tickets like a veteran soldier's campaign medals.

A skier cop, Rhyme reflected. That seemed odd, though he couldn't say why exactly. Maybe something about the dangers of hurtling down a mountain with a hair-trigger 9-millimeter pistol under your bunny suit.

'Where's the furnace repair guy?' Rhyme snapped to his aide.

'He said he'll be here between one and five.' Thom was wearing a tweed jacket, which Rhyme had given him last Christmas, and a dark purple cashmere scarf, which had been one of Sachs's presents.

'Ah, between one and five. One and five. Tell you what. Call him back and—'

'That's what he told—'

'No, listen. Call him back and tell him we got a report there's a crazed killer loose in his neighborhood and we'll be there to catch him between one and five. See how he likes them apples.'

'Lincoln,' the patient aide said. 'I don't—'

'Does he know what we do here? Does he know that we serve and protect? Call him and tell him that.'

Pulaski noted that Thom wasn't reaching for the phone. He asked, 'Uhm, you want me to? Call, I mean?'

Ah, the sincerity of youth . . .

Thom replied to the young officer, 'Don't pay him any attention. He's like a dog jumping up on you. Ignore him and he'll stop.'

'A dog?' Rhyme asked. '*I'm* a dog. That's a bit ironic, isn't it, Thom? Since here *you* are biting the hand that feeds you.' Pleased with the retort, he added, 'Tell the repairman I think I'm suffering from hypothermia. I really think I am, by the way.'

'So you can feel—' the rookie asked, his question braking to a halt.

'Yes, I goddamn well *can* feel uncomfortable, Pulaski.'

'Sorry, wasn't thinking.'

'Hey,' Thom said, laughing. 'Congratulations!'

'What's that?' the rookie asked.

'You've graduated to last-name basis. He's beginning to think of you as a step above a slug . . . That's how he refers to the people he really likes. I, for instance, am merely Thom. Forever Thom.'

'But,' Sachs said to the rookie, 'tell him you're sorry again and you'll be demoted.'

The doorbell sounded a moment later and first-name Thom went to answer it.

Rhyme glanced at the clock. The time was 1:02. Could it be that a repairman was actually prompt?

But, of course, this wasn't the case. It was Lon Sellitto, who walked inside, started to take his coat off, then changed his mind. He glanced at his breath billowing from his mouth. 'Jesus, Linc, with what the city coughs up for you, you can afford to pay your heating bill, you know. Is that coffee? Is it hot?'

Thom poured him a cup and Sellitto clutched it in one hand as he opened his briefcase with the other. 'Finally got it.' He nodded at what he now extracted, an old Redweld folder disfigured with faded ink and pencil notations, many of the entries crossed out, evidence of years of frugal municipal government reuse.

'The Luponte file?' Rhyme asked.

'That's it.'

'I wanted it last week,' the criminalist grumbled, the inside of his nose stinging from the cold. Maybe he'd tell the repairman he'd pay the bill in one to five months. He glanced at the folder. 'I'd almost given up. I know how much you love clichés, Lon. Does the phrase "day late and a dollar short" come to mind?'

'Naw,' the detective said amiably, 'the one I'm thinking of is "If you do somebody a favor and they complain, then fuck 'em".'

'That's a good one,' conceded Lincoln Rhyme.

'Anyway, you didn't tell me how classified it was. I had to find that out on my own, and I needed Ron Scott to track it down.'

Rhyme was staring at the detective as he opened the file and browsed through it. He felt an acute sense of uneasiness, wondering what he would find inside. Could be good, could be devastating. 'There should be an official report. Find it.'

Sellitto dug through the folder. He held up the document. On the cover was an old typewritten label that read *Anthony C. Luponte, Deputy Commissioner*. The folder was sealed with a fading piece of red tape that said, *Classified*.

'Should I open it?' he asked.

Rhyme rolled his eyes.

'Linc, tell me when the good mood's going to kick in, will you?'

'Put it on the turning frame. Please and thank you.'

Sellitto ripped open the tape and handed the booklet to Thom.

The aide mounted the report in a device like a cookbook holder, to which was attached a rubber armature that turned the pages when instructed by a tiny movement from Rhyme's finger on his ECU touch pad. He now began to flip through the document, reading and trying to quell the tension within him.

'Luponte?' Sachs looked up from an evidence table.

Another page turned. 'That's it.'

He kept reading paragraph after paragraph of dense city government talk.

Oh, come on, he thought angrily. Get to the goddamn point . . .

Would the message be good or bad?

'Something about the Watchmaker?' Sachs asked.

So far, there'd been no leads to the man, either in New York or in California, where Kathryn Dance had started her own investigation.

Rhyme said, 'It doesn't have anything to do with him.'

Sachs shook her head. 'But that's why you wanted it.'

'No, you *assumed* that's why I wanted it.'

'What's it about then, one of the other cases?' she asked. Her eyes went to the evidence boards, which revealed the progress of several cold cases they'd been investigating.

'Not those.'

'Then what?'

'I could tell you a lot sooner if I wasn't interrupted so much.'

Sachs sighed.

At last he came to the section he sought. He paused, looked out the window at the stark brown branches populating Central Park. He believed in his heart that the report would tell him what he wanted to hear but Lincoln Rhyme was a scientist before all else and distrusted the heart.

Truth is the only goal . . .

What truths would the words reveal to him?

He looked back at the frame and read the passage quickly. Then again.

After a moment he said to Sachs, 'I want to read you something.'

'Okay. I'm listening.'

His right finger moved on the touch pad and the pages flipped back. 'This is from the first page. Listening?'

'I said I was.'

'Good. "This proceeding is and shall be kept secret. From June eighteenth to June twenty-ninth, ninety seventy-four, a dozen New York City police officers were indicted by a grand jury for extorting money from shopkeepers and businessmen in Manhattan and Brooklyn and accepting bribes to fail to pursue criminal investigations. Additionally, four officers were indicted for assault pursuant to these acts of extortion. Those twelve officers were members of what was known as the Sixteenth Avenue Club, a name that has become synonymous with the heinous crime of police corruption."'

Rhyme heard Sachs take a fast breath. He looked up and found her staring at the file the way a child stares at a snake in the backyard.

He continued reading. '"There is no trust greater than that between the citizens of these United States and the law enforcement officers who are charged with protecting them. The officers of the Sixteenth Avenue Club committed an inexcusable breach of this sacred trust and not only perpetuated the crimes they were meant to prevent but brought inestimable shame upon their courageous and self-sacrificing brothers and sisters in uniform.

'"Accordingly, I, the Mayor of the City of New York, hereby bestow upon the following officers the Medal for Valor for their efforts in bringing these criminals to justice: Patrolman Vincent Pazzini, Patrolman Herman Sachs and Detective Third-Grade Lawrence Koepel."'

'What?' Sachs whispered.

Rhyme continued reading. '"Each of these officers risked his life on a number of occasions by working undercover to provide information instrumental in identifying the perpetrators and gathering evidence to be used in their trials. Because of the dangerous nature of this assignment, these commendations are being presented in a closed proceeding, and this record will be sealed, for the safety of these three courageous officers and their families. But they should rest assured that, although the praises for their efforts are not being sung in public, the gratitude of the city is no less."'

Amelia Sachs was staring at him. 'He—?'

Rhyme nodded at the file. 'Your father was one of the good guys, Sachs. He *was* one of the three who got away. Only they weren't perps; they were working for Internal Affairs. He was to the Sixteenth Avenue Club just what you were to the St James crew, only he was undercover.'

'How did you know?'

'I didn't *know*. I remembered something about the Luponte report and the corruption trials but I didn't know your father was involved. That's why I wanted to see it.'

'How 'bout that,' Sellitto said through a mouthful of coffee cake.

'Keep looking, Lon. There's something else.'

The detective dug through the folder and found a certificate and a medal. It was an NYPD Medal for Valor, one of the highest commendations given by the department. Sellitto handed it to Sachs. Her full lips parted, eyes squinting, as she read the unframed parchment document which bore her father's name. The decoration swung from her unsteady fingers.

'Hey, that's sweet,' said Pulaski, pointing at the certificate. 'Look at all those scrolls and things.'

Rhyme nodded toward the folder on the turning frame. 'It's all in there, Sachs. His handler at Internal Affairs had to make sure that the other cops believed him. He gave your dad a couple thousand a month to spread around, make it seem like he was on the take too. He had to be credible – if anybody thought he was an informant, he could've been killed, especially with Tony Gallante involved. IAD started a fake investigation on him so it'd look believable. That's the case they dropped for insufficient evidence. They worked out a deal with Crime Scene so that the chain-of-custody cards were lost.'

Sachs lowered her head. Then she gave a soft laugh. 'Dad was always the modest one. It was just like him – the highest commendation he ever got was secret. He never said a thing about it.'

'You can read all the details. Your father said he'd wear a wire, he'd give all the information they needed about Gallante and the other capos involved. But he'd never testify in open court. He wasn't going to jeopardize you and your mother.'

She was staring at the medal, which swung back and forth – like a pendulum of a clock, Rhyme thought wryly.

Finally Lon Sellitto rubbed his hands together. 'Listen, glad for the happy news,' he grumbled. 'But how 'bout we get the hell out of here and go over to Manny's. I could use some lunch. And, guess what? I'll bet *they* pay their heating bill.'

'I'd love to,' Rhyme said, with a sincerity that he believed masked his absolute lack of desire to be outside, negotiating the icy streets in his wheelchair. 'But I'm writing an op ed piece for the *Times*.' He nodded at his computer. 'Besides, I have to wait here for the repairman.' He shook his head. 'One to five.'

Thom started to say something – undoubtedly to urge Rhyme to go anyway – but it was Sachs who said, 'Sorry. Other plans.'

Rhyme said, 'If it involves ice and snow, I'm not interested.' He supposed she and the girl, Pammy Willoughby, were planning another outing with the girl's adoptee, Jackson the Havanese.

But Amelia Sachs apparently had a different agenda. 'It does,' she said. 'Involve snow and ice, I mean.' She laughed and kissed him on the mouth. 'But what it doesn't involve is you.'

'Thank God,' Lincoln Rhyme said, blowing a stream of wispy breath toward the ceiling and turning back to the computer screen.

'You.'

'Hey, Detective, how you doing?' Amelia Sachs asked.

Art Snyder gazed at her from the doorway of his bungalow. He looked better than when she'd seen him last – when he was lying in the back-seat of his van. He wasn't any less angry, though. His red eyes were fixed on hers.

But when your profession involves getting shot at from time to time, a few glares mean nothing. Sachs gave a smile. 'I just came by to say thanks.'

'Yeah, for what?' He held a coffee mug that clearly didn't contain coffee. She saw that a number of bottles had reappeared on the sideboard. She noted too that none of the Home Depot projects had progressed.

'We closed the St James case.'

'Yeah, I heard.'

'Kind of cold out here, Detective,' she said.

'Honey?' A stocky woman with short brown hair and a cheerful, resilient face called from the kitchen doorway.

'Just somebody from the department.'

'Well, invite her in. I'll make coffee.'

'She's a busy lady,' Snyder said sourly. 'Running all over town, doing all kinds of things, asking questions. She probably can't stay.'

'I'm freezing my ass off out here.'

'Art! Let her in.'

He sighed, turned and walked inside, leaving Sachs to follow him and close the door herself. She dropped her coat on a chair.

Snyder's wife joined them. The women shook hands. 'Give her the comfy chair, Art,' she scolded.

Sachs sat in the well-worn Barcalounger, Snyder on the couch, which sighed under his weight. He left the volume up on the TV, which displayed a frantic, high-definition basketball game.

His wife brought two cups of coffee.

'None for me,' Snyder said, looking at the mug.

'I've already poured it. You want me to throw it out? Waste good coffee?' She left it on the table beside him and returned to the kitchen, where garlic was frying.

Sachs sipped the strong coffee in silence, Snyder staring at ESPN. His eyes followed a basketball from its launchpad outside the three-point line; his fist clenched minutely when it swished in.

A commercial came on. He changed channels to celebrity poker.

Sachs remembered that Kathryn Dance had mentioned the power of silence in getting somebody to talk. She sat, sipping, looking at him, not saying a word.

Finally, irritated, Snyder asked, 'The St James thing?'

'Uh-huh.'

'I read it was Dennis Baker behind it. And the deputy mayor.'

'Yep.'

'I met Baker a few times. Seemed okay. Him being on the bag surprised me.' Concern crossed Snyder's face. 'Homicides too? Sarkowski and that other guy?'

She nodded. 'And an attempt.' She didn't share that she herself had been the potential victim.

He shook his head. 'Money's one thing. But offing people . . . that's a whole different ball game.'

Amen.

Snyder asked, 'Was one of the perps that guy I told you about? Had a place in Maryland or something?'

She figured that he deserved some credit. 'That was Wallace. But it wasn't a place. It was a thing.' Sachs explained about Wallace's boat.

He gave a sour laugh. 'No kidding. *The Maryland Monroe?* That's a pisser.'

Sachs said. 'Might not've broken the case if you hadn't helped.'

Snyder had a millisecond of satisfaction. Then he remembered he was mad. He made a point of rising, with a sigh, and filling his mug with more whiskey. He sat down again. His coffee remained untouched. He channel-surfed some more.

'Can I ask you something?'

'I can stop you?' he muttered.

'You said you knew my father. Not many people're still around who did. I just wanted to ask you about him.'

'The Sixteenth Avenue Club?'

'Nope. Don't want to know about that.'

Snyder said, 'He was lucky he got away.'

'Sometimes you dodge the bullet.'

'At least he cleaned up his act later. Heard he never got into any trouble after that.'

'You said you worked with him. He didn't talk much about his job. I always wondered what it was like back then. Thought I'd write down a few things.'

'For his grandkids?'

'Something like that.'

Reluctantly Snyder said, 'We never were partners.'

'But you knew him.'

A hesitation. 'Yeah.'

'Just tell me: What was the story on that commander . . . the crazy one? I always wanted to know the scoop.'

'*Which* crazy one?' Snyder scoffed. 'There were plenty.'

'The one who sent the tactical team to the wrong apartment?'

'Oh. Caruthers?'

'I think that was him. Dad was one of the portables holding off the hostage-taker until ESU found the right place.'

'Yeah, yeah. I was on that. What an asshole, Caruthers. The putz . . . Thank God nobody was hurt. Oh, and that was the same day he forgot the batteries in his bullhorn . . . One other thing about him: He'd send his boots out to be polished. He'd have the rookies do it, you know. And he'd tip 'em, like, a nickel. I mean, tipping uniforms is weird to start. But then five goddamn cents?'

The TV volume came down a few bars. Snyder laughed. 'Hey, you wanta hear one story?'

'You bet.'

'Well, your dad and me and a bunch of us, off duty, were going to the Garden, see a fight or game or something. And this kid comes up with a zip gun – you know what that is?'

She did. She said she didn't.

'Like a homemade gun. Holds a single twenty-two shell. And this poor fuck mugs us, you can believe it. He sticks us up right in the middle of Three-four Street. We're handing over wallets. Then your dad drops his billfold, accidental on purpose, you know what I'm saying? And the kid bends down to pick it up. When he stands up he shits – he's staring right into the muzzles of our pieces, four Smitties, cocked and ready to unload. The look on that kid's face . . . He said, "Guess it ain't my day." Is that classic or what? "Guess it ain't my day." Man, we laughed all night about that . . .' His face broke into a smile. 'Oh, and one other thing . . .'

As he talked, Sachs nodded and encouraged him. In reality she knew many of these stories. Herman Sachs wasn't the least reluctant to talk to his daughter about his job. They'd spend hours in the garage, working on a transmission or fuel pump, while stories of a cop's life on the streets reeled past – planting the seeds for her own future.

But of course she wasn't here to learn family history. No, this was simply an officer-needs-assistance call, a 10–13 of the heart. Sachs had decided that former detective Art Snyder wasn't going down. If his supposed friends didn't want to see him because he'd helped nail the St James crew, then she'd set him up with plenty of cops who would: herself, Sellitto, Rhyme and Ron Pulaski, Fred Dellray, Roland Bell, Nancy Simpson, Frank Rettig, a dozen others.

She asked him more questions and he replied – sometimes eagerly, sometimes with irritation, sometimes distracted, but always giving her something. A couple of times Snyder rose and refilled his mug with liquor and frequently he'd glance at his watch and then at her, his meaning clear: Don't you have someplace else to be?

But she just sat back comfortably in the Barcalounger, asked her questions and even told a few war stories of her own. Amelia Sachs wasn't going anywhere; she had all the time in the world.

Author's Note

Authors are only as good as the friends and fellow professionals around them, and I'm extremely fortunate to be surrounded by a truly wonderful ensemble: Will and Tina Anderson, Alex Bonham, Louise Burke, Robby Burroughs, Britt Carlson, Jane Davis, Julie Reece Deaver, John Gilstrap, Cathy Gleason, Jamie Hodder-Williams, Kate Howard, Emma Longhurst, Diana Mackay, Carolyn Mays, Tara Parsons, Seba Pezzani, Carolyn Reidy, Ornella Robbiati, David Rosenthal, Marysue Rucci, Deborah Schneider, Vivienne Schuster, Brigitte Smith, Kevin Smith and Alexis Taines.

Special gratitude, as always, to Madelyn Warcholik.

Those interested in the subject of watchmaking and watch collecting will enjoy Michael Korda's compact and lyrical *Marking Time*.

About the Author

Former journalist, folksinger and attorney Jeffery Deaver's novels have appeared on a number of best-seller lists around the world, including *The New York Times*, the *Times* of London and the *Los Angeles Times*. His books are sold in 150 countries and are translated into thirty-five languages. The author of twenty-one novels, he's been awarded the Steel Dagger and Short Story Dagger from the British Crime Writers' Association, is a three-time recipient of the Ellery Queen Reader's Award for Best Short Story of the Year and is a winner of the British Thumping Good Read Award. He's been nominated for six Edgar Awards from the Mystery Writers of America, an Anthony Award and a Gumshoe Award. His book *A Maiden's Grave* was made into an HBO movie staring James Garner and Marlee Matlin, and his novel *The Bone Collector* was a feature release from Universal Pictures, starring Denzel Washington and Angelina Jolie. His most recent books are *The Twelfth Card*, *Garden of Beasts*, *The Vanished Man* and *Twisted: Collected Stories*. And, yes, the rumors are true, he did appear as a corrupt reporter on his favorite soap opera, *As the World Turns*. Readers can visit his website at **www.jefferydeaver.com**.

Kathryn Dance will return in *The Sleeping Doll*
July 2007

THE SLEEPING DOLL

*Dance noticed too that Pell put his hands, tipped with long,
clean nails, on the table at the word 'relatives'. This was a
deviation from baseline behaviour. It didn't mean lying, but he
was feeling stress. The questions were upsetting him.*

Eight years ago, Daniel Pell, a murderer obsessed with
Charles Manson, viciously slaughtered four family
members in a seemingly motiveless attack. The youngest
daughter asleep in her bed and hidden by her dolls, was
the only one to survive. The public came to know her as
the Sleeping Doll.

Now, Pell has escaped from prison and kinesics expert
Kathryn Dance must use her skill in reading body language
to find the Sleeping Doll before Pell comes back to finish
the job he started all those years ago . . .

HODDER &
STOUGHTON

Chapter
ONE

The interrogation began like any other.

Kathryn Dance entered the interview room and found the man sitting at a metal table, shackled, looking up at her closely. Subjects always did this, of course, though never with such astonishing eyes, their color a blue unlike sky or ocean or famous gems.

'Good morning,' she said, sitting down across from him.

'And to you.' His voice soft.

A slight smile on his bearded face, the small, sinewy man sat back, relaxed. His head, covered with long, gray-black hair, was cocked to the side. While most interrogations were accompanied by a jingling soundtrack of handcuff chains, as subjects tried to prove their innocence with broad, predictable gestures, Daniel Pell sat perfectly still.

To Dance, a specialist in interrogation and kinesics – body language – Pell's demeanor and posture suggested caution, but also confidence and, curiously, amusement. He wore an orange jumpsuit, stenciled with 'Capitola Correctional Facility' on the chest and 'Inmate' unnecessarily decorating the back.

At the moment, though, Pell and Dance were not in

Capitola, but rather a secure interview room at the county courthouse in Salinas, thirty miles away.

Pell continued his examination. First, Dance's own eyes – a green complementary to his blue – and framed by square, black-rimmed glasses. He regarded her French-braided, dark-blonde hair, the black jacket and beneath it the thick, un-revealing white blouse. He noted too the empty holster on her hip. He was meticulous and in no hurry. Interviewers and interviewees share mutual curiosity. (She told the students in her interrogation seminars, 'They're studying you as hard as you're studying them – usually even harder, since they have more to lose.')

Dance fished in her blue Coach purse for her ID card, not reacting as she saw a tiny stuffed bat that either twelve-year-old Wes or his younger sister Maggie, or both conspir-ators, had slipped into the bag that morning as a practical joke. She thought: how's this for a contrasting life? An hour ago she was having breakfast with her children in the kitchen of their homey Victorian house in idyllic Pacific Grove, two dogs at their feet begging for bacon, and now here she was, sitting across a very different table from a man who'd murdered four family members eight years ago for reasons never made clear.

Dance found the ID and displayed it. He stared for a long moment, easing forward. 'Dance. Interesting name. Wonder where it comes from. And the California Bureau . . . what is that?'

'Bureau of Investigation. Like an FBI for the state. Now, Mr Pell, you understand that this conversation is being recorded.'

He glanced at the mirror, behind which a video camera was humming away. 'You folks think we really believe that's there so we can fix up our hair?'

Mirrors weren't placed in interrogation rooms to hide

cameras and witnesses – there are far better high-tech ways to do so – but because people lie less frequently when they can see themselves.

Dance gave a faint smile. 'And you understand that you can withdraw from this interview anytime you want and that you have a right to have an attorney present?'

'I know more criminal procedure than the entire graduating class of Hastings Law rolled up together. Which is a pretty funny image, when you think about it.'

More articulate than Dance had expected. More clever too.

She wasn't pleased to be sitting this far away from the subject, with a table separating them. Anything between interrogators and subjects gives them an added layer of defense.

With the prisoner's violent past, though, security took priority.

The previous week, Daniel Raymond Pell, serving a life sentence for the 1999 murders of William Croyton, his wife and two of their children, apparently approached a fellow prisoner due to be released from Capitola and tried to bribe him to run an errand after he was free. Pell told him about some evidence he'd disposed of down a Salinas well years ago and explained he was worried that these items would implicate him in the unsolved murder of a wealthy farm owner. He'd read recently that Salinas was revamping its water system. This jogged his memory of the items he'd ditched and he grew concerned that the evidence would be discovered. He wanted the prisoner to find and dispose of it.

Pell picked the wrong man to enlist, though. The short-timer spilled to the warden, who called the Monterey County Sheriff's Office. Investigators wondered if Pell was talking about the murder of farm owner Robert Herron, beaten to death a decade ago. The murder weapon, probably a claw hammer, was never found. The Sheriff's Office sent a team to search all the wells in that part of town. Sure enough, they found a tattered t-shirt, a claw hammer and an empty wallet, with the initials 'R.H.' stamped on it. Two fingerprints on the hammer were Daniel Pell's.

The Monterey County prosecutor decided to present the case to the grand jury, and had asked CBI agent Kathryn Dance to interview him, in hopes of a confession.

Dance now asked, 'How long did you live in the Monterey area?'

He seemed surprised that she didn't immediately begin to browbeat. 'A few years.'

'Where?'

'Seaside.'

A town of about 30,000, north of Monterey on Highway One, populated mostly by young working families and retirees.

'You got more for your hard-earned money there,' he explained. 'More than in your fancy Carmel.' And examined her closely.

His grammar and syntax were good, she noted, ignoring his fishing expedition for information about her residence.

He continued, 'And now my home is beautiful downtown Capitola.'

Dance continued to ask him about his life in Seaside and in prison. Observing him the whole while: how he behaved when she asked the questions and how he behaved when he answered. She wasn't doing this to get information – she'd done her homework and knew the answers to everything she asked – but was instead establishing his behavioral baseline.

In spotting lies, interrogators consider three factors: non-verbal behavior (body language, or kinesics), verbal quality (pitch of voice or pauses before answering) and verbal content (what the suspect says). The first two are far more reliable indications of deception, since it's much easier to control what we say than how we say it and how our body responds when we do.

The baseline is a catalog of these behaviors exhibited when

the subject's telling the truth. This is the standard the interrogator will compare later to the subject's behavior when he might have a reason to lie. Any differences between the two suggest deception.

Finally Dance had a good profile of the truthful Daniel Pell and moved to the crux of her mission here, in this modern, sterile courthouse on a foggy morning in June. 'I'd like to ask you a few questions about Robert Herron.'

Eyes sweeping hers, now refining their examination: the abalone shell necklace, which her mother had made, at her throat. Then Dance's short, pink-polished nails. The gray pearl ring on the wedding band finger got two glances.

'Where were you living in January of 1996?'

'Monterey.'

'What street?'

He pursed his lips. 'Beats me. North part of town, I think.'

Interesting. Deceptive subjects often avoid specifics, which can be checked and which you can recite back to them later if they offer a contradictory statement at trial. And it was rare not to remember where you lived. Still, his kinesic responses weren't suggesting deception.

'How did you meet Robert Herron?'

'You're assuming I did. But, no, never met him in my life. I swear.'

The last sentence was a deception flag. Once again, though, his body language wasn't giving off signals that suggested he was lying.

'But you told the prisoner in Capitola that you wanted him to go to the well and find the hammer and wallet.'

'No, that's what *he* told the warden.' Pell offered another amused smile. 'Why don't you talk to him about it? You've got sharp eyes, Officer Dance. I've seen them looking me over, deciding if I'm being straight with you. I'll bet you could tell in a flash that that boy was lying.'

She gave no reaction, but reflected that it was very rare for a suspect to realize he was being analyzed kinesically.

'But then how did he know about the evidence in the well?'

'Oh, I've got that figured out. Somebody stole a hammer of mine, killed Herron with it and then planted it to blame me. They wore gloves. Those rubber ones everybody wears on *CSI*.'

Still relaxed. The body language wasn't any different from his baseline. He was showing only emblems – common gestures that tended to substitute for words, like shrugs and finger pointing. There were no adaptors, which signal tension, or affect displays – signs that he was experiencing emotion.

'But if he wanted to do that,' Dance pointed out, 'wouldn't the killer just call the police *then* and tell them where the hammer was? Why wait over ten years?'

'Being smart, I'd guess. Better to bide his time. Then spring the trap.'

'Why would the real killer call the prisoner in Capitola? Why not just call the police directly?'

A hesitation. Then a laugh. His blue eyes shone with excitement, which seemed genuine. 'Because *they're* involved too. The police. Sure . . . The cops realize the Herron case hasn't been solved and they want to blame somebody. Why not *me*? They've already got me in custody. I'll bet the cops planted the hammer themselves.'

'Okay. Let's work with this a little. There're two different things you're saying. First, somebody stole your hammer before Herron was killed, murdered him with it and now, over ten years later, dimes you out. But your second version is that the police got your hammer *after* Herron was killed by someone else altogether and planted it in the well to blame you. Those're contradictory. It's either one or the other. Which do you think?'

'Hm.' Pell gave an easy smile. 'Okay, I'll go with the second one. The police. It's a set-up. I'm sure that's what happened.'

She looked him in the eyes, green on blue. 'Okay, let's take the situation apart: first, where would the police have gotten the hammer?'

He thought. 'When they arrested me for that Carmel thing.'

'The Croyton murders in ninety-nine?'

'Right. All the evidence they took from my house in Seaside.'

Dance's brows furrowed. 'I doubt that. Evidence is accounted for too closely. No, I'd go for a more credible scenario: that the hammer was stolen recently. Where else could somebody find a hammer of yours? Do you have any property in the state?'

'No.'

'Any relatives or friends who could've had some tools of yours?'

'Not really.'

Which wasn't an answer to a yes or no question; it was even slipperier than 'I don't recall.' Dance noticed too that Pell put his hands, tipped with long, clean nails, on the table at the word 'relatives'. This was a deviation from baseline behavior. It didn't mean lying, but he *was* feeling stress. The questions were upsetting him.

'Daniel, you have any relations living in California?'

He hesitated, must have assessed that she was the sort to check out every comment – which she was – and said, 'The only left's my aunt. Down in Bakersfield.'

'Is her name Pell?'

Another pause. 'Yep . . . That's good thinking, Officer Dance. I'll bet the deputies who dropped the ball on the Herron case stole that hammer from her and planted it. They're the ones behind this whole thing. Why don't you talk to them?'

'All right. That explains the hammer. Now let's think about the wallet. Where could that've come from? . . . Here's a thought. What if it's not Robert Herron's wallet at all? What if this rogue cop we're talking about just bought a wallet, had

'R.H.' stamped in the leather then hid that and the hammer in the well. It could've been last month. Or even last week. What do you think about that, Daniel?'

Pell lowered his head – she couldn't see his eyes – and said nothing.

It was unfolding just like she'd planned.

Dance had forced him to pick the most credible of two explanations for his innocence – and proceeded to prove it too wasn't credible at all. No sane jury would believe that the police fabricated evidence and stole tools from a house hundreds of miles away from the crime scene. Pell was now realizing the mistake he'd made. The trap was about to close on him.

Checkmate . . .

Her heart thumped a bit and she was thinking that the next words out of his mouth might be to suggest his willingness to accept a plea bargain.

She was wrong.

Daniel Pell attacked her.

His eyes snapped open and bore into hers with pure malevolence. He lunged forward as far as he could. Only the chains hooked to the metal chair, grounded with bolts to the tile floor, stopped him from sinking his teeth into her.

She jerked back, gasping.

'You goddamn bitch! You have no idea what it's like to be set up! You're part of it too! Oh, yeah, blame Daniel. It's always my fault! I'm the easy target. And you come in here sounding like a friend, asking me a few questions. Jesus, you're just like the rest of them!'

Her heart was pounding furiously and she was afraid but noted quickly that the restraints were secure and he couldn't reach her. She turned to the mirror behind which the officer manning the video camera was surely rising to his feet right now to help her. But she shook her head. It was important to see where this was going.

Then suddenly the fury was replaced with a cold calm. He sat back, caught his breath, and looked her over again. 'You're in your thirties, Officer Dance. You're somewhat pretty. You seem straight to me, so I guarantee there's a man in your life. Or has been.' A third glance at the pearl ring.

'If you don't like my theory, Daniel, let's come up with another one. About what really happened to Robert Herron.'

As if she hadn't even spoken. 'And you've got children, right? Sure, you do. I can see that. Tell me all about them. Tell me about the little ones. Close in age, and not too old, I'll bet.'

This unnerved her and she involuntarily thought of Maggie and Wes. But she struggled not to react. He *doesn't* know I have children, of course. He can't. But he sure acts as if he's certain. Was there something about *my* behavior he noted? Something that suggested to him that I'm a mother?

They're studying you as hard as you're studying them . . .

'Listen to me, Daniel,' she said in a pond-calm voice. 'An outburst isn't going to help anything.'

'I've got friends on the outside, you know. They owe me. They'd love to come visit you. Or hang with your husband and children. Yeah, it's a tough life being a cop. The little ones spend a lot of time alone, don't they? They'd probably love some friends to play with.'

Dance returned the gaze, never flinching. She asked, 'Could you tell me about your relationship with that prisoner in Capitola?'

'Yes, I could. But I won't.' His emotionless words mocking her, making clear that, for a professional interrogator, she'd phrased her question carelessly. In a soft voice he added, 'I think it's time to go back to my cell.'

Chapter
TWO

Alonzo 'Sandy' Sandoval, the Monterey County prosecutor, was a handsome, round man with a thick head of black hair and an ample moustache. He sat behind a desk littered with files in his office, two flights above the lockup. 'Hi, Kathryn. So, our boy . . . Did he beat his breast and cry, "*Mea culpa*"?'

'Not exactly.' Dance sat down, peered into the coffee cup she'd left on the desk forty-five minutes ago. Non-dairy creamer scummed on the surface. 'I rate it as, oh, one of the least successful interrogations of all time.'

'You look shook, Boss,' said a short, wiry Anglo, with curly red hair and wearing jeans, t-shirt and plaid sports coat. TJ's outfit was unconventional for an investigative agent with the CBI – the most conservative law enforcement agency in the Great Bear State – but so was pretty much everything else about him. Around thirty and single, TJ lived in the hills of Carmel Valley, his house a ramshackle place that could have been a diorama in a counter-culture museum depicting California life in the 1960s. TJ tended to work solo much of the time, surveillance and undercover, rather than pairing up with another CBI agent, which was standard procedure. But Dance's regular partner was in Mexico on an extradition and, when the Pell case came up, TJ jumped at the chance to meet the Son of Manson.

'No, just *curious*.' She explained how the interview had been going fine when, suddenly, Pell turned on her. Under TJ's skeptical gaze, she conceded, 'Okay, I'm a *little* shook. I've been threatened before. But his were the worst kind of threats.'

'Worst?' asked Juan Millar, a tall, dark-complexioned young detective with the MSO – the Monterey County Sheriff's Office, which was headquartered not far from the courthouse.

'*Calm* threats,' Dance said.

TJ filled in, '*Cheerful* threats. You know you're in trouble when they stop screaming and started whispering.'

The little ones spend a lot of time alone . . .

Dance forced the recollection of Pell's words away.

'What happened?' Sandoval asked, seemingly more concerned about the state of his case than threats against Dance.

'When he denied knowing Herron, there was no stress reaction at all. It was only when I had him talking about police conspiracy that he started to exhibit aversion and negation. Some extremity movement too, deviating from his baseline.'

Kathryn Dance was often called a human lie detector, but that wasn't true; in reality she, like all successful kinesic analysts and interrogators, was a stress detector. This was the key to deception; once she spotted stress, she'd probe the topic that gave rise to it and dig until the subject broke and told the truth.

But there are different types of stress, and the sort that Dance had observed Pell exhibiting didn't suggest deception.

She explained this and added, 'My sense was that he'd lost control of the interview and couldn't get it back. So he went ballistic.'

'Even though what you were saying *supported* his defense?'

Lanky Juan Millar scratched his left hand absently. In the fleshy Y between the index finger and thumb was a scar, the remnant of a gang tat.

'Exactly.'

What, she wondered, was bothering him so much? Was it that—

Then Dance's mind made one of its curious jumps. A to B to X. She couldn't explain how they happened. But she always paid attention. 'Where was Robert Herron murdered?' She walked to a map of Monterey County on Sandoval's wall.

'Here.' The prosecutor touched an area in the yellow trapezoid.

'And the well where they found the hammer and wallet?'

'About here, make it.'

It was a quarter mile from the crime scene, in a residential area.

Dance was staring at the map.

She felt TJ's eyes on her. 'What's wrong, Boss?'

'You have a picture of the well?' she asked.

Sandoval dug in the file. 'Juan's forensic people shot a lot of pics.'

'Crime Scene boys love their toys,' Millar said, the rhyme sounding odd from the mouth of such a straight-arrow. He gave a shy smile. 'I heard that somewhere.'

The prosecutor produced a stack of color photographs, riffled through them until he found the ones he sought.

Gazing at them, Dance asked TJ, 'We ran a case there six, eight months ago, remember?'

'The arson, sure. In that new housing development.'

Tapping the map, the spot where the well was located, Dance continued, 'That development is still under construction. And that—' She nodded at a photograph. 'is a hard-rock well.'

Everybody in the area knew that water was at such a

premium in this part of California that hard rock wells, with their low output and undependable supply, were never used for agricultural irrigation, only for private homes.

'Shit.' Sandoval closed his eyes briefly. 'Ten years ago, when Herron was killed, that was all farmland. The well wouldn't've been there then.'

'It wasn't there *one* year ago.' Dance muttered. '*That's* why Pell was so stressed. I was getting close to the truth – somebody *did* get the hammer from his aunt's in Bakersfield and had a fake wallet made up. Only it wasn't to frame him.'

'On, no,' TJ whispered.

'What?' Millar asked, looking from one agent to the other.

'Pell set the whole thing up himself,' she said. 'He couldn't escape from Capitola.' That facility, like Pelican Bay in the north of the state, was a high-tech superprison, reserved for the most dangerous prisoners. 'But he could from here.'

Kathryn Dance lunged for the phone.

Have you discovered the other
Lincoln Rhyme thrillers?

THE BONE COLLECTOR
THE COFFIN DANCER
THE EMPTY CHAIR
THE STONE MONKEY
THE VANISHED MAN
THE TWELFTH CARD

Introducing Kathryn Dance.
Coming soon in

THE SLEEPING DOLL

HODDER

THE BONE COLLECTOR

It wasn't a branch sticking out of the ground: it was a hand. The body'd been buried vertical and the dirt piled on until just the forearm, wrist and hand protruded. She stared at the ring finger; all the flesh had been whittled away and a woman's diamond cocktail ring had been replaced on the bloody, stripped bone.

Lincoln Rhyme is one of the world's foremost forensic criminalists. And a quadriplegic. And planning suicide.

Then he gets a call he can't ignore.

A single human hand has been found, belonging to someone who got in a cab at the airport and never got out. And the driver was the Bone Collector.

As the minutes count down towards each successive death of an innocent, Rhyme and the female police officer acting as his arms and legs race to locate the victims by unravelling the clues the Bone Collector leaves.

Slowly the criminalist begins to narrow the noose around the kidnapper.

But it appears the Bone Collector has other plans . . .

THE COFFIN DANCER

The most dangerous and elusive hitman in the world is visiting New York City – on business . . .

Percey Clay, one of America's foremost pilots and the uncompromising owner of a struggling charter flight service, was in the wrong place at the wrong time.

Now she's the target of the Coffin Dancer.

Brilliant quadriplegic criminalist Lincoln Rhyme knows the killer only too well. He's a man who's raised murder to a form of high art; whose deadliest weapons aren't guns or knives but his uncanny knowledge of human nature . . .

And Rhyme must combat both the hitman's amoral genius and Percey's headstrong determination if he is to save her.

And keep himself alive.

THE EMPTY CHAIR

She came here to lay flowers at the place where the boy died and the girl was kidnapped.

She came here because she was a heavy girl and had a pocked face and not many friends.

She came here because she was expected to.

Ungainly and sweating, twenty-six-year-old Lydia Johansson walked along the dirt shoulder of Route 112 . . .

She easily found the place she was looking for; the yellow police tape was very evident through the haze.

This spine-chilling thriller pits renowned criminalist Lincoln Rhyme against the ultimate opponent — Amelia Sachs, his own brilliant protégée.

THE STONE MONKEY

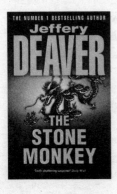

Only one thing is more terrifying than seeing the Ghost.

Surviving.

As they enter the terrifying world of Chinese organised crime, quad-riplegic detective Lincoln Rhyme and his partner and lover Amelia Sachs face an ultimatum from the west, evil from the east and a brand new threat – from within.

Having tracked down a cargo ship carrying illegal Chinese immigrants, Rhyme and Sachs find the capture of the notorious killer behind the human smuggling goes terribly wrong. Now the detectives have just 48 hours to find the two surviving families before the Ghost does.

And as the assassin's threat grows clearer, Amelia is forming a connection that endangers the very fibre of her relationship with Rhyme . . .

THE VANISHED MAN

Sachs studied the young blond woman, lying on her back ten feet away, belly arched up because her bound hands were underneath her. Even in the dimness of the theatre lobby Sachs's quick eyes noted the deep ligature marks in her neck, the blood on her lips and chin – probably from biting her tongue, a common occurrence in strangulations.

A killer flees the scene of a homicide at a prestigious Manhattan music school and locks himself in a classroom. Within minutes, the police have him surrounded. Then a scream rings out, followed by a gunshot. The police break down the door. The room is empty.

As the fatalities rise and the minutes tick down, Rhyme and Sachs must move fast to prevent a terrifying act of vengeance that could become the greatest vanishing acts of all.

THE TWELFTH CARD

Sixteen-year-old Geneva Settle is running from death. She's just a bright high school kid researching a paper on one of her ancestors, but someone out there sees her as a threat. Someone who will stop at nothing to prevent her digging up the past. Someone on a mission to kill.

Lincoln Rhyme and his partner Amelia Sachs are called to the case. They've tracked down some of the world's most brilliant criminals, but this particular hunt is posing more questions than answers. Where will their prey strike next? What is the historic secret he's so desperate to protect? And how can anyone catch a killer who leaves no trace?

'Deaver's investigators are two of crime fiction's most enduring characters, and once again he spins a fascinating and intriguing story. A certain hit.'
Independent on Sunday